fro Mil...
from
Julian

April 1998

Novel
SPC to
Milos (Je66)
F 1r d/~
↑2ⱴ

The Social Comedy

THE
SOCIAL COMEDY

Julian Fane

Constable · London

First published in Great Britain 1998
by Constable and Company Ltd
3 The Lanchesters
162 Fulham Palace Road
London w6 9ER
Copyright © Julian Fane 1998
ISBN 0 09 4785201
The right of Julian Fane to be identified as the author
of this work has been asserted by him in accordance with the
Copyright, Design and Patents Act 1988
Set in Linotron Palatino 10.5pt
by SetSystems Ltd, Saffron Walden, Essex
Printed in Great Britain by
St Edmundsbury Press Ltd
Bury St Edmunds, Suffolk

A CIP catalogue record for this book
is available from the British Library

To

BEN GLAZEBROOK

my publisher and friend

Contents

PART ONE

A Mother's Love

'What can be wrong with my darling daughter? She's being so tiresome.'

The speaker was a woman, to be precise a lady, Lady Meavy, the society hostess Florence or Florrie Meavy, widow of the wealthy baronet and explorer Sir Eldred Meavy and the mother of their only child Fay, who was twenty years old.

Florrie was speaking on the telephone to her cousin, contemporary, friend, assistant and dependant Mildred Chaffcombe, a reluctant spinster aged forty-eight. Mildred lived in a flat in the East Wing of St Eo – pronounced Ee-o – the ancestral Meavy home in Hampshire, and, notwithstanding her feyness, was expected to supervise the household in the absence of her ladyship.

The time was nine-thirty a.m., the day Thursday, the season late summer or early autumn, and Florrie was seated at the desk in the first floor sitting-room of her house in London, located on the sunny side of Buckingham Square, and the main topic of her conversation with Mildred was the forthcoming weekend party at St Eo.

She continued: 'I mean it's not fair. I'm beginning to be afraid that Fay no longer loves me best, as I love her. She's lost weight, she's growing unforgivably pretty, she tells me nothing and gives me the widest possible berth, she's treating me as badly as most daughters treat their doting mamas. And I refuse to face facts, I do not recognise her right to love my rival, I've never given her permission to fall in love, and I hate whoever's presumed to alienate her affections.'

Mildred giggled and scolded: 'Oh Florrie!'

Florrie as usual ignored her and demanded with mock solemnity: 'What are your thoughts on the subject? What are your suggestions?'

'My suggestion is that it's exciting.'

'Are you confirming that Fay's in love? Has she told you she is?'

'No.'

'Well, it may excite you – you're incorrigibly romantic and unselfish – but I'm far from ready to lose a daughter or to imagine a son-in-law would be any sort of gain. Let's postpone consideration of a future that looks even blacker from my point of view – the present's bad enough. Fay isn't coming to St Eo tomorrow, she believes she has better things to do than to spend the weekend helping her mother to entertain a group of old codgers.'

A looking-glass hung on the wall above Florrie's desk, and she studied her reflection in it. Her hair was plentiful, still naturally brown and provocative of the scepticism of other women, and was cut stylishly short. Her face was heart-shaped under her cap of shiny wavy hair. Her eyes were dark blue and slightly hooded, and her lips beautifully modelled, sensitive, refined, neither too thick nor too thin. She was smiling at herself in the mirror, not merely to show off her pretty white teeth but because her temperamental inclination was to do so. She sat straight-backed and trim-waisted on a stool, holding a silver pencil in one elegant hand with polished pink fingernails and the telephone in the other.

'Who will be staying?' Mildred asked.

'Sylvester Kexmoor for one,' Florrie sighed.

'You didn't manage to put him off?'

'He's incommunicado. With luck he may be dead. He's not on the telephone – I don't know his address – he must be over eighty by now – and twenty years ago we used to call him Kexmoor the Boor. Artists in general are the bottom, socially speaking they're wreckers to a man and probably to a woman, they're even more destructive than politicians and journalists.'

The subject of this exchange, the painter Sylvester Kexmoor, had been briefly lionised by society, whence his acquaintanceship with Florrie. But as a result of his drunken offences, including a tendency to punch art-lovers on the nose, he was cast into outer darkness. He had also ceased to be fashionable, he had gone back

to painting proper naturalistic pictures and the critics were unfor-
giving. He consoled himself with successive wives and mistresses
on a houseboat on the Norfolk Broads. His letter to Florrie had
arrived out of the blue, and its single sentence was written in
Indian ink on a piece of tracing paper: 'I want to see you again,
and will arrive at St Eo on next Saturday evening and leave at
three on Sunday afternoon.' Her efforts to trace him and tell him
that she did not want to be seen were unsuccessful, and she
decided it was less trouble to try to grin and bear his projected
visit.

She glanced down at a piece of paper on her desk and half-
closed her eyes in order to read her writing: she refused to wear
spectacles.

'Anyway,' she remarked, 'he'll have Helen to flirt with and Anna
to flatter him, so he won't have much to complain about.'

The first name referred to Helen Islebeck, another widow,
although differing from Florrie inasmuch as she had had several
husbands, who survived: rumour had it that she entertained all
her husbands to lunch on Sundays. She was older than Florrie, and
suspected of having reached pensionable age: if she really was
sixty she could have won a prize for being the prettiest of
pensioners. Time had not robbed her of the talents essential to a
career as a siren, good looks and the constitution of an ox: her face
and her figure had withstood a surfeit of love and rich food. Her
intelligence, such as it was, troubled no one, and her unfailing
amiability was an addition to her range of social assets.

Anna, who was expected to stop Sylvester Kexmoor complaining, had bagged her seat as it were at the top table mainly by
means that were the exact opposite of Helen Islebeck's: instead of
being praised she did the praising. She was the daughter of a
backwoodsman peer, Lord Hulcott, and cleverly made the best of
the bad job of her lack of physical attractions. She was large and
clumsy, had been spotty in youth and in middle age was pock-
marked. Long ago a Polish gigolo hustled her into matrimony,
impregnated her, stole most of her money and deserted her;
without too much difficulty she steered clear of sex from then on.
She reverted to her maiden name, liked to be addressed as the
Honourable Anna Hulcott, changed her son's name by deed poll

[5]

from Stanislas Wisniowieski to Stanley Hulcott, and concentrated on dishing out soft soap to those more loved and envied than she was.

'The other men are Geoffrey and Philip, of course,' Florrie said.

'Of course,' Mildred echoed, laughing.

'And finally T.D. and Roger. Can you bear to keep T.D. under your wing? I know your wing's quite small, but he does like to get as much of himself as possible under it.'

Mildred laughed again in her giggly way.

The two jokes would not have been seen by strangers. Geoffrey was Geoffrey Oldcoate, and Philip was Philip Mozergh, pronounced Mozer: they were Florrie's perennial admirers and social stand-bys. The object of their devotions was the only thing they had – or more accurately did not have – in common.

Geoffrey Oldcoate's unusual surname suited him, and was said by malicious people to have a bearing on the treatment meted out to him by Florrie. He was in his seventies, tall, loose-limbed and short-sighted. He had worked for a charity that helped refugees, and years ago encountered possibly his first and certainly his last love at a meeting of some fund-raising committee. Theirs was an unlikely attachment. Yet his inexhaustible reserves of gentle good-will made up for his lack of sophistication, and he personified the available single man that no hostess can do without, while she was not so spoilt as to fail to appreciate the dedication of himself to her service. He lived in the back of beyond in Bayswater, and, since the demise of his mother and his own retirement, was always at the beloved's beck and call. Admittedly she used him to escort her here and there and to sit next to the dim wives of the interesting men she liked to entertain; but, to put it another way, she filled the empty bowl of his existence, which he held out to her, with fun and romance.

Philip Mozergh was Austrian by extraction, the son of refugees too well-heeled to have required assistance from Geoffrey's organisation, and was a round-faced red-cheeked black-eyebrowed and rotund businessman in his late fifties, whose middle-European charm was the vehicle that deposited him in all the worthwhile English drawing-rooms. His business was the manufacture of trinkets for millionaires, and understanding luxury as he did he was bound to fall in love with Florrie. After meeting her twice he

[6]

declared himself in semi-commercial terms: she was so well-made, the ultimate article of quality, a perfect gemstone in the alternative settings of Buckingham Square and St Eo, that he must possess her instantly or perish.

But Sir Eldred Meavy was alive at the time, and, although he chose to absent himself in outlandish places, his wife did not require intimate attentions from a suitor who was older, shorter, heavier, less good-looking and less distinguished than her husband. On the other hand she was not averse to vaguely emotional relationships with members of the opposite sex. By means of procrastination and tact, by the grant of minor favours and by social bribes, she persuaded Philip not to perish; and if Geoffrey was her bread and butter in this extra-marital context, he became her jam.

Philip continued to pay her the compliment of the odd proposition, but satisfied his grosser appetites elsewhere, and was inclined to make a virtue of necessity by telling her that sex would have ruined their friendship.

Florrie Meavy and Mildred Chaffcombe on the telephone laughed at the notion that Geoffrey and Philip might not be spending the weekend at St Eo – of course they would be present – they nearly always were.

The next exchange referred to T.D. Faulkbourne, Florrie's solicitor and adviser, who was widely known by the initials of his Christian names, Theobald Duncan. T.D. was again a single man, but a widower. He was old and deaf, a dour and pawky Scot, not quite a skeleton at every feast since he was large and stout and ate like a horse, but an oppressive influence in his dark three-piece suits and with his great head of lustreless white hair.

Florrie used T.D. to deal on her behalf with stockbrokers, accountants, bank managers, and she invited him to her jamborees partly to save herself the trouble of communicating with him by post or telephonically. She would hand him a carrier bag full of unopened envelopes, brown and otherwise, almost as he entered her houses; she would then restrict dull discussions of them by pointing to the other people she was duty bound to amuse; and she would soften the impact of his personality by laughing at it. When he interrupted a sparkling conversation to remind her that she had to sign her Tax Return, she would transmute dross into

[7]

gold, or at least into gilt, for instance by addressing the assembled company thus: 'T.D. has the memory of an elephant, he never forgets that life is short, and he's always ready to remind us why we're eating and drinking and being merry.'

The last guest mentioned by Florrie was Roger Ryther, much younger than the other members of the party, thirtyish, resolutely boyish, and an interior decorator by trade. Roger was another single man, he sometimes seemed too obviously single, at any rate in his forays into society; and his blonded hair complete with highlights was rather embarrassing, as were certain mannerisms – Philip Mozergh's witticism was that he should spell his name Writher. But he was unfailingly polite and appreciative, and his gossip helped to make a party go.

'Shall I just run through the list of guests?' Mildred asked.

'Do!'

'The men are Sylvester Kexmoor, Geoffrey, Philip, T.D. and Roger – five of them, and four of us.'

'Well, I can't be bothered to get hold of another female, because Fay may relent and come to the aid of her mother. She may yet prove her pretty feet aren't made of clay. After all, she's never smoked like a chimney or drunk like a fish, or played with pills or injected her veins with poison for fun. She never went to university, where girls are mainly taught to love boys. She doesn't wear rings in her nose like a pig, or dye her hair green, or dress like a scarecrow. And she isn't anorexic or bulimic or neurotic or psychotic. I've no cause for complaint, and I know it. There! Shall we go through the weekend menus?'

Florrie's drawing-room was painted yellow, and furnished with thoughts of hospitality in mind. There were sofas and chairs in groups and numerous occasional tables bearing protective coasters on which glasses of iced liquid could be placed. A portrait of her late husband hung over the mantelpiece, his face wedgelike and aristocratic, his eyelids narrowed as if he were spying out a new and ever more remote horizon. He had looked like that when he condescended to notice her at a ball in London, and to ask her to dance, and she was suddenly able to see nothing except his challenging and commanding grey eyes.

She was then twenty-two and he was forty-four. She was an orphan, had lost both her parents in a car crash before she knew

[8]

them, had been brought up by a Chaffcombe uncle and his wife in Devon, and was living with an aunt, her mother's unmarried sister, in Chelsea. She worked as receptionist in a picture gallery, went to parties, laughed a lot, was kissed a good deal and occasionally kissed back, and might have looked to a casual observer like an ordinary middle class type of debutante; but she already had her differences from most other girls of her age. She was in no hurry to lose her virginity, for one thing; she was unusually optimistic, she believed in true love, and her temperament was at once outgoing and reflective. She was sane, curious, principled, tolerant and sociable, all to marked degrees. Her personality was as charming as her appearance, and she had emerging qualities of leadership.

She recognised her destiny instantly, and her assurance was another departure from the norm. Eldred Meavy had no time to waste: he was about to return to the Brazilian rain forest. He proposed to her at their fourth meeting and she accepted with fervour. She was undaunted by his twenty-two years of seniority, his reputed eccentricity, his warnings that she might never see much of him, and the task of running St Eo, possibly without his assistance. She disregarded the doubts of her relations, and their pleas to do nothing in haste. She was the opposite of a gold-digger, but had been sufficiently poor and was sufficiently sensible to have no inhibitions about marrying money. She became the wife of her marvellous mad hero, and proved she had not been wrong.

He was as good or as bad as his word: he was hardly ever at home. He spent long periods of the fifteen years of their marriage alone, abroad, searching for Atlantis, Eldorado, the Abominable Snowman, the source of some South American river, and cohabiting with head-hunters. As a rule he returned to Florrie on a stretcher, suffering from a dozen diseases, and had to be nursed back to health. They were happy together nonetheless; and her successes in the nursing line could be called counterproductive, since no sooner was he fit than he was off again. She did not stop him, she knew she could not stop him, and although she missed him she did not repine. She brought up their daughter, entertained, formed her circle of friends, and became a sort of byword.

Her husband died in Brazil – his body was not recovered. He had been attempting a feat worthy of, but perhaps too preposterous for, Tarzan: to travel about a hundred miles through the jungle without putting a foot to the ground.

Fay, aged nine, did not miss him much more than usual, and Florrie's individualistic version of fidelity to her husband did not alter or end with his death. She continued to talk about him so fondly and vividly that his daughter never felt entirely fatherless.

Mildred Chaffcombe, after settling the weekend's fare with Florrie, and the allotment of bedrooms for the guests, reverted to the subject of Fay's romance.

'Are you sure it's love?'

'No – I'm hoping it's glandular fever.'

Mildred giggled again.

'I'd be thrilled if Fay found a lover who was worthy of her,' she said.

'Don't get carried away, for pity's sake! If a man's causing all the trouble, and she was proud of him, she wouldn't be secretive. I've a nasty feeling he's an idealised oaf. She has no experience to speak of, she could have lost her head as well as her heart, and the worst of it is she might turn out to have a single-track mind like mine.'

Mildred giggled once more and said: 'But first love's so fragile and poignant – you won't crush it underfoot, will you?'

'Don't talk nonsense, Mildred! More often than not first love's fatal – look at Romeo and Juliet!'

A Daughter's Difficulties

Buckingham Square was a stone's throw away from Buckingham Palace. It was said to be London's smartest address, and was central yet secluded, having a single access road – a narrow cobbled alley of a road – from Value Lane that ran along behind Wellington Barracks. Parking there was for residents only, and residents were discouraged from using their own cars by often getting stuck in jams while driving in and out: taxi drivers dropped customers bound for the Square in one of the main thoroughfares. The houses were Queen Anne, terraced, uniform, their brickwork mellow and their windows sashed with small panes. Front rooms looked at a circular railed garden, where a pair of splendid plane trees over-hung meagre grass and some evergreen shrubs.

All the houses were in single occupancies, and the pristine state of their exterior paintwork and the quality of their net curtains told a tale of well-heeled inhabitants. In the evenings, hot summer evenings when windows were open to admit a little more polluted air, and the early dusks of winter, lit rooms could be seen into by passers-by, if any: they glowed like treasure chambers. In the mornings cars driven by long-suffering chauffeurs manoeuvred into the square to pick up blue-suited executives with bulging briefcases. The front elevations of each house sported a metal box bearing the name of a burglar alarm company; but they might have been superfluous in that burglars were deterred by innumerable locks, by living-in staff, by the unpredictable coming and going of guests, and by the problems of getting away with loot.

Lady Meavy's London home was number seven: it had been acquired by Sir Eldred's father. A Filipino couple, Maria and

[11]

Barney, had the basement to themselves. On the ground floor were an entrance hall, lavatory, dining-room and kitchen. The first floor had a landing for sitting in as well as the drawing-room. Florrie's bedroom, bathroom and closet were on the second floor, and on the third were Fay's quarters and a spare bedroom and bathroom.

It was the day after Florrie and Mildred had talked on the telephone, nine o'clock on Friday morning, and the mistress of the house, fully clothed and cleverly made-up as usual, was descending the stairs while Maria and Barney, each carrying a tray, were ascending them. They met according to custom in the drawing-room, halfway between Florrie's bedroom above and the ground floor kitchen below.

Maria was a small person with a big personality: she was middle-aged. Barney was foolish, hen-pecked, clumsy and well-meaning, and they were both keen Roman Catholics. They had already looped back the curtains in the drawing-room, and cleaned and tidied and puffed the cushions and opened a window. The sun shone and the sky was cloudless over the crowns of the plane trees.

Greetings were exchanged, and the trays were deposited on coffee-tables in front of the two sofas. Maria addressed Florrie as 'My lady', rather possessively than with more conventional respect. Barney, who had not learnt to speak English after living in Buckingham Square for twenty years, could only manage to call her 'Lady'. They drew attention to the tray waiting for Fay, which had a boiled egg on it covered with a garishly coloured egg-cosy,

'To keep Missy's eggy warm – Missy home very late last night,' Maria explained with a wide warm smile.

Florrie thanked them and looked at the morning paper. She was grateful for the services rendered by her employees in town and in the country, and particularly fond of Maria, whose ever-expanding family in the Philippines she supported. But not for the first time she regretted Maria's readiness to communicate unwelcome news.

She tackled her own breakfast of tea and toast. She had not slept well: she had been to see a bad new play with Geoffrey Oldcoate and dined at a restaurant afterwards, returned to Buckingham Square round about midnight, and lain awake surely for hours, listening for Fay's step on the stairs. In the end she decided that Fay must be safely asleep in her own bed, and had herself dropped off. But the egg-cosy disillusioned her.

[12]

Fay appeared at nine-forty-five, by which time Florrie was at her desk. The door burst open and a tall plump girl with lots of curling brown hair gave her mother a puppyish hug and said: 'Oh good, I haven't missed you!' She wore a long white T-shirt, jeans and trainers, and looked nice in every way, although her attire was in sharp contrast to Florrie's silk shirt, pencil skirt, stockings and court shoes. She was all energy and vivacity, and flung herself down on her sofa, saying: 'Sorry I overslept!' The egg-cosy caused her to pull a face and exclaim: 'Heavens! This is something new, isn't it?'

Florrie laughed and replied: 'Maria knitted it for you to stop your egg getting cold.'

'I see. How sweet of her! What was your play like?'

The significant words of this little speech were the first two. I see, she had said – and the grey eyes inherited from her father ceased momentarily to dance as she saw the point that Maria had expected her to oversleep and that the reason why she had done so was common knowledge.

Florrie answered Fay's question: 'A fiasco, a catalogue of curses – this fashion for swearing in plays and books is infantile and I do wish the writers would grow out of it. Geoffrey was embarrassed and I was yawning. How was your evening?'

'Fine! You're going down to St Eo today, aren't you?'

'Yes, this morning. The question is, will we survive without you? But I'm not saying you shouldn't do as you please, darling. You'll be staying here, won't you?'

'Probably – I may be in and out – you know – and I may not be in when you telephone – I don't want you to worry.'

They both laughed again. Their laughter was an acknowledgment that they were fencing, playing a game, and that Fay's last somewhat lame gambit was a counsel of perfection.

'Oh I never worry,' Florrie said in her best ironical style. 'I raise no objections to your being on the loose in London, lodging here when it suits you, disappearing in the daytime, keeping late hours, and I never have a moment's anxiety because we're in such nonstop telepathic communication that I'm fully informed of every single move you make.'

'Oh Ma!' Fay scolded with amusement in the same tone of voice in which Mildred had frequent cause to say 'Oh Florrie!'

[13]

She poured milk on her bowl of Corn Flakes, and Florrie resumed: 'My darling, I love you having your head, I approve of your free spirit, I'm in favour of your sabbatical year or two, I think you're right to be giving serious consideration to the problem of privilege, and I'm delighted and flattered that you haven't abandoned me. All the same, London seems to grow more frightening daily, and we're told that young people do more and more disgusting things to themselves and one another and the rest of us. Perhaps I shouldn't say so, especially to your father's daughter, but I can't help feeling at one with the majority of mothers in the middle of the night, and a trifle uneasy about my ewe lamb.'

Fay took it well. Although she wriggled a bit, she continued to smile and munch her cereal.

However, her comment was on the defensive and evasive side: 'I only muck about with friends – I follow your example,' and she removed the egg-cosy and studied its varicoloured wools.

'You go to pubs and discos, don't you? I don't muck about with my friends in pubs.'

Fay giggled and said: 'Too true, Ma. But pubs can be good fun – I'll take you to one and you'll see what I mean – and I don't go to pubs alone. Honestly, I try not to do anything dangerous. My friend Jenny's got a flat of her own and we meet there sometimes, and we have met in Sue's home when her parents were on holiday.'

'Why don't you bring your friends here? I'd do my best not to disgrace you, or you could wait till the cat's away.'

'It's not that.' She decapitated her egg with a knife in a gesture rendered slightly savage by embarrassment. 'They'd be afraid of breaking stuff, and they'd probably think the house was swanky.'

'Don't they have swanky homes?'

'Not as swanky as ours.'

'Well – I remember Jenny and Sue – they were charming little girls when you were at school together – and I expect they're charming big girls now. I'd love to see them again. But you know what Mrs Bennet's next question would be – Mrs Bennet in *Pride and Prejudice* – don't you? Are you shy of asking your friends in because they're your social inferiors?'

'Oh good heavens, Ma, that's just so old-fashioned!'

'No, no, darling – the preoccupations of mothers with daughters never have changed and never will – we've always hoped and prayed that our little ones are going to love and marry the right type – which means a man who passes muster mentally, physically, morally, financially, and any woman would be proud of. Wait and see, wait until you're in my shoes, God willing! You're so idealistic, you'd prefer not to pigeonhole people in classes, you love every-body and want to break down barriers, and you think high society died out in the dark ages, and snobs only figure in Victorian novels. It's not true! Revolutions cut off the heads of kings and queens and shoot tsars in cellars in the name of classlessness, which lasts for about ten minutes – new classes bob up, and society's reconstituted and reinforced by new blood. I'm not worldly, I am realistic – and I long for you to find someone to love and be loved by who's as good as you are, who at least has a similar background, and you can admire as I admired your papa. Is your egg edible?'

'Delicious!'

'Sorry to lecture you so early in the day, my sweet; but I do dread your throwing yourself away. You will beware of pity, won't you, which misleads so many kind girls?'

'Ma,' Fay began hesitantly and carried on with diffident deter-mination; 'I don't think any of my friends are inferior, but none of them have smart houses in this part of London as well as stately homes in the country.'

'No – I don't suppose they do – and I can see that St Eo might make a difference between you and them. I told your father I couldn't ever live in such a grand place when I first set eyes on it, and he said he understood, he'd sell it and someone else could live there. He was very persuasive and, believe it or not, capable of hard-headedness: he said he'd get rid of his money and let other people be rich, and taught me not to be squeamish about our advantages. Social guilt's a chronic affliction – and to attempt to cure it by redistributing wealth in general and yours in particular, by taking vows of poverty and dossing down in a hovel, is futile, because someone else is always ready and willing to fill the vacuum created. We've maintained the fabric of St Eo, and pro-vided employment and tilled the land, and welcomed hordes of members of the public – our record's nothing to be ashamed of.'

Fay tried to be reasonable. 'I'm not ashamed – but I don't want a label hung round my neck, I'd rather be anonymous, at least until I can answer questions about my future. Anyway,' she giggled

[15]

forgivingly and made the ambiguous statement, as if getting to the heart of the matter while complaining that her mother had already got there; 'I can't imagine how marriage counselling's crept into our conversation.'

Florrie seized her opportunity, perhaps as she was intended to, and said: 'It's partly your looks, darling.'

'What?'

'Who are you becoming beautiful for?'

Fay was pleased to deny it, blushing: 'I'm not beautiful – I'll never be a patch on you.'

'I'll leave it to your lover – or lovers in the plural – to change your mind. But thank you for the compliment. Actually, it's not your looks alone – telepathy isn't needed for me to have an inkling of what you're up to – girls don't stay out so late with girlfriends as you do sometimes – last night, for instance. Sorry, my sweet! There are two flies in the ointment of our living together, one for each of us: you can't be private and I can't be inquisitive. Otherwise, from my point of view, the arrangement's perfect.'

Fay was simultaneously apologetic and excited.

'I do long to confide in you, and I would if I could.'

'Don't torture me then – you know my nosey inclinations. As long as you're happy, I'll hold on to the thought that all's for the best. Have some more toast! You see how good I can be.'

'I've never felt like this before, although I was always happy in another way. It's the first time.'

'The first time for what?'

'No – not that – for caring – for possibly caring. Nothing's happened really. And the things you've been saying reinforce things I've thought.'

'But I talk too much, darling, and never can remember what I've said. I hope I haven't been a spoilsport.'

'I'm afraid you wouldn't approve in principle. He's not a society person.'

'Oh dear – am I? If I had been, would I have been singled out by your father, whose attitude to the society he was born into was summed up by his preference for living on rats and worms in jungles? Yes, I'm sociable, and I go in for friendship, and because I like to keep in the swim I can't steer clear of a whole shoal of

[16]

acquaintances; but I'd prefer not to think I'm a socialite. Being a widow doesn't mean I'm a merry one.'

'I meant that Mrs Bennet might not approve.'

'Are you saying he's somehow inferior?'

'No! He's the finest man I've ever known – he's so strong and wise – but he's utterly different from everyone else.'

'You're frightening me. Is he a freak?'

'Different from the men I know, and better.'

'How old is he?'

'Twenty-four.'

'That's a relief. I was beginning to think he was an OAP. Twenty-four-year-olds aren't wise as a rule.'

'Exactly! It's just that he isn't what people are probably expecting.'

'You're frightening me again. You're not engaged to him already, are you?'

'No – worst luck, maybe – we haven't seen all that much of each other – it's not easy considering his work – but what's so amazing is that he seems to like me – he's my friend.'

'Listen, sweetest, you can't stop now, you've said too much to stop – I'll die of curiosity if you do. What is his work?'

'It's temporary. You won't jump to conclusions and make jokes, will you?'

'Do I ever make jokes?'

'Often.'

'Funny jokes?'

'Yes and no.'

'I'm glad to know some are funny. But sorry – I promise to behave – and please!'

'He's foreign.'

'Foreign! What colour is he?'

'Oh he's a white Caucasian, as they say in American films – he's a Caucasian all right.'

'American?'

'No – Orezanian.'

'Where's that? What's that? I've never heard of it. You make him sound like a breed of monkey.'

'Don't, Ma! Orezan, or Orezania in English, was part of the

Soviet Union. It's an island in the Black Sea between Georgia and Turkey, a bit like the Isle of Wight.'

'It can't be very like the Isle of Wight if it's full of Georgians and Turks. Why is he here? What's he doing in London?'

'He's a waiter.'

Lunch in the Country

Florrie's involuntary exclamation, 'A waiter!' was expressive of shock and horror, and she lived to regret it.

Fay would not say a word more on the subject. She blushed, her eyes filled with tears, she apologised for being silly and swore that her mother did not need to apologise, she promised she understood, but declared repeatedly and unrelentingly that she had already said too much.

'Please don't press me, Ma – I'll tell you when I can, if I have anything to tell. Good heavens, is that the time? I must rush, honestly! Have a lovely weekend – I'll see you next week – goodbye!'

Florrie was miserable. She hated secrets, she hated not to be in on them. She was especially hating the unwonted experience of being shut out of her daughter's life, and having the door slammed and bolted. She hated herself for upsetting Fay, for her tactlessness, and for having sounded and seemed so crassly snobbish.

'But a waiter,' she inwardly repeated with a shudder of foreboding. And what could his secret possibly be? A waiter was a waiter, however attractive his looks and pleasant his character; and Fay's one was most unlikely to be the paragon that many people thought she deserved.

It was unthinkable, unthinkably sad, and matters were not made better by Fay popping her head round the drawing-room door in order to beg her mother, to beg and command her, not to discuss the affair with anybody – or with everybody, as she knowingly put it.

Florrie prepared to leave London: Barney had informed her that her chauffeur Crisp was waiting in the Jaguar. What should, what could she do? She had no idea where Fay intended to spend the weekend, she only had disagreeable suppositions. She must not try to trace her daughter via Jenny and Sue, or act the detective. She said her goodbyes to the Filipinos.

In the Jaguar she sat in the back instead of the front passenger seat – she was not in the mood to chat even to dear Crisp. And her reactions to the sunshine, the car's smooth ride, the metropolitan crowds enjoying the weather, the verdant landscape that was more summery than autumnal, and at St Eo, as she was driven towards its porticoed entrance, the good tourists who had contributed to the upkeep of her property, and their toddlers and the omnipresent signs to their toilets – her every reaction was uncharacteristically jaundiced.

The Meavy family home was a huge redbrick house standing on a gentle eminence in the middle of undulating parkland. The building was mid-nineteenth century. It had elaborate Victorian chimneys and plate glass windows set in stone mullions. There was no formal flower garden: instead, ancient cedars grew out of a considerable area of mown lawn in positions calculated to be most pleasing to the eye. The surrounding landscape was agricultural, and sheep safely grazed in the meadow reaching to the South Terrace – several reception rooms with a southern outlook were reserved for Lady Meavy's use while the house and grounds were open to the public.

The interior was either beautified or wrecked in the opinions of visitors by Victorian plasterwork and architectural details. Oak was much in evidence – various overmantels and the staircase were heftiest oak. The decoration of the rooms was grand and shabby, a compensatory combination. The absence of curtains in the dining-hall, where severe shutters alone were closed at night-fall, seemed to remind assembled companies that they would have to sing or anyway talk for their supper, yet the sofas with threadbare covers beside the fire promised comfort and ease.

Florrie was exclusively busy for the remaining hours of daylight, talking to Jean Watson her housekeeper, to Mrs Withgill her cook, to her butler Wilson, then to Ben Simmonds in the garden and to Angus Macrae, her land agent or factor, in the Estate Office. She had to inspect guests' bedrooms, approve menus, choose wines, arrange the seating at meals, and do a dozen vases of flowers. She also fitted in three telephone calls. She rang Buckingham Square and was told by Maria that Fay was out; she invited neighbours called Gristhorpe to lunch on Sunday; and she asked Mildred to join her for a snack at eight o'clock in her small sitting-room.

It was another mistake. She broke the bad news, then was doubly annoyed by her cousin, who, having listened to it with eagerness, reprimanded her for blabbing, for being so indiscreet, and secondly insisted that Fay might well live happily ever after with an Orezanian waiter.

Florrie was always made to feel pessimistic by Mildred's optimism; and on this occasion so much so that she had to invent an excuse and withdraw to her bedroom.

On Saturday morning Helen Islebeck and Anna Hulcott, and Philip Mozergh, Geoffrey Oldcoate, T.D. Faulkbourne and Roger Ryther arrived. Florrie was depressed to notice how badly Philip carried his years. He looked unhealthy – he had such dark rings under his eyes – and foreign into the bargain. And Geoffrey seemed to have aged in the week or so since she last saw him. But they all got through lunch, and in the afternoon Helen rested upstairs, Anna walked with Geoffrey and Roger, Philip worked at business papers in the library, and T.D. obtained Florrie's signature on innumerable cheques and documents.

At six o'clock Sylvester Kexmoor joined the party. Sylvester now resembled a gaunt old outsize eagle rather than the young lion she remembered. He had downy fluff on his head, and moles like flowerpots sprouting white hairs on his cheeks and neck. He was wearing a rag of a shirt, a paint-stained suit of corduroy, no socks and splitting plimsolls. He disseminated anti-social odours and, although he had kissed Florrie in a way that was surprisingly libidinous, he took an offensive lack of interest in his fellow-guests – Helen Islebeck was put out not to receive her dues of admiration.

Half an hour after arriving he was tipsy enough to say to Anna Hulcott, who had gushingly hoped he was not going to bury himself for ever in the watery grave of the Norfolk Broads, that his art was more important than clowning around for a clique of arrogant philistines. At dinner he drank the fine wines as if they were water, and bored everybody with his hackneyed lament: that the public was moronic, and critics should have their eyes, tongues

[21]

and other means of communication removed surgically. The burden of his personal complaint was that he had been loved by the artistic establishment while he painted like a child of four, and hated for the forty-odd years during which he had tried for ten hours a day to paint like Leonardo.

Brandy brought out the beast in him. He captured Florrie's hand and would have guided it under the table towards proof that he was still virile if she had not tugged it away in the nick of time. A few minutes later he accused Helen Islebeck of being a chocolate box for display purposes with fake chocolates inside – an insult no doubt indicative of a similar sequence of events. He finally slumped backwards in his chair and was thought for a moment to have passed over as well as out. But he came to and was assisted up to his room by Roger Ryther, who writhed to hear himself repeatedly addressed as 'Nancy'.

Even Mildred's tendency to look on the bright side was not altogether equal to these events. Anna Hulcott said Florrie was a saint to entertain such a naughty old boy; Philip suggested that Sylvester's surname should be changed to Vexmore; Geoffrey predicted that Sylvester would be unwell in the morning; and T.D. Faulkbourne delivered himself of the cryptic aphorism that 'artists never get anywhere by living in the country'. Sympathy was extended to Helen for having been at least verbally assaulted; but she shrugged her shoulders and smiled her brave and beautiful smile – she had received another compliment, when all was said, and had confidence that the chocolates in her box were not fakes.

A blight having been cast on the party, too early to flatter the hostess everyone agreed it was time to retire to the county, meaning in the dialect of society folk the county of Bedfordshire, or, in plainer English, bed.

At eight-thirty the next morning Florrie was warned by Wilson that Mr Kexmoor had just frightened Mrs Withgill by appearing in the kitchen in his pyjamas and demanding a jug of black coffee in his bedroom, where he intended to remain until his taxi turned up at three.

At nine o'clock her four other male guests joined her in the dining-room – Helen and Anna had opted for breakfast trays in their rooms, and Mildred was in her flat. The consensus of the advice she sought and received was that she should let Sylvester

[22]

stew in his own juice, and she followed it to the extent of broaching the subject of the Gristhorpes.

'Who might they be?' Philip inquired.

Neighbours, she replied.

'Old neighbours, or new young pretty ones?'

She was not in the mood to swap banter with Philip, and never liked his hints of licentiousness.

'They've been here for quite a few years,' she replied seriously. 'When he retired they bought the Old Rectory here, in the village of St Eo. I believe she's written a book or two.'

'Have you asked them in to entertain us, or are we meant to entertain them, and if so why?'

'Does there have to be a reason?' she returned, smiling but unable to exclude a testy note from her voice. 'All you have to do is to be polite.'

'My dear Florrie, we're polite in other people's houses. In yours, we let our hair down if we have any – witness your rude absent friend nursing his hangover upstairs.'

Geoffrey intervened at this point.

'The name Gristhorpe rings a faint bell, I fancy.'

And Roger, who knew or claimed to know everybody who was anybody, chipped in: 'It's probably faint because it's ringing in Bloomsbury.'

The problem was solved: Mona Gristhorpe was formerly Mona Bardswell, and had hacked out a niche for herself in the public eye by writing repeated accounts of her necking session with Virginia Woolf, her one night stand with Clive Bell, and her application of lipstick to the bearded lips of Lytton Strachey when he donned the apparel of the Virgin Queen, Queen Elizabeth I.

'The Bloomsburyites called her Mona Bedswell,' Roger added, 'but I guess they were exaggerating.'

T.D. cleared his throat loosely and contributed the following: 'Harold Gristhorpe was our ambassador in Turkey.'

'Quite right,' Florrie admitted, adding in order to stop the questioning: 'but I can tell you no more about them, I've only met them once or twice – you'll have to wait and see!'

She then excused herself – she was determined not to be more indiscreet than she had already been; dealt with household chores; met Mildred by arrangement and attended Matins in the chapel,

[23]

which also served as the church of the village of St Eo; was introduced to the nice new vicar and the agent of Mildred's unwonted interest in religion, a widower named Aubrey Millard-Jones; and rejoined her guests, who had spent their Sunday morning in secular activities such as reading the newspapers with disapproval and drinking Bloody Marys.

Mr and Mrs Gristhorpe arrived too punctually. It was unimaginable that she could ever have merited the nickname or epithet Bedswell: she had become a bundle of old clothes with a heavy head poking out at the top and a grumpy grey face. He had two dominant features, grizzled eyebrows that met over his nose and a wobbling dewlap.

Mona Gristhorpe betrayed her connections with the so-called Bloomsbury Group by the sharpness of her tongue. She responded to Florrie's welcome by saying: 'Thanks for letting us see the inside of your house at last.' Mercifully, her husband was more diplomatic by training, whether or not by temperament. He sat next to Florrie, but the conversation was general and she did not get a chance to pick his brain in private.

When the company returned to the drawing-room, she poured coffee from a silver pot and proffered a cup to Mr Gristhorpe as she asked: 'Should I have called you Ambassador, or may I call you Harold?'

He replied with a gallant wobble of his double chin: 'Harold, if you please.'

'Only on condition that you call me Florrie.'

'I'm honoured to accept your condition,' he smirked.

'You ruled our ambassadorial roost in Turkey, didn't you?'

A modest yet incongruous snigger signified his assent.

By now a hush had descended – Florrie's friends were waiting to hear why she had compounded the error of Sylvester Kexmoor by feeding the Gristhorpes.

'How fascinating,' she fibbed with an encouraging smile.

Indeed, he agreed; it had been his last tour of duty; and he launched into a series of superfluous reminiscences.

'Did you ever get to Orezania?' she gently interrupted.

'We did. We obtained permission to spend a holiday there.' He leant across and spoke loudly to his wife. 'We're talking about Orezania, dear.'

[24]

'Horrible spot,' she retorted.

Harold Gristhorpe ignored her in a matrimonial manner and volunteered geographical data.

'Orezania is an island in the Black Sea, five or six miles off the Crimea, and due south of Balaclava, which gave its name to the headgear worn by our troops during the Crimean War.'

'And now by criminals,' Philip Mozergh murmured.

'It's twenty-two miles long from north to south, and twelve from east to west. My figures are approximate – I fear the metrical system defeats me. The landscape is a mixture of hills and mountains, formerly volcanic, and fertile valleys. But why do you ask? Do you, Florrie, know it? Do any of you know it?' He lifted his heavy eyebrows interrogatively.

Heads were shaken.

He assumed that he was meant to continue: 'The island has a long and tragic history. It was invaded and occupied by Greeks, Romans, Ukrainians, Romanians, Turks, and each occupying power seems to have liquidated the ruling class of its predecessor; but apparently immigrants were tempted by the rich rewards of Orezanian agriculture to repopulate the land. In the nineteenth century a grouping of politicians raised the flag of freedom from the Turks, and attracted the support of a majority of the islanders, uniting them despite the diversity of their origins. The uprising was successful, Orezania became an independent state under the control of the rebel chieftain or self-appointed King, and for sixty or seventy years flourished, growing richer and more civilised until October 1917.'

Mona Gristhorpe interrupted here. 'High time we were going,' she grated impatiently. But Florrie led a chorus that shouted her down.

Harold was easily persuaded to resume. 'After 1917, the Bolsheviks in Russia were too paranoid to permit a successful monarchy to operate almost within their territory. Lenin's gangsters disposed of every member of the Orezanian royal family, swamped the island with troops, incorporated it into the Soviet Union, turned it into a fortified outpost of their empire, and to all intents and purposes destroyed it. We obtained our visas to travel there in the 1970s, and were depressed by the contrast between the beauty of the scenery and the plight of the terrorised and impoverished natives. The capital Orez had become a slum, its opera house was a pile of rubble, fit young men were conspicuous by their absence, and people were obviously starving in the midst of what had been and could have been plenty.' He turned to his wife for confirmation. 'I've been saying that our visit to Orezania was not a very happy experience, dear.'

'They should drop a bomb on it,' she suggested.

Philip asked: 'What's happened since the break-up of the Soviet empire?'

'Nothing good, I regret to say,' Harold Gristhorpe answered.

'But the Commies have been booted out, haven't they? That can't be bad.'

'Orezania was fortunate to be allowed to secede from Russia. On paper, it has become an independent state. But all the politicians who stepped forward with offers to run the country were ex-communist civil servants, *apparatchiks* for whom might was still right. They grabbed the arms and munitions left behind by the Soviet forces, formed armies and declared war on one another. My present understanding is that no one's come out on top as yet, and that between them the three warring parties, the Blues, Whites and Reds, inevitably supported by foreign mischief-makers and commercial interests, are doing even more damage to the fabric of the island and its remaining inhabitants. Although the fighting may be intermittent, I'm sure it would conform to the proud and fierce character of the people; and should you have thought of visiting the island or spending a holiday there, I would regrettably counsel you not to do so.'

Philip turned to Florrie and inquired: 'Have you been thinking of a holiday in Orezania? What have you been thinking of?'

Her other friends now put a variety of oars in: Anna Hulcott said Florrie was too precious to be permitted to travel in a war zone; Geoffrey that a study of the archaeology of the region might be rewarding; Helen Islebeck, inconsequentially, that a diet of Turkish apricots was supposed to work wonders for the complexion; and Roger that Florrie ought to buy Orezania.

The Gristhorpes, who were being hustled as it were from centre stage into the wings, took their leave.

Florrie saw them off and braced herself for Philip's further interrogation.

[26]

'What's going on, my dearest? I scent scandal, and you can't blame me for giving tongue. Come on, you know you can't keep any secret, let alone a secret from us. I bet you love's at the bottom of it.'

'Don't be disgusting,' she said.

'Well, what about a bet?'

'No.'

'In that case name the brute.'

'I'll do nothing of the sort.'

'Well, you're bound to spill the beans sooner or later. At least admit that a heart must have its reasons to prompt this obsession with a molehill in Asia Minor.'

'I'll only admit that it's not my heart.'

'Whose then?'

'A friend's.'

'Oh yes,' he agreed sarcastically. 'We all have friends on whose behalf we ask our awkward questions. I dare you to deny that the person with the heart and a yen for Orezania has the initials F.M.'

Florrie was speechless. She was too taken aback to hide her confusion, for her initials and Fay's were the same. Had he somehow hit on the truth?

She hesitated and the drawing-room door was thrown open. Sylvester Kexmoor stood in the doorway. He did not enter the room, just stood there, and growled out the embarrassing proposition: 'Florrie, I want you.'

Love in the Afternoon

She forgave him. She laughed at the earthiness of his phraseology. She was glad to get away from Philip pulling her in one direction towards betrayal of Fay's secret, and Mildred frowning at her and pushing her in another.

Sylvester's taxi waited at her front door. But she said to him: 'Don't go for a moment – come for a tiny stroll!' And she put her warm soft arm through his heavy bony one, and they began to promenade on her sprung lawns in the autumnal afternoon sunshine, and then in the shade cast by the cedar trees.

'Are you feeling better?' she asked.

'My days of feeling better are gone for good,' he growled in reply, but with wry humour instead of yesterday's aggressiveness. 'I'm back to being the degrees below par I'm used to. I suppose I owe you an apology – I couldn't face the social music, and I had no appetite for lunch – I'd been poisoned by your rich food – my staple diet is bread and cheese.'

'Saying sorry doesn't suit you,' she laughed and squeezed his arm, 'and don't think you can get away with saying it was my food that poisoned you.'

His chesty bark, signifying amusement, sounded painful.

He said: 'I was under the impression that you'd floated off my planet, but you seem to keep a toe on the ground.'

'Is that a compliment, Sylvester?'

She stopped and smiled up at his battered but undefeated countenance under his broad-brimmed straw hat worn at a rakish angle.

He shrugged his shoulders and replied: 'I came here to see if there was anything left of my Florence.'

[28]

'What's your verdict?'

'I can recognise you in spite of the flummery.'

They moved on as she commented: 'Not bad, coming from you. I'll pay you a compliment in return – in that hat you look like a proper artist instead of a fish out of water. And at least you don't suffer from the real killer disease of today, hypocrisy. Most people who call my life-style flummery are either angling for invitations or angry because I haven't invited them, believe it or not. Besides, I like your pictures – your later pictures, not the ones that seem to have been done in a kindergarten – I've several in London, you know – they're fine.'

'Thank you. You're one of the few who buy them, and the not many more who like them.'

'Wait till you're dead – you'll enjoy the spectacle of pundits eating their hats yet again.'

He now stopped and, turning towards her and dredging up amorous emotion, said with gruff force: 'You're still beautiful.'

She returned his gaze, narrowing her hooded eyes against the sun and smiling sceptically.

He persisted: 'Last night I wished you'd told me where your bedroom was.'

She burst out laughing. 'It wouldn't have been much fun for either of us if I had.'

'Come and see me in Norfolk!'

'On your boat?'

'We'd be alone there.'

'And I'd be seasick.'

He yielded to her resumption of mobility and seemed to leave his idea of love or lust behind.

He said with grim thoughtfulness: 'Flummery and flippancy are the enemies of art. I ran away from society before its flummery destroyed me and my work. Interrupting my routine to stay with you was a mistake.'

'Now now,' she scolded him good-humouredly, 'don't bite the hand that would have fed you if you hadn't got so tipsy! Society isn't to blame because you no longer have the energy to be sociable and creative at the same time. Tell me, are you short of money? Can I help you?'

'No. I thought you could, but no such luck. I'm stuck, Florrie, that's the long and short of it. I'm seventy-three and stuck. and I came to you for inspiration – I need sex or a kick in the pants. But I can afford to keep body and soul more or less together. Money's not the problem.'

'Same here.'

He barked mockingly.

'Your problem, Florrie, what may that be? You've your beauty and wealth and health, you've had one good husband and you're not stuck with a second bad one, you shouldn't have a care in the world.'

'Silly old Sylvester,' she said.

His response to the dryness of her tone of voice was to ask: 'Am I wrong?'

'Of course,' she returned with another of her easy-going smiles.

'Seriously?'

'No,' she reassured and mocked him in her turn. 'An artist doesn't change his blind spots. I was never your Florence, and I've never been ready to receive you in my bedroom. And although I'm glad I give you the impression of being carefree, I wonder how a man of your age can believe any woman of mine is free of care. You forget that I've a nubile daughter. No questions! My lips are sealed. But I must find out before you disappear into a world of your own: are you looked after by someone?'

He ignored her question, and observed: 'They say children are more troublesome than lovers.'

'I wouldn't know about that.'

'Wouldn't you just! Sorry, Florrie! Not your fault that you only inspired me to get damn-fool drunk. I'd better cut my throat on a dark night.'

'You will not! I hate such stupid talk. Pull yourself together!'

He laughed and said: 'You're a better friend than I am.'

'Artists are no good at friendship – it's love or nothing – and they spell trouble always. Are you looked after?'

'By a woman, you mean? I'm acquainted with one of many broads on the Broads – put it that way.'

She reached up and planted a kiss on his rough cheek and said: 'My daughter would tell you to take care. That's the latest way to say goodbye – it replaces ta-ta and toodle-oo. Be careful anyway!'

[30]

He replied: 'Some hopes!' – and clambered into his taxi and did not look back as he was driven off.

She re-entered the house and the drawing-room, where Philip Mozergh awaited her.

He explained that Geoffrey, Roger and T.D. had taken Helen, Anna and Mildred for a walk, and asked proprietorially: 'What have you been doing?'

'Shall I tell you? Or shall I give you the answer you sound as if you deserve?'

'Which is?'

'Nothing.'

He laughed. His laughter and Sylvester Kexmoor's were different: in edible terms, Sylvester's was like a mouthful of lumpy porridge, and Philip's like a chocolate cake with cream. He was lounging on a sofa in a lascivious attitude, powerfully masculine despite his pensionable age and the shadows round his eyes.

'I'd prefer you to come here and give me a chance,' he said.

She was standing in front of the smouldering fire – keeping her distance – and returned: 'What I will give you is ten out of ten for trying.'

'Be kind for a change, Florrie!'

'And you beware, or I'll give you ten out of ten for being trying, too!'

'I know what you were doing anyway.'

'Your question was even more out of order in that case.'

'How could you kiss that toothless water rat?'

'Sylvester isn't toothless, not completely, and he isn't a water rat though he did rat on me at lunchtime. He used to think he loved me – I was one of the hundreds of women he thought he loved – but his heart was never in it – his heart was in art, and now art's let him down, he's run out of the steam he needs to paint his pictures. As a result he threatens to make the ultimate nuisance of himself. He's a typical man of talent, a quite glorious failure, and if you were less self-centred than he is you would have profited from meeting him.'

'Drunken ravings aren't profitable, believe me. And what with anti-social shenanigans at dinner last night, and your uncivilised neighbours at lunch today, and dim Geoffrey and grim T.D. – it

[31]

hasn't been your most brilliant party. But I've kept smiling for your sake, and now I'm submitting my bill for services rendered.'

'How can you complain when Helen's around to dazzle and charm you with her time-honoured tricks?'

'But I'm tired of kissing Helen, and Anna's attractions aren't kissable, and Mildred's a different kettle of fish. I'm reminding you that I'm a cad who has his price and is prepared to take steps to be paid it. I've suffered, Florrie, compensate me! I'll turn nasty if you don't.'

'You're incorrigible, and I don't know why I love you.'

'Love me a little more.'

'Love me a little less,' she retorted.

'Very well, you were warned. Tell me, my dear – have you a new friend from Orezania?'

She sat down abruptly on the stool in front of the fireplace and said: 'I knew you wouldn't be considerate, I knew you'd blunder in.'

'Was it considerate of you to force us to mix with the Gristhorpes so that you could obtain information about an island that nobody in his or her right mind has ever had the slightest interest in or desire to hear about? But love is blind and deaf to boredom. Who is F.M. if not Florence Meavy?'

'Drop it, Philip!'

'Fay, I suppose?'

'I can't say.'

'Won't, you mean. Fay's fallen for an Orezanian. Hard lines, Florrie!'

'You're jumping to conclusions. Why do you sympathise with me? If you thought you were right, you'd crow.'

'I sympathise because the men of that region aren't noted for their sensitive treatment of women. Their idea of sex is rape, and wives are mere vassals – or should I say vessels? As for mothers-in-law, they're fed to the dogs.'

'Oh do stop!'

'Fay's ample proportions would be more to the taste of a full-blooded Orezanian youth than to his English equivalent who wants a girl to look like a boy. And maybe she's more sensual and responsive than her mother. I haven't mentioned the money side of things. Wait till Fay brings her dark-eyed young man to St Eo and he sees the size of her dowry!'

'You're horrible, Philip.'

'But am I far wrong? Am I wrong to pity you?'

'You're wrong to tease me.'

'How strange! You've taken the words out of my mouth. I tease you – what do you think you do to me? You tease me to distraction. Have you any idea how many females have benefited from my passion for you which you've frustrated?'

'Poor things!'

'Listen, Florrie, Florrie my darling, if Fay leaves you to consort with a foreigner you'll be lonely and you'll need me as never before. Why not pay me something on account by way of a retainer?' He stood up and approached her. 'A kiss would be better than nothing.'

She also stood, and she placed her hands on the lapels of the jacket of his dark business suit at once affectionately and in readiness to repulse him.

'Haven't you worried me enough?' she asked. 'Besides, we're too old for kisses.'

'Not too old when you look at me as you are looking.'

'No, please.'

'You're stealing my lines, Florrie – please please me. And may I remind you, because you seem to have forgotten to remember in your solitary state, that love can express itself in different ways?'

They were interrupted: voices and footsteps were audible.

'Here are the others,' Florrie said on a note of relief and broke away, and Philip's murmured curses caused her to laugh forgivingly.

Mildred, re-entering the drawing-room, said hullo and goodbye, she had invited Mr Millard-Jones to have tea in her flat before Evensong. Philip went upstairs to pack his case alone, and the others followed his example, except for Geoffrey, who had packed and placed his suitcase in the hall together with his folded mackintosh and his trilby hours ago.

Florrie asked him if he had had a nice walk.

'It would have been nicer if you'd been with us.'

His tribute was slightly laboured. His mild eyes glowed at Florrie with doglike devotion.

'It certainly would have been nicer for me,' she said.

He was concerned.

'Oh, but I wouldn't have left you in the lurch if I'd thought you were in difficulties.'

'I know – you're so sweet to me, Geoffrey, and I'm so grateful.'

'You were with Sylvester Kexmoor when we set out. Was he being tiresome again?'

'Not really – he'd recovered from his hangover – and although he's as hopeless as most artists I've still got a soft spot for him and I do admire his work. Philip's been telling me that I shouldn't have subjected you all to the company of drunks and bores.'

Geoffrey disagreed.

'Philip's very wide of the mark so far as I'm concerned, and he certainly shouldn't have distressed you in such ungrateful terms. I'm not surprised that Philip should be critical of poor Sylvester – charity isn't his strong suit. But Harold Gristhorpe's discourse on the subject of that island was extremely worthwhile, and, again, Philip should not have made some sort of personal issue of it. It was most embarrassing when he accused you of having ulterior motives in front of strangers. At any rate I've thoroughly enjoyed my weekend, Florrie, as I always do enjoy every opportunity to be with you.'

She smiled thanks in his direction, and said: 'Geoffrey, in the context of Orezania, will you help me?'

'If I possibly can.'

'It's Fay.'

'Ah!'

His gloomy exclamation called forth a quick denial.

'It's not that bad! She's only struck up a friendship with an Orezanian.'

'Which could be instructive, I'd have thought.'

'Not necessarily – not in a suitable way – he's a man.'

'Ah!' he repeated, and she caught him up with a touch of testiness: 'Don't, please – you sound so ominous.'

'Forgive me! I was appreciating the fact that a male Orezanian of unknown origins might be a mistake from a mother's viewpoint. What age is he?'

[34]

'Young – I'm not sure – I haven't liked to demand details – she mentioned him at the end of a long chat and I tried not to jump out of my skin.'

'Is she in love with him?'

'Probably – she looks as if she might be – but I'm sure about nothing.'

'Where did they meet?'

'At a restaurant, I believe.'

'You mean dining together?'

'Not exactly. He's a waiter. Don't say "Ah", Geoffrey!'

'I was going to ask how I could help.'

'Sorry! Advise me! What am I to do? Listen, this is very confidential, I haven't confided in a single other soul.'

'I understand and give you my word of honour that I'll always respect your confidence, which greatly flatters me. Now, my first piece of advice is never to trust Philip. As likely as not, he would dine out on the story. After all, setting aside the emotional aspects, a great estate is involved.'

'Fay's not married, Geoffrey – you needn't worry about the marriage settlement yet. What I want to know is how to play the game with Fay. Am I to forbid her to meet her man? Am I to lock her up in the cellar of Buckingham Square?'

'Good gracious no!' Geoffrey laughed discreetly at the exaggeration.

'Should I have a discouraging heart-to-heart? But discouragement is like pouring petrol on the fire of love, isn't it?'

'Too true,' Geoffrey nodded sagely, as if fully cognisant of such fires.

'What then?'

'I'm rather of the opinion that silence might be the wisest response.'

'And let her sleep with the beast under the impression that I'm in favour of the love affair, and bring home an Orezanian half-caste, and have her heart broken and her future blighted?'

'Oh my dear, you misunderstand me. I would never knowingly make a suggestion that could have undesirable repercussions on yourself. My thoughts were all for Fay and for what would best serve mother and daughter. Every alternative to silence, to your keeping your own counsel, would compel Fay to choose between

[35]

her beloved Mama and her lover, and her choice would be bound to be sad and bad for one of you and therefore both. Remember your own simile of the petrol – speaking a piece of your mind would be like pouring petrol over your boats and lighting a match in the vicinity. My humble opinion is that the maintenance of good relations with Fay has to be your number one priority.'

'Thank you, darling Geoffrey. You're right, that settles it – silence is always golden – mum's the word – not a single squeak will escape me – I promise to hold my tongue. Will that do? You're my friend and the best of bricks.'

She patted his cheek and hugged him as she had been careful not to hug his rival.

A Cry in the Night

As soon as she was alone she rang through to Buckingham Square. But Fay was not there: Maria said she had been gone the whole weekend.

Florrie spent the rest of that Sunday evening quietly, that is to say on the telephone, returning calls, issuing and responding to invitations, and at her desk, catching up on correspondence.

On the Monday morning she had her customary session with Mildred, who was expected not to let the house fall down until the following Friday. She handed over a sheaf of memoranda and gave instructions in an unusually sharp tone of voice: Mildred after her tea for two with the Reverend Aubrey Millard-Jones seemed to be in a dream of love, whether religious or secular.

At ten-thirty Crisp brought the Jaguar to the front door, Wilson stowed it with luggage and country comestibles, and Jean and Mrs Withgill emerged to say goodbye to her ladyship.

Mildred, more wakefully, did ask her kinswoman as they walked towards the car: 'Oh – Fay – are there any developments?'

Florrie shook her head and put a finger to her lips.

She was then driven to London and welcomed by Maria and Barney, not by Fay, at Buckingham Square.

Her luncheon engagement was with Roger Ryther in his basement flat in the outback of Battersea. Afterwards Crisp took them to the Tate Gallery to see the winning entry for the Turner Prize, a glass case containing a plate of food and a pile of ordure separated by some animal or possibly human intestines. Roger thought it was seriously interesting. Florrie said it was revolting and hurried to her hairdresser's.

She dined out on the Monday evening. Her host was the billionaire socialist M.P. Solomon Windsor. He was a big oppressive financier by trade with hair so black that it was surely dyed, and his wife Wilma was a match for him in size and had crimson cheeks and an exuberant manner: they were both Hungarian by extraction. Their residence in London was a rambling maisonette in Belgrave Square furnished and decorated with the best taste that money could buy, and they had invited their friends, most of whom, like Florrie, were actually acquaintances, to meet the composer Theodore Hildwitch.

Florrie had known Theodore for ages, and several of his wives. The music he composed was modern and a pain for her to listen to: as someone who also loathed it had said, the only bearable bits were the silences that separated the rattles and squawks. He was now getting on for eighty, a short spry septuagenarian with a trim white moustache and imperial beard, a great success, acclaimed by the critics and loaded with decorations – he had reasons galore to be as pleased as he was with himself.

Florrie sat between Solly and Theodore: neither took much notice of her. Conversation was general, predictable, about political skulduggery and funding for the arts, competitive and loud – she could not have made herself heard if she had had anything to say or any wish to say it. But she smiled dutifully, and might have compared the occasion to bread and butter without jam if the meal had not consisted of five rich courses cooked by a French chef. One short sentence differed from all the meaningless hot air so far as she was concerned: Theodore boasted that he was bringing the folk songs of the Caucasus up to date. It was a disagreeable reminder of Fay's waiter. As soon as possible Florrie, entitled by precedence to be the first to leave, said good night: her excuse that she must not take advantage of her chauffeur could hardly be challenged by a representative of the working man.

She was back at Buckingham Square by eleven-thirty, and immediately climbed the stairs to the top floor of the house. But for the second time in the day she found Fay's door open and her bedroom empty. Downstairs, in her own bedroom, she changed into her night attire uneasily, straining her ears for sounds of her daughter's arrival. But the house was quiet, except for an occasional creak of floorboards. A sudden chorus of goodbyes as guests departed from a neighbour's house rose above the hum of distant traffic and the soughing of the large leaves of the plane trees in the garden of the Square.

Just before midnight the telephone rang. It startled and frightened her: friends only rang so late in an emergency. What could have happened? What might have happened to Fay? Dread possibilities crossed her mind.

She lifted the receiver shakily.

'Ma!'

'Where are you?' she said.

'Don't worry! I'm at St Eo.'

'St Eo! Why? Why on earth are you there?'

'I'll explain. Am I disturbing you?'

Florrie had to laugh.

'Of course not! I haven't known where you were – you wanted to be in London while I was at St Eo – you go to St Eo after I've gone to London – you tell me too much and too little – I thought you must have been murdered and I've scarcely closed an eye for the last three nights – of course you haven't disturbed me – why should I be disturbed? Are you alone?'

'Quite alone. I'm in your sitting-room at the moment. I've tried to reach you, but Maria said you were out.'

'Is anything wrong?'

'No! Were you having dinner with people?'

'The Windsors.'

'Heavens!'

'Not our royal family – its Hungarian branch – Solly and Wilma Windsor in Belgrave Square – a good socialist address. I'd have boasted till I was blue in the face if I'd been asked to mix with royalty.'

They had both been laughing, but now Florrie thought they were cut off.

'Fay?'

'Yes?'

'Did you hear the line go dead? I couldn't hear you for a moment.'

'Yes – possibly. Was it fun?'

'Routine – the slap-up mixture as before – and I'm spoilt and ungrateful – and much more interested in your arrangements and why you're at St Eo.'

'Nothing's arranged, Ma, and I promise I'm not avoiding you – it isn't like that at all – and I'm ringing because I was afraid you'd jump to bad conclusions if I didn't turn up for breakfast in the morning. But I know I haven't kept in touch, and now it's late – sorry!'

'Don't you worry, my sweet! I've just been dying to talk to you.'

'What about?'

'Well . . . Are you sleepy, darling?'

'No.'

'Well, I've thought things over, I've had second and third thoughts, and I wonder if you'd mind my trying to put them into words – to speak out would do me a power of good whatever it does to you?'

'Go ahead!'

'You don't sound very receptive, and I don't blame you, I remember the boredom of advice from officious hasbeens.'

'Oh Ma! I'm listening, I really am.'

'Thank you, darling. My message is a kind of confession. Philip Mozergh calls me cold-hearted, but that's the opposite of the truth – it's the people who fall in and out of love on a daily basis who have the cold hearts. I hadn't loved anybody properly when I met your father – I believed I had, but, thanks to him, I discovered I hadn't. Everyone was against our marrying, and in principle they were right because our marriage was so unusual. He left me for the first time a month after our honeymoon to go and risk his neck in some swamp in South America, and was incommunicado in the Antarctic when you were born. His absences weren't easy, but I wasn't tempted to look to right or left – I used to think I was like Penelope waiting for Ulysses to come home. Eldred was legally acknowledged to be dead eight years ago, although he was never found, and I haven't married again. I can't imagine myself getting involved with another man, not deeply – your father still seems to be enough for me. That's my temperament – there should be an extra sign of the zodiac for me named Fido. Can you see my drift? I may have passed it all on to you, and if so please be, you must

[40]

be, careful about committing yourself. Fay? I've talked too much, haven't I?'

'It's not that, Ma. I will be careful. Is that all?'

'I suppose so. No! I can't help saying one or two other things. But is this telephone on the blink?'

'I can hear you very well.'

'Darling girl, have you any idea of the difficulties that are added to marriage by choosing to marry a foreigner? I know a lot of drivel is talked about citizens of the world, and an end to nations and nationality and sovereignty and suchlike. But races differ in spite of the do-gooders, they're as different as they look, and references to the land of one's fathers aren't meaningless, our native landscape shapes us or we somehow fit into it – anyway to break the rules of nature is bound to be dangerous – think of mules, which lose the power to reproduce themselves! I can give you human examples: Sibell Hurlingham's girl married a Moroccan who locked her up in their bedroom and stuffed her with food for five years – when she was rescued she weighed twenty stone.'

'No, Ma – '

'It's true! Tabitha Hurlingham may not be completely human, but Lettice Mappleby is or was – and she married a Tibetan and had four disastrous children who only grew to be four feet tall with slanting Tibetan eyes and enormous English feet.'

'You're so funny, Ma.'

'Well, the attribute that hardly ever crosses a frontier is a sense of humour. Timothy Leigh married that American girl and went to work in Wall Street, and his own mother told me that one of his main reasons for returning to England was to have a laugh. And you're so good at seeing a joke, Fay! I'm serious!'

'And I'm not laughing any more.'

'What?'

'I'm listening.'

'The other thing is class. Forgive me for repeating myself, dearest girl – and God forgive the wicked fools who brainwash simple people into believing classlessness is possible. The effects on love of pretending we're all lumped together in a single class can be tragic. Sex may bridge the gap for a short while if a couple are cast adrift on a desert island, but sooner or later there's bound to be friction over backgrounds and memories and manners and habits. Naomi Wickens spent a year in a tree with her lover who wanted to stop somebody cutting it down – he was a professional protester and never washed – but although she swore she was perfectly happy, the moment Johnny Linkinhorne proposed to her she climbed down and scampered off to Harrods to order her trousseau. And Willy Haddenham's marriage to that nice little girl came to grief because the members of her family were embarrassed by his posh accent and he couldn't bear to watch them eating with their mouths open.'

'Ma, you're wide of the mark.'

'No, darling – I hate to disagree with you, but at the risk of seeming to be materialistic I have to say I'm not that wide. Apart from the emotional and cultural sides, there's the financial one to be taken into consideration. I'm thinking of your expectations, of St Eo and our dependants.'

'Please stop, Ma!'

'You're not ill, are you?'

'No.'

'Have I gone too far?'

'Farther than you need to go.'

'What do you mean?'

'You've been talking about Alexander, haven't you?'

'Is your friend called Alexander?'

'Yes.'

'The Orezanian friend?'

'Yes.'

'I've worried so, darling – you deserve better than a foreign waiter.'

'He isn't exactly a waiter, he isn't only a waiter.'

'Don't tell me he's a crook.'

'He's not a crook, he's a king.'

'I couldn't catch your last word?'

'A king – he's the King of Orezania.'

'You amaze me.'

'In the circumstances, Ma, the question of class is more his concern than ours, because we're the social underdogs and obviously he shouldn't marry beneath him.'

'Wait a tick! Now you're going too far and fast for me. And

[42]

you're mocking me! Do you believe Alexander? Masses of lunatics have imagined they were kings of somewhere or other.'

'I believe him absolutely – he isn't mad and doesn't tell lies – and he's shown me documents and seals.'

'They could be stolen, evidence can be faked. He might be another Anastasia.'

'Never!'

'I'm sorry, my sweet – I happen to know that every Orezanian royal was knocked on the head by the Russian secret police, who'd had a lot of practice after all.'

'How do you know that?'

'I've had it on good authority.'

'Who from? Who have you been gossiping to, Ma?'

'I haven't been gossiping, but I did ask Harold Gristhorpe to lunch, and he provided a potted history of the place in return.'

'Isn't he a neighbour?'

'Exactly – and his wife's cashed in on having some rather disgusting links with the Bloomsburyites – they've been to Orezania. They came to lunch yesterday.'

'Did you ask him about Orezania in front of everyone?'

'I was as discreet as possible, I promise you.'

'Oh dear!'

'Don't be upset – the one person I mentioned your name to was Geoffrey, who gave me a word of advice – and he's like the grave for secrets, and always has our best interests at heart.'

'What did Geoffrey advise?'

'He told me to mind my own business.'

Fay laughed and caused laughter by commenting in the satirical family style: 'I'm glad you followed it.'

'Your Alexander, darling, why is he here and working in a cut-price restaurant if he's King of Orezania?'

'He's a refugee – there's an awful civil war in his country – some of his countrymen would kill him if they could.'

'Well, I won't give him away.'

'You would, Ma – but you can't – because he's in hiding – he's had to disappear.'

'That's terrible! Poor young man! Now you're not to tease too much – but, obviously, his being a king, if he is a king, makes a difference to the Mrs Bennet in me. A king isn't a foreigner in the

[43]

common sense, and I'm certainly not against the principle and possibility of self-improvement – women would be in an even worse pickle than they are, and always have been, if they weren't allowed to marry above their stations. I always hoped you'd do well, my darling – that's why I couldn't settle for a waiter – but I never expected to see you on a throne. Good Queen Fay, fancy that! I knew I could trust you, and I wasn't wrong, was I?'

'Maybe.'

'What's the matter, darling? You don't sound happy.'

'Ma, you're counting a whole flock of chickens before they're hatched. I'm not engaged to Alexander, we met only thirteen days ago, and now he's vanished.'

'Are you saying he led you up the garden path?'

'It was more the other way round.'

'Tell me, Fay.'

'We spent Sunday together – he took me boating on the river, he hired a boat at Maidenhead and rowed for miles – and it was so sunny and lovely, it was my happiest day – and in the evening he declared himself and I said yes, same here, and for a while everything was perfect. Then he told me who he was.'

'How romantic!'

'He told me who he was, and I backed out.'

'Wasn't that a mistake?'

'I was shocked – I mean it was such a shock! And he was terribly honest. He warned me of the difficulties ahead, and specially ahead of me – he was more alarming than you've been, which is saying something. He might be assassinated at any moment, he told me, or kidnapped and tortured and maimed – and I would be in danger, too, and our children would have to be guarded night and day. And supposing he regained his birthright, which was extremely unlikely, because he would have to defeat three armies, but just supposing he had been crowned King, and I'd consented to be his Queen, we'd lose the right to live our own lives, to live for each other, and to stop smiling or get cross or yawn or wear comfy clothes, we'd belong to Orezania and become the slaves of obligation. He explained that I'd have to renounce my nationality and religion and home, and that in Orezanian law an engagement to marry was blessed in church and marriage was for ever and divorce was against the law. And his warnings got mixed up with

[44]

yours, Ma, and I remembered I wasn't of his class and he wasn't of mine, that our backgrounds were oil and water, that he was a foreigner and could always be penniless, that St Eo could be no more than a consolation prize for him, and, worst of all for me, that I'd be loving a man who might not be monogamous in our sense and anyway sharing him with his country. So I said no.'

'Proper men don't take no for an answer.'

'I'm afraid kings do,' Fay sniffed audibly.

'Why are you afraid?'

'He was so sad. He dropped me back at Jenny and Sue's at about ten o'clock and said good night and goodbye in Orezanian, which I believe also means adieu. I went indoors and worried and changed my mind and tried to ring him in his hotel or hostel in Clapham. Somebody told me he'd paid his bill and cleared out. This morning I went to the restaurant where he worked and was shown a note he'd written to the manager and delivered overnight saying he had to go abroad.'

'Is that why you're at St Eo?'

'I thought I couldn't talk to anyone, even to you,' Fay said between sniffs; 'but I changed my mind about that, too.'

'Thank heavens you did, my sweet. I'm full of sympathy for you. But do remember where marriages are made, and don't despair.'

'What I'm trying my hardest and failing to remember is that all may be for the best.'

Florrie now mingled an audible sniff with Fay's.

'And Ma,' Fay added in a strangulated voice, 'if I'm exactly like you, Alexander would be my last love and I've lost him' – at which both mother and daughter cried.

The Royal Box

Florrie's telephone conversation with Fay continued until they were able to dry their eyes, and resumed the following morning.

Emotion was kept to a minimum, neither of them had slept well, and they talked in lowered voices.

Fay explained that Alexander's family name was Orez; also that Orez was the capital of his kingdom, and that Orezania itself was so-called after his forebears. But as his father was dead he bore dozens of titles, Archduke of this and Grand Duke of that, the humblest of which, Baron Nix, figured in his British passport. Yes, she assured her mother, although she had not seen his passport he had told her it was British: apparently Alexander's grandfather took the precaution of obtaining alternative nationalities for his children, hoping thus to conceal their identity and perhaps save their lives. The Bolsheviks, nonetheless, caught and executed the majority of the members of the royal house; only Alexander's father, a baby some months old, escaped – he was smuggled out of the palace of Orez by his wet-nurse and brought up in a shack in the mountains. He lived to marry and to sire Alexander. But the stooges of Moscow in the Orezanian seats of power heard of the young woodcutter to whom court was being paid, and despatched officials to investigate in the good old Bolshevik manner: that is by murdering the youth and his relations and friends. Alexander survived the bloodbath: he had been spirited away by soldiers of the monarchist secret army and was packed off to England to complete his education and await fate's summons to the throne of his ancestors.

It was or was like a fairy tale, and Florrie almost believed it. She

[46]

wished to please Fay and was half-persuaded by Fay's conviction. Yet scepticism compelled her to quote the experience of the daughter of her acquaintances the Linklaces of Linklace Abbey in Herefordshire. Young Cissie Linklace who worked for Greenpeace had married a black African under the impression that he was the ruler of the state of Nambkha and the chieftain of all the Namb-khaians. Her first letter home disabused her proud parents: Cissie's new address was to be, Beneath the Old Apple Tree, Nambkha, and she told them she was living in a mud hut with three of her rat-poor husband's other wives.

Fay was not amused: Alexander was poor for the time being, but he had jolly well earned his daily bread, and he possessed royal warrants and rings and things. Florrie was not disposed to argue. She merely mentioned the coincidence of Fay boating with genuine King Alexander while her mother was dining with the bogus Windsors, and asked where the young people had met.

At the restaurant where Alexander was working, The Greek Experience, located in a suburb of London that Florrie had never heard of. Fay had gone there thirteen days ago with a group of her friends.

'Wasn't the Greek experience homosexual?' Florrie blurted out apprehensively.

'Was it? Does it matter?' Fay replied.

'Alexander's not that way inclined, is he?'

'He is not.'

Fay's reply was firm and her smile possibly nostalgic, and Florrie held her peace.

Evidently the restaurant was the informal type, guests and staff mingled freely, and Fay had been drawn to Alexander and vice versa by irresistible force, and they had fallen for each other on the spot.

'I didn't know who he was, and he didn't know who I was – if I am anybody – but nothing made any difference, we just under-stood each other.'

'Does he speak English?' Florrie asked.

'Yes – he's been in England for ages – he was at some university up north – he speaks English much better than we do – he's so brilliant,' Fay declared.

'Where has he been living?'

[47]

Florrie went on to refer to the unusual circumstances of a king in a hostel or obscure hotel where someone was willing to answer Fay's telephone call in the middle of the night.

The defensive reply was: 'I don't exactly know, I haven't been there, Ma – it seems to be a place for commercial travellers to arrive at and leave whenever they like.'

'What about now?'

'What do you mean?'

'Where do you think Alexander is now?'

'I'm trying not to think.'

'I'm sure he'll come back to the charge.'

'Are you? I'm not – I was frightened when he told me those home truths.'

'But you'd make the loveliest queen.'

Fay murmured repressively and changed the subject.

'I've reached another decision, Ma. I'm going to do a nursing course.'

'Oh – well – that's admirable – but rather you than me, I'm hopelessly squeamish – won't you faint at operations?'

Time would tell, Fay answered; and she would find out if she should do it in town or in the country, based in Buckingham Square or at St Eo.

'Are you all right, darling?'

'Oh yes. I will be.'

'Shall I come down to be with you?'

'No, no, Ma, thanks.'

'Will you promise to ring me again if you're feeling wretched?'

'Will you promise me not to broadcast my news?'

They both laughed, and soon said goodbye.

Florrie dialled Mildred Chaffcombe's number.

Mildred sounded sleepy: she read poetry until the small hours and was a slow starter in the mornings.

'You've got Fay in the house,' Florrie began.

'So I've just been told by Wilson. I can't imagine why Fay rang the Wilsons' doorbell instead of mine at nine o'clock last night – I was here and my lights were on.'

'She wanted to be alone.'

'Is anything wrong?'

'Yes – her love affair – but it's meant to be a deadly secret.'

[48]

'I'm surprised she told you in that case,' Mildred giggled, then asked: 'What secret, Florrie?'

'Her boyfriend's disappeared. He's foreign, you know.'

'No – I don't know anything.'

'He's Orezanian.'

'What?'

'It doesn't matter – I can't say more – I mustn't or she'll kill me – but if she should confide in you, for goodness sake don't whisper a word against her young man.'

'I thought we were all meant to pray she'd ditch him as soon as possible.'

'Who told you that?'

'You did.'

'Oh – well – I can't be responsible today for what I said yesterday. Plead complete ignorance and encourage her in that order, if you get a chance. I'd rather she married well than turned herself into a nurse.'

'Is she thinking of becoming a nurse?'

'Oh dear – I'd better ring off – forget I said so – ignorance is the best policy, Mildred – remember, please!'

Later that morning, after making more telephone calls and paying even more bills, Florrie walked from Buckingham Square northwards to the Everyman Hotel behind Oxford Street. She supposed exercise was good for her and tried to take it regularly; but today she travelled by shanks' pony instead of by chauffeur-driven Jaguar in order to cogitate. She was strangely stirred, as well as upset, by Fay's vicissitudes. Almost hallucinatory images of crowns, sceptres, coats of arms, palaces and liveried flunkeys were superimposed on Niobe-like images of her daughter, all tears, deserted and deceived; at the same time her heart beat a little faster with an unwonted interest in love. It was vicarious – she was merely entering into Fay's feelings – she was convinced that her interest in the opposite sex had died at Eldred's death – she had said as much to Fay, and to go back on her word and as it were weaken would complicate her existence unbearably.

Horrendous possibilities crossed her mind. If she were to re-enter the lists of love, she would lose friends left, right and centre. Philip Mozergh was right – she would not see him for dust if she ever let him have what he said he wanted – he would have nothing to sit

[49]

up and beg for; and it would be positively cruel to tell Geoffrey Oldcoate she was willing. Moreover wives would not like her to take an active, as distinct from a social, interest in their husbands; and the professional paramours like Helen Islebeck would not be so appreciative of a mean competitor as of a generous hostess.

The summer sun shone on her in the open spaces of Hyde Park, and in the shade under the trees the air was balmy. She shook herself: what nonsense! There was nothing wrong with her life. She was the luckiest person in the whole world, her life could not be improved upon, and she must not fall into the trap baited by discontent and greed.

She arrived at The Everyman and was directed to the Banqueting Room, where she was to lunch with the organisers and patrons of the charity bearing the name: 'Say No!' She had paid through the nose for the privilege: she was an unfailing donor to charities and had suppressed expensive yawns at many fund-raising functions. Her motives were not so much interest in charitable work, or faith that it would do any good, as reluctance to resist the appeals directed at her more or less oppressively by acquaintances and sometimes even by friends.

She joined a queue and was at long last greeted by Brenda Slawston, the old Countess of Slawston of Slawston Court in the Brecon Beacons and the President of 'Say No!', which aimed its efforts at drug abuse in inner cities.

Brenda thanked Florrie for coming, exhorted her idealistically to have fun, and pointed out Anna Hulcott amongst a group of ladies in hats. T.D. Faulkbourne lumbered in later and the three friends bagged places together at one of the dozen or so tables for ten.

Anna was not looking her best, in plainer language she looked ghastly, chinless and loose-lipped with colourless lank hair and large uncontrolled bosom. But she was as enthusiastic as ever and again sang the praises of her weekend at St Eo.

Florrie, who knew Anna was not flush with money, interrupted: 'It's very decent of you to cough up for a do of this sort.'

'Oh but Brenda's so marvellous to patronise such a cause.'

Florrie's feelings for Anna were perverse: she appreciated Anna's honey-sweet talk, and admired her for not being bitter, yet was inclined as if for culinary reasons to squeeze a little lemon over their exchanges.

With reference to Brenda she now said: 'And she knows so much about the inner cities after living for thirty years in splendid isolation at Slawston Court.'

Anna hooted. She was too clever to compound the effects of her ugliness by being nasty, but she adored – as she put it – to listen to Florrie calling a spade a bloody shovel.

She chipped in provocatively: 'Brenda's such a compassionate person.'

'The questions are,' Florrie returned in a judicious undertone, 'should Brenda show compassion to drug addicts, and should we all dig deep and eat over-priced lunches in order to save their lives?'

'You'll get us shot,' Anna warned, laughing behind her hand.

'Seriously – it's ridiculous – I feel compassionate about poor diabetics having to inject themselves with insulin – diabetics dread having to do it, and ninety-nine point nine percent of the population would run a mile from a hypodermic needle if they could – but drug addicts inject themselves for a lark, and behave suicidally for pleasure, and cost the rest of us swingeing taxes. I think the sensible answer, satisfying for everybody, would be to distribute the drugs free and rid ourselves of a disgusting and dangerous social element.'

'You're priceless, Florrie,' Anna laughed, and deftly turned the conversation in the direction that interested her; 'no wonder those gentlemen of our acquaintance are your devoted slaves. I saw Philip turn green at St Eo, even after so many years, when you were keen to know about Orezania. Was he right to suspect he had a rival rising in the east?'

Florrie denied it, and shifted round to talk to T.D., who was also Brenda Slawston's solicitor.

T.D. growled more thanks for the St Eo weekend, and Florrie asked him: 'May I talk business here?'

He bent his heavy head to signify assent, and she said: 'I was going to ring you up – we were intending to transfer a nice round sum into Fay's name, weren't we?'

He either replied in the affirmative or cleared his throat.

[51]

'Can we wait a bit? Can we postpone?'

'I always encourage my clients to seize every opportunity not to spend money,' he said, peeping at her through the hedge of his eyebrows. 'Are whys and wherefores likely to be forthcoming?'

'Not at this stage,' she told him with a bewitchingly mysterious grimace, and summoned Anna to participate in frothy tripartite talk.

The meal dragged on; but everything comes to an end. At three o'clock the chief executive of the charity concluded his speech by threatening to change its name, 'Say No!' He explained with unintentional humour that too many appeals for money were returned minus cheques and in unstamped envelopes with the following words scrawled across them 'I am saying no'.

Florrie kissed a large number of people goodbye and was kissed by more, then walked to her dressmaker's for a fitting.

She returned to Buckingham Square at five-thirty, decided with difficulty not to ring Fay, but made and answered other telephone calls, eventually had a bath and donned the black evening dress with sequins laid out on her bed by Maria, clamped on a diamond brooch and hurried downstairs and into the Jaguar, beside the open front passenger door of which Crisp was waiting.

She had been invited to the opera at Covent Garden by Bobby Ireby, a member of the board of directors of the opera house. She was late and suspected that she would displease her host. Sir Robert Ireby was at once big in business and small in stature, an ominous mixture. He had won not only his spurs but also his knighthood by being a high-class nagger in boardrooms, and in society he was a busybody and martinet. He had reduced his wife Rosamund to a zombie-like state, and as a rule kept her down in the country. He had bullied Florrie into accepting his second or third invitation to the opera because he was keen to be invited to St Eo.

Crisp deposited her at the door in Floral Street, the entrance for the royal box, the use of which was an occasional directorial perk, and said he would find and fetch her at the end of the performance. One attendant ushered her up a red-carpeted staircase and another into a brightly lit empty room and through a doorway into the dark of the box. The house-lights had been extinguished and the audience was clapping the advent of the conductor of the orchestra.

[52]

Florrie could not see very well for a moment and was almost startled when Bobby Ireby on his tiptoes kissed her.

She hissed at him: 'I'm so sorry,' and he hissed back irritably: 'You're not the only one who should have been here earlier,' and escorted her, or rather shoved her, into a free-standing upright chair.

Her eyes were soon accustomed to the darkness, and she made out several guests sitting on the other chairs ranged alongside the parapet – unexpectedly Rosamund had been permitted to join the party, but she was seated in the one with the worst view. The place of honour on the left, next to Florrie's chair, was at present unoccupied; and Bobby and a couple of his dinner-jacketed friends sat on elevated chairs behind her.

The great introductory chords of the overture to *Don Giovanni* thundered out. Florrie knew and loved that opera; but the anticipated pleasures of seeing and hearing it again deteriorated into pain, or at least disappointment. The producer had not deigned to let the music set the scene and as it were speak for itself, he had seen fit to enliven the overture with happenings, curtains opening and closing, gauzes playing tricks, bits of scenery flying up and down and lights flashing. The action began: in accordance with some half-baked political theory, Leporello, the servant, was made to act like a lunatic, and Don Giovanni made to look like a tramp – the leading singer had two days' growth of beard and wore rags. And Donna Elvira was sluttish, and Donna Anna was obviously meant to be a lesbian.

Florrie was familiar with the theatrical fashion for turning texts on their heads and for trying to reduce high art to some low common denominator. She called it the look-at-me school of production: in the case of *Don Giovanni* the producer was instructing the audience, 'Forget Mozart, to hell with da Ponte, composers and librettists are neither here nor there, anything they've done I can do better – look at me!'

The vandalism of it did not appeal to her, and she marvelled at the tolerance or bad taste of the paying customers. The mercy was that the music had not been rewritten by the producer, and she listened and averted her eyes from the stage. The chair beside her remained empty until Don Giovanni was practising his wiles on the innocence of Zerlina. The door of the reception room opened,

[53]

admitting a momentary shaft of light into the box. Florrie was aware of a hushed commotion behind her and, half-swivelling round, was surprised to see a man in a sky-blue suit.

She had expected the latecomer to be the husband of a more punctual guest, wearing conventional clothing. But his sky-blue apparel was actually a military uniform, and he was also wearing a dark blue sash and a complex cross set with twinkling precious stones at his neck. Her surprise did not end there: she essayed a polite gesture of greeting as he sat down in the chair reserved for his use, and was dazzled by his smile in reply, his handsome features, smooth silvery hair and the almost cannibalistic glisten of his large strong teeth.

Throughout the rest of the first half of the opera she was disturbed by his proximity. He was restless, and she sensed that he stared at her a good deal. Who could he be? – No doubt one of those diplomats in the marble halls of whose embassies Bobby liked to attend receptions for visiting dignitaries. But he seemed more confident than a consul or a first or second secretary, or even than an ambassador from the third world. He put the finishing touches to her lack of interest in the proceedings onstage, and she waited impatiently for the interval and the chance to have a closer covert look at him.

The operatic party in Don Giovanni's house ended with his escape from his accusers, and the audience applauded and the houselights came on.

Florrie stood and Bobby Ireby appeared and cleared her chair away and said to her neighbour: 'Sir, may I introduce Lady Meavy?'

To Florrie herself he explained as if with a verbal bow and scrape: 'His Majesty King Michael of Orezania!'

Who's Who?

She omitted to curtsy. She was a woman of the world, and not an ignoramus, yet she was stunned, dumbfounded, and blushed and perspired like a debutante, as she had hoped she never would again. She was suffering for Fay's sake; at the same time she was afraid the King might mistake her discomfiture for love of himself at first sight, or for signs that she was going to be sick. In fact her sudden rush of unspeakable questions to the brain did induce a wave or two of nausea.

But she recovered herself to some extent. Bobby was introducing his other guests to the man in pale blue, whom she was loath to call a king – she could not be so disloyal to Fay as to recognise his claim to the Orezanian crown. But the horrible possibility was that he had right on his side: if so, Alexander was the impostor – she had suspected it from the word go – and Fay was in the toils of a conman, of a Balkan adventurer, of a bloodsucker from Dracula's part of the world, who would do her down financially and probably do her in. How was she – Florrie – to know? She could not ask this smooth fifty-year-old Ruritanian-style hand-kisser.

She was now being herded by Rosamund Ireby out of the box and into the reception room, where a rectangular table was laid for supper. At the head of it Bobby had already seated the royal guest in accordance with courtly etiquette, resigning his position as host. Rosamund was summoned to sit on the kingly left and Florrie was hustled into the chair on his right, while the other members of the party took their places. Bobby, before he sat down, made a superfluous speech.

He and his wife were honoured to entertain His Majesty, he said.

Unfortunately he had never had the pleasure of visiting Orezania, but understood it to be a fascinating island, and nothing would stop him rushing there as soon as peace broke out. He explained in a sort of aside, through a general murmuring of respectful agreement with his sentiments, that he had met King Michael in the line of business.

The latter had knocked back one glass of sherry and another of white wine, and tucked hungrily into a dish of chicken, by the time Bobby finished. He was an animalic feeder, to put it as mildly as Florrie could, and he had looked about him in a rude manner, not paying attention, throughout Bobby's address. His sudden stare at herself – his swimming fierce brown eyes fastened upon hers – had been disconcerting, and had tightened the screw of her unease.

He spoke. His loud bass voice had a Russian edge, and his English was fractured but fluent.

'Orezania not at war, so peace not possible. Terrorism only in Orezania – we are catching and killing terrorists. I am in London for money to buy guns to shoot enemies of my people. Sir Ireby will sell me guns when I have money.'

Bobby was embarrassed, he had not expected to be publicly branded a gun-runner in return for his hospitality, and he subsided on to his chair between two sniggering females. As if to cover his confusion a male guest chimed in with a question.

'What does Your Majesty think of this production of *Don Giovanni*?'

The King or the pretender looked up from his plate, chewed and swallowed a mouthful noisily, swigged more white wine, and delivered his verdict.

'Singing okay, but where is noble? Don Giovanni is noble, not guttersnip.'

He then smiled with self-satisfaction round the table, showing his big moist teeth and causing muted laughter. Some pedant muttered 'guttersnipe' correctively, Bobby mounted a muddled defence of the producer's equally muddled intentions, and Florrie murmured agreement with the critical regal view.

He again subjected her to a disturbing stare, but instead of acknowledging her overture he withdrew a sheet of paper from his pocket, unfolded it with supple brown fingers, read and at length inquired: 'You are Meavy Lady Florence?'

[56]

'I'm Florence Meavy, yes,' she replied.

'You are rich woman?'

Florrie could not help bridling.

'Well, not as rich as all that.'

'All what?'

'Not so very rich.'

'Sir Ireby writes that you have big estate.'

Florrie showered mental curses on the head of her host and said: 'I have a house in the country, that's true.'

'Also house in London?'

'Yes.'

'I go there?'

'What did you say?'

'You invite me?'

She was appalled, and floundered. 'That would be nice – thank you for thinking of it – but I don't believe I have the staff to cope with a king's visit.'

'What is staff?'

'Servants – or would you call them serfs?'

'I bring,' he offered. 'We eat Orezanian dinner and after you give me money.'

'We'll have to see about that.'

'House in London better for me,' he added, signalling to a waiter to replenish his glass.

Rosamund Ireby came to the rescue at this point. She aimed a sympathetic glance at Florrie and tried to engage their neighbour in a discussion of English weather, ignoring his terse responses and preoccupation with his food and drink. The neighbour on Florrie's other side, an unappealing Civil Servant called Wilberforce, told her he had paid to get into St Eo and what he liked and disliked about it.

She answered automatically – the conversation was not a novelty – and did her best to control her agitation. Could it be that that beautiful uniform disguised an ugly customer? He was bloodthirsty, he was crude and coarse; and although Florrie was sufficiently well-versed in history to know that kings were seldom good, she was amazed that a modern monarch in an egalitarian world, moreover a monarch waiting to be crowned, fighting for the throne of his forefathers, almost a nobody in the meanwhile except

[57]

in the snobbish eyes of a social climber like Bobby Ireby, would dare to be so arrogant as he was.

Dirty plates were swapped for clean ones and fruit salad was handed round and had to be eaten in a rush.

Back in the box she was relieved to sit safely between men who were kings of nowhere. The opera restarted and her inner argument monopolised her attention. She must not allow this Michael person to cross any threshold of hers: to do otherwise, to supply his demands, above all to give him a single penny, would be an act of dire disloyalty to Fay. There could not be two crowned heads of one kingdom: whence the conclusion she jumped to that Michael might well be buying guns from Bobby with which to shoot Alexander and make a premature widow of her daughter.

Florrie recalled the information supplied by Harold Gristhorpe. A civil war raged in Orezania, Harold had said – Michael's denial was a lie – he must be a liar and might be a fake – which meant that Alexander perhaps was the real thing. But she could not be sure. She simply had to play safe, and extend no encouragement whatsoever to the man who could turn out to be the murderer of Fay's beloved.

The question was, the salient point was: how? How was she to bar her door against the forceful wretch? How was she to reject his appeal for money? Her best answer amounted to a feeble hope that she could escape from Covent Garden without having to commit herself and thereafter hide, refuse to answer the telephone, seek refuge somewhere or go abroad until her coast was clear. She waited on tenterhooks for the curtain to fall, hating Bobby Ireby who had sacrificed her to serve his own unscrupulous ends and placed her in a frightful predicament.

Her plan went awry. Her path was blocked by coffee and liqueurs, so to speak. Royalty required refreshment, and protocol and Bobby's servile attitude combined to restrain her until royalty was refreshed and ready to leave. And he was in no hurry: he drank two embarrassing toasts in cognac, the first, looking straight at her, to millionaires, the second to the downfall of his enemies, accompanying it with the smiling dumbshow of slitting a throat. At length Rosamund had the nerve to tell him that the opera house was closing for the night.

Bows and curtsies having been acknowledged with condescending nods of his head, he stopped in front of Florrie, reached into his pocket, produced a visiting card and pointed at it stabbingly.

'You telephone here,' he informed her.

'Thank you,' she said; 'but I won't be in London, I'm afraid – I'm off tomorrow.'

'What is off?'

'Elsewhere, not at home – I'm sorry.'

He frowned, lowering his sleek eyebrows, which were more iron-grey than silver, and intoned the reply, at once haughty and threatening: 'My people will telephone in morning.' He then appropriated her hand, pressed the card into her palm, closed her fingers on it and raised her fist in order to kiss the back with noticeably hot lips.

She felt obliged to bob half an erratic curtsy, and the Irebys conducted him down the stairs.

She followed them as soon as she was sure he had gone, and said her own hasty goodbyes – she could not wait to get out of the place.

In the Jaguar she was asked by Crisp: 'Pleasant evening, milady?'

'Not my best by a long chalk,' she answered.

'Was the gentleman in uniform a member of the party, milady?'

'He calls himself the King of Orezania.'

Crisp's comment was either insular, an opinion of foreigners in general, or perspicacious recognition of a confidence trickster: 'One of them, is he?'

She was too concerned to enter into a discussion.

Crisp added: 'It wasn't a king's car he climbed into.'

She registered this piece of information, but continued to rack her brains silently, wondering what to do next, who could help her, who to ring up, and when.

They arrived at Buckingham Square, and she thanked Crisp and, so far as dignity allowed, dashed indoors.

The time was eleven-thirty and she had decided it was not too late to ring Geoffrey Oldcoate. He had been telling her for years that his aim in life was to be of use to her – well, his chance had come, she reflected egotistically.

She hurried up to her bedroom, switching off the lights that

[59]

Maria had left on for her, and sat on the edge of the bed with her nightdress laid out on it and jabbed at the relevant buttons on her telephone.

She was seized by a new anxiety, that if her daughter should ring her while she was ringing Geoffrey their lines could get crossed. He did not answer, and she began to think his unavailability might be a blessing and she had better replace the receiver.

'Hullo?' he demanded in the loud voice of someone emerging from a dream. 'Who's that, who's there?'

'It's me.'

'Florrie!' He paused to control his displeasure, and popped in the afterthought: 'My dear!'

'You were in your beauty sleep – I'm sorry.'

He regained his gentlemanly tone of voice and replied: 'Not very much beauty about it, I fear. But a call at this hour must signify trouble?'

She sought assurances that he was fully awake, then told him her tale, evoking increasingly melodramatic exclamations.

She ended: 'So Fay has her King, who's missing, and I have mine, who'll be ringing me in a few hours, and is determined to force his way into my house and get his hands on my money. What am I to do?'

'Ah,' he remarked.

'Geoffrey,' she scolded, 'you'll have to break yourself of this bad habit of saying "Ah"! Seriously, I've had enough "Ahs" in the last few days to last a lifetime.'

'Forgive me! A temporary reprieve would be to leave a note for Maria instructing her to take messages in the morning.'

'But what do I do about the messages?'

'A diplomatic illness would be one option.'

'Shall I ask Maria to tell people I'm dead?'

'I can't laugh at such a suggestion, my dear.'

'And I daren't put ideas into the head of fate.'

'Far be it from me to make you ill, Florrie – please forget my suggestion! With regard to the money side of things, you could refer the beggar to T.D. Faulkbourne, you could say that T.D.'s in charge of the purse strings.'

'Well done, Geoffrey – he'll put a flea in His Majesty's ear if

[60]

anybody can, T.D. will serve him right! Do I still have to feed the brute?'

'I think not. I see no reason why you shouldn't say our Foreign Office has issued strict instructions that, to safeguard our trading relationships with the Balkan neighbours of Orezania and until he is installed on the Orezanian throne, the impression that he is supported by Britain must not be created and he is not be entertained formally by leading British citizens.'

'I'm not a leading British citizen, Geoffrey.'

'In my eyes you are, Florrie – and is this savage likely to know better than me?'

'I'll do it,' she said, giggling excitedly, and made a different point. 'I'll stand with my flaming sword downstairs and keep him out of my house and my life.'

'Your life? I wasn't aware that interest of that sort was involved.'

'Don't be a goose, Geoffrey – my one and only interest is to avoid involvement with the enemy of Fay's boyfriend and consequently of Fay. I've told you I'll be brave and do as you say. And I won't worry Fay. There! Thank you again – go back to sleep – good night!'

She rang off. She had not been sufficiently grateful. She had been put out by his implication that her attitude to one king bore a similarity to Fay's attitude to another, and she realised with regret that she had nipped, if not bitten, the hand of friendship. She was thinking of having a further kinder word with him, and vaguely hoping that he might have the same thought, when the telephone rang.

She lifted the receiver and said: 'Geoffrey?'

'It's Fay, Ma.'

Her heart missed a beat. She was not prepared to play dodgy games with Fay. But how was she to tell the truth? She wished, like Mona Gristhorpe, that Orezania was at the bottom of the sea.

'Oh my darling, hullo!'

'Were you waiting to speak to Geoffrey? Shall I ring later?'

'No, no! I wondered if Geoffrey might be ringing back – but that's neither here nor there and doesn't matter. How are you?'

'Better. Is it too late to talk?'

'Not for a minute.'

[61]

'You were out earlier.'

'Yes.'

'Somewhere nice?'

'At the opera.'

'Who with?'

'The Irebys. But tell me what's made you better.'

'You have, really, Ma.'

'How's that, for heaven's sake?'

'You told me I'd made a mistake to turn Alexander away.'

'Did I?'

'Don't you remember? You weren't too keen on a waiter, but thought a king would do.'

'Oh dear, you make me sound like Snobby Bobby Ireby.'

'You were being Mrs Bennet, you were being sensible – I see that now, and agree with you.'

'Has Alexander reappeared?'

'No – but I'm keeping as calm as possible, I'm determined not to fuss. Now that I know he's worth waiting for I feel completely different, Ma, and prepared to be patient.'

'Darling girl, don't you think you're rather young to dedicate yourself so wholeheartedly? I mean monogamy's all very well – but you've hardly ever met other young men, who might not vanish into thin air.'

'Please – please don't say you've changed your mind again – I've been such an idiot and so miserable – how could I have let him go? – but although I've lost him for the time being I've felt happier today – doubts have taken a back seat, and I've sort of seen my way ahead clearly – and I'd be happier still to know you're on my side.'

'I'm on your side whatever happens.'

'Oh thank you, Ma! You are the very best Ma. I've never told you how much I love Alexander. It really was love at first sight for me, and he says for him too, and the other almost incredible thing is that it was so easy, being in love was much easier than not being in love, all the difficulties that I anticipated melted into nothingness and I suppose nature took over. He's my better half, Ma – I don't deserve him, I know, but I do appreciate him – he's the most wonderful man that ever was, except for Father – and so strong and brave – I can't believe he would let me or anyone else down,

[62]

and I'll never disappoint him again if I can possibly help it. The trouble was I panicked. My friends think I'm terribly old-fashioned, but I belong to my generation after all, and was more at home with a waiter than I thought I would be with a king. I shied away from the prospect of danger and limelight, and duty and ceremonial if we were lucky, and goodness knows what if we weren't. I said no, and behaved as if he'd deceived me on purpose. But after we parted and I talked to you, and specially after I realized that I might have lost Alexander, not just mislaid him, it dawned on me that I loved him on any terms and that we'd both actually misunderstood each other: for he was wrong to think my negative was final, and I failed to realise he was offering to make my dearest dream come true. I've always dreamed of having a cause to live and fight for, and the cause of Alexander, who'd be such a great good king, couldn't be improved upon, although I was too silly to see the point to begin with. My friends would probably scoff, they're against privilege and don't like authority much; but that's just a passing fad, isn't it, Ma? Besides, a king's only a leader. Alexander's my leader anyway, and I'd be happy ever after if I could find him. Oh dear! I'm so sorry to gas on like this – but I longed to tell you – sorry to be so self-centred. What about your evening? What was it like? Who was there?'

Florrie replied: 'My darling, the guest of honour was King Michael of Orezania.'

Plots and Plans

'Oh Ma!'

'I had no idea he'd be there, I mean I wasn't sent a list of the Irebys' guests, I was introduced to him in the interval, and had to sit next to him at dinner, and I've dreaded having to tell you.'

'He's a cheat.'

'You know that and I believe you, but he seems to have persuaded quite a lot of people that he isn't – Bobby Ireby slavered over him, and the other people present kowtowed for all they were worth.'

'What's he like?'

'Middle-aged, middle-European, a B-picture romantic gangster with a touch of the international terrorist, wearing a fancy uniform and a blue sash and the jewelled insignia of some order hanging round his neck.'

'You can buy those insignia for tuppence in gift shops. What did you talk about at dinner?'

'I can't remember – nothing.'

'Come on, Ma!'

'He wants me to entertain him.'

'Is he in love with you?'

'Don't be funny, darling – he's after my money, nothing else.'

'Money! You mustn't give him money to pay people to kill Alexander – please, please, Ma!'

'It's all right, I'm not going to, and I won't have him here, in our house, I won't – I've spoken to Geoffrey and worked out exactly what to say when he rings up tomorrow morning.'

[64]

'Oh no! He's ringing you? How friendly did you get with him? I may be ill at any minute.'

'Don't, my darling – and don't punish an innocent party – you couldn't have found fault with my behaviour – I was as stand-offish as possible in the circumstances. If I'd refused to shake hands and unmasked the villain, I would have had to answer questions, your connection with Alexander would have come up, then you'd be kidnapped and Alexander would be blackmailed and so would I, and I'd probably receive parcels containing pieces of your anatomy. This man's dominating and determined, but, rest assured, he's not as determined as I intend to be.'

'Does Geoffrey know all my secrets now?'

'Well – I was so flustered by my evening that I had to consult somebody. Geoffrey's sufficiently in the picture to know what's what.'

'What is what?'

'I'm to say the Foreign Office won't let me invite an uncrowned king to dinner.'

'He won't swallow it, Ma – no one would – I wouldn't. You don't look like a politician, thank goodness – and you're obviously not a buttoned-up diplomat – why should the Foreign Office take the slightest interest in your guests? But listen, I remember Alexander mentioning a man called Miklos or Michael, one of the warlords, the Blue one, an old communist and a new claimant to the throne. Alexander said he was an unreconstructed swine, and I'm afraid he'll fight his way into Buckingham Square and fight his way out with the swag.'

'You're not showing much confidence in your mother, darling. What I had to tell you wasn't nice, I know – it was nasty and unsettling – but we're living in England in peacetime, not in Orezania where there's civil war with no holds barred – so even a weak woman like me ought to be able to run rings round a man, and two of us should be more than a match for anything in trousers. Look on the bright side! Michael can't get his hot hands on my money unless I sign my name, and I swear I won't sign any document that does him a favour. The pressing question is tomorrow – what's to be done? Let's try to be constructive, if not logical. In view of your feelings for Alexander, shouldn't we take his likely wishes into consideration? What would he want us to do about Michael?'

[65]

'Clever Ma, you're right! I'm sure he'd want anybody in the queue for the crown to be kept out of his kingdom.'

'Then I'd better cooperate with Michael and, provided I use a very long spoon, have him to dinner. He'll ring up to invite me to invite him, and I'll make a date as far ahead as possible. What do you think?'

'You won't be alone with him, will you, Ma?'

'No – I wasn't born yesterday, more's the pity – I'll hand-pick a group to meet him and protect me and serve our interests. Will you join in?'

'I'd rather not. Actually I couldn't bear to, if you don't mind. Besides, I've begun my crash course in nursing at a St John Ambulance place in Gloucester. I drove there today and signed on, and I'll be busy for the next week or so.'

'Isn't Gloucester miles from St Eo?'

'It is, and I've wondered if I should fix myself up in local lodgings for the duration.'

'We must have friends in that area – Brenda Slawston's pigging it in fifty rooms just across the Welsh frontier. You could certainly stay with Lady Slawston.'

'No, Ma – I'm not in the mood to mix with your friends – thanks all the same.'

'You're as independent and stubborn as your father, and I love you for it. I'll keep you informed of all developments, and do my best.'

'And I'll give everyone my telephone number if or when I move out of St Eo. And there's a more important if: will you ask Maria and Barney to tell Alexander where I am if he tries to contact me? I've given the same instructions in case he rings St Eo. The name will be Alexander Nix – don't forget!'

Florrie said she never would, and swapped sympathy and reassurance for the sweets of fond filial gratitude until they bade each other good night.

But Florrie's night, or rather morning, for they had talked till past twelve, was not good. She saw things more clearly in the dark, and seemed to hear what had not been discussed. But she struggled to concentrate exclusively on her maternal responsibilities. Via various changes of mind she had come round to fostering her daughter's relationship with this unknown quantity from Orezania.

[66]

Fay was a lovely lovable girl with great expectations, who could pick and choose and was bound to be chosen over and over again – and her mother was encouraging her in her twenty-first year to settle for a presumptuous youth who might or might not reciprocate her feelings, who was at best the King-in-exile of an ungovernable island in the Near East, and at worst an ex-waiter with an eye on the main chance.

Florrie hated politics and would neither countenance political argument in her own houses, nor go to the parties of other hostesses whose social objective was to set man against man and to turn women into fishwives for the purposes of entertainment. She was not against debate, but when it deteriorated into argument she called it bad manners. Her social aim was to please, give pleasure, rest weary souls and feed hungry ones, and turn tears into laughter if she could. Yet here she was on the point of asking to dinner the sort of politician who argues with guns, guns moreover that he wanted her to pay for, and probably the guns with which to shoot the man loved by her only child. It was madness – she had weighed up the alternatives and reached the decision that the best course was to lead or be led by Fay into the quicksands of Balkan belligerence.

Her worries were like the globule of mercury in a child's puzzle: they kept on dividing and branching off in unintended directions. Geoffrey had provided another piece of advice she was not going to follow. Far from wriggling out of an engagement with this damn King she was about to welcome him with almost open arms. And she realised that Geoffrey was not capable of protecting her from Michael – one was a rabbit and the other a stoat. She would have to call on Philip to provide protection from the risks that Geoffrey had urged her not to run – and assuage Geoffrey's jealousy before it provoked a quarrel with Philip.

How complicated! What a muddle! She was acting in opposition to her character, judgment, principles, habits. And the word jealousy, the concept of the jealousy she was on the point of arousing, and her consequent sense of guilt, brought her out in a sweat. She felt guilty not only with regard to Geoffrey and Philip, but also with regard to Fay. For she had not been altogether honest, she never ever could be – and she was a truthful forthright person and notoriously bad at keeping secrets. That seductive devil in the

[67]

royal box must have hypnotised her with his swimmy black eyes. She cursed him yet again for muddying the issue and disturbing the even tenor of her widowhood.

The telephone rang. She was not aware that she had been asleep and had no idea of the time. She switched on the bedside lamp and squinted at the clock: eight o'clock. Her hand shook as she lifted the instrument to her ear.

A disappointingly English voice with a half-Cockney half-American accent said: 'Hi there! The name's Vic Pullent and I represent King Michael of Orezania in the U.K. May I speak to Lady Florence Meavy?'

'Lady Meavy speaking.'

'Morning! The name's Vic Pullent.'

'Good morning, Mr Pullet.'

'It's Pullent with an n, and the n means a lot to me, I can tell you – Vic Pullent, got it?'

'I'm sorry, Mr Pullent.'

'No problem – anyone can make a mistake at this time of day! Sorry I'm early, but the order was to be sure to catch you – I understand you're leaving London in a hurry. His Majesty's willing, that's the message – and I'm checking on the type of visit you had in mind.'

'I see. Hold on while I open my diary!'

She reached for her bag. Why not ring off and let this cheeky travesty of a courtier get the engaged signal until she could run away and hide? But somebody would be bound to betray her in one way or another – there were no hiding places for a hostess – and Fay wanted her to delay Michael's return to Orezania for as long as possible.

'Hullo?' she said. 'Could His Majesty dine here one evening?' And she mentioned a date a month ahead.

'No way! His Majesty's going to be needed back home by then – he's got a war to win. And he isn't taking it easy here, believe you me. He might rearrange his schedule so as to be free for dinner next Monday.'

A spot of haggling ensued – Florrie put forward the Friday of the week in question, the man said Tuesday, she proposed a compromise on Thursday, and a provisional deal was done.

'His Majesty's expecting dinner for two – okay?'

[68]

She spoke loudly as if to muffle the note of hysteria. 'That's out of the question – I've already asked people who have an interest in Orezania to meet the King – we'll be a party of twelve or fourteen.'

'He won't like it, I know he was wishing for words in private – but maybe he'll lump it. I'll see if His Majesty's prepared to grant you an audience before supper or more likely after.'

'Mr Pullet', she began and bit her tongue – she was so stupidly nervous she could not speak straight. 'I know,' she corrected herself, 'I'm sorry again. Mr Pullent, I must tell you that my financial and legal affairs are entirely in the hands of my advisers, who would have to be present if the King expected to talk business. Now,' she hurried on before he could interrupt, 'shall we say eight-thirty at number seven Buckingham Square, and black tie?'

Vic Pullent returned that as H.M. was the C.O. of the Blue army in Orezania he would wear military togs, and that he would be accompanied by two bodyguards, who would also have to be fed. He then gave Florrie the telephone number and the address at which he himself could be reached in an emergency – 119 Sidney Webb Buildings. Catford, London SE6 1CF – and said cheeribye.

Immediately she rang Philip Mozergh's house and, when he answered, burst out in a voice quivering with emotion that she needed to see him without delay.

'My darling!' he exclaimed hopefully, increasing her agitation by misunderstanding her. He then bewailed the fact that he had meetings all morning and promised to be with her not a minute later than twelve-thirty.

She mumbled no, it was not like that, and yes, thank you, come to lunch, and she would explain everything.

In due course he arrived, was admitted by Barney, pounded up the stairs, and in the sitting-room embraced her with unacceptable eagerness. But her deflating laughter and pleas for his attention rectified matters, and she managed to sit him in a chair with a glass of white wine and to pour out her story, begging belatedly for his assistance.

He gave it thus: 'You must keep your dealings with this man to a minimum.'

[69]

She quite agreed, resisting the temptation to tax him for stating the obvious.

'For Fay's sake,' Philip said.

'Exactly,' she agreed again, hating her hypocrisy.

'You say that according to Crisp he was driven to Covent Garden in a Mini-Minor, not a vehicle one would expect to find a king in – and I've never heard of a courtier living in a council flat in Catford. They must be a couple of cheap crooks.'

'The Pullet could hardly be cheaper.'

'Well, I'll make inquiries, but meanwhile what's certain is that you don't want to give money to finance a civil war.'

'How not to give it, or not to let him take it, is what's worrying me.'

'You can tell him that your trustees only disburse Meavy money to registered charities in accordance with the terms of your husband's will.'

'That's not true.'

'My dear, it's better to be tactful than truthful.'

'Is it really?'

He overruled her doubt as if at a board meeting. 'The aim of the dinner party, as I understand it, is to detain Michael here so that he can't spoil Alexander's chances of becoming King there, provided, of course, that Alexander's still alive and kicking. Am I right?'

'Yes, but wrong to make my flesh creep, and wrong again to overlook the fact that Michael terrifies me.'

'We'll have to collect a group of people who'll serve our purposes and keep him at bay – is that better?'

'Much,' she said, and, in response to Barney's knock and announcement that lunch was served, she stood up, held out her hand and led Philip downstairs to the dining-room.

They ate breadcrumbed fillets of sole, followed by a chocolate soufflé and cheese, and drank more white wine and then coffee, sitting at a round table in the red-painted room while they selected the members of the forthcoming dinner party.

The names that Philip scribbled on a page of his pocket memo-pad were F.M. and K.M., the initials of Florrie and the King, himself and Helen Islebeck, Geoffrey Oldcoate and Anna Hulcott, also, complete with question marks, Roger Ryther, Agatha Grize-

[70]

beck, Adam and Melanie Crabhouse, and Guy and Jane Shokerbrooke.

Florrie had sworn she would flee the country if Philip and Geoffrey were not in attendance on the evening in question. She objected to Helen, who was so vacuous and a dead loss conversationally; but Philip insisted that Helen might prove to be more protective of Florrie than anybody else by entangling the monarch in the silken net of her charms. As for Anna, she could be depended upon to pour complimentary oil on troubled waters. Roger would come in handy if His Majesty happened to share his amatory orientation. And Agatha Grizebeck, the unmarried daughter of Florrie's acquaintances and a don in an unfashionable university, was a linguist apparently fluent in forty-seven languages, although somewhat inarticulate in her mother tongue.

At least, if the King should be lost for a word or in need of an interpreter, Agatha could fill the bill, which would be a nice change for her. Adam Crabhouse was better known as 'Argus', a nom-de-plume deriving not from the superannuated dog that recognised Ulysses after his long absence, but from the all-seeing character with a hundred eyes in classical mythology: he was a gossip columnist. He scratched his living by peddling the secrets of his friends to readers of the gutter press. Although Florrie was against him, she had to admit he was not slow to spot a scandal, and that his talent for unpleasantness of the journalistic type might exercise a restraining influence over delusions of royal grandeur. Guy Shokerbrooke was included in the company because he was one of the Dragons Pursuivant at the College of Arms and would be able to shed light on Michael's lineage. Jane Shokerbrooke and Melanie Crabhouse were the price that would have to be paid for the interest of their husbands.

Florrie's dining-room table could be extended to seat two more guests, making fourteen in all, and she and Philip wondered whether somebody political plus partner ought to be invited. But as neither of them knew a politician who was trustworthy they discarded the idea.

When they returned to the sitting-room Philip confided in his juiciest accents that he had the time and inclination to climb one more flight of stairs. Florrie had to laugh at the eccentric phrasing of his proposition, but could repay him for his assistance with no more than a quick kiss, since she was already late for the meeting of potential donors to Millicent Brighton's charity. Millicent was an impecunious old fool who raised money for starving Africans that enabled her to travel widely in the African continent.

The Dinner Party

Florrie Meavy left Buckingham Square, following lunch with Philip Mozergh, feeling bad. Why did she let him kiss her? She was not obliged to do so, she was not his wife. She was struck by the squalor of the transaction: on her side part-payment for services rendered, on his a sort of long-term investment that might pay off, and a sop to the vanity of the 'serial kisser', of which nickname he was proud.

It was disgusting, or at any rate ridiculous – she could not remember why she had ever sanctioned the practice, and wanted it to stop.

She felt no better at Millicent Brighton's social bash, where a cup of tea cost her five hundred pounds. She was aware that the main beneficiary of Millicent's charity was Millicent herself. She could afford the price of her compassion for her poor friends with rich tastes: besides, some of the money might feed a few of the millions of hungry Africans. But today she resented the charities that appealed for her donations to more or less good causes by means of ritzy galas, glossy brochures, costly and seldom read paperwork, unsolicited videos, and other administrative expenses.

Later on the same day she received a brief telephone call from Fay.

'My darling, how lovely! Where are you?'

The answer was: in a payphone in a b-and-b in Gloucester, where she had begun her course.

'What's a b-and-b?'

'Honestly, Ma – bed and breakfast!'

'But where do you get dinner in the evening?'

[73]

'Oh – somewhere – it's not important.'

'Well, I think the people you're nursing are lucky.'

'I'm not nursing anyone yet – it's only First Aid at present. Did that man ring you?'

Florrie told the story of the Pullet and the party she had planned, and hoped she did not sound embarrassed.

Fay seemed to approve. But she said people were queueing to use the telephone, and that it would not be easy for her to speak to her mother or be spoken to until the Thursday of the week ahead: 'My course finishes with a visit to an operating theatre on that day.'

'How jolly!' Florrie commented. 'Will you be watching an operation?'

'We're meant to – and you'll be having your dinner party.'

'But, darling, will you be able to stand the horror?'

'Will you?' Fay batted back with a tense little laugh and in quite a snubbing manner. She hurriedly added: 'Sorry, Ma – he's not the true King.'

'I know, sweetie – but I thought I was supposed to keep him out of mischief by entertaining him for Alexander's sake. If you'd rather I didn't, please tell me! I've been wondering if it's wise to steer clear of politics at home and get involved in them in Orezania.'

'Don't worry, Ma – and thank you for helping. I'll have to fly. Mildred has a telephone number in case of emergency – otherwise wait till you hear from me – good luck with the party and best love!'

Florrie was bewildered. For her daughter's sake she had erred and strayed into the position of an irresponsible matchmaker and a string-pulling meddler in a foreign civil war; yet she seemed to be failing to please Fay. Had her attitude to Michael been insufficiently hostile? Was she suspected of hedging her bet on Alexander? And what was the point of this nursing business? Who did Fay expect to have to nurse in the foreseeable future?

The fact had emerged, the fact remained, that she and her daughter were drifting apart. Fay was keeping her distance and, Florrie feared, belatedly repudiating her, as all her friends' adolescent daughters had repudiated their mamas. The only hope was that they would draw closer, would be themselves again, perhaps

[74]

not immediately, but when Michael had been wined and dined, had done his worst and was out of the way.

Meanwhile, in the interim before next Thursday, life had to be lived. Florrie had dresses to try on, things to buy, hair to be washed and nails to be manicured, engagements to keep, and so on. She went to a recital of unmelodious songs at the Wigmore Hall and afterwards had dinner with the Culkertons, delighted parents of the aspiring soprano who had sung them. She spent hours with T.D. Faulkbourne in town and Angus Macrae in the country, and added a codicil to her will just in case Fay should wed an avaricious husband. She spent time at St Eo, and checked that everything was under control and in order. She discussed Fay with Mildred and was not cheered up by her cousin's spinsterish enthusiasm for love at any price. And she made the mistake of honouring an engagement to stay the Saturday night with Eric Hinxton.

Eric was like Sylvester Kexmoor in two respects and unlike him in a third. He too was a friend of Florrie from earlier days, and another artist, a literary one, in difficulties; the difference was that he was effeminate. He lived beyond his means at Hinxton Grange in the village of Hinxton in Dorset, was sixtyish and, in appearance, a peculiar mixture of country squire and lady bountiful – he was tubby and red-faced and wore three-piece tweed suits, but had tiny hands and feet and a melting manner.

Florrie had not wanted to stay with him, she had memories of uneasy weekends at Hinxton; but he pleaded with her and refused to take no for an answer. In the event she found the house full of a company as mixed up as the host, including a couple of lusty young carpenters who cannot have been there to do joinery. Intercourse of the social kind was a strain, dinner on Saturday was no fun, and on Sunday morning Florrie was set upon by Eric, metaphorically speaking.

He had writer's block: how could he write when nobody reviewed, read or, for that matter, was prepared to publish his books? He had lost his job as a critic: he was against the vogue for lengthy tomes, and had confined his opinions of some fictional blockbusters to listing their respective weights, for which exercise of common sense he was given the sack. As a result he had been stripped of his privileges in the literary pigsty, where backs were

[75]

scratched on an exclusively reciprocal basis. He was at a loss professionally, bankrupt or nearly in artistic and in financial terms, living beyond his means with nothing to do, and in dire need of what was rudely called a kickstart – what did she suggest?

She mentioned money.

'No, thank you, dear – I still have my pride,' he contradicted himself by claiming.

She tried to reconcile him to his lot; said she was sure his books were good although in truth she had read none – she had no time to read books; said he might well be famous in a hundred years; and undertook to continue to puzzle over his problem.

'Problems in the plural, dear,' he said with pursed lips, and added: 'You're sweet to take me seriously, nobody else does – but I'll bob up – and thank you for listening to my caterwauling – you're my friend in need, my need if not yours.'

She was due to leave Hinxton Grange at eleven o'clock. Crisp and the Jaguar were a welcome sight, and in the car on the road to St Eo a scenario that she would have called defeatist a month ago presented itself to her. She would renounce society, the social treadmill, the lit candles of London, and retire to some hermitage in the country and never leave it. She would be able to buy a dog and would live with it happily ever after. She loved dogs, she had had one of her own when she was a girl, a Welsh collie called Tip, whose eyes burned with affection for her and with fidelity. But when she went to boarding school Tip pined, fell ill, had a sort of breakdown, ran amok, chased sheep and was shot by a farmer; and in the tragic aftermath she vowed solemnly not to have another dog until she could look after it properly and permanently. Had that time come? Was she ready to exchange human for canine company?

Not immediately, it transpired, for everyone had accepted her invitations to the dinner party on Thursday. She talked to Maria about food, asked Crisp if he would be kind enough to help Barney hand it round, wrote out menus and place-cards, ordered special wines and spent hours choosing flowers and arranging them. She received encouraging telephone calls from Geoffrey and Philip, had her hair done on the Thursday afternoon, and in the evening put on her new dress and her pearl choker and best diamond

[76]

bracelet and her rings with particular care. But any possible sport she might have derived from these preparations was spoilt by her relentless examination of her motives; and she wished harder than ever, but again in vain, that Fay would ring up and throw her a kind or conciliatory word.

Her guests bar one had all arrived by eight-fifteen. She performed introductions and supervised the distribution of drinks. When the doorbell rang she hurried down to the front hall, the door was opened by Barney and two men in dark suits, looking like all-in wrestlers and carrying mobile phones, crowded together on the doorstep. They were the royal bodyguards, who, instead of acknowledging her tentative greeting, peered paranoiacally in all directions, then stood aside, creating a gap through which Florrie could see King Michael struggling to climb out of a car. She recognised the Mini-minor, and was recognised by the chauffeur holding open the passenger door – he called out without much regard to courtly etiquette, 'Hi! I'm Vic, Vic Pullent – how's yourself?'

His Majesty was in purple, a purple uniform jacket with a raised collar and black braid all over the place and a coruscating medallion in the form of a sunburst on the left breast, and purple plus-fours with black side-stripe tucked into knee-high black boots. He would have looked absurd, a chocolate soldier, the villain of a comic strip, if he had been less handsome and dignified. He marched towards Florrie, devastating her with his suntanned complexion, glistening eyes and great white teeth; and holding her hand, which must have been as cold as her feet, in his warm one he bowed and pressed his lips to it while she wobbled into a curtsy.

They mounted the stairs, she leading the way self-consciously – Barney and Crisp between them were taking care of the body-guards. After being introduced to everybody, the king demanded vodka, a large undiluted measure of which he swallowed in a single gulp. Dinner was announced and they all trooped down-stairs and seated themselves round the full oval extent of the dining-room table, elegantly laid with silver candelabra, lit candles under red shades, gleaming glass and cutlery, and linen napkins folded into the shape of water lilies.

[77]

Clear soup was served, followed by a dish of lobster, then saddle of lamb, lemon mousse and fresh fruit. The wines, in order, were white and dry, red, sweet, and liqueurs were also on offer.

It had gone sufficiently well to permit Florrie a degree of relaxation. She might have been pleased if the King had not taken an irritating shine to Helen Islebeck and insisted on talking individualistic English to Helen as well as to his hostess throughout the meal, thus isolating several of his fellow-guests conversationally. But he did not broach the subject of money, nor did he distress anyone with overtly amorous attentions.

By the time the coffee came round, however, Florrie noted uneasily that the volume of the voices had been turned up by the consumption of alcohol, and was startled to see Agatha Grizebeck rise to her feet.

She must have been a changeling. Her parents, Reggie and Marigold Grizebeck, to whom Florrie had been introduced by Eldred, lived in Leicestershire, were respectively a JP and a big noise in the WI, hunted to hounds and had not a single intellectual interest or attainment between them; yet they had brought forth this academic paragon and social catastrophe. Florrie had asked her to dine partly in case translation should be required and partly out of pity. But Agatha's electric-blue velvet dress, her thirty-five years, her long hair piled on top of her head untidily and her gawky shyness failed to find favour with her neighbours at the dinner table, and, noticeably and ominously, she had assuaged the embarrassment of sitting in silence by emptying her various glasses as soon as they were filled and refilled.

Her reason for standing was to toast His Majesty in crème-de-menthe. Before Florrie could restrain her, she had raised her glass in his direction and was spouting weird vowels and syllables that sounded like water running out of a bath. He scowled at her, and slightingly turned away as if not listening, and when she finished said something dismissive and guttural that could have been a curse.

Florrie called out: 'Thank you, Agatha,' and frowned and indicated in dumb show that she should shut up and sit down.

But Agatha had already blushed beetroot-red, and was apparently shattered by the King's response; at the same time she probably suspected that her precious reputation was at risk, and

[78]

she stammered defensively in English: 'Your Majesty must be familiar with the language that was always spoken at court!'

Silence fell.

His Majesty asked Florrie, nodding his head at Agatha: 'What is she?'

Florrie laughed, Philip on her other side joined in, Geoffrey initiated a resumption of chatter, and Agatha subsided on to her chair.

Florrie's answer and apologia, including details of Agatha's linguistic skills and distinctions, fell on deaf ears since the regal attention, as if to punish her, switched to and was firmly fixed on Helen Islebeck.

Florrie was furious, she knew she never should have invited Helen: but at least she had a chance to question Philip about the meaning of Agatha's exchange with the king.

Philip had found out and whispered the explanation into her ear: 'His nibs swore at Agatha in the Orezanian equivalent of French *argot* – and he doesn't seem to know the polite language of his country. Maybe he's not kosher after all.'

Philip now spoke louder and silenced the desultory chatter. 'Sir! May I congratulate you on having survived the attempt of the Russian Bolsheviks to murder your entire family.'

'What you say?'

His Majesty swivelled round in order to look across Florrie towards Philip instead of at Helen.

The tribute was repeated and rephrased and eventually understood.

'I thank you,' His Majesty replied.

'How did you survive? Would you like to tell us?'

'I survive because I am strong, I am King through strength.' A royal leer at Florrie accompanied this boastful statement.

'But did you remain in Orezania during the Russian occupation?'

'I am leader of my people. I will not surrender.'

'Where did you hide? Surely the Russians regarded you as public enemy number one. How did you manage not to be caught?'

His Majesty stared at Philip forbiddingly, then summoned a smile, or at least bared his teeth, and said: 'You talk too fast, you talk too much, you are chatbox, I think.'

'My apologies, sir – I'll speak more clearly – and ask one more question, if you'll allow me.'

King Michael threw up a hand in a generous gesture of assent and winked at Florrie, as if to suggest that he had got and could get the better of Philip.

'The civil war in Orezania, who is fighting it and what for, and who is winning, sir?'

'I have win, I am Blues – Reds are Bolsheviks, Whites are nothing. Reds capture Orez, my best city, my capital, but I fight, I kill Reds, many Reds, and now Orez mine – Blues are for Orezania. We are killing more Reds all day.'

Anna Hulcott, whose talent for admiration stopped at nothing, emitted an exclamation that could be construed as a bravo.

His Majesty added with his cannibalistic smile round the table: 'I am in England for guns to kill Reds and Whites, many many Whites – liberals, you call. Lady Florrie has money for me to buy more guns for killing enemies.'

A murmur of dissent and a snigger of laughter arose. Jane, the wife of the Dragon Pursuivant and doubtless a reader of The Guardian, drew the line at the idea of liberals getting it in the neck, and Melanie Crabhouse, wife of Adam, was laughing nervously. Roger Ryther passed the word along that they would all be lucky to save their skins in Buckingham Square, and Florrie intervened.

'Philip, you know my rules – no politics! Your Majesty, I don't let my guests talk politics in my house, and I'm sure you'll be grateful not to have to discuss the sad situation in your country. Shall we change the subject? Will you have something more to drink?'

He understood the last word without difficulty and shouted: 'Vodka!' Barney was sent to fetch the bottle. Florrie tried to explain to His Majesty that she had never observed the barbaric English custom of separating ladies and gentlemen after dinner. His reply was unexpected and unwelcome: 'You give me money now.' She hesitated and he seized her hand and squeezed it painfully tight and lifted and kissed it with his warm persuasive lips. A glass containing ice cubes was placed in front of him and vodka was poured in. He released her and grabbed it, and Guy Shokerbrooke had something to say.

[80]

'Your Majesty!'

Guy was the opposite of a dragon in appearance, being short and slight, and in colour pink and white. His scholarly eyes glinted with the hope of ferreting out another esoteric fact or two.

'I am a genealogist, Your Majesty.'

Angela Grizebrook was as it were raised from the dead in order to interpret the sentence for the benefit of the King.

'Before meeting Your Majesty,' Guy proceeded, 'I looked into the so-called bible of the nobility of Europe.'

The King downed his glass of vodka and queried repetitively: 'What is?'

'I'm referring to *The Almanach de Gotha*, sir – of which I'm proud to possess a copy of an edition published soon after the turn of the century.'

'Is Christian Bible?'

'No – *The Almanach de Gotha*, sir – which traces the ancestry of the noble families of Europe – it's very well known.'

The King shrugged his shoulders and turned to smile at Helen Islebeck.

'Sir,' Guy insisted, 'I should be grateful if you would trace your line of descent from Grand Duke Paul Orez, King of Orezania, who must have perished in the massacre of the members of your family by the Russian secret police in nineteen-twenty. I can find no record of the royal house between then and now, and assure you that our College of Arms would be extremely glad to have information that you alone may be able to supply.'

Angela put this speech into more accessible terms. As she did so, the King's face darkened alarmingly, and without further warning he banged his fist on the table.

Everybody jumped.

'Lady,' he accused Florrie, 'you have bad people here.'

He frightened her – his anger was so alien – she could not meet his savage black eyes – and she dithered and was tongue-tied. Guy Shokerbrooke was making apologies, Philip was trying to defend Guy, Jane Shokerbrooke was squeaking and Geoffrey Oldcoate protesting for their respective protective reasons. The almost falsetto voice of Adam Crabhouse rose above the babble.

'I represent the newspaper industry, sir,' he piped.

[81]

Adam was a big bald ugly man in granny glasses whose articulation in his high voice was precise to the point of prissiness.

The King glared at him, smoothing his uniform jacket and patting his pockets agitatedly.

'Would Your Majesty object to publication of the story that you refuse to justify your claim to the throne of Orezania?'

The reply verged on incoherence.

Angela had ventured to translate.

The King raged and bellowed in his language or the slang of it, and somebody knocked and the door burst open and a bodyguard burst in and bent down to speak to him.

He instantly stood and without a word to anyone marched out of the room.

Florrie, pursued by Philip and Geoffrey, followed him. In the hall, where one bodyguard was holding the front door ajar while the other loomed large on the doorstep, he hastily went through the motions of kissing his hostess's hand.

'I have news from my country,' he said. 'I go to my people now, tonight – Whites attack Orez – it is crisis – goodbye, lady – come to see me!'

He ignored her reply, also her friends, disappeared into the night, and the door was banged behind him.

Philip said: 'If he's what he pretends to be I'll eat my hat,' and Geoffrey chimed in: 'A slippery customer certainly!'

The other guests emerged from the dining-room. The consensus was that the King was a commoner, and a common commoner at that. Everyone sympathised with Florrie for having to entertain such a beast and thanked her for a particularly enjoyable evening.

Florrie, relieved to be on her own, mounted the stairs to her bedroom – she had already thanked Maria and Barney, who were locking up the house, and Crisp who had gone home.

She sat on the edge of her bed, took off her earrings, and punched in the telephone number of St Eo, where Fay, having finished her course, might be spending the night. After three or four rings Mildred's sleepy voice came on the line: the St Eo telephone system was usually switched through to Wilson's cottage if the big house was empty, or to Mildred's flat if Wilson was not going to be at home.

'I've woken you,' Florrie said unrepentantly. 'But I'm dying to talk to Fay – the dinner party for you-know-who has just finished here.'

'Oh Florrie, what happened?'

'Lots of things – Michael was shown up – everybody thought he was dreadful – which is a step in the right direction even if it doesn't prove Alexander really is the King-in-waiting – and Fay will be delighted. Where is she, Mildred?'

'I don't know – she came back from Gloucester this morning, we had a bite of lunch together, and she left this afternoon – I didn't like to ask too many questions – and I assumed you were fully informed. There is an envelope addressed to you, but she said it's not urgent.'

'Oh God! She wasn't depressed, was she?'

'No – the opposite – in high spirits.'

'Where's the envelope?'

'In my sitting-room – but I'm sure you needn't fuss – she was perfectly calm.'

'Do me a favour – fetch the envelope and read me whatever's inside! Quick, please!'

During the pause that followed Florrie sat very still, listening to the thump of her heart.

The letter read out by Mildred ran as follows.

'Darling Ma, Don't be cross with me. I'm going to Orezania. I've heard nothing from A and I'm not pursuing him, in fact I'm far from sure where he is, but I'm going to Orezania just the same. I decided some time ago, that's why I've done the nursing, so as to be able to make myself useful if necessary. Whether or not I ever see A again, I'd like to have a look at the country I might have been the Queen of! That's a joke. I'll communicate when I can. Sorry, Ma. I'm afraid I'm not Father's daughter for nothing. You've been a wonderful Ma to me. With best love from Fay.'

[83]

Consequences

At seven-thirty the next morning Florence Meavy rang Philip
Mozergh.

She could have done so the evening before – she knew she
would not be able to sleep, and that he suffered from insomnia;
but she was as it were paralysed by Fay's letter, and she was
always afraid of interrupting nocturnal activities she preferred not
to know about.

She had no such inhibitions in the morning: she spoke Fay's
name and began to cry.

Philip elicited the latest chapter of the story of Fay, and had to
stop short of telling Florrie that her tears were unreasonable. The
fact was that a winsome fair-skinned girl was venturing, apparently alone, by irregular means of transport, and with scarcely a
word of the Orezanian language, into an island engulfed in civil
war and peopled by a race of men not noted for their chivalrous
attitude to the weaker sex. Besides, her attachment to an Orezanian
king or waiter or whoever he was, who had loved and left her,
seemed to be reaching the proportions of an obsession.

Philip said they must find out how she might be travelling to
Orezania, and gather information about the circumstances of
existence there.

Florrie cried again.

She sobbed out that her party was on her conscience, too, because
it had been shameful to bait King Michael, an offence against the
laws of hospitality, and she should not have allowed everyone to
pick on him as they had, especially considering the responsibilities
on his shoulders and the danger he was in. Philip laughed at her.

Her tears were wasted on Michael, he said, who was a double-dyed rotter if ever he saw one. The important thing was to trace Fay: he would look into the practicalities of her project, while Florrie made inquiries amongst her friends.

She agreed. They rang off. But before keeping to her agreement she spoke to Geoffrey Oldcoate. Characteristically and traditionally he advised her not to follow Philip's advice, but, roughly as before, to do nothing.

'Your dear daughter's an adult, who knows her own heart better than anyone and is of age and entitled to live her life as she pleases. My prophesy is that she'll emerge unscathed, and gain from her experience, provided she doesn't have to interrupt it to reassure you.'

Once more Florrie agreed. Of course he was right. Yet not for the first time she behaved as if he were wrong. Inertia was not in her nature, she was unwilling and unable to wait and see. Geoffrey was feeble – she would have to do something or she would burst.

She tried to reach Vic Pullent at his Catford address, but the telephone was not answered. She spent hours tracking down Jenny Bowditch and Sue Cartwright, Fay's girlfriends, who were not in the flat they shared in Stockwell, nor at home with their parents, nor in the offices where they worked. Jenny was out of town, decorating the interior of a house in Sussex, and Sue was cooking for directors in a City office. She spoke to Sue eventually at four in the afternoon.

No, she told Florrie, they had not known Fay was planning a trip to Orezania. They were aware that she had gone out with Alexander, and had heard the rumour that he thought he was a king or something, but were under the impression that she was not that hooked on him. Sue concluded, speaking for Jenny, that they would be frightfully envious of Fay's holiday in a pretty fascinating part of the world.

Florrie's conversation with Mildred was equally unconstructive. Mildred continued to take a romantic view of the episode, and envisaged not Fay robbed, raped, wounded, dying, but Fay falling into the arms of Alexander and living ecstatically for the rest of her days with the Orezanian crown on her head. And her single piece of relevant information was depressing: she said Fay had left her car at St Eo and taken a taxi to wherever she was bound. In other

[85]

words Fay had deliberately covered her tracks, for she could have asked Wilson or a member of the outdoor staff to drive her to her destination.

Florrie said tersely that she would see Mildred later: as usual on a Friday she was going down to St Eo in the afternoon. She then went to a ladies' luncheon given by Wilma Windsor with the declared object of raising money for the homeless in Solly Windsor's constituency in the Midlands. She had thought of chucking, she was disinclined to be bribed by too much unhealthy food to support another questionable cause while her daughter was probably in trouble: but she would have been even more anxious on her own, and more impatient to hear from Philip.

Wilma's other guests might have been clones of herself. They were large dark fleshy women with red cheeks, disarmingly glad to have got rich quick. Florrie, on impulse, yielded to the temptation to confide in them that her daughter had gone on the wildest of wild goose chases, and was perversely cheered by their lamentations and accounts of their comparable maternal heartaches. When she handed over her donation, Wilma undertook to have a word with Solly, who had been born not far from Orezania as the Hungarian crow flew and was still in touch with friends and relations in the area, and Florrie reflected that her money could turn out to have been well spent for a change.

But Philip's telephone call, received in Buckingham Square in the early afternoon, was discouraging. Fay would not have been detained by having to apply and wait for a theoretically essential visa, since there was no Orezanian government office with the power to issue visas at present operational in the UK. Her possible itinerary was a flight on one of several international airlines either to Odessa in the Ukraine, or Bucharest in Romania, or Istanbul in Turkey, and travel onwards by sea or land to the southernmost point in the Crimea. She would then have to hire a boat to ferry her across to the island, or else pay for a passage on some smuggler's craft.

Realistically, therefore, Fay was untraceable while in transit, unless the police were called in and had a lot of luck. And telephonic and even radio links with Orezania, at any rate for private individuals and for the time being, had completely broken down.

[86]

Florrie thanked him for these glad tidings. She was not fond of Philip in what she called his 'Götterdämmerung' mood.

He on the other hand loved to be the subject of her irony. But he checked his laughter, and tried to say something more acceptable.

'The good news is that Michael won't be bothering you any more.'

'Is he dead?'

'No – I don't think so – I don't know – but his office in Catford has shut up shop – he must have scuttled back to Orezania, taking his staff with him – though whether or not he's gone to polish off or to be polished off by Alexander remains to be seen.'

She ended the conversation abruptly, said she could not keep Crisp waiting a moment longer, dredged up a few affectionate sentiments, and allowed that they might have another talk on the Sunday morning.

She replaced the telephone with relief; was glad not to have invited Philip to stay for the weekend; reissued strict instructions to Maria and Barney to pass on any messages; and was driven to St Eo.

It was blessedly peaceful there. She looked in on Mildred, but refused her offering of supper – she could not bear a prolonged discussion of Fay's folly and fate. She slept badly again, but counted and recounted the blessing that only Geoffrey Oldcoate was arriving on the following afternoon. On Saturday morning she pored over impersonal documents with Angus Macrae in the Estate Office, and when Geoffrey turned up she explained that she had an awful headache, which was not quite a white lie, and, having persuaded him not to summon a doctor and an ambulance, she retired to her bedroom between tea and dinner and as soon as she politely could afterwards.

At last she slept. She slept as if for hours, and woke refreshed, and saw it was two o'clock in the morning. She rose and drew her curtains and sat on the window seat, gazing out at the fitfully moonlit scene of cedar trees and the black shadows they cast on the pale expanse of lawn.

Questions circulated in her head like a not very merry merry-go-round: what was she to do, what was she doing, what had she done with her life since Eldred made a widow of her? She and Fay were connected not merely by their natural relationship and

[87]

mutual devotion, they were entangled in thornier senses; and her conscientious morality linked her weakness for the rival and foe of Alexander with the worry and woe imposed upon her by the girl who loved him. She had such a lot to pay for – great good fortune, good looks, health and nerves, a good husband, a good child, and recently some bad ideas. Had the time come for destiny to submit its account, which could not be settled by a signature on a cheque?

At an unearthly hour she reached a sort of decision – at least she rebelled against indecisiveness. Michael had gone simultaneously east and probably west, he was either leading his army into battle or dead, he had anyway bowed out of her life, and she had no further reason to bother about him. In the dark she saw that she loved her daughter better, she loved her best, must never lose track of that priority, and had to share everything with her, risks included.

In short she would follow Fay to Orezania.

Her arrival on the scene might complicate matters – but to count the costs was to dither. She had resources at her disposal which could be Fay's salvation, cash, contacts, experience, and she was determined to place them at her dearest one's disposal instead of reserving them for her own trivial uses. Notwithstanding the unsuitability of the metaphor, it did occur to her that she was about to kill several birds with one stone, for instance to settle the Michael question and to rescue herself as well as Fay. The obstacles ahead, and trials and tribulations, would not be just another novelty, a new amusement, they held out possibilities of reforming the unsatisfactory parts of her existence and, in an unfrivolous word, of redemption.

Sunday dawned. She was up and about early, sleepless yet no longer tired. She cleared her desk before breakfast, and when Geoffrey appeared she attempted to justify her bad habit of disregarding his advice.

'Forgive me – but you couldn't seriously expect me to sit back here while Fay's in peril in the middle of nowhere, could you? You know me better than that, dear Geoffrey. I'm ever grateful, and have enormous respect for your wisdom, but I'm begging to differ, and I'm going to act on the difference – will you understand?'

She put forward her plan.

'We'll get there somehow, and won't stay for more than a day or

[88]

two – and either find Fay, because the island's so small, or leave messages and money for her – and I'll have a preview of the country – and possibly catch a glimpse of Alexander – and it'll be an adventure and terrific fun – and you're to come with me, Geoffrey, and be my right hand man.'

She covered her ears with her hands in order not to hear his cautious queries and objections, and hurried away to telephone Harold Gristhorpe.

'Hullo, Harold – it's Florrie Meavy – can we talk?'

The gravelly voice returned: 'I'm Mona Gristhorpe. Who are you?'

Florrie apologised and reintroduced herself.

'I'm travelling out to Orezania, and seeking guidance from your husband,' she explained.

Mona's response was a disagreeable apothegm. 'People who live in palaces can never wait to go slumming.'

It was not like that, Florrie said – and could she speak to Harold?

Mona's parting shot was: 'Good luck to you, you'll need it.'

Harold came on the line.

He grasped the object of the exercise, that Florrie was anxious to pursue and protect her daughter who had taken it into her head to visit Orezania; but said the journey would be fraught with difficulties, and that in some areas of the island rapine and pillage had replaced the rule of law.

'What's happening in Orez?' Florrie asked.

'I have no up-to-date information. Orez has changed hands repeatedly throughout the civil war, and strange to relate, perhaps because successive victors occupied it and used its amenities, the heart of the city was spared bombardment and continued to function after a fashion for a number of years. But I cannot believe that would still be the case.'

'Supposing I flew to Orez, just supposing, wouldn't I bypass some of the rapists and pillagers? I could fly there direct, jump into a taxi, have a look around, and fly back without getting involved in any nastiness.'

'My dear lady, you'd have to charter an aeroplane, moreover an aeroplane capable of flying so far without stopping for fuel; and you'd need to obtain permission to fly through the airspace of half a dozen countries; and in the end, since Orez Airport has been out

[89]

of commission for many months, you'd reach your destination only by parachute. I'm sorry to have to be a wet blanket. Your daughter's no doubt a wilful girl. I can only hope she's done her research, and that you'll have second and even third thoughts before you waste a great deal of money.'

Florrie thanked him without meaning it, and gritted her teeth and forced herself to pursue her inquiries.

'Does the name Alexander mean anything to you in the context of Orezanian politics?'

'Indeed.'

'Do you mean yes?'

'I do.'

'And Michael?'

'King Michael, the commander-in-chief of the Blue faction?'

'Well, yes. Can you tell me who has the right to wear the crown of Orezania, Alexander or Michael?'

'My considered opinion is that Alexander could be compared to the Young Pretender.'

She rang off, and wondered: what next, what now?

Her telephone rang.

Solly Windsor wanted to hear more about her Orezanian problem: Wilma had instructed him to render assistance if he could.

Florrie poured out an abridged version of the story and carried on: 'It's kind of you to trouble, Solly, and you'd be even kinder if you could tell me how to spirit myself on to that inaccessible island – everybody says don't and can't.'

'Everybody's usually wrong.'

'Are you by any chance saying do and can?'

'Everything has its price, whether or not everybody has theirs.'

'Continue, please – I feel I'm going to be beholden to you for ever.'

He did so: he had spoken to Bobby Ireby, who had business dealings with King Michael and with some of the other political and military leaders. Apparently the three sides in the civil war had agreed to repair the runways at Orez Airport; within the last few days it had become possible for a smallish private jet to land; and fuel could be made available, and a tourist bearing a large amount of foreign currency was bound to be the welcome guest of

[90]

a government, whatever its colour, trying to cope with inflation of fifty percent a year.

She asked: 'What time do we leave?' – and he laughed and supplied practical particulars.

An international company, *By Air to There*, had long-haul jets for hire, and trained its air-crews to cope with hazardous assignments. According to Solly's informants, an extraordinary feature of the capital was that two institutions remained intact after being fought over and even fought in for years, the Orez Ritz Hotel and the Orez Natwest Bank. In the last two battles of the war, the Blues had ousted the Reds from Orez and its Ritz, and recently the Whites had ousted the Blues, which meant that the top brass of the White army would now be comfortably quartered in the hotel; but nobody else, no paying customers, could afford the prices, therefore rooms would certainly be vacant and available, and the National Westminster Bank in London would surely be able to get a message through to its branch manager, who could make the necessary reservations. Last but not least, he felt honour bound to warn her that the trip she contemplated would be costly, and the potential expenses of travel in a country governed by brigands were astronomical.

She was thrilled, she was eternally indebted to Solly, she could not care less about the money, she said goodbye.

When Philip Mozergh rang as planned she did nearly all the talking, as a result of which he promised to lunch at Buckingham Square on the next day, Monday, and help her to pick the people she should invite to accompany her to Orezania.

The rest of her Sunday was busy. She had to prepare for a period of absence, however brief. She persuaded Mildred that a dose of abroad would do her a power of good, then had to arrange with Jean, Mrs Withgill and Wilson that St Eo was never empty. She spoke for an hour to T.D. Faulkbourne, who would be looking after her financial interests. She summoned Angus Macrae and discussed estate business. She chucked engagements right, left and centre, and late in the evening rang Jenny and Sue.

They had returned to the flat in Stockwell from their country homes. Jenny, who sounded exactly like Sue, said they had been thinking a lot about poor old Fay. Although Florrie was surprised

[91]

by the erroneous adjectives chosen to describe her daughter – she had always been surprised that Fay's special friends should be so unlettered and seemingly silly – she was touched by Jenny's sympathy and sweetness. She revealed her plan and expressed a hope that the girls might like and be able to join in the jaunt, if it could be organised.

Jenny said they would adore to – it was so frightfully kind of Lady Meavy – she was sure they could wangle a spot of extra holiday – they were dead keen to help to search for Fay – and a private jet was fantastically glamorous.

Florrie drew attention to the dangers, the war, and the threat to pretty girls of their age posed by soldiery in general and Orezanian soldiery in particular.

Jenny giggled and replied: 'How exciting! We're not frightened, Lady Meavy. Both of us love those swarthy men – we might encounter Mr Right out there, or maybe Mr Wrong.'

'Yes,' Florrie agreed.

PART TWO

Unhappy Landings

The chartered aeroplane damaged one of its wheels when it landed at Orez Airport, and Captain Jenkins warned that he would not be able to fly home until the wheel was in working order.

There were twelve passengers aboard. The ladies were Florrie and Mildred, Anna Hulcott, Angela Grizebeck, Jenny and Sue, and the gentlemen, in a manner of speaking, were Geoffrey Oldcoate, Roger Ryther, Adam Crabhouse, and Theodore Hildwitch, Sylvester Kexmoor and Eric Hinxton. Philip Mozergh had refused to come along, having failed to persuade Florrie not to go; and Helen Islebeck had not been invited.

Captain Jenkins had a nameless co-pilot, and the two stewardesses were called Tracy and Nicky.

The local time was 1800 hours on the Friday after the Sunday on which Florrie had decided to follow Fay to Orezania. The party had assembled at Gatwick; everybody praised her generosity and was grateful; they seemed to be pleased to meet one another and laughed at the perils of sightseeing in a country at war; and the four and a half hours of the flight were passed in enthusiastic conversation and the consumption of considerable quantities of alcohol and victuals. But the landing was a shock, and Captain Jenkins' warning was another. Florrie had to ask Geoffrey to reassure everyone that the wheel would be mended in time for them all to leave as planned after three full days on the island.

Night was falling fast and the eerily deserted airport was not well lit. However, the smells of alien tobacco, flowers, garlic and drains, combined with the presence on the tarmac of the manager of the Orez Natwest, Mr Wilfred Hamilton, had a calming effect on the travellers. They straggled through Passport Control without having to show their passports – the desk was unmanned – and the Customs Hall, where only a grandmotherly black-clad cleaner was on duty, and piled into a bus puffing out clouds of diesel fumes.

Captain Jenkins and his crew were left behind. They would guard the aeroplane, an extremely expensive machine, so adapted as to provide the facilities for sleeping and eating if or when it might be at risk.

Florrie shared a seat with Mr Hamilton on the bus. He was a middling sort of man, quiet, neat, neatly dressed with neat flat brown hair perfectly parted in the middle. She bewailed the damaged wheel: he was sure it was nothing serious. She asked if he had heard from Fay: not yet, he replied with a confident smile.

'You know my daughter's making her own way to Orezania?'

He did – a Mr Mozergh had explained the position.

'Will she be safe? That's what worries me.'

Mothers were inclined to worry, he observed neutrally.

'But what can be done to protect her? And how am I to find and meet her?'

He had obtained an appointment at the Department of Immigration on the next day, at eleven o'clock, which should set her mind at rest.

Adam Crabhouse piped squeaky questions at Mr Hamilton – what was the pound-slozar rate of exchange, were international telephone calls possible? – and Florrie looked out of the window. Electric light was again in short supply in the empty streets. She could just see houses bearing the imprint of war, roofs caved in, windows blown out, a curtain fluttering from a black rectangle, a notice nailed to the remnants of a door; and then gaps in terraces filled with rubble. Here and there a faint orange luminosity emanated from a window still in place – candles must be burning within. Where were the shops, she wondered. Occasionally, momentarily, the huddled shape of a woman hurrying somewhere was revealed.

Without warning they roared and bumped into a garish square jammed with civilian cars and camouflaged vehicles. The Orez Ritz occupied the whole of one side of it, an unmistakable hostelry with a solid awning over marble steps. A church, actually the

[96]

cathedral, reared up on the opposite side. The illuminations were dazzling after the gloom – the floodlighting, more light glaring through plate glass, lit windows and wandering beams of head-lights and red rear lights. The chauffeurs and soldiers standing about, and the crowds of people on the move were also a surprise. Instead of a commissionaire, two teenage youths in khaki with their fingers on the triggers of machine pistols lounged on the top step.

Mr Hamilton escorted Florrie into the foyer, which had a black and white marble floor that needed cleaning, and, at the reception desk, introduced her to the manager of the hotel, an agitated bald man in heavy horn-rims, who answered to the name of Mr Wilko and was supposed to speak English.

'Good morning,' he said.

His agitation was partly due to having to inform Lady 'Mivvy' that six of the twelve bedrooms booked by Mr 'Mossaq' had been commandeered by General Salbych, the White general using the hotel as his HQ, for officers on his staff.

Predictably, two members of Florrie's party objected to the prospect of having to share a room. The composer Hildwitch demanded privacy because he needed to be able to sing intermit-tently throughout the night, and the painter Kexmoor refused to sleep with any member of his own sex, let alone a flatulent old one. The others were amenable: Mildred would shack up with Florrie, and Anna with Angela, who might be sweet enough to teach her the rudiments of Orezanian, and Jenny with Sue, while Geoffrey meekly submitted to the nocturnal company of Adam Crabhouse. As for the writer Hinxton, the third representative of the arts and the awkward squad, he had made friends with Roger Ryther, and they were looking forward to bed-time.

Eventually Theodore and Sylvester resigned themselves to the inevitable. They saw the point, reinforced by the wringing of Mr Wilko's hands and the mopping of his brow, that in Orez civilians could not and should not attempt to prevail against literally superior forces – the foyer was full of forbidding black-eyed soldiers with white badges in their green berets and white flashes on the shoulders of their antiquated khaki battledress.

Mr Hamilton was glad that the bedroom issue had been settled to everyone's satisfaction. He had engaged a guide to conduct a

[97]

tour of the sights of the city from ten o'clock onwards tomorrow, and he would return to the Ritz at ten-thirty to escort Lady Meavy to the Department of Immigration. The bank, he added, had slozars, dollars and gold that he could release as required – and he tendered his wishes for an enjoyable evening. Florrie led her party up the marble staircase in the wake of Mr Wilko fiddling with keys and superannuated pages humping luggage. The interior of the hotel retained some remnants of Ritz-like charm, pink-shaded wall-lights and kitsch plasterwork; and a short first floor passage containing neither more nor less than the relevant accommodation created an impression of privacy. But the six doors that were unlocked and opened showed box-like rooms with narrow twin beds and cracked windowpanes, and without wash-basins or bedside lamps. Moreover the nearest bathrooms were only two in number, and both bath-plugs were missing. Although Florrie's guests had been warned that the trip would be no picnic, the words 'dog kennel' and 'pigsty' were audibly bandied about by Theodore and Sylvester.

Mr Wilko did not improve matters by speaking of 'hair-rides', meaning air raids, of shelter in the 'collar', meaning cellar, of 'diner' at 'eight o'click' and 'carfew' at eleven. He departed in haste with everybody's 'dickumints' and, when luggage had been sorted out and a rendezvous agreed, the bathrooms were bagged and unpacking began.

Florrie closed the door of her room and, leaning back against it, said to Mildred: 'I must have been mad.'

Mildred offered anti-climactic consolation: Orezania was interesting and different, and they would not be in it for long.

Florrie disagreed: Orez was ghastly, the Ritz squalid, the White army sinister, and she had led or misled eleven friends into the front line – how could she have failed to foresee it all? Fay was a needle in a haystack, she continued; Fay's urge to involve herself in Orezanian affairs was even madder than her mother's; and finding Fay – ever finding Fay – more than likely a lost cause.

Mildred begged Florrie not to become one of those mothers who underestimate their children.

'But I overestimate Fay, that's why I'm so afraid of losing her,' Florrie retorted.

Mildred said it was too soon to despair, and was told: 'Too late, you mean! We might have been killed in our aeroplane, and I bet it won't be ready to fly us home. What will the third disaster be, for pity's sake?'

Mildred's comfort boiled down to the foolproof suggestion: 'You never know,' and Florrie promised to try not to cry over spilt milk.

But philosophy failed her intermittently as they distributed the contents of their suitcases.

She said: 'I imagined I was doing those artists a favour – Theodore could ruin a few harmless folk songs – Sylvester and Eric could pack up their troubles for a change – and between them they'd be my cultural excuse for coming to Orezania. But Sylvester's more than likely to do in Theodore if they're locked into that room for any length of time, and Eric and Roger should be kept apart, not thrown together . . . It's all a fiasco, and Orez is simply tragic – I feel we're like clowns at a funeral . . . And this hotel should be called an Officers' Mess in every sense of the words.'

They descended the stairs, negotiated the crowded foyer, passed through portals over which a neon sign in English advertised Lounge Bar, and joined the rest of the party in a large bright room, bearing some resemblance to a village hall. It must have been built on to the original edifice, had a low ceiling and linoleum on the floor, and mostly empty chairs arranged round formica-topped tables, and not many bottles were in evidence.

Nevertheless a better mood prevailed. Geoffrey had managed to have a nap: Adam Crabhouse had succeeded in speaking to his editor in London and was ordering more celebratory champagne, for which Florrie was asked to sign her name; Sylvester and Theodore were drinking deep and amicably; Jenny and Sue had put on war paint and their own form of battledress, and were issuing ocular challenges to a group of soldiers, in whom Eric and Roger were also taking an interest; and Anna had at least had a good wash in a bath, and Angela was enjoying guttural intercourse with the barman.

The latter retailed the news she had gleaned. The Whites had turfed the Blues out of the Ritz just as the Blues had turfed out the Reds six months ago, according to the barman, who said the Reds were the biggest drinkers and the Blues were next best – his view of the civil war was exclusively professional. General Salbych, pronounced Salbeek, was living in the hotel until he could move into Orezu, the royal palace ten miles or so from the centre of Orez beside the River Zu.

Florrie asked if the barman knew what had become of King Michael.

Angela passed on the question, then replied: 'Apparently there's a big price on his head, but if he's still alive he's probably in his camp in the hills, preparing to fight another day.'

They were interrupted by the sound of music. It was the Palm Court type, the signal that dinner was served, Angela said. Florrie shepherded her flock, including Jenny and Sue whose glances over their shoulders invited the soldiers to follow them, into the dining-room.

Pretty old tiles covered the floor here, and light fittings composed of alabaster bowls were suspended from intricate plaster rosettes in the ceiling. The band consisted of a middle-aged lady pianist with bare arms like hams that quivered, a gipsy violinist in a patched tail-suit, and a tall thin mournful double-bass player.

Florrie's group sat at a round table for twelve. Soldiers sat at other large tables, at one of which some chairs were as yet unoccupied. The native civilian element was confined to several pairs of businessmen, and half a dozen over-made-up and under-dressed girls in an alcove. Waiters wove in and out with various courses of the set menu, cabbage soup, goulash, sweet pancakes, cheese, fruit and coffee, and were cheered and applauded for pulling corks. Florrie had instructed Geoffrey, who was on her right, to order liquid refreshment; but Adam on her left, having been primed by Angela, repeatedly shrieked the Orezanian word for wine and more wine.

At some point the soldiers stood up, and a stout grizzled version of the younger men, oozing perspiration and bonhomie, waddled in at the head of a troop of nine or ten senior officers and seated himself in one of the empty chairs. He immediately rose to his feet, smiling and bowing at Florrie, who was urged by Sylvester in not very attractive language to return the compliment: 'He's the big bug – you don't squash him – let him crawl over you.'

General Salbych seemed to be satisfied. Florrie's party settled down to the suspect goulash. The orchestra played Strauss waltzes. Then a waiter staggered over with six bottles of champagne on a tray, French champagne not the ersatz sort served in the Lounge Bar, and another waited arrived with twelve champagne glasses and a white card on which was written: 'Avec mes regrets pour les six chambres.' Florrie's eye was caught by the general, more smiles and bows were exchanged, and in due course toasts were drunk across the room, and the band changed its tune, and the character of the evening likewise.

The measured whine and thump of Greek melody was greeted with cheers and rhythmical clapping. Two or three soldiers began to dance Greek style, linking arms over one another's shoulders and moving backwards and forwards in line with more or less complicated steps. Tables had to be hurriedly moved to create space as the line of dancers lengthened, and a couple of young soldiers marched over and in the international lingo of their attractive looks and outstretched hands invited Jenny and Sue to participate. The four of them formed a charming line of their own – the boys swarthy enough to please the girls, who laughed and stumbled with grace as they were initiated into the rules of the game. The professionals from the alcove were also on the cleared area of dance floor, and a soldier was dragging Agatha on to it too, despite her protests in different languages.

The fun grew furious, and now General Salbych approached Florrie and indicated that she was to dance with him. She agreed, she obeyed – there was really no alternative. He was short and hot, and stank of garlic, and the heavy arm that was meant to be round her shoulders ended in her armpit; but he smiled up at her with broken teeth and bounced about as if on springs, and sang and tried to teach her to imitate his neat footwork. She could not do it, she had not done any dancing for years, and was sure she was making a fool of herself, especially as she glimpsed the antics of some of her friends. Mildred's bosom was not suited to the requisite up and down movements, and Agatha had loosed her bun and her hair was all over the place. Roger was having a high old time between two soldiers, and the gaunt features of Sylvester as he shook a leg seemed to be a reminder of the dance of death. Luckily Anna Hulcott was restraining Theodore at his dangerous age from joining in.

The music whined unstoppably and faster, and the Orezanian dancers snatched bottles from the tables in passing and poured wine down their own and others' throats and even over faces. Everybody was dancing now, even Geoffrey, and Florrie was in the partial embrace of a major as well as a general, and she wondered how much more of it she could stand. Time had passed, drunkenness was beginning to ruin the proceedings, and sex was raising its also intoxicating head. Adam, shamelessly oblivious of his absent wife and the mother of his children, dim and dumb Melanie, was doing something disgusting to one of the hostesses in a dark corner, and Jenny and Sue were being kissed to bits against a wall.

Without warning, theatrically, the lights went off and, after a ten second blackout, on again. The band struck up a rousing march – the national anthem, respected by all three contending armies, Angela whispered in a loud aside – and the soldiers stood to attention, the other Orezanians froze in deferential attitudes, and the irreverent cries and laughter of the tourists petered out. The anthem was being broadcast from rooftops throughout the city, the noise outside clashed with the noise within, and as the musicians finished Mr Wilko ran into the dining-room and began to hustle the waiters through one door and his paying customers towards another. General Salbych spoke incomprehensibly to Florrie, bowed, kissed her hand, and, with a sly facial expression that could be the Orezanian equivalent of a wink, directed her attention to his finger and thumb which he was rubbing together – the gesture meant money, probably her money, and that he was after it. She had to smile, he was so disarming, so tubby and jolly; and he retreated at the head of his troops. Mr Wilko was flapping his arms at the English contingent and shouting: 'Carfew – go, please – blickout soon – carfew!'

Adam Crabhouse swore at him with alcoholic venom in his falsetto voice. The artists were also rebellious. But Florrie and Geoffrey helped to shoo them out of the dining-room, and the lights going off and on again had a persuasive effect. The party wandered and lurched across the almost empty foyer and mounted the stairs, Florrie and the sober ones making haste to reach bedrooms and bathrooms before the blackout was permanent, the others dragging their feet and alternately laughing and cursing.

[102]

'Good night,' Florrie called by her bedroom door. 'Good night, everybody, and sleep well.'

Similar cries echoed along the passage, and doors were opened and closed or in some cases slammed, and English voices mingled with Orezanian ones in other parts of the hotel, and the electricity supply was suspended altogether.

Sylvester banged on Florrie's door and was told to go away sharply. Mildred voiced the controversial opinion that the evening had been fun, and fell asleep before she could be disagreed with. Moonlight poured through the cracked windowpanes, and Florrie was sorry she had disregarded all the advice to stay at home.

She was not sure she had slept when the attack began, and she could not see the time. Orez was being shelled, shells whined and exploded, shaking the hotel to its foundations, and machine-gun fire rattled and tracer bullets described crimson arcs through the sky. And there was fighting at close quarters, vehicles roared in the square, guns were fired outside and within the hotel accompanied by yelling and screaming – and soldiers were shooting, running and tramping even on the upper floors.

Florrie was afraid and nonplussed: what should she do, what could she do? Mr Wilko had spoken of a cellar: but how was she to collect her people and find it in the pitch dark during a blitzkrieg? How was she to rouse them? Mildred had not stirred, and although she was renowned for sleeping deeply Florrie wondered if she was in receipt of a stray bullet until reassured by snores. Aeroplanes seemed to be dropping bombs on the city, and the cries of the wounded were awful. She lay as if paralysed, feeling craven and guilty, and yearning for Buckingham Square or St Eo.

At least the war was short – half an hour perhaps, no more. Relative silence fell and her ears ceased to sing, she was no longer sweating, her heart regained its rhythm, and she considered the possibility of action.

Somebody knocked on her door.

'Who's there?' she demanded, suspecting Sylvester of returning to the charge.

It was Geoffrey.

She scrambled into a dressing-gown and opened the door.

[103]

'Are you safe, my dear?' he asked.
'Thank God! Are you?'
'Yes, I am.'
'Is someone hurt? What's the matter, Geoffrey?'
'Jenny and Sue have disappeared.'

Bad to Worse

Her reaction was that common verbal denominator of crisis.

'What?' she said.

Geoffrey began again, and she heard herself ask another foolish question: 'How do you know they've disappeared?'

He had a small torch and conducted her along the passage – he was wearing his Burberry over his striped pyjamas, and warm sheepskin slippers. The door of the girls' room was open, and the glimmer of light through the windows showed that the twin beds were disarrayed.

'Where could they be?'

'Where indeed!'

'Have they run off with those soldiers?'

'Do you think it likely?'

'Oh Geoffrey!' she scolded him for his ignorance of the facts of life, modern life in particular. 'They're sweet girls but giddy – haven't you noticed?'

'They might be sheltering somewhere.'

'Without telling us?'

'Or might they be in the soldiers' rooms?'

'Which soldiers? Which army's in control of the hotel?'

'Perhaps I should investigate.'

'You'll do nothing of the sort. This is the third disaster – I was waiting for it – but I won't be responsible for a fourth.'

Roger Ryther burst out of his room in a visibly yellow satin dressing-gown, saying: 'Is that you, Florrie? Are we still alive, dear? Lucky us!' But then he sensed the mood of the meeting and inquired: 'What's happened?'

[105]

Anna Hulcott and Agatha, the latter with a bathcap over her mop of hair, emerged and asked similar questions. Eric Hinxton came out complaining of the location of the Ritz in No Man's Land, and Sylvester, ghost-like, draped in a sheet, complained because he had forgotten to pack his pyjamas. They were all present, except for Mildred, Theodore who apparently slept in ear-muffs and a face-mask and had registered nothing, and Adam sunk in alcoholic stupor.

The fate of Jenny and Sue took precedence over their fears – recent and future – for their own lives. The sound of activity downstairs reached them, and Florrie backed up by Angela and Roger followed the beam of Geoffrey's torch to the landing above the foyer: Anna and Eric agreed to stay with Sylvester. The purpose of the reconnaissance was to seek information and, if possible in connection with the missing girls, assistance.

But the scene below put paid to it. Old-fashioned paraffin hurricane lamps held by unidentifiable soldiers in a line shed light on dead bodies being carried out of the hotel. The luminosity was limited and golden, and melodramatic moving shadows were cast, as in some terrifying masterpiece of painting. Stretchers and body-bags were conspicuously absent. Most corpses were being swung by arms and legs between two soldiers – heads drooped and bobbed and dripped blood on the marble floor; some were simply thrown over a soldier's shoulder, and limp hands flapped against the back of his knees. They could have been killed – executed – either in the Lounge Bar or the dining-room, where they had danced and flirted not long before: they were borne out of those doorways, and Florrie thought she recognised an occasional moribund feature or a head of curly or wavy black hair.

She tugged at Geoffrey's sleeve, and they stole away by common consent. No one was prepared to wade into the middle of that grisly undertaking – no hotel employees were on duty – it was already past three in the morning – they would have to wait for a few hours to set the search for Jenny and Sue in train.

They rejoined the others. Adam had regained consciousness, and Sylvester had taken it on himself to rouse Theodore – 'I thought he was a goner,' he said. Geoffrey and Roger told the tale of the Orezanian version of body-snatchers, and Florrie controlled her involuntary trembling and started to apologise.

'I shouldn't have brought you here, I didn't realise we'd be in so much danger, I'm sorry.'

She was as it were shouted down in loyal and lowered voices. Geoffrey said she was blameless, Anna Hulcott that she was everybody's benefactor, and Angela that Orezania was educational. Roger pointed out that she had not shot anybody, and Eric that Jenny and Sue were probably having a nice time. Adam piped and slurred the chilly epigram that blood and tears were his bread and butter, and Theodore grumbled controversially that it seemed to be a storm in a teacup and he was going back to bed.

They all adjourned to their bedrooms. Mildred – who must have dormice in her family tree, Florrie reflected – was still asleep. Footsteps thumped overhead, boards creaked, doors were opened and shut, and the noise of traffic in the square below had not abated. Florrie lay awake, counting not sheep, nor her blessings, but dead bodies and the relentless minutes fraught with unwonted emotion, with fear and regret, each one of which would be doing damage to her appearance.

At seven o'clock the Orezanian anthem boomed and roared across the city, ending the hours of curfew. Mildred woke, and Florrie washed, dressed and felt duty bound to check that the hotel was functioning normally.

She tiptoed along to the landing above the foyer. A grandmotherly cleaning woman was on her knees, washing the black and white floor, and soldiers were criss-crossing it, leaving dirty footprints. No sign of sudden death, or of any change, was visible. She was hailed in English – that is in American cockney.

'Hi there, Lady Florrie Meavy!'

She jumped and looked round. A soldier had come down the stairs from an upper floor. She did not know him. His face bore a resemblance to a rat's – the nose was pointed, the chin recessive and stubbly. He had blue flashes on his black beret and his shoulder, and a major's crown on the epaulette of his battledress.

'Buckingham Square not so long ago.' he reminded her; 'and I've spoken to you on the blower – I was King Michael's dogsbody in the UK.'

'Mr Pullent,' she said, taking care to include the n in the name and hoping he might have his uses: 'what are you doing here?'

'What are you could be more interesting,' he retorted, but then answered her question. 'I'm with His Majesty and we rule the world now – Blues gave Whites a hiding last night and he's king of the castle again.'

'Should I congratulate you?'

'Why not? It's better to do in than be done.' They began to descend the last flight of stairs side by side. 'Are you on your ownsome, Lady Florrie?'

'No – I have friends with me – there are twelve of us – or there were.'

'How did you get here?'

'I hired an aeroplane.'

'All right for some!'

'Mr Pullent, I need help.'

'Don't we all?' he quipped.

'Two members of my party, guests of mine, two girls, disappeared in the night, probably during the fighting, and I must find them – I must! What shall I do?'

'Naughty girls?'

'Not that naughty.'

'My bet is the Whites nabbed them for hostages – bargaining counters, they're called. I'll tell His Majesty.'

'Please don't bother King Michael.'

'No bother – he'll be pleased to know you're in town.'

'Really?'

'Sure – and he'll be on your side if you're on his.'

They had reached the bottom of the stairs by now, and Florrie proceeded to give the names and descriptions of Jenny and Sue to Mr or Major Pullent, who jotted them down on the clipboard he carried.

'Thank you,' she ended.

'His Majesty's going to be the grateful one – he's down on crime – he's set on turning Orezania into a tax haven and tourist trap – the boys who took your girls, when they're caught, he'll boil them in oil in public. I tell you true, he doesn't pussyfoot, like the politicians back home. But what's the story, Lady, what brings you to the land of peace and prosperity?'

She replied: 'I'm hoping to meet my daughter – Orezania was suddenly where she wanted to be – I don't know why. But I was keen to see the island too – and one of my friends is a linguist, she

[108]

speaks the language, and three of them are artists of one sort and another – I thought a short trip would be good for everyone as well as fun – I thought so until last night.'

'You didn't like the fireworks?'

'Not much. I was terrified – it was terrifying. Then dead soldiers were being carried across the floor we're standing on.'

'Oh well, you can't make an omelette without breaking eggs. Have you met up with your daughter?'

'Not yet. I'm keeping an appointment at the Department of Immigration in an hour or two – the people there may know where she's got to.'

'Hang on! That's the Slutzk show.'

'What do you mean?'

'General Slutzk is in command of Immigration. He's a half-pint, but poison. Mind how you go! Talking of going, I'd better say bye-bye till the next time.'

He left her, and she was joined by Agatha Grizebeck. They approached the Reception Desk and inquired if they could have a word with Mr Wilko.

Agatha translated the clerk's answer: 'Mr Wilko has retired.'

'He must have been shot,' Florrie said. 'Ask if Mr Wilko was shot!'

Agatha did so and translated: 'Mr Wilko's retired into the country.'

'Into a hole in the ground in other words. Who's in charge now – ask him!'

'He says he is – he's Mr Djuro.'

Florrie eyed Mr Djuro, who was a hirsute youth with spots wearing a black jacket several sizes too big for him, and remarked: 'I've a funny feeling he was a page-boy yesterday, and he's got hold of Mr Wilko's clothes as well as his job by fair or foul means. Ask if he knows anything about Jenny and Sue!'

The answer was no – Mr Djuro lived with his mother – he was therefore unable to comment on whatever had happened within the hotel during the hours of darkness – but he was sure the young ladies would soon be having a big breakfast with their friends.

Florrie with Agatha's agreement gave up, she was not prepared to listen to more lies and be leered at, and demanded the use of a

[109]

telephone. She dialled the numbers of the Orez Natwest and then Mr Hamilton's home – all she obtained was an ear-splitting screech. Belatedly Mr Djuro supplied the information that the central telephone exchange had been put out of commission by the White army as it retreated.

Geoffrey Oldcoate now came downstairs with Mildred, Anna, Eric and Roger in tow, and, when news or the absence of good news had been discussed, they moved into the dining-room and began to have breakfast. In the course of the meal Florrie aired the increasing number of her concerns: for Jenny and Sue; more than ever for Fay; for the crew of the oddly named Gulfstream IV aeroplane out at the airport – they might be dead, it might have been appropriated; and not least for her friends.

They must leave Orezania, she said – she had decided that as soon as the wheel of the plane was in working order her friends must fly home or else to some more civilised country – she greatly appreciated their readiness to remain at their posts, in a manner of speaking, and support her and keep her company – but she would be relieved to know that they at any rate were safe, and she believed she would do better on her own with a little help from Mr Hamilton.

Theodore, Sylvester and Adam appeared, complaining respectively of having had his night's rest interrupted, of the coldness of the hot water in a bathroom, and of a hangover. Florrie paraphrased her speech for their benefit, at which everyone began to argue with her. The artists said she was not getting rid of them so easily; Roger looked at Eric and pleaded to be counted in; Adam squeaked objectionably, Geoffrey objected fondly; Agatha expressed a negative in Orezanian, Anna was consoling and Mildred optimistic. As for Jenny and Sue, uncharitable interpretations were put upon their absence or absenteeism: they were a tarty pair at best, and at the worst inconsiderate and ungrateful.

Florrie slipped away, whispering to Mildred that she would be in the cathedral across the square if needed, for instance if the girls turned up or communicated.

She passed the armed guards outside the hotel, who looked exactly like yesterday's except that their badges were blue rather than white. The houses on her right and left were old, painted in

[110]

bright colours, picturesque and apparently inhabited. In the middle of the square, behind the parked military vehicles, there was a patch of tired grass. Beyond, the front of the cathedral blackened by time and its tiered roofs rose to an onion dome with worn gilding. The autumn weather had the peculiarly penetrating chill of unaccustomed climates.

She entered by antique doors of thick oak and was engulfed in darkness. A deep voice in the distance was intoning prayers, which were responded to by the fervent chorus of a considerable congregation. She saw a golden glow issuing from a side chapel, and as her eyes adjusted to the dark she made out shapes of kneeling worshippers. Black-clad women, backs bent and heads covered, and men rendered visible by grey and white hair or by baldness, were attending the service in progress in the chapel. Florrie joined them – she found a place on an empty pew at the back, and sat there for a few minutes, watching the scene of bearded priest in brilliant vestments attended by altar boys in white surplices. The language meant nothing to her, and she supposed the ritual was either Russian or Greek; but the flames of innumerable votive candles and paraffin lamps, their reflections in gold and silver crucifixes, candelabra, sacred vessels and sunbursts, and the passionate cadences of the prayers and heartfelt entreaties of the faithful, combined together to affect her as she was not affected by Matins conducted by mild-mannered Aubrey Millard-Jones at St Eo.

She knelt. She had come to the cathedral to pray for assistance. She thought of herself as a reasonably religious person, she liked the traditions of Christianity, she was unquestioning and quite dutiful, and had often derived comfort from praying along the old lines. Now the difference was that she felt she could not receive anything from God, she did not deserve to, until she had given Him something as important to her as were the coins being put into boxes and plates by these poor Orezanians. And even in a formal way she did not like to plead for forgiveness, since she was unable to promise not to repeat the offence. Instead of praying for Fay and the others, her thoughts turned inward and she could not project them away from herself. The potential sin on her conscience was an absurdity, a figment of her imagination, a whim, a threat

[111]

although unlikely ever to be carried out, a brainstorm that could only end badly. But her existence had been empty for too long, she argued or pleaded in extenuation.

Her dialogue with God, or rather her monologue, continued. She was reminded, perhaps because of the subject, perhaps because of circumambient perils, and notwithstanding the one-sidedness, of conversations with her husband before he again risked his neck and her happiness – she had to try to say everything, everything that had been unsaid since Eldred died.

The service concluded, candles were snuffed, her fellow-members of the congregation shuffled out, and she postponed the moment when she would have to face reality at the Ritz Hotel. At last she exchanged the reassuring gloom scented by incense of her sanctuary for the grey daylight fouled by diesel fumes and the smell of dust and burning homes.

Her party had already left for their guided tour. Geoffrey's explanatory note, awaiting her in the keeping of Mr Djuro, also informed her that Jenny and Sue had not materialised.

At eleven, by appointment, Mr Hamilton arrived. In the back seat of his chauffeur-driven car, metaphorically and with the greatest respect, he applied soothing platitudes to the sore spots of Florrie's Orezanian experience. He agreed that it had been a noisy night; that to be the spectator of a battle was never pleasant; that the scrapes young persons were apt to get into nowadays were upsetting for their parents and guardians; and that the breakdown of a telephonic service was disadvantageous. On the other hand, he assured her, visitors to the island were popular with the natives and usually treated well.

She asked if he had ever heard of someone called Slutzk.

Mr Hamilton bowed his neat head affirmatively and said yes, he was a Blue general, a short gentleman who spoke English, had once been a jockey at Newmarket, was rumoured to have served under the Red flag, and was now in charge of law and order for the Blue administration.

The Department of Immigration was like government offices everywhere – had a pompous exterior, was grim and dirty within, and seemed to be over-staffed. But when Mr Hamilton gave in his name and Lady Meavy's, an obsequious clerk stepped forward and escorted them past long queues and through waiting-rooms packed with wretched people, knocked on an obviously important door and ushered them into a big bright office with a carpet on the floor and a kneehole desk in the window.

General Slutzk was speaking on the intercom on the desk, which was piled high with files and papers. Florrie thought he was sitting down, but he was standing up: he rang off, strutted towards her, shook her hand and nodded at Mr Hamilton. He was about the size of a boy of ten, pale, black-haired with black eyebrows and double rows of black eyelashes, wearing battledress without head-gear, and extraordinarily authoritative, suave, impatient and alarming.

'Slutzk,' he said, clicking his tiny heels. 'How do you do? What can I do for you?'

'Good morning, General Slutzk.' Florrie said. 'You must be terribly busy.'

'Yes.' He was cutting her short. He did not offer chairs.

Florrie began to say two young friends of hers, English girls, had gone astray.

'Send me written descriptions,' he cut in again and changed the subject. 'You have a daughter?'

'Yes.'

'In Orezania?'

'Well, I believe so. She was making her own way here.'

'How was she entering the country? I hope she was not entering Orezania illegally.'

'No – no, I don't think so.'

'Send me her name and full description. I will tell you when we have traced her. What is the purpose of her visit?'

Florrie hesitated. She was frightened and started to sweat. Fay's link with Alexander, the enemy of this horrible cruel midget, must on no account be revealed.

'Tourism, I suppose you'd call it,' she said. 'We're all tourists.'

'I see.' She was sure he disbelieved her. 'You are acquainted with His Majesty King Michael?'

'What? Yes, we have met, we met in London briefly.'

'Thank you, Lady Meavy.' He spoke to Mr Hamilton. 'I shall be paying you a visit.' He clicked his heels again and turned his back on them.

They left the room and the building, and in the car Florrie

exclaimed: 'What a disgusting creature! I wouldn't put my money on him if he was still a jockey. Why was he so rude, and why was he nasty to you?'

'The general was not pleased because I arranged our interview with his White predecessor, Colonel Petso.'

'I see. What about his visit to the bank?'

'He'll come to fine us for our dealings with the other armies, just as the Whites did and Reds have done. He may also wish to be remunerated for protective services rendered.'

'You take his nastiness very calmly.'

'The bank is vital to the Orezanian economy, and I feel sure will prove to be more durable than General Slutzk.'

'You mean he may not last long?'

'That would be an historic repetition.'

'How do you manage to live, Mr Hamilton, how does anyone survive in such a dangerous corrupt environment? How long have you been here?'

'Just short of six years, Lady Meavy. And if I may say so, the island has compensations.'

'I can't imagine what they are.'

'In my own case, Mrs Hamilton happens to be Orezanian.'

'Oh Mr Hamilton, I'm sorry.'

'Please don't mention it, Lady Meavy.'

After a short pause for embarrassment, Florrie apologised for reverting to her personal problems. She said she wished to organise the removal of the majority of the members of her party to a safer place without delay. She spelt out her newest worry that Slutzk would get his bony little hands on Fay and do unthinkable things to her. She had reason to be sceptical of Mr Hamilton's truism that money moved mountains in Orezania as elsewhere.

They reached the hotel. He gave her directions to the Natwest, she promised to advise him of her plans. They both hoped the telephone would be mended, and with thanks on her side and euphemistic regrets that she was being inconvenienced by the war on his they said goodbye.

Mr Djuro presented her with two messages when she asked for the key to her room.

One was from Captain Jenkins, her pilot, and informed her that the Gulfstream IV was now operational, but that the fuel required

[114]

to fly it anywhere was not available. The other commanded the attendance of Lady Meavy and friends at a reception at the Orezu Palace at nine o'clock that evening to celebrate the reinstatement of King Michael on the throne of his ancestors.

'Okay?' Mr Djuro inquired.

'No,' she replied. 'Orezania's nothing like the Isle of Wight.'

The Difference between
Victory and Defeat

The royal command would be obeyed. No member of Florrie's party thought of disobeying it. They were curious, they wanted to see the inside of the Palace, perhaps some of them were snobbish, they were all determined to attend the reception. They took the views that Jenny and Sue's absence was temporary, that the girls' parents would have to wait to be warned of developments, and that for the time being nothing could be or needed to be done about Fay or about fuel for the aeroplane.

Spirits rose at luncheon. Everyone was not only looking forward to the evening, they had also derived benefits of one sort and another from the tour of the city. The artists were inspired to practise their arts in the afternoon. Theodore Hildwitch, having modestly claimed that his reinterpretation of the folk music of Eastern Europe would be superior to anything done by Dvorak, went upstairs to his room to compose with the aid of a Swanee whistle. He was extremely keen on this instrument, a cross between a recorder and in principle a trombone, which could be carried in a pocket. Sylvester went to paint out of doors, accompanied by Anna Hulcott, whose enthusiasm for culture and the opposite sex had been unified in a willingness to oblige him even to the extent of bearing his heavy easel. He had shouted one of his graceless artistic explanations at the luncheon table: 'By God, Florrie, your wealth has bought me some great scenes of poverty!' Eric Hinxton, in search of copy for the journal he was writing, which he compared with Captain Scott's Log of his last expedition, returned to a slummy area of the city he and Roger had discovered. He was delighted to have broken through his literary blockage and to be describing the massacre in the night and the hopeless plight of the Orezanian populace.

Geoffrey seized his opportunity to have an undisturbed siesta. Adam Crabhouse had heard tell of a club where journalists congregated, and had gone to find it and to gossip and carouse as if he had been in Fleet Street.

Agatha was obstinately keen to track down a retired Orezanian academic of international renown who was reputed to speak even more languages than she did, and Mildred had agreed under pressure to tag along. Florrie walked with them as far as the Orez Natwest, where she reported the possibly ominous grounding of the Gulfstream IV, and, after Mr Hamilton had said he would see to it, whatever he might mean by that ever-welcome phrase, proceeded to a hairdressing salon recommended by a bank clerk and had her hair done.

They reassembled in the Lounge Bar at seven, and, uncertain as to whether or not food would be served at the Palace, had a snack in the dining-room. Dress was various: the ladies wore their best day-dresses, they had no evening attire, except for Agatha who appeared in an ankle-length garment made of clashing-coloured fibres and monkey hair and acquired on the Tibetan plateau. The gentlemen were in suits, creased but respectable, although there was again an exception: Theodore had put on the black tailcoat and white tie that he always packed in case he should be asked to step on to a podium and conduct an orchestra at short notice.

He – Theodore – was in sprightly form notwithstanding the burden of his years: that is to say he was particularly pleased with himself. He had stood up better than some to the vicissitudes of the trip, his egoism as it were wrapped him in cotton wool, and although he had disturbed Eric's writing with his shrill whistles and percussive taps, and intemperate words had been exchanged, his white moustache and imperial now bristled as he boasted of having dashed off another masterpiece.

Sylvester was forced to admit that he too had done passably well: Anna Hulcott, who was permitted to watch him at work, heaped praises on the picture he had succeeded in painting before the trouble started. The trouble, she confided in Florrie, was that

[117]

the paupers were not so charmed by the artist as he was by them, and had chased him back to the hotel.

The fly in the ointment of a tacit and democratic decision to make the best of a bad job, or, to put it another way, the threat to Florrie's evening, was Adam Crabhouse. Geoffrey had marvelled at her looks, Mildred had dinned it into her that even the Orezanian story might have a happy ending, Roger planned to visit her super hairdresser, but Adam was drunk and a journalist – he was already arguing that Michael deserved to be debunked.

They piled into their fume-filled bus at eight forty-five. Florrie sat with Geoffrey and pretended that the noise ruled out talk: she clutched her invitation card and shivered apprehensively. They drove through unilluminated streets for twenty minutes and joined a queue of cars and camouflaged trucks. The Palace was even more of a shock than the Ritz had been the previous evening: it was not only floodlit, but also beautiful. Behind its crested railings and beyond its area of parade ground, the classical facade was pale green and pink, white plasterwork framed the long windows through which lit chandeliers sparkled and glowed, and above the pierced parapet huge blue flags bearing the royal coat of arms furled and unfurled in the breeze.

A disturbing thought occurred to Florrie while the bus trundled across the parade ground and through an archway into a courtyard: would Fay live here one day?

She banished it and, when the bus squeaked to a stop under a portico, led her people between lines of heavily armed guards, up a stained red carpet on shallow steps, through a sort of sentry post where she had to show her invitation, and into a hallway.

The scene was chaotic. A crush of soldiery and loud women milled about amongst garbage bins overflowing with rubbish, discarded furniture, office equipment, carpets and even clothing as in a flea market. Guests were divesting themselves of unwanted garments, cloakroom attendants had their hands full, men were roaring with no doubt congratulatory laughter, and nobody was perceptibly moving in any direction.

Vague sounds of music in the distance could be heard. Angela came to the rescue: spouting the Orezanian equivalents of 'Excuse me!' and 'Beg pardon!' she cleared a passage to a staircase, and Florrie and the others mounted it. Guards wearing the same khaki

[118]

battledress as their White enemies, apart from the blue shoulder-flashes, lolled against the banister rail at intervals, fingers on the triggers of their stubby guns. A wide corridor at the top was packed solid with guests; but the combination of Angela's exclamatory injunctions and outlandish attire again enabled Florrie and her group to squeeze through to a large room, a ballroom in fact, lit by innumerable real candles in huge coruscating chandeliers. Her entry seemed to coincide with a hushing of the raised voices, a shuffling of feet, a clicking of heels, applause and cheers that sounded like the barking of dogs.

King Michael had entered the room and was progressing at a stately pace in order to receive the first fruits of his victory, adulation, heads and knees bent in homage, fists shaken and boots stamped on the floor. It was impressive but also primitive. He wore a spotless royal blue uniform, its neckband embroidered with gold thread, and starry orders and rows of medals. He caught sight of Florrie and, as aides and bodyguards roughly pushed her fellow-guests aside, walked towards her. He was changed, unshaven, yet more regal somehow, more dominant or tyrannical. His features relaxed, he smiled, showing those big white hungry-looking teeth, and instead of kissing her hand he took it in both of his and said in a triumphant tone of voice: 'You have brought me money.' Then he tucked her hand in the crook of his arm and led her, almost dragged her along in his wake towards a long table spread with a blue cloth.

She blushed, and because she was so embarrassed, not least to be blushing at her age, she grew even hotter and more bothered. They reached the centre of the table and he dumped her on a gilt chair, literally pushed her down on it. A waiter approached, bearing a silver tray of glasses of champagne. The King seized one, raised it high and growled a toast to the assembled company, drained it, threw it over his shoulder and smashed it, whereupon a wild shouting broke out and the band – perched on a balcony, and having ceased to play during His Majesty's lap of honour – struck up again.

He sat beside her and stared at her and said: 'You have come to me – I am glad.'

She shook her head, she did not know how to counter his assumption, she had put herself in an impossible position. More-

[119]

over her trained eye noticed he was tipsy and might soon be drunk, therefore capable of every sort of bad behaviour – drunkenness was the curse of the sort of people she entertained who were meant to be polite.

'You will give me money now,' he said with the false solemnity of drunkards.

She laughed not very convincingly: what else can women do when cornered by men? She was afraid of what he would say next, she could not trust him. She had never wished to be either his Queen or his banker. And she hated the limelight, she was attracting too much attention – her friends were looking lost and directing interrogative glances at her – and she could not meet those dark eyes which were paradoxically moist and hot, she seemed to be paralysed by the royal proximity, and was even more constrained by the recollection that she had asked for it.

Soldiers advanced and saluted the King, and an officer bent down and addressed him.

He frowned, waved the messenger away, spoke to Florrie in an intimate and authoritative manner, 'Stay here, do not move!'- and stalked off with unnatural care.

Her relief was only partial. His retreating figure was so shapely and lithe as to militate against her better judgment. How was she to get through the evening? The artists had commandeered another table in a less exposed situation and were bagging extra chairs, and Geoffrey and Roger were beckoning to her to join them. She hesitated, then disobeyed His Majesty and sidled through the crowd and had to answer awkward questions: why had the King made such a fuss of her, was he in love with her, or vice versa? Adam was drinking too much champagne; the band, composed of the same musicians who had performed at the Ritz, were playing their Greek and Russian repertoire, and guests began to dance to it; and Florrie was disappointed by Geoffrey's ruling that she could not leave just yet. Soldiers were rigging up a microphone on the balcony, and suddenly the music was amplified to such an extent that conversation became an ordeal.

She refused Roger's invitation to dance with him: he made do with Eric Hinxton. She would not dance with the officers who clicked their heels and held out their hands. She tried to control her nerves and be patient. But her study of the interior of the ballroom was not exactly calming. Pieces of plasterwork must have been used for target practice – the heads of cherubs were missing, and the horns of unicorns in a representation of the regal coat of arms. On closer inspection the chandeliers had streamers of glass lozenges unhooked and dangling disconsolately. There were life-size portraits of gentlemen in uniform, monarchs, grandees, hanging on the walls, where the remnants of political posters were also visible. One of the portraits was of a younger man in the civilian clothes of the turn of the century. The subject, the model, was not in fact a subject: she could read the inscription, unexpectedly in English, on the base of the frame – Alexander the Third of Orezania. It shocked her – he was or he might be the forebear of Fay's Alexander – and Fay's Alexander might have inherited his aristocratic elegance and wise eyes – and here she was, Fay's mother, fraternising with her possible son-in-law's arch enemy.

Theodore Hildwitch sat down beside her and at the top of his wheezy old voice enumerated the reasons why he was excited by regional harmonics. She was not interested, could not hear him, did not attend, had more important and even more depressing things on her mind.

He said: 'I have composed a variation on the national anthem of Orezania.'

She heard enough to ask him to repeat the sentence.

He did so and added: 'I look forward to having my piece played to His Majesty.'

'Oh no, you mustn't do that,' she advised spontaneously.

She had heard enough of his music. Although critics praised it to the skies, she was sure that normal people found it painful to listen to. His reputation seemed to be one of those miracles of modern art, created more by showmanship than talent.

'My dear lady!' he expostulated.

She suffered a spasm of accumulated exasperation, and warned: 'The King won't see the point of your sort of composition, I'm afraid – they're behind the times here – and their anthem means a lot to them. Listen, please, Theobald, we're in a hornets' nest already – don't infuriate the hornets!'

He was outraged, his face turned purple and his chin with the badge of his vanity on it – his imperial – quivered.

He retorted cuttingly: 'You amaze me,' and struggled to his feet.

She was about to detain him and apologise, to try to mend at least one fence, when she became aware of a small shadowy presence claiming her attention.

'General Slutzk,' she exclaimed.

'We meet again, Lady Meavy,' he replied, taking her hand, bowing over and dropping it – he travestied the act of kissing a hand with studied insolence. 'His Majesty will rejoin you shortly. His Majesty is impatient to join you. If I may say so, you acted the role of his consort with distinction.'

'I'm afraid I don't understand you.'

He was undeterred by the stiffness of her response, and shrugged his narrow shoulders. 'We Orezanians are waiting for a queen to reign over us, Lady Meavy.'

She suspected she was being mocked, teased at any rate, but his unblinking eyes behind the stiff black lashes and half-smile told her nothing for certain.

'I don't know what you're talking about,' she said.

He continued: 'A pity your daughter wasn't here to see the show.'

'Has she arrived in Orezania?'

'Were you expecting her to arrive?'

'No – I've told you – I came to Orezania on the off-chance of meeting her – we made no definite plans to meet.'

'Excuse me, but I have difficulty in believing that a rich English debutante would wish to travel alone in this country for no specific reason, and even more difficulty with your spending so much money to stay in a one-star hotel in a wreck of a town in the middle of a war in the very vague hope of running into her.'

'General,' she batted back gamely in spite of her mounting unease and fears, in particular the fear that she was betraying her guilt, 'I hardly think your attitude's likely to encourage tourism in your country. I asked you a civil question, which you haven't answered – instead, you level accusations at me.'

'Please forgive my interest.'

'Is my daughter in Orezania?'

'To the best of my knowledge, no.'

'Thank you.'

King Michael was coming back. The band stopped playing and the dancers ceased to dance; but he signalled energetically at the musicians, who resumed, and there was general applause and more throbbing noise.

General Slutzk said to Florrie: 'Time will unravel the mystery,' and before she could think of a suitable rejoinder His Majesty assailed her verbally from another quarter, saying: 'You moved from table – why? I order you not to move.'

He was pouring with sweat, wilder-eyed than he had been, drunker no doubt, and more alarming.

'I'm sorry,' she began.

He seized her by the upper arm and gripping it painfully tight yanked her to her feet and said: 'You sit with me, at my table – we drink together – I will be nice to you.' And he dragged her in the direction of the table draped in blue.

She resisted, she was inhibited by the slurs of Slutzk, and by the senior officers and their wives at that table, and by being the centre of attention.

'Sir, sir – wait a minute, please! Some of my people want to fly home – can I buy fuel for my aeroplane?'

She had to repeat and rephrase her plea – he could not hear, he would not listen.

'No – you stay in Orezania – all stay – no fly home,' he bawled at her.

'But sir – '

'This no good,' he interrupted, meaning the circumstances of the party; 'tomorrow you eat with me in countryside, not town – in country house like yours – all come tomorrow.'

'Thank you, sir, but our aeroplane – '

He turned to her, or rather turned on her, frowning and furious, and said so fiercely and loudly that her legs seemed to liquidise: 'You will not leave Orez!'

Everyone was angry with her – she was not used to it – she felt miserable – and a new menace loomed on her horizon in the shape of Adam Crabhouse.

Adam was making for the King, stumbling and reaching out and articulating with attempted precision in his absurdly squeaky voice: 'Let me pat you on the back, Your Majesty, you've got to the top of the greasy pole, old boy – I love a cheat, let me shake your hand!'

One event followed another in quick succession. A member of

the royal entourage, a bodyguard probably, stepped forward and banged his fist on the top of the head of Adam, who slumped to the floor. All the activity, music included, ground to a halt. Florrie knelt by the unconscious hulk of Adam, and was joined by Mildred and Anna. Meanwhile the King rapped out Orezanian words, and a strange sound swelled in volume and became recognisable as hissing. Florrie imagined for a second or two that it was caused by and aimed at Adam and herself and the rest of them, was a xenophobic demonstration against foreigners, and looked round apprehensively: she did not want to be lynched on top of everything else.

A horrible scene was in train. A bedraggled man in a khaki shirt and trousers far too big for him that he held up with one hand was advancing towards His Majesty between two lines of soldiers hissing and making hateful gestures. The man was bruised and battered about the face, and his other arm hung oddly limp and might be broken. He seemed to be scarcely able to walk, and was propelled forward by two thuggish guards. King Michael swore at him, cursed him, and pointed at a certain exit, whereupon the soldiers cheered and the prisoner was prodded in the direction indicated.

He was General Salbych, the jolly little White general who had danced with Florrie at the Ritz. He had obviously been tortured and was going to be shot, and Michael must have presided over the beating and the breaking of his bones, and had issued the order for his execution.

Florrie cried.

Dinner Orezanian Style

She did not cry for long. By bending over Adam in his prone position she managed to conceal her involuntary tearful hiccups from the circle of Orezanian spectators, although Mildred, kneeling beside her, noticed and gave her a cousinly squeeze of the hand. She recovered herself, brushed away her tears, helped Adam to his feet, and, when Geoffrey had mobilised the other members of her group, led their exodus from the Orezu Palace. Nobody tried to detain them. His Majesty had lost interest and moved off – he probably thought he had better or worse things to do.

The views expressed in the bus were predictable in so far as they were audible. Adam boasted with addled ire that he had the power of the press behind him and would wreak revenge on that swindler of a king, expose, dethrone, ruin and consign him to kingdom come. The three artists wanted somebody, or perhaps everybody, to be cut into little pieces. Agatha sought to explain the Orezanian character. Anna was torn between sympathising with Florrie, Adam and His Majesty. Mildred was glad that Adam had more or less regained his senses, and hoped that General Salbych would soon be feeling better.

Geoffrey, sitting with Florrie, and having been given an account of her conversations with Slutzk and Michael, summed up the evening accurately in two words: 'Oh dear!'

They arrived at the Ritz and dispersed, wishing one another at least a peaceful night.

Mildred said to Florrie in their bedroom: 'I've never seen you cry before.'

[125]

Florrie's reply was a repressive half-truth or quarter-truth: 'I was so sorry for that poor wretch.'

Mildred did not inquire any further, she could be and was being tactful. Besides, she was as tired out by events and emotions as her cousin was clearly disconsolate, and when the overhead light was switched off she soon fell asleep.

Florrie could not. The questions in her head were more like accusations or judicial sentences. She had never expected to witness the effects of severe torture or to see an acquaintance on his way to his execution. Mildred might be pleased to think that Salbych was indisposed or had been hurt in an accident, but the facts of the matter were that he had been tortured and condemned to die – and Michael was responsible. She had not told anyone that her request for aeroplane fuel had been turned down flat, and that she and her friends were now detained by the equivalent of force and had become hostages and prisoners – and again Michael was responsible.

But it was her fault that she was embroiled with Michael, acquainted with Salbych, in Orez, and that Adam had been hit on the head, that Jenny and Sue had disappeared, that her other friends were at the mercy of barbarians, and that Fay was in greater danger than might have been the case if her mother had stayed at home.

She heard the bells of the clocks of Orez chime the hours, and tossed and turned between two extremely uncomfortable bedfellows, obligation and inclination. Dawn was like rescue, and when Mildred stirred at last and asked if she had slept well she answered in the affirmative. Fibs were easier to justify than the division of her loyalties, and on no account must she drag innocent parties deeper into the vortex of her own predicament.

She met her guests at breakfast. Morale was better than might have been expected. Adam attributed his hangover to the usual cause, not to any external agency. He was congratulated by the artists, who thought it was more important to flout authority than to be sober. The fate of General Salbych seemed to have been hidden from the view of some by the soldiers crowding round, and perhaps others found its nastiness unthinkable; at any rate nobody dwelt on it. And, while Florrie remembered to keep quiet, agreement was reached that everyone would be glad to get out of Orezania sooner rather than later.

Mr Hamilton, calling in on his way to work, reinforced the atmosphere which Sylvester compared with the perverse Anglo-Saxon response to calamity known as the 'Dunkirk spirit'. His information was that the telephone system should be repaired shortly. Radio contact with the outside world might also be available, he said – possibly it had been jammed as a military tactic. Perhaps fuel could be ordered into the island telephonically – he would attempt to find out. He expected the two young ladies or their kidnappers to communicate – kidnap followed by a ransom demand was a common feature of the civil war. He was counting on a sign of life from Miss Fay Meavy.

Before he had concluded his catalogue of pious hopes, a missive was delivered to Florrie – the promised invitation to dinner that evening at Kraga, the rural residence of Orezanian Kings. She wanted not to go but did not say so; and the consensus was that they might as well get a free meal out of His Majesty as they were not getting much else. Adam was prepared to be beaten to a jelly for the sake of his journalistic calling, and Mr Hamilton settled the question by suggesting that the occasion would be festive and attendance diplomatic.

The day proceeded. Florrie ordered a taxi to take her to the airport, where she checked that the Gulfstream IV was still in one piece and Captain Jones and his crew were safe. Geoffrey insisted on accompanying her, and in order not to be alone with him she had to beg Mildred and Anna to squeeze in for the ride. Agatha had run her philologist to earth, and was sharing a midday sandwich with him in the vestibule of a seat of learning. The artists had their art to keep them out of mischief. Roger was amusing himself by helping Eric with his researches into the degradation of dwellers in the backstreets, and Adam's morning constitutional led him straight to his drinking club.

Florrie and Mildred rested in their room in the afternoon. At four o'clock the former began to prepare herself for the evening, at four forty-five the latter powdered her nose, and at five the whole party congregated downstairs in the foyer – they were invited for six – apparently Orezanian dinners began early and ended late.

[127]

The drive in the bus was prolonged by two inspections of their passports by the military, and eventually by a traffic jam in a dusky forest of silver birch trees. They had to walk across the car park in a field to reach Kraga, which looked more like an extended seaside cottage than a royal residence – its exterior was all verandahs and carved wood.

The entrance hall and a series of reception rooms were low-ceilinged – Kraga was actually a bungalow. Nobody greeted Florrie and Co., and more and more people packed into the limited space. Relays of waiters proffered small glasses of unrecognisable spirits – nothing non-alcoholic – and dishes of hunks of salt fish on sticks and raw onion hoops. The noise increased in volume, and women's scent was overpowered by the smell of perspiration, and immovable men in uniform with rolls of fat at the back of their necks ate, drank, smoked and laughed raucously, and the time was half past six and then a quarter to seven.

Eventually double doors were thrown open in the distance, part of the crowd surged into another room, a path was cleared in Florrie's vicinity, a hush descended and the King with his train of attendants advanced slowly, returning curtsies and bows with wolfish smiles and gracious nods of his sleek head. He was wearing a pale blue uniform similar to that which he had worn at Covent Garden, high-necked and with the darker blue sash, and he not only put the men in drab battledress and their wives in the shade, he also revived the impression he had made on her in the royal box. Her resolutions were superseded, and she sank into an obeisance.

He raised her up, thus fulfilling one of her two contradictory wishes. He reached out his smooth brown hand, and she simply took it and was extricated from the crowd and led between the lines of his subjects and through those double doors into a huge room in which a horseshoe-shaped table was laid for dinner for a hundred or more.

The King escorted her to a chair in the outer curve of the horseshoe and left her there. He had not spoken a word to her, and he now deserted her without warning or compunction; yet he was not drunk, and his attentions had changed the appearance of her personal landscape.

[128]

She sat in her chair and collected her wits. She was the only seated guest, and started to feel embarrassed rather than excited. The room was low-ceilinged again, bare-walled, painted white but grubby, and with a platform at the far end. People were flooding in and standing behind the chairs ranged round the external side of the horseshoe, waiting for the royal signal to sit down, while waiters and waitresses in the middle charged wine glasses. Florrie wondered whether or not to stay put, then had other things to worry about.

Four figures had stepped on to the platform, the three musicians from the Ritz and the Orezu Palace, the female pianist with the quivering upper arms, the gipsy violinist, the tall thin double-bass player and Theodore Hildwitch in his penguin suit. What on earth was Theodore up to, what was he not capable of?

At the same time a loud but unmusical foursome caught her ear and eye, Adam Crabhouse again the worse for Orezanian refreshments, Sylvester reeling and roaring and causing a commotion, and Eric and Roger laughing immoderately as they supported and deposited him in the nearest empty chair, to which, judging by the reactions of more important guests in the vicinity, a bad-mannered foreign civilian was definitely not entitled.

Geoffrey, Mildred, Agatha and Anna hove into view, and exchanged signals with Florrie: they were indicating the difficulties of dealing with Sylvester and urging him to get or be got to his feet, and she was appealing to Agatha to come over and cope with linguistic emergencies.

'Evening, Lady Florrie!'

It was the Pullet, leaning over the back of the chair next to hers and smiling craftily.

'Vic!' she exclaimed, almost as if she loved him dearly. 'I'm in bad trouble.'

'How's that?'

'My friends over there are drunk and disorderly.'

'They're only a bit previous – we'll have everybody under the table before the party ends.'

'But they're artists, they stop at nothing.'

'Don't you fret!'

'Vic, I am fretting – couldn't you remove them before they cause a riot? Please help me! Now my aeroplane's grounded or impounded or whatever you call it, and we're stuck here for ever so far as I can see. Can you help with fuel for the aeroplane?'

'Sorry, not my pigeon.'

'Whose then?'

'The gent in powder blue.'

'He won't listen to me.'

'He's waiting for your daughter to turn up. He'd like a chat with her, he wants to know what brings her to Orezania and who's she's been mixing with – and you're the cheese in the mousetrap.' He grinned and continued: 'I tell you true, it's no fun being a king out here – you have to mind your back.'

Someone was striking a glass with a knife. Florrie, in a new access of misery, because of Fay, because of everything, gazed blindly through the centre of the horseshoe. The uniformed figure at the bottom end, standing and waiting for the noise to subside, forced himself into her consciousness. He was tiny, and even across the twenty or thirty yards of empty space the blackness of his eyebrows and the shadowy setting of his eyes made a dramatic impression.

He spoke in Orezanian. At the end of his announcement he brandished his hand as if introducing the next act at a circus and stood aside. Through a door on the right men were emerging and shuffling towards another door on the left. They were passing – parading or being paraded – across the opening of the horseshoe; they were prisoners, shackled by leg-irons, wounded, all cowed, but nonetheless guarded by soldiers with guns; and as they reached the left-hand exit they were pulled and pushed through it by rough types, three or four of them, wearing odd neck-to-ankle leather aprons.

The duration of the episode may have been a minute. Florrie hardly had time to adjust to the shock of it. And then King Michael was down there – General Slutzk had stepped aside and Michael was haranguing his guests hoarsely as the prisoners were hissed and whistled at and hustled to their doom by the warders or executioners.

The sound of another knife on glass rang out. She redirected her gaze and saw Sylvester Kexmoor and Eric Hinxton struggling to their feet. They were protesting against the show of prisoners: a cabaret of cruelty, Sylvester barked and bellowed. The Blue army a bunch of sadists, he bellowed ungrammatically, and Eric chimed in that he hoped the Reds would pay them out and punish them; whereupon, like a drunken double-act on the stage, they subsided on to their chairs, Sylvester shaking his fists at everyone and being patted on the back by Adam, and Eric giggling with Roger.

General Slutzk was translating their outburst for the King, who shouted back in angry Orezanian at his English critics, and the royal retort was now translated for their benefit.

In so far as it was audible above the hisses and jeers, its burden was that the prisoners were war criminals, responsible for killing and maiming many people, that they had been tried in accordance with the laws of the land, found guilty, condemned to die and in short treated just as Great Britain had treated the Nazis at Nuremberg.

His Majesty continued to shout and Slutzk to translate. His Majesty was determined to learn from the mistakes made in the decadent west and create a better Orezania. He would not be kinder to criminals than to the victims of crime, he would not be so cruel as to keep homicidal maniacs in cages for year after year, nor so undemocratic as to disappoint the hopes of the majority in respect of law and order.

Furthermore, Slutzk translated, King Michael was outraged by the behaviour of his British guests. He had welcomed them into his country, honoured them with invitations to his palace and his dacha, and was repaid with unjust accusations and insults, and with sedition, seditious activities, offences carrying the severest penalties.

The reaction of the company to the above was a reverberating chorus of hostility with hissing and stamping of feet thrown in.

Florrie wanted to offer ocular apologies to Michael and turn away his wrath if she could, but he had vanished, he was not where he had been; and Slutzk was saying something more in English while another soldier translated each sentence into Orezanian. He had a pile of paper in his hand, somebody had produced and passed it to him, and he was shaking it in the face of Eric, who was looking alarmed and then shattered.

'Here is the diary of a visitor to our country and the recipient of our King's hospitality,' he said. 'This British writer describes

[131]

Orezania as "hell on earth", and Orez as "an abomination best served by the bomb and bulldozer". His opinions are that our long struggle for liberty and justice is nothing more than an excuse to shoot our enemies, and that the common denominator of Orezanians in general is bloodlust, and that our beloved sovereign and leader is – and I quote – "a tuppenny-ha'penny despot with the appearance of an inebriated wog and the culture of a snake in the grass". No – wait – silence if you please!' One of Sylvester's canvases was the next exhibit – Slutzk held it up in his left hand and resumed. 'This picture by a British painter is entitled "The Spoils of War, Orez" – it's written on the back. What is the subject? A street scene shows a squalid shanty built of cardboard and sacking – the father of a family has lost a leg and an arm and sits on an orange box, his wife is in rags and has been cooking on a brazier, her three almost naked children gather round, waiting to be fed – they are all obviously starving – and an open sewer runs through the foreground. I'm sorry, what they will eat for dinner is too small to be visible from a distance – the woman of this household of our compatriots is holding it up by its tail – it is either a small rat or a big mouse.'

Hubbub ensued. Those who had understood the speech were translating it in angry voices. The noise became more threatening when Slutzk lowered the canvas to the floor and kicked his little knee-high boot through it, and began to tear up the paper. The artists protested, and were being jeered and howled at. And the King reappeared – he was beside Florrie, they were standing together at the top of the horseshoe of the table, and she was clutching his arm and begging him to control the hullabaloo, and suddenly the introductory chords of the national anthem were thumped out on the piano.

King Michael and the assembled company, even including the foreigners, froze. But, Florrie was appalled to hear, the band was playing Theodore's version of the tune.

Instead of the semi-sacred martial harmonies, bold masculine rumbling of the double-bass, lively continuo of the piano and inspirational leadership of the violin, instead of the music that seemed to unite the Orezanians whatever the colour of their political allegiance, rude noises, booms and burps, discord, unlinked squawks and squeals disfigured the original, and Theodore's contributions, his Swanee whistle's hoots and swoops that sounded like wolf-whistles, made a mockery of it.

He obviously thought he was being funny. He moved his head in a humorous manner as he worked the plunger of his instrument, he almost conducted with his white imperial, and winked and opened his eyes wide at the more outrageous passages. His musicianship must have persuaded the band to participate in the risky performance, though no doubt money had exerted its usual influence, and his tasteless travesty might have amused the musical establishment in London. To the layman it was nonetheless a nasty racket that ridiculed the patriotic ideal; and its audience was not sophisticated, not afflicted with the aural equivalent of jaded palates, but soldiers who had marched to the unreconstructed form of the anthem into the cannon's mouth.

Florrie thought she would melt with mortification and apprehensiveness. She stole a sideways glance at the King; but his aquiline profile and wing of silver hair told her nothing.

At last one ordeal ended for her, and the next began. The ultimate whistle-cum-toot was drowned by a deep swelling sound, the voice of a lynching mob, and suddenly chairs were falling over, boots were scraping on the floor, many men were making for and converging on Theodore. He was preparing to bow, to accept the plaudits he was accustomed to receive – a complacent self-important figure with a trim paunch, whose healthy old age might have been attributable to an obliviousness of the feelings of others. He smiled, he beamed, he was surprised that no one was clapping, then his smile turned into a grimace of fear, he was surrounded by an audience with a difference, and sank out of sight.

It happened in a second or two. Florrie watched, meant to intervene somehow, gasped, and was distracted by Vic Pullent on her right speaking into her ear.

'Never a dull moment, is there? Time to pay the price, that's my advice,' he said.

She turned back to the scene at the farther end of the hall.

Theobald and his fellow-musicians were missing. They had disappeared, there was nobody on the platform. nothing, and the men in and out of uniform who had assailed it were returning to their chairs, talking, laughing. Moreover Sylvester and Eric were also gone, and Anna, Mildred, Agatha, Geoffrey, Roger and Adam, previously their neighbours, were signalling at her, signalling and urging her inaudibly to plead the cause of their companions and compatriots with the King.

'Sir, sir,' she begged him, and rushed on rather incoherently. 'Please forgive my friends – I apologise for them – but they're artists, and you know what artists are, always troublesome – please release them – I'll pay damages – I'll pay for the fuel for the aeroplane that could take them home – I'll pay whatever it costs.'

She stopped because of his discouraging regard. He was only half-looking at her out of the corners of his impenetrable brown eyes. He was not relenting, on the contrary: he was suspecting, accusing, punishing her in an autocratic way.

'They are criminals,' he said.

'Oh no, sir, they didn't mean it – you must understand – they're idiots – I'd get them out of Orezania if you'd let me.'

'You are criminal too.'

'What?'

'You not honest woman.'

'But I've committed no crime – not knowingly – I promise – and I'm just as annoyed with my friends as you are.'

'What for your daughter come to my country? Maybe she is enemy. What for you? Maybe you give money to my enemies. You do not tell – I do not trust you.'

She struggled not to betray the swelling lump in her throat.

'I came to Orezania because you asked me,' she said. 'If you just want money, let my friends go.'

He now fixed his eyes fully on her and, assuming a new crafty expression, suggested: 'Criminals expensive – many millions – yes!' While she wondered what he meant and whether the millions mentioned were in his inflated currency, he licked his red lips and continued: 'You stay in Orezania – you meet me private – tell me secrets – have good time.'

His expression had changed again, as hers had doubtless: she could recognise lust when she saw it.

'You agree?' he inquired. 'You pay me for good time, you pay with many millions – you not agree, no deal – okay?'

She shielded her eyes with her hand. She cried behind her hand, and hoped nobody noticed, the King in particular. He had averted

[134]

his face to listen to some message imparted across the width of the table by General Slutzk. When the latter clicked his heels and withdrew, he caught hold of Florrie's arm, gripped it tightly, and announced in a flat voice: 'That old man dead.'

Post Mortem

His Majesty, ignoring Florrie, gave orders and instructions, whereupon chairs scraped on the floor, people sat on them and began to
jabber, waiters were everywhere, the outsize lady pianist and the
two fiddlers reappeared on the platform and struck up a tune as if
their lives depended on it, which might have been the case, and
Sylvester and Eric, looking pale and persecuted, materialised and
rejoined Geoffrey's group away on the left.

Meanwhile the King, having conferred with General Slutzk
across the table, stood, turned his back on Florrie and precipitately
left the hall.

She had ceased to cry. She herself was on the move, she could
not carouse over Theodore's corpse, she was too shocked and hurt
to sit tight, and Vic Pullent was shepherding her towards one of
the reception rooms.

They were all together there, and had the room to themselves.
Sylvester, being fussed over by Anna, and Eric by Roger, proved
they were both still alive and kicking with characteristic utterances.
Sylvester glowered and growled: 'At least they take art seriously
enough to shoot artists in this country, which is more than can be
said for our home-grown philistines,' and Eric quipped: 'Those
boys play rough – if Theodore hadn't toddled upstairs, I don't
know what they might not have done to me.' Geoffrey was
concerned about Florrie, Adam was cautiously threatening Orezania with the fire and brimstone of his journalistic connections, and
Mildred kept on saying: 'Poor Theodore! Was he really shot for
being silly?'

An unknown officer in uniform entered the room and spoke

[136]

Orezanian. Agatha translated: the late gentleman had died of a coronary thrombosis at such-and-such a moment in a waiting-room of the country house of His Majesty King Michael, and a certificate would be issued to that effect by the Department of Health. Sylvester disagreed: 'He died of fright,' and Eric put his oar in: 'Some waiting-room! It had bars across the window, and we were locked in.' The officer was proceeding and Agatha confined her translation from Orezanian into English. The gentleman, she explained, could be viewed by his friends and would be ready for collection in an hour or two, when he had been prepared for burial.

Sylvester demanded: 'How are we meant to collect him, and what are we meant to do with him?' Eric and Roger giggled, and Anna thanked goodness inconsequentially that the two other artists had been spared.

The officer now stepped out and General Slutzk strutted into the room.

He said: 'His Majesty wishes me to express regret for the unfortunate incident. However, King Michael is glad that Mr Hildwitch did not suffer summary justice at the hands of those who were forced to listen to his extremely offensive treatment of our national anthem, but died naturally of old age.'

Sylvester muttered: 'Stuff and nonsense!' Adam squeaked dissent, and Eric said: 'I must object to the theft of literary material from my room at the Ritz, and its destruction which amounted to a denial of free speech in Orezania.'

'Please!' The general silenced the rebellious murmurings. 'Mr Kexmoor and Mr Hinxton will be relieved to hear that His Majesty has decided to waive the punishable charges that could be levelled against them, provided they desist from seditious activity, supply affidavits that they will never again publish negative descriptions of Orezania, and leave our country.'

Geoffrey cleared his throat authoritatively and introduced an element of diplomacy into the exchanges.

'General Slutzk,' he said, 'I'm sure I speak for Lady Meavy and the rest of us when I apologise to yourself for the artistic expressions that have given offence. I'm sure we would all like you to convey our regrets to His Majesty and to his other guests and, if possible, to the Orezanian people. We understand and accept that Theodore Hildwitch died by misadventure, that his death was an accident and not preventable. The trouble is that Mr Kexmoor and Mr Hinxton can't go anywhere except by air and our aeroplane has run out of fuel. Secondly, the composer Hildwitch was a man of considerable renown in the musical world and cannot be buried in a rush in Orezania. If your telephone system was in working order we'd be able to summon external aid. As it is, solutions of these problems would be welcome.'

The general, having stood as still as some small hunting reptile throughout, now as it were snapped at the olive branch.

'Our telephone system will be mended – the breakdown is due to Red sabotage,' he said.

Adam cheered in his hooligan style, while Geoffrey stuck to sweet reason.

'We can't postpone the departure of the body of Theodore Hildwitch for very long.'

'Naturally. Fuel for the aeroplane is available.'

'Ah!'

'Supplies have recently reached us, and are for sale.'

'At a price, I expect?'

'Why not? We cannot afford to subsidise the rich.'

'How much?'

'A quarter of a million sterling.'

Gasps and groans greeted the announcement, somebody said 'Highway robbery!' and somebody else 'Blackmail!'

Geoffrey objected thus: 'I imagine that figure's negotiable?'

'You imagine wrong,' General Slutzk retorted.

At this point Florrie seemed to recover her composure and her wits.

'I'll pay,' she said.

Geoffrey led the chorus of voices telling her she should not, it was too much and too bad, she was too generous, and they would not let her.

'No, I'll pay,' she repeated, adding with a watery smile at her friends: 'It's nothing but money after all.'

General Slutzk had a question for her or a command: 'But you will do us the honour of remaining in Orezania?'

She directed her response at Geoffrey and the others, she could not bear to look at the grimly smiling manikin confronting her.

'Of course I'll be staying behind to wait for Jenny and Sue.'

[138]

'And for your daughter,' he reminded her, surely with malice aforethought.

She ignored him and inquired: 'How soon can our aeroplane be ready to take off?'

'As soon as I receive the requisite assurances from your bank.'

'General Slutzk,' she began, as if about to crush him for not believing her word was her bond and for his general unpleasantness. But she changed her mind, she dealt with him more subtly, she added: 'Tell our bus-driver that we're ready to return to the Ritz.'

He submitted. He clearly did not like to be treated as a menial, but he duly clicked his little heels and did her bidding. And Florrie took the bony arm of Geoffrey and led her party out of the place

In the bus it emerged that not only Florrie's feelings were mixed. Her guests were more or less embarrassed by the sum of money she was about to spend to ransom them, and by the probable packet already spent: the veil that was usually drawn across the profligacy of smart social life had been ripped aside. Geoffrey shook his head sadly over the two hundred and fifty thousand pounds; Anna bewailed the fact that she would never be able to repay Florrie for her kindness; Agatha professed not to know that anybody had so much money to burn; Eric was tickled to work out that he had a price of sixty-odd thousand pounds on his head, and Adam squeaked that he would almost prefer to stay in Orezania and have the cash. The majority said that Florrie was certainly not to be alone at the Ritz, but Eric was quick to make the point that he was the subject of a deportation order and therefore could not volunteer to keep her company, and Sylvester indicated that he too had no choice in the matter. She saved a few blushes by firmly rejecting definite offers of companionship and protection.

Soon Sylvester and Eric seized their chance to describe their sojourn in detention, having first ascertained that the bus-driver knew no English. They had thought they were for it, for a dose of lead to the head, as the Russian victims of Marxism referred to capital punishment, they shouted above the drumming of the diesel engine. The room they were taken to was actually a cell in a prison, and they were convinced that the men in the peculiar leather aprons were butchers of men, and that, to be precise, the prison was a human abattoir. Eric said he had read a book about such Leninist-Stalinist institutions, and expected momentarily to be fetched, escorted along a dark passage, then shown into a blindingly bright sound-proofed chamber, swivelled round to face a wall and shot at the base of the skull.

He admitted he was shaking like the usual aspen leaf, and Sylvester owned up to discovering that he liked life better than he had imagined he did. Theodore's fear was different, they said: what caused his heart to stop was not the imminence of death, at his age he was used to its imminence, but the experience of an audience so unappreciative of his music that it wanted to tear him limb from limb.

Sylvester pronounced a verbal obituary which was typically professional: 'Theodore had two talents, one for music and the other for luck, and he cashed in on a fashion, like the so-called painters who sell white canvases for big bucks, but Orezanians aren't fashionable and his luck ran out tonight.'

Eric struck a lighter note by saying: 'Thank God the critics who loathe my books express their opinions on paper.'

Sylvester and Eric, Adam and Roger and even Geoffrey, united in a chorus of condemnation of Orezanian cruelty and belligerence. The death of Theodore, the prospect of departure in the morning, removed inhibiting factors such as loyalty to Florrie who was paying for their opportunity to disapprove of Orezania, and fear of incurring the displeasure of agencies with hair-trigger mentalities and unbridled power. Those manacled men, a sort of appetiser at a dinner party, were representative victims of every war, especially every civil war, fought to glorify ambitious and callous politicians and doing more immediate harm than any conceivable good in the future. That nice General Saltbeach, they said, meaning Salbych, was another casualty of blood-lust, and the corpses being carried out of the Ritz in the dead of night were those of more sacrifices to the gods of selfishness. Blues and Whites, there was probably not much to choose between them, and Reds were reputedly worse; and how childish as well as wicked they all were, they were as pitiless as only children and retarded adults can be!

The bus arrived at the hotel, and Florrie with help from Agatha succeeded in ordering sandwiches and apples, which were served in the Lounge Bar. Drinks loosened tongues further, and the talk turned personal. For safety's sake, in case defamatory remarks

[140]

should reach Orezanian ears and be understood and reported, the names that were bandied about were Tom Thumb and the Big Cheese. Anna broke the habit of a lifetime of speaking well of everybody by acknowledging that Tom Thumb was creepy, and Mildred admitted that he gave her the heebyjeebies. Agatha deplored his Orezanian accent. Geoffrey said he disgraced the Blues, Sylvester that he was a psychopath, Eric that he was certainly a naughty boy, Roger that he was a turn-off, and Adam mumbled that he meant to get equal in print.

But the consensus was that the Big Cheese was a jumped-up nobody who, if the punishment were to fit the crime, should be shot at dawn.

Florrie changed the subject as soon as she could. It was not very late, she said, but the day had been disastrous, she had heaps of arrangements to make with Geoffrey, who would be going home in the morning, she hoped she would be forgiven if she lured him into a quiet corner, and she wondered if the others or some of them would like to retire to the county.

They took the hint. They drained glasses, thanked her again, said how awful they felt and so on, hoped Fay would join her soon and Jenny and Sue would return to the fold, kissed her good night and headed for the foyer and staircase, still enumerating Michael's vices and sins.

Florrie and Geoffrey sat down closer together. They were the last customers in the neon cheerlessness of the room. The barman remained at his post, but was busily washing glasses and out of earshot.

'Oh my dear,' Geoffrey said. 'I'm happy to have this moment alone with you. Dearest Florrie, my heart's bled for you this evening – I knew how hard you were taking Theodore's death – I've imagined how unhappy you must have been ever since we landed in Orezania for that matter – but, do believe me, you are not the author of our chapter of accidents – they could not have been anticipated – and in the final reckoning Theodore's sudden death at his age may be regarded as a blessing in disguise – and when the girls are under your wing once more, the whole expedition may be seen in a more favourable light. Meanwhile may I ask you a great favour? Please permit me to stay here with you.'

'No, Geoffrey.'

'I've seen so little of you in Orezania, I've had scarcely a word with you in private, and I always see too little of you to my way of thinking. I know you have people queueing up for some of your time, and you've been more than ever preoccupied recently – but if we were together in Orez even for a few days, you and I together, it would make up for everything. The danger means nothing to me – and the object of my existence ever since we met, for nearly twenty-two years, has been to care for and take care of you. What is it, my dear? What's the matter?'

'Forgive me!'

'Good gracious, Florrie dear – is it something I've said?'

'No – I'm being silly – I'm such a fool – you're my best old friend – but I can't bear to think of how much I have to make up for!'

'What? I didn't mean you were indebted to me – the debt is all on my side – I was merely saying that I'd love to be with you and help you after everyone's gone – I was asking you to do me the favour of letting me stay. Please, I don't like to see you cry!'

'I never cry, and now I can't stop.'

'Shouldn't I offer you my handkerchief?' She laughed at him and waved it away, and he continued. 'I'm afraid you're overtired – overtaxed and overtired – you have been looking tired, if I may say so.'

'Oh Geoffrey, don't you even know that you should never tell a woman she looks tired? And I'll have to give you a lesson in how to present a handkerchief to a woman in tears. No, thanks, I don't need yours now – I've stopped – crying's just escapist – forgive me for that, too!'

'I do, I will, if you wish it, though I'm quite baffled. Am I not the one in need of forgiveness for having inadvertently upset you?'

'No – we're at cross purposes – don't worry. I'll go to church tomorrow and try to explain, not excuse, myself. But Geoffrey, open your eyes a little wider! You're so wise, can't you see any reasons why Orezania should have forced me to draw odious comparisons? I'm not the same person, don't you see that?'

'Perhaps I would, if you'd tell me more.'

'I can't. No! But half the story is that I've led too nice a life. I had nice well-to-do guardians who sent me to a nice school, I married a gentleman who was exceptionally nice and rich, we did all the nice traditional things like having a nice daughter, and when I was on my own I went on seeing nice people who were nice to me. It's true, Geoffrey – I've won life's lottery, and had the health and strength to keep nastiness at arm's length. I haven't let politics or politicians spoil my sport, I haven't had to fight anybody or deny myself anything, or flee an oppressor, or divorce a husband, or wonder where the next meal was coming from. It couldn't go on for ever.'

'My dear, you're exaggerating. I know you're sad about Theodore, but you'll recover your equilibrium soon. Think of all the people who love you, and all the people you've been kind to!'

'Theodore's a footnote. Don't be shocked! Yes, I've been kind enough to give people what I don't need, and sign cheques in their favour. I've been kind enough to entertain and be entertained by the people who go to dinner parties in London and stay for the weekend in stately country houses. As for love and loving, they're the other half of the story. Don't ask me questions! Listen, listen instead! Orezania's caught me out. I came here because I wanted to, as usual I did what I wanted to do, and the consequences are dreadful, and in Orezania there's no sand for me to bury my head in. I've had to watch nastiness in action. I've condoned and now I'm rewarding nastiness with my money. I've bought and brought shame on myself. And the worst of it is I'm afraid I can't stop.'

'Stop what, Florrie? Please elucidate! I disagree wholeheartedly with your self-accusations, and can't follow you.'

'Don't follow me! I haven't been good to you, I haven't repaid you for your more than friendship, and it must have been painful for you to love someone who's bad. No – I know what I'm talking about – and I think you should give me up for lost. Sorry, Geoffrey, sorry – and can I borrow your hanky after all?'

She cried again for a minute or two, and was begged not to, comforted, patted and treated to fond assurances.

When she was approximately back to normal she succeeded in brushing aside further interrogation.

She said with touches of her customary winning briskness: 'I would do you that favour if I could, but if you were here with me who'd contact Theodore's relations, if any, and the organisations he was connected with, and perhaps supervise his burial, who'd talk to the parents of Jenny and Sue and keep them calm, who'd

[143]

break the news to T.D. that I've spent a quarter of a million and may have to spend a lot more, who'd deal with *By Air to There* and persuade it to send another aeroplane to Orezania to ferry the rest of us out, and who'd tell Philip I'm still in the land of the living? It's another tall order, especially asking you to confer with my friend who isn't yours, but you ought to be flattered by it: I trust you as I trust no one else. Artists are not to be depended on, Roger's hardly the undertaker type, Adam's vocation is to be offensive – and I'm old enough to think the capabilities of ladies and gentlemen are not interchangeable. Will you oblige me once more?'

'Yes and no, my dear – yes in this instance, no in that I hope to oblige you more than once.'

The curfew of the national anthem now blasted across the roofs of Orez. The barman stood to attention, and Florrie and Geoffrey also rose to their feet to listen for the second time that evening to an example of the music that had been the death as well as the life or the living of Theodore Hildwitch.

The Seamy Side

Mildred had slept through it. She was fast asleep when Florrie reached their bedroom; but she was woken by the anthem eight hours later, and the cousins chatted in the greyness of the dawn.

'Poor Theodore,' Mildred said.

'If everything goes according to plan,' Florrie returned in a tone resistant to sentiment, 'Geoffrey's agreed to accompany the coffin back to England and see to the funeral.'

'Are all the others homeward bound?'

'I'm hoping so.'

'Leaving you alone here?'

'Yes. Geoffrey wanted to stay, but I talked him out of it.'

'You shouldn't be alone.'

'Whyever not? It's what I want, I'm used to being on my own, I'll be fine, and relieved to think you and the others are out of harm's way.'

'What about the King?'

'What about him?'

'He's got his eye on you, that's no secret and not surprising, but if you were alone it might be more than his eye.'

'Nonsense, Mildred!'

'Don't you mind – or shouldn't I ask?'

'Of course I mind. Of course I do. He's unbearable, he frightens me, and Orez and Orezania are frightening. But he's probably got fifty wives, and anyway he's too busy killing people to bother with me. I'll manage – the missing persons may turn up – with any luck I won't be here for long – and His Majesty hasn't been particularly

[145]

attentive yet. All the same, I admit I've made enough mistakes to last me a lifetime.'

'Are you saying I can stay?'

'Aren't you in a hurry to get home?'

'Well – you and Fay really mean home – you're my family – but I'll willingly go back to St Eo if you think I should be there.'

'I don't think that. We'll have to be careful not to hurt Geoffrey's feelings.'

'Yes,' Mildred agreed; 'and Fay's feelings for Alexander, too.'

'Exactly.'

By these ambiguous exchanges the cousins seemed to reach a new understanding.

They dressed and went downstairs. Anna and Agatha, Geoffrey, Eric and Roger were already in the foyer, informing Mr Djuro that they were leaving Orezania and would vacate their rooms later in the day. The telephone was still out of order: Agatha interpreted Mr Djuro's view that the Reds were responsible. They adjourned to the dining-room for breakfast.

Geoffrey sat next to Florrie, and Florrie said to him: 'You don't have to worry any more, Mildred's going to keep me on the straight and narrow in Orez – you'll be doing all the things I should be doing in London, and Mildred will be doing all the things for me that you would have done if you were here.'

He swallowed it. He was a man made by nature or by long experience for back seats, and he altruistically expressed relief that his beloved had chosen to favour somebody else.

The others were again tendering their regrets to Florrie for deserting her. But if anyone had shed a tear it would have been the crocodile sort, for in fact an unmistakable atmosphere of excitement prevailed. Agatha would be able to deliver her lecture on the Orezanian language to a group of English polyglots, and Anna announced coyly that she was looking forward to having her portrait painted by Sylvester. Eric and Roger also meant to keep up with each other: Eric would escape from Hinxton Grange to stay with Roger in jolly old London, and Roger would get out of his cramped basement flat to spend weekends and spread himself at the Grange. Moreover the prospect of not being subject to the vagaries of a self-appointed king whose hands were dripping with blood was a relief, despite the ambivalent opinion shared by Eric and Roger that Michael was a handsome beast.

By the time Sylvester and Adam joined the party the Orez Natwest would be open for business, and Florrie with Geoffrey in tow went upstairs to fetch an overcoat before sallying forth to authorise the payment for the aircraft fuel. Five minutes later, as she descended the stairs, she was startled to see General Slutzk crossing the foyer backed by a detachment of six of his soldiers.

He marched into the dining-room and she was sure he was doing something disagreeable to her people. Geoffrey had delayed in his room, and was too old to be asked to intervene, and she felt weak at the knees and indecisive.

But long before she expected it the mini-general with his outsize henchmen reappeared, and caught sight of and greeted her, smiling mirthlessly.

She met him in the foyer and bade him good morning in the steadiest voice she could muster, while he extracted a page of writing paper from a leather wallet, presented it to her, waved it almost in her face, saying: 'I'm glad to know that your friends have enjoyed their stay in Orezania. Please read their statement – it will be of great assistance to our tourist industry.'

The writing paper bore the address of the Orez Ritz, and ran as follows: 'We, the undersigned, have had an unforgettable holiday in the historic and unspoilt capital city of this treasure island, the people of which have been reconciled and united by their popular and charismatic sovereign, King Michael. We have relaxed in peace and security, in the mild and sunny climate, in superb hotel accommodation, and seen beautiful sights, travelled comfortably by regular bus services, spent too much money on tempting goods at bargain prices, and today we are sad to leave Orezania, although we sincerely hope our goodbye is only au revoir.'

She handed back the affidavit, blushing with sympathy for the signatories, Sylvester, Eric and Adam: they were professional communicators and could never publish or paint the truth about Orezania after putting their names to that pack of lies.

She said: 'General, the truth is, as you very well know, that my

[147]

friends can't wait to leave your country. How soon are you going to keep your promise to refuel our aeroplane?'

'As soon as I receive assurances that you will keep your promise to pay for it,' he retorted.

'I'm on my way to meet Mr Hamilton now.'

'If or when Mr Hamilton brings the equivalent of two hundred and fifty thousand pounds sterling in British banknotes or American dollars or in gold either to me at the Department of Immigration or to the officer in charge of Orez airport, your friends will be free to fly out with the remains of the composer.'

'Thank you, but I have no witness to that statement.'

'I have no witness to your claim that you're going to the bank.'

'Goodbye, General.'

'Goodbye, Lady Meavy.'

She had never before encountered such steely impudence, and was nonplussed by it. She was also angered and alarmed; but her feminine nature was mainly annoyed with herself for getting on the wrong side of the little bully.

Geoffrey joined her and was given a rueful account of the incident as they hurried to the bank. Mr Hamilton was already there and ushered them into his neat office. His affirmative reply to her unceremonious question – could the bank produce the money she had pledged more or less while she waited? – lifted one worry from her shoulders.

He then put another in its place.

He said: 'I was on my way to the hotel, Lady Meavy, to tell you that I received a telephone call at home yesterday evening. Strangely enough, someone somehow got through to me on the line that's automatically switched from the bank to my house out of office hours, and I heard the name of your daughter and a query about funds available.'

Florrie's reaction was to reach for and grip Geoffrey's hand tightly.

'Was it Fay speaking?'

'I'm sorry to say I'm unable to confirm that – the voice was muffled by interference – whoever it was might have been using a mobile or a military radio telephone.'

'Was the voice female?'

'Possibly.'

[148]

'What did she say?'

'The conversation was one-sided, and consisted of Miss Meavy's name coming through a fog of sound and the query with regard to funds. The whole extent of it, so far as I can recall, was "Fay Meavy ... funds available at bank ..." The caller might have been a lady or a gentleman, and before I could discover if I was being asked a question, or indeed could give any answer, the line went dead.'

'You mean the caller rang off?'

'Yes, Lady Meavy – or was cut off.'

'Cut off by whom? What do you mean?'

Geoffrey now spoke up.

'Is your telephone tapped, Mr Hamilton?'

'I believe it was when the Reds were in power, but whether or not the Blues have had time to reinstate a monitoring agency with the power to interrupt or divert telephone calls is a moot point.'

'How else could the caller have been cut off?'

'Possibly by a fault on the line.'

'Did you think it was a long distance call?'

'My impression was that it was local.'

Florrie intervened: 'Fay would never talk of "funds available", she'd say "money at the bank". She must have been kidnapped – it must have been her kidnapper checking on her funds.'

Mr Hamilton managed to be at once frank and soothing.

'That is again a possibility, Lady Meavy. But, as I have informed you with references to the other young ladies, kidnap victims are treated well in Orezania and may even be safer than they would be if they were at liberty. Supposing Miss Meavy were detained in one of the northern camps, and the telephone call was the beginning of a dialogue on the subject of ransom, we shall no doubt be approached again shortly.'

Florrie said: 'Money, Mr Hamilton, can we talk about money for a moment?'

He acquiesced, he listened, while she raced through the events at Kraga the previous evening, which seemed so remote, so superseded, that she was surprised when Mr Hamilton pulled a long face and offered his condolences for the sad loss of Mr Hildwitch.

And when he pointed out that she would be paying far in excess of the market price for aircraft fuel she was impatiently dismissive.

[149]

'Yes, yes, too true, I know,' she said, and explained why she had settled for daylight robbery – Theodore rotting in his coffin, and other risks – then sought assurances that she herself had 'funds available' for every conceivable emergency.

The essence of his reply was that she had and he had: Head Office in London had instructed him to grant Lady Meavy unlimited credit, and his bank-vaults were chock-full of every currency except Orezanian slozars – the sum in question could be counted and stowed in suitable receptacles in next to no time.

It was arranged that he would summon the tourist bus and at, say, eleven o'clock arrive in it with Mr Hildwitch, the money and some security guards, pick up Mr Oldcoate and the others, drive to the airport, supervise the exchange and report back to Lady Meavy when her friends were airborne.

She thanked him and said she would see him later.

Out in the street she was subjected to a mild interrogation by Geoffrey.

'You didn't divulge the secret of Fay's connection with the other King of Orezania.'

'No,' she agreed, but also in a questioning tone of voice.

'Alexander might have had something to do with the telephone call.'

'Yes,' she agreed again.

'Are you going to confide in Mr Hamilton?'

'I don't know.'

'Ah,' he said.

'Please, Geoffrey – no "ahs"!'

They reached the hotel. Florrie urged her friends to finish their packing and waited for something else to go wrong. But in due course the bus and temporary hearse chugged to a stop under the hotel awning, and they all said their goodbyes.

Sylvester was predictably ungracious. He growled, 'What a fiasco!' as he planted a prickly kiss on the cheek of his hostess and clambered into the bus before anybody else. Anna followed him, carrying his heavier painting gear and gushing thanks for a delightful holiday. Agatha Grizebeck's shy and convulsive pecks were too close to head-butts for comfort, and Roger Ryther's kisses smelt of lilies of the valley, which was preferable to Adam Crabhouse's that stank of yesterday's wine. Eric said: 'Sorry and

[150]

all that, my dear, but the best thing an artist can do in Orezania is scram.' Geoffrey embraced her according to his paradoxical custom, that is with warmth from a distance, clutching her shoulders with outstretched hands and bending over to press his cheek against hers.

An hour passed eventually. Mr Hamilton brought Florrie good news for a change. He had a receipt for her money, and the Gulfstream IV had taken off at noon.

The empty bus had chugged away in a cloud of black smoke. Florrie restrained herself from disarraying Mr Hamilton's neat person with a hug. Instead, standing in the open and presumably out of earshot of inquisitive people, she asked him to tell her about the northern camps.

'To the best of my knowledge, Lady Meavy, the Blues, Whites and Reds have impregnable bases in the hilly and even mountainous area of the island, where they recruit and train their conscripts. The armies only wage war in the lowlands, and regrettably no victory is either total or final since the defeated troops can always retreat to their camp and live to fight another day.'

'There are three camps, you say?'

'Three at least.'

'Is there a fourth?'

'There may well be.'

'Would it be Alexander's?'

'I beg your pardon?'

'The camp of the real King?'

'You have heard of Alexander Nix, Lady Meavy?'

'Yes. I'm speaking very confidentially, Mr Hamilton, you do understand that, don't you? Alexander is a friend of my daughter, they may have met here in Orezania for all I know, and a consequence of their meeting could have been the telephone call you received last night.'

'Perhaps one should not jump to conclusions, Lady Meavy.'

'Perhaps you're right.'

'Alexander is a controversial figure.'

'What do you mean?'

'The word is that he's attracting considerable support. Within a short space of time, notwithstanding his youth and his assertions that Orezania is his kingdom, he seems to have become the leader of a type of People's Crusade. As a result he has a high price on his head, and many Orezanians of every colour would resort to any trick in order to obtain it. I hope that General Slutzk, for example, is unaware of Miss Meavy's friendship with Alexander.'

'So do I – that's the point! Listen, if Fay should contact you she must be warned not to come to Orez or try to join me just yet. And if anything happened to me, you'd give her money, wouldn't you, whatever she needed to keep her safe in Orezania and help her out of it? I'm sorry, Mr Hamilton, I'm afraid I'm overwrought. Thank you for all you've done – I'd better go and pull myself together.'

He claimed that he understood, promised to carry out her instructions, said that he would call at the hotel should there be further developments, expressed hopes that she would soon feel better and that all was well with Miss Meavy and the Misses Jenny and Sue and the group in transit, and took his leave with the suspicion of a respectful bow.

She was relieved to be alone, but unable to arrest the confused and confusing spin of her imaginings. She sought out Mildred – contrarily she preferred her cousin's undemanding companionship to the solitary struggle to pull herself together. And she inwardly blessed Mildred's lack of curiosity or polite reluctance to invade another's privacy. They celebrated the exodus of their fellow-travellers and consoled themselves for their isolation and everything else with wine at luncheon. They rested on their beds in the afternoon – restlessly in the case of Florrie – and waited indoors on the off-chance that Geoffrey might ring through from London. But not altogether surprisingly the telephone remained out of order. They had supper and again retired to the bedroom they had agreed to continue to share, and not only Mildred but Florrie too, the latter as if acknowledging the impossibility of solving her problems, fell asleep.

She was woken by a knocking on their door, and called out: 'Yes? What is it?' – Mildred did not stir.

'Telephone,' a foreign voice informed her.

'Oh – one moment,' she called.

Her heart thumped: was it Geoffrey, was it Fay? And she had to hurry before the telephone system went phut again.

She was wearing pyjamas and she pulled on slacks and slippers and thought she looked sufficiently decent and opened the door.

No one was there, so she ran along to the landing and down the stairs.

General Slutzk and two soldiers emerged from the recess beneath the staircase.

He gazed up at her darkly, extended his clawlike hand, took hers, gripped and pretended to kiss it, clicked his heels and said: 'Good evening, Lady Meavy. His Majesty requests the pleasure of your company.'

She stammered: 'Who was on the telephone?'

'We didn't want to alarm you,' he explained with his untrustworthy smile. 'Shall we go?'

'Go where? I'm not ready, I'd have to change – it's too late – what are you doing?'

She had tried to extricate her hand from his grip, but could not, and the soldiers stepped forward and were bumping against her, one on each side. As she attempted to adjust to the situation they expertly propelled her towards the door, squeezing her with their hard shoulders, almost lifting her. And out of doors, again so quickly that she had no time to protest or even to comprehend exactly what was happening, she was pushed into a car, into the centre of the back seat, with a soldier on her left and right and General Slutzk in the front passenger seat beside the driver.

The car whirled away at speed.

'What are you doing?' she repeated, but her heart was in her mouth and her vocal chords were constricted.

'King Michael wishes to see you. It's an honour – you are a lucky woman. Please don't talk,' the general answered tersely.

'How ridiculous,' she managed to exclaim. 'I would have accepted a proper invitation from the King. Why does he behave like a gangster?'

'I cannot hear you,' he said.

They were travelling very fast – there was no traffic on the roads. The soldiers smelt of garlic, and the headlights picked out landmarks that surely belonged on the route to Kraga. She tried to take deep breaths and prepare herself for whatever lay ahead.

They stopped under the recognisable Kraga portico. She climbed out of the car obediently – soldiers were everywhere, what else could she do? She was ushered into the hall and with General Slutzk in front of her and the soldiers close behind marched

[153]

through room after room. Her legs weakened – she was afraid not least of having to be supported by her captors. At length the general opened a door and stood aside, she entered a large empty softly lit library or study, and was shut in.

Bookshelves lined the walls; a thick rug covered the floor; a table spread with papers had a light with a green shade on it; the furniture was upholstered in red leather, and the room was warm.

The King added to her agitation by coming through a different door that was disguised as a bookcase and swung open noiselessly. He looked sober for a change. But she might have felt better if he had been dead drunk, and if he had not been in a state of undress similar to her own. He wore a collarless white shirt, pale blue trousers, black braces and black socks – no shoes: he must have been at some function in his full-dress uniform.

She could not trust herself to curtsy; but he seemed not to expect it. Without preliminaries he said, as if continuing a conversation, 'I want you talk' – a beginning either ominous or ungrammatical. He was far from courtly; he was oppressive, and he stood by the desk, shuffling papers.

'It's very late,' she responded.

'No,' he contradicted her. 'I have no time to look at clocks,' he deigned to explain. 'I have no time for nothing. You are tired – I give you pick-up.'

He abruptly padded across the room, opened another false bookcase, revealed a cocktail bar with a bottle of champagne in an ice bucket, and started to uncork it with his strong brown hands.

'Made for kings,' he said, indicating the features of the room and the furniture with an expansive gesture. 'Is good, is luxury – Reds like it best – Reds give water to people and drink champagne – Reds like luxury better than kings did.'

He laughed and showed his big gleaming teeth. He poured glasses of champagne and, turning round, saw that she had perched on the edge of a chair.

'No – on sofa, please – sit on sofa.'

She did as she was told, and he handed her a glass and sat beside her.

'Thanks for money. You pay me for petrol, I pay you for money.' He clinked his glass against hers. 'You kind lady, no? You lonely lady and I busy man, we have pick-ups and make happiness.

[154]

Drink!' He raised his glass to his red lips with one hand, and slapped his other hand down on her thigh. 'First we talk,' he said, changing the subject he had seemed to be discussing with his allusive English and forthright body language. 'Where is daughter?'

'I don't know, sir.'

'Is in Orezania now.'

'Is that true?'

'You will meet soon.'

'I know nothing – she doesn't know I'm in Orezania – we had no plan to meet – I shall go home when I've found the two girls who were kidnapped.'

He ignored her and said: 'You will bring daughter to me.'

'Sir, are you asking me if she's here or telling me?'

'I kill enemies,' he declared. 'She will help me. She is friend of my enemy.'

'Why do you say that? What makes you think that?'

He lifted the hand on her thigh and tapped the back of his head and said: 'Have oyes here.' He meant eyes. 'Oyes and earies everywhere.' He meant ears. 'I see and I listen. Daughter friend of criminal Alexander. I kill him if she help me. Maybe I do not kill her.' He raised his glass again and said with callous inconsequentiality: 'Cheers!'

Florrie forced herself to repeat the unmajestic toast, then, scarcely noticing the hand that was back on her inside leg, appealed to and pleaded with him: 'You wouldn't harm my only child, sir – I can't believe you would ever hurt me so much – she's young and innocent and has done nothing wrong, she's never done wrong – you'll kill me if you harm her – and you like me a little, and I like you – please don't make me hate you – I'll pay more money, much more money, so that you don't involve her in your politics and do cruel things to both of us.'

He was apparently unmoved.

'Alexander in my country,' he said; 'daughter in my country, I think. One day she look for mother – you bring her to me – we kill him – okay? You stay till he is dead. I do not kill mother or daughter if necessary.' She hoped he meant if possible. 'You have good money, you pretty woman, we have time to be happy now, you better alive. Take off clothes!'

[155]

'Not like this, please.'

'What say?'

'Your thugs drag me here against my will in the middle of the night, and you threaten to kill my daughter and blackmail me. I won't be treated so horribly! Don't you understand anything? It doesn't have to be like this.'

He drained his glass, took hers from her trembling hand, threw the glasses over his shoulder, and, smiling at her with a sly victorious wolfishness, placed his hands behind his 'earies'.

'Quiet, see?' he asked. 'Nobody hear – soldiers far – doors automatic locked – you and me alone – do you understand?'

She did.

She said: 'Not now, please – let me go back to the hotel.'

'What for you go there? I am here.'

In spite of her anger, fear, nearness to tears and longing to escape, she had to smile and surrender to that extent to her excitement.

He stood up.

'I will wait in bedroom.' He pointed to the door through which he had entered. 'You join me sooner, you will be happier, afterwards go to hotel, and never forget.'

Two Way Stretch

She was in her own bed at the Ritz by four-thirty, and she immediately slept deeply and dreamlessly, and better than she had for weeks, until the national anthem of Orezania blared.

Mildred also woke. She had heard nothing at all – her sleeping was more like concussion or a coma. When she wished to know what sort of a night her cousin had had, she was told 'a good one'. Florrie was thankful for the small mercy of having to say no more.

They went downstairs to breakfast and were assailed by an unusual sound. The telephone on Mr Djuro's desk was ringing. Yes, he informed them in a tone of self-justification rather than apology or relief, it was working again.

While they ate their black bread and oily butter and drank their coffee with its suspicious taste of acorns, Florrie was summoned to the phonebox in the foyer.

Her calmness drained away, her uncertainties rushed in, she lifted the receiver with dread and said: 'Hullo?'

It was Geoffrey Oldcoate – and the telephone was not working all that well since his name was chopped up into syllables: 'Geo – off – re – ey.'

'Darling Geoffrey,' she shouted back emotionally, gratifying him no doubt because he happened not to be somebody else.

'Are you safe?' he inquired in thin slices.

'Yes! Are you?'

'The flight was uneventful.'

'What a relief! I'm glad.'

'Any news of the girls?'

'None.'

'Thankfully we can talk now.'

'After a fashion.'

'What! Can you hear me?'

'Just.'

'Florrie?'

'Yes?'

'Philip is helping to arrange Theodore's funeral.'

'Thank you both.'

'Is His Majesty behaving better?'

'This line's bad, Geoffrey.'

'I'll try again.'

'Yes, but I may not be here, I don't know where I'll be.'

'I'll try anyway. Give Mildred my love.'

'I will.'

'Goodbye, my dear.'

'Goodbye.'

She rejoined her cousin, said that Geoffrey was the caller, passed on his message, and described the faultiness of the reception.

'At least you don't have to worry any more about Geoffrey and the others,' Mildred observed in her encouraging vein.

'That's right,' Florrie agreed.

'Even a wonky telephone is an improvement on no telephone.'

'Of course,' Florrie said, although she was far from sure that it was.

'Geoffrey's so dependable and such a pet,' Mildred added perhaps with a hint of reproach, and Florrie echoed perhaps with a hint of defensiveness: 'Yes, he is.'

On safer ground they wondered in unison how they would pass the time. Ostensibly and to the best of Mildred's knowledge they were waiting for Fay, and to be contacted by Jenny and Sue or their kidnappers, therefore they had to remain available and were not to leave the hotel for long. But Florrie seemed to have exhausted her reserves of power to take decisions. They were both at a loss – they were lost without their seven companions to get rid of. Mildred thought she might have another shot at reading the short pamphlet she had been lent by Aubrey Millard-Jones entitled *The God of Africa*; and Florrie said she might pay another visit to the cathedral if Mildred was really going to be on call. They agreed that they were not particularly keen on walking through the lawless streets of Orez.

Florrie's choice was counterproductive: she was unable to concentrate on her prayers, and she grew more confused, not less, in the stifling religious murk, filled with incense and the muttered pleas of other sad people. She had forgotten to tell Mildred to warn Fay to keep her distance. How could she still entertain the far-fetched hope that she would rescue her daughter and evade Michael and his minions? She had been in cloud-cuckoo-land altogether. And Michael was past praying for. He was fatal in a sense, but, she argued profanely as she sat there sweating, he was not her fate – she must not allow him to be that. He did not know the meaning of courtship and consent – his world was made up of those who could be bent to his will and those who could not and had to die. She sought to repress her recollections of the dormant passion he had stirred in her after all the years of habit-forming chastity, even as she squirmed with a mixture of excitement and embarrassment: she and Eldred had not gone in for such antics, and she had never dreamed she could be so undignified.

A male figure was taking an unwelcome interest in her: for a moment she fancied that her train of thought had emitted a sexual signal. Then she recognised Mr Hamilton, and her ardour was instantly exchanged for guilt and anxiety.

'What's happened?' she asked.

'Excuse me, Lady Meavy, might we have a word?'

She felt worse – he had used the phrase that strikes fear into the heart of every employer – but she said yes and that she would join him out of doors.

He demurred: if she would not mind, the cathedral itself, to which he had been directed by Miss Chaffcombe, could well be the safest place for a brief confabulation.

'Please tell me quickly,' she said as he sat down beside her in the pew.

'I've received another communication from whoever asked about Miss Meavy's funds.'

'What was it?'

'"Confirm Lady Meavy at Orez Ritz Hotel now."'

'Nothing more?'

'I think not.'

'Can we begin at the beginning? When did you get the message?'

'An hour ago – I walked to the hotel as soon as I could leave the bank.'

'Were you at the bank when you got it?'

'Yes – the call came through on the telephone that rings in my office in the daytime and in my home while the bank's closed.'

'Who would know that telephone number?'

'Anyone – the number in question is printed with two more on the bank's stationery.'

'Would Fay know it?'

'If Miss Meavy spoke to our foreign exchange people about travelling to Orezania, she would have been advised to apply to the Orez Natwest in an emergency.'

'Was it Fay on the telephone today?'

'That is not my opinion. The line was no better than the last time – I'm inclined to believe the caller was male.'

'But I've spoken to London this morning – the line wasn't too bad – why are these calls you're getting so indistinct?'

'The explanation that's been given me by a colleague with an interest in telecommunications is that somebody has devised a method of bypassing the normal channels and tapping into the telephone system with primitive apparatus.'

'What did you hear him say?'

Mr Hamilton repeated the sentence and added: 'I half-heard two more words – "house" or "horse" and "all" – they were in a second sentence that sounded more informative than interrogative – but I was unable to catch the meaning.'

'He must be after money – he must want to tell me Fay's been kidnapped – and the ransom will have to be delivered to a particular house.'

'Beg pardon, Lady Meavy, but "house" could have been "horse". And why haven't the kidnappers submitted their demands more promptly and clearly? Not many Orezanians can afford to wait to be paid.'

'What am I to do, Mr Hamilton? I'm sorry to ask an unanswerable question. You see, I could now charter another aeroplane, but I can't leave Orez because my daughter's obviously in Orezania, probably in trouble, kidnapped or ill, and needing me or my money. As a matter of fact I ought to leave, because I happen to have found out for certain that the Blues are using me to lure Fay into their clutches and would then use Fay to lure Alexander to his doom; but I can't until I've recovered Jenny and Sue. I should be strong enough to acknowledge that Fay would be better off without me, I should desert her for her own good, and sacrifice her friends to her safety. But I'm weak and growing weaker, I can't, I can't even bear to ask you to tell her I've gone when I haven't, while I'm waiting for Jenny and Sue, although I dread to think of her coming to Orez to look for me and putting herself in danger of God knows what.'

'Orezania specialises in such dilemmas, I regret to say, Lady Meavy. On the other hand, Orezania also offers a method of resolving them. I've received reports of increased activity in the northern hills, which probably means that General Zaporag is on the warpath. He's the leader of the Reds, and according to the law of averages it's his turn to regain control of Orez and, at least in principle, the island. He would or he will oust the Blues who are threatening you and your daughter, he wouldn't or won't know about Miss Meavy's connection with Alexander, and I'm confident that he will again recognise the advantage of having high-spending tourists in his capital city.'

'Are you saying that it might be safer to stay put than to try to leave?'

'I wish I could be so dogmatic. No, I'm suggesting that it might be more difficult, both practically and emotionally, to leave in the meanwhile than to stay.'

'Thank you, Mr Hamilton. I appreciate your gift for saying the right thing.'

'May I add, Lady Meavy, that I can detect no sign of weakness in your attitude to the shocks and setbacks of your visit to Orezania?'

'Oh well – setbacks aren't the whole story.'

His reaction to her odd statement was invisible in the gloom. He stood up and withdrew in his unassuming way.

Half an hour later she followed him out of the cathedral, crossed the square, re-entered the foyer of the hotel, was greeted by Mr

Djuro indicating that she was again wanted on the telephone, and, with faltering steps that would have disillusioned her dear bank manager, tottered over and shut herself in the phonebox.

'Hullo?'

'My love, at last!'

'Philip!' she returned anti-climactically.

'Yes, my darling. Can you hear me?'

'Quite well.'

'How are you?'

'Quite well again, thanks. And you?'

'Quite ill – I've been buying black ties. I would have rushed to your rescue, but because your aeroplane was virtually hijacked I couldn't persuade any other charter company to fly me to Orezania. I've been frustrated and furious, and now I've heard from your Oldcoate I'd like to string up the author of your woes and mine.'

'Be careful what you say, Philip!'

'Oh my God! Why did you have to visit a place still sunk in the dark age of communism? Sorry – we'll talk in a civilised language that no Orezanian could understand. How dare Rex put the squeeze on you?'

'I think we should change the subject.'

'Can I come and get you out?'

'No, definitely not – I'm waiting for people – ask Geoffrey! The last straw for me would be to have you here throwing your weight about.'

'You describe me in flattering terms.'

'I meant that I daren't risk your life as well.'

'Hildwitch's funeral is planned for the day after tomorrow. Don't blame yourself for his death – he was damn lucky to live as long as he did – a lot of people who had to listen to his compositions would have liked to wring his neck.'

'Philip, you don't understand what life's like in Orezania. I didn't, I still don't, and can't believe the awful things I've witnessed have actually occurred – it's like a nightmare. Theodore was frightened to death – and I'm frightened – and you don't get used to it – fear's cumulative and you grow more afraid. I was so naive – I'm ashamed of my determination not to know how the other half lives, the half at the mercy of evil politicians. Thank you

[162]

for offering to come here, but don't, please don't even if you can't reach me on the telephone or find out where I am.'

'No promises, Florrie – your word may be law – but I'm not the law-abiding type. Incidentally, Rex must be the nastiest piece of work in Asia Minor.'

'It's difficult for me to go on talking, Philip.'

'What's wrong?'

'I can't explain – thank you for ringing.'

'But I haven't finished.'

'Goodbye!'

She replaced the receiver and waited in the phonebox until she was breathing more easily. Then she found Mildred and confessed that she had felt estranged from Geoffrey and Philip and was sorry; also that she seemed to have formed an unbreakable habit of playing fast and loose with others' lives.

Mildred's solace included denials and comforting prognostications that they would all muddle through, and a hint that they should have something to eat. The day wore on. They strolled into the square, but rain fell on them. They drank tea in the Lounge Bar, and returned to their room. They told each other they were relaxing, having a badly needed rest; but Florrie could neither control nor conceal her tension, which was aggravated by the approach of darkness and night, and Mildred was affected by it. They looked into their books and were easily distracted by sounds within and without the hotel that might mean trouble. They filed and buffed their fingernails, and their desultory snatches of conversation referred to irrelevant matters.

At six o'clock someone knocked on their bedroom door.

Florrie's heart thumped with terror, elation, uncertainty, indignation, her face burned, she signalled at Mildred and whispered at her forcefully: 'Say I'm out, say I'm not here!'

Mildred called: 'Yes? Who is it?'

A male voice answered in English in an undertone: 'Lady M.? Open up quick!'

'Who are you?'

'Vic Pullent – private business – not to worry!'

Florrie addressed Mildred: 'We'd better let him in.'

He was in uniform and armed with a machine-pistol, but he carried a bulging civilian backpack.

[163]

'What do you want?' Florrie asked warily.

'It's hullo and ta-ta, Lady M.,' he explained, dumping his stuff on the floor. 'Pardon the armament – it's only for show – I can't shoot straight or stand the sight of blood – but a gun's a passport in Orezania and could be a help with Plan A. Evening, Miss,' he said to Mildred, revealing his ratlike teeth in a smirk.

Florrie shut the door and inquired: 'Where are you going?' – she had recovered a degree of composure.

'Home sweet home – full speed – and won't be stopped – but don't tell anyone!'

'Are you deserting King Michael?'

'I'd put it different – I'm looking for a permanent position – I've read the writing on the wall – "Save your skin before the Reds rip it off you."'

'Oh heavens!' Mildred exclaimed.

'Not to worry, Miss – so long as Lady M.'s got her cheque book you'll be popular – Reds are mad for money though they won't let no one else have any.'

'How are you going home?' Florrie asked.

'On my flat feet, along with all the other refugees and with luck. Point is, Lady M., your two missing girls could be in the hills where I'm heading – the Whites have been trying to peddle them – thought you'd like to know.'

'Not my daughter?'

'No – but she'll be worth an extra bob or two – and nobody wastes money in this island.'

'Please explain!'

'Michael won't bite – he's got more on his mind than foreign fillies – or he will have soon – but number two, the titch, he'll have a nibble, I shouldn't wonder. He'll make out he can supply the goods provided you pay in advance. I'm partly here to warn you – not a penny till you see the girls are in good nick. And take your time – your cash'll buy twice as much when the shooting starts again.'

An apprehensive squeak was Mildred's response to his assumption that the shooting would start. He tossed his head at her cheerily and heaved his backpack on to his shoulder.

Florrie said: 'Can't you wait a moment?'

'Half a mo, more like.'

He winked at them and swung the backpack on to his other shoulder.

'Will Michael be defeated? Will they kill him?' she asked.

'They'd like to. But he's a few of his nine lives left. He didn't have a throne to sit on when he lodged with my people in Catford, he was buying guns but square meals were another matter. What next, says you? My guess is the other King, the one they're dying to kill, your daughter's boyfriend maybe, who's doing too damn well.' He was interrupted by what might have been a remote roll of thunder. 'Told you so,' he added.

'It was a bomb,' Mildred squeaked.

Florrie thanked Vic for his trouble as he picked up his firearm.

'Goodbye, ladies – here's hoping we die in our own beds – and don't buy nothing from Slutzk without seeing it's alive!'

He put his finger to his lips, opened the door, listened and slipped out.

An explosion rocked the hotel. Suddenly guns were going off near and far, booming and rattling, shaking the window in its frame, causing the ceiling light to dance on its flex.

'Do you want to go down to the cellar?' Florrie shouted at Mildred.

'Do you?' Mildred shouted back.

Florrie said no, and Mildred signified agreement with a pale grimace. They covered their ears with their hands and sheltered on their beds from the possibility of flying glass.

It was a bombardment such as they had gone through on their first night in Orez. Experience did not render it any easier to bear, on the contrary. Mildred cowered and occasionally cried out, and Florrie trembled not only on her own account. Conversation and even trains of thought were impossible. But they survived for half an hour and then an hour.

It stopped as it had started, suddenly and completely. The time was seven-thirtyish. They were not convinced the battle was over, their nerves continued to jangle, they stayed away from the window and scarcely spoke. At last Florrie dared to crawl across to the door and peep through it. The lights were still on, and the sound of fairly normal voices in the foyer reached her. They waited in their room for another half-hour, and, partly spurred by hunger, decided to venture downstairs.

[165]

The Blue officers resident in the Ritz must have retreated strategically, and other ranks were humping kitbags and official files across the marble floor of the foyer. Hotel staff were helping and hurrying them, no doubt to facilitate preparations for the arrival of their Red counterparts. But the scene was not especially sinister. Mr Djuro called to the ladies with a happy smile: 'Peace – no war!' – and the head-waiter was standing at the door of the dining-room and making welcoming gestures.

They tried to eat a little dinner and soon returned to their room. Their appetites had proved unequal to the additional strains of finding that they were the only guests in the dining-room and to being fussed over by six waiters and a chef, most of whom were keen to practise their English. For some irrational reason they felt safer on the first than on the ground floor, and by themselves they could at least listen for the progress of the lethal projectile that might have their names on it.

They scarcely discussed the intervention of the Pullet. They postponed analysis of his throwaway mixture of good and bad news – they as it were held their breath until the next phase of the battle began. But nothing bad happened, and at about nine o'clock they switched off the overhead light and retired to their beds for the night.

The knock on the door came at about the same time as yesterday's.

Florrie, who had anticipated it and every complication it was likely to lead to, urged Mildred to wake up.

A man, possibly the man who had delivered the last misleading message, spoke with an Orezanian accent.

'Telephone – important!'

Mildred was awake by now, and Florrie issued more orders.

'Please go down and answer it – say I'm ill. Don't ask why, I'll tell you later.'

Mildred complied, she put on her overcoat and slippers and left the room.

Florrie could not stay still. She paced the floor bare-footed, wrung her hands, stepped into the passage and strained her ears, and thought of hiding in the bathroom.

Mildred came back sooner than expected.

'Was it General Slutzk?' Florrie demanded.

[166]

'No,' Mildred replied in some bewilderment; 'were you expecting him to ring?'

Florrie ignored her question and posed two questions of her own.

'Was it a real telephone call? Who was it then?'

'It was Fay.'

'Oh my God! Are you sure?'

'Absolutely, although I couldn't hear much.'

'How can you be sure in that case?'

'She wanted you and asked who I was, and when I told her she said "Mildred, golly!"'

Frying Pan and Fire

They talked in the dark: somebody had warned them that Orezanian soldiers liked to shoot at lit electric bulbs visible from the street.

'What did she say, Mildred?'

'I heard the word "hospital" and she seemed to be saying "all" – it could have been "all at hospital" or "all well at hospital: or even "come to hospital". I'm sorry, Florrie, I was so surprised that it was Fay speaking, and the line was dreadful.'

The bombardment began again and rudely interrupted their conversation.

During a momentary intermission Mildred inquired: 'Do you think all the soldiers know that the Ritz is not to be blown up?'

And later Florrie remarked: 'The man who rang Mr Hamilton this morning must have said "hospital", not "house" or "horse". The man and Fay must have used the same rotten old telephone. But where are they, and what hospital are they talking about? And is Fay ill in it?'

The answers to these questions were the strains of the national anthem punctuated by the sounds of murder and maiming.

Then Mildred, uncovering her ears in another relatively silent patch, again expressed interest in Florrie's reference to General Slutzk.

'Were you expecting that devil to ring you?'

'No – it wasn't like that.'

'How was it?'

'He played a dirty trick on me yesterday evening.'

[168]

'How and why? Sorry, I don't understand.'

'You were asleep at the time. He had me summoned to the telephone, and I rushed downstairs thinking it might be Fay.'

'But it wasn't?'

'No.'

'Who was it?'

'No one.'

'Don't you want to tell me, Flo?'

'Slutzk and his men bundled me into a car and took me to Kraga.'

'To Michael?'

'Yes.'

'Did he seduce you?'

'He forced me.'

'You mean he raped you by force?'

'You could say so.'

'Oh Florrie, how terrible!'

But Florrie veered off at a tangent. 'I've been so mean to Geoffrey and specially to Philip for years and years, and now this had to hit me at my time of life!'

'It wasn't your fault.'

'Everybody tells me that. But it is my fault – I needn't have come here and needn't have brought you or the others.'

'You did it for love of Fay.'

'Did I? Well, that was a mistake, too. Fay was my excuse.'

'You're very hard on yourself.'

'I know what I deserve. Keep my secrets, please – don't shame me any more than I am ashamed.'

'Of course, I promise. Anyway, judging by the Pullet's words and actions, Michael won't bother you again.'

Florrie's murmur either signified gratitude for Mildred's sympathy or was a somewhat tearful gulp.

They were interrupted by exterior noises, bangs, bumps, sirens, engines revving furiously, shots, shrieks.

Florrie then said: 'You'd sleep through this if I didn't keep you awake. War seems to act on you like a sleeping pill.'

Mildred giggled and replied: 'I'm not as sleepy as sometimes. I'm thinking of all you've been through. You weren't physically injured, were you?'

[169]

'No. I suppose I'm none the worse. And it's par for the course in many countries. How can I complain?'

Another pause was imposed on them by more fighting.

Mildred took advantage of a blessed silence to ask: 'What time did you get in last night, or was it this morning? It worries me that I wasn't capable of looking after you.'

'About four.'

'Four o'clock!'

'I can't remember precisely.'

The next query was tentative and perhaps wistful: 'Do you like him, Flo? Did you like him?'

The answer was slow and carefully phrased 'Once maybe – too foolish – a disaster considering Fay's Alexander and from every other point of view. I'm blushing – nothing of the sort had ever happened to me – but it was over as soon as it began, if you know what I mean – I was afraid that the telephone call you took would deliver me to His Majesty again – so I didn't speak to Fay, I missed the point of our expedition to Orezania, which has cost one life and two kidnaps and trouble and tears and money galore. So many mistakes!'

'Everybody makes those,' Mildred commented, probably rueing her own talent for loving the wrong man and hoping Aubrey Millard-Jones was the right one.

Florrie said: 'And now I've made another by being egoistic.'

They exchanged assurances and apologies, and Mildred asked: 'Do you want Fay to marry Alexander?'

'What I want now is not to decide anything for anybody, or advise or organise or interfere or boss about. I just want to creep into my shell and lead a private life.'

'You'll never do that,' Mildred laughed.

'We'll see.'

The battle raged once more.

When the racket subsided, Florrie said: 'The hospital that Fay mentioned . . .' and stopped. Mildred was breathing with recognisable depth and regularity. And strangely, exceptionally, as if to prove the rule of the Orezanian combatants' disregard for human life and happiness, a truce seemed to have been agreed in order not to disturb her slumbers. Instead of shelling and shooting, the sweet chimes of city clocks and the melodies of church bells were again audible. Florrie was sceptical; but gradually her tight muscles released the blood to warm her hands and feet. She realised how tired of it all she was, and dropped off.

The national anthem woke and recalled them to care. But it was another day and a fine one, and Mildred took the view that peace or at least armistice had broken out, while Florrie wondered whether Michael had survived the Red onslaught.

They dressed and proceeded along the passage to the top of the stairs. Down in the foyer, but not looking up at her, was General Slutzk, flanked by the two robotic heavyweights who had coerced her into the car to Kraga.

She hesitated. Could he be bringing her an acceptable message? Had the Blues repulsed the Reds? But there were not enough people in the foyer to provide protection, and she had no nerve for a fight.

She dragged Mildred back to their room, explained that she feared the worst, wished they had a decent lock on their door, and held and squeezed her cousin's small damp hand.

He had followed them, and he knocked.

'You can't come in, sorry!' Florrie called out.

'General Slutzk speaking, Lady Meavy.'

'I'm sorry – it's not convenient.'

'Open the door, please.'

'No, I can't do that.'

'Lady Meavy, can you hear me? We are at war, and I have no time to argue. I have news of Miss Bowditch and Miss Cartwright, and I refuse to talk to you in this manner.'

She looked at Mildred and Mildred looked back: they were undecided.

Something heavy, someone heavy in fact, bumped against the door, which burst open, and the general strutted in. His men remained in the passage.

Florrie released Mildred's hand and addressed the intruder. 'Not a good example of Orezanian chivalry, General.'

He was unamused, took no notice, and raising his shadowy black eyes to hers said: 'Whites have offered to release the girls for five hundred thousand sterling.'

[171]

Mildred snapped with the occasional courage or foolhardiness of the timid: 'So it's five hundred thousand this time round – how outrageous!'

Florrie asked: 'Are they all right?'

'Yes.'

'Where are they?'

'They're held by the Whites, but I've been given to understand they could be exchanged for the money at short notice.'

'Why haven't the Whites contacted me?'

'Lady Meavy, I have traced these persons with effort and expense, and negotiated an offer which, I assure you, is advantageous. If you were to be approached directly by the White negotiators the price would be one million. Therefore you will deal with me.'

Mildred again thrust her oar in.

'Goodness gracious, you're expecting us to trust you with all that money?'

General Slutzk acknowledged her existence by a faint flicker of his eyelids, and, removing his flat leather wallet from under his arm, unzipped it with long white bony fingers and produced a typed sheet of paper.

'This document authorises me to draw the money from your bank. It states that you have not appended your signature under duress. I have brought with me two witnesses.'

'Witnesses!' Mildred exclaimed on a derogatory crescendo, at which the general frowned at her.

He resumed: 'You will be reunited with your friends no later than midday provided you sign now and your bank does not delay the transaction – that is my personal guarantee.' He pulled a fountain pen from the wallet and unscrewed the top, and a shell or bomb or landmine exploded in the vicinity of the hotel. The ladies almost involuntarily shrank away towards the corner of the room where they thought they were screened from splinters of glass. He flinched but did not move, and added: 'I'm sure I don't need to remind you that hostages can become more trouble than they're worth.'

'How dare you make such a vile threat? How dare you blackmail us?' Mildred demanded irrepressibly, and Florrie tried to drown her provocative questions by insisting in a loud voice: 'I couldn't

[172]

sign anything – nothing – not possibly – before I've spoken to the manager of my bank. No, listen! I appreciate your offer, and I promise to speak to Mr Hamilton if you leave us alone. Please – I'm not feeling well – and I don't know what money I can afford or get hold of.'

General Slutzk retorted with impatience: 'I must teach you to take me more seriously,' and issued an order to the men in the passage, who shouldered their way into the room and shut the door behind them.

Mildred began to scream. Fear and outraged gentleness combined to strip her of inhibition and revolt against oppression.

'Get out, get out,' she screamed.

The general spoke in Orezanian. One of the men, unshaven and impassive, advanced on Mildred and caught her by the arm. He yanked her towards the door, but she reached out to Florrie with her free hand. A tug-of-war ensued. Then the other man chopped his great red hand down on the arm that was clinging to Florrie. Mildred emitted a different sound, a cry of pain, and had to let go, and the soldiers between them pulled her through the door which the general was holding open.

He shut it and said: 'Here is my pen, Lady Meavy.'

'No, no – free my cousin immediately!'

He gave a knock on the inside of the door, a signal to the soldiers outside. Mildred's moaning became a long-drawn-out high-pitched sobbing groan of agony.

'Stop it!' Florrie shouted at the torturer-in-chief, with his panda-like eyes and peaky countenance. 'Stop hurting her!'

'That's up to you.'

'I'll report you to King Michael.'

He smiled. He was disdainful and she was taken aback. What did he know that she did not? She now noticed that the shoulder flashes on his uniform were no longer blue. They were red – he had changed sides – he was a traitor – King Michael had become his enemy.

He raised his hand as if to knock on the door again.

'I'll sign,' she said.

An explosion occurred at extremely close quarters to the hotel. The bang was like concussion, and the blast caused Florrie to crash into a wall and General Slutzk to finish on his knees. The door had burst open, and Mildred was sprawled on the floor of the passage and the soldiers had reeled aside. Something was bleeping – the general's pager – and a black cloud of dust began to obscure the daylight. There were sounds of panic downstairs and in the street, yelling, commands, ambulance bells, a rattle of small arms fire, engines roaring.

General Slutzk addressed Florrie: 'I have to go. Where are the back stairs?'

She heard him although her ears sang, but gestured to indicate that she could not care less, and attempted to brush past him to hurry to the aid of her cousin.

He caught her by the arm, his fingers were like pins digging into her, and perhaps standing on tiptoe, anyway reaching up to bare his teeth in her face, he said: 'This is a postponement, nothing more. Don't try to escape. Remember I'm looking for your daughter – don't tempt me to punish her.'

He pushed her aside with surprising force and scampered into and along the passage – the patter of his tiny feet resembled a sort of obbligato to the pounding of his soldiers' hobnailed boots.

Florrie knelt by Mildred, who managed to say: 'Thank God for bombs.'

Her left arm had been twisted nearly to the point of dislocation: Orezanians did not bother with high-tech contraptions that ripped off fingernails, brute force served their purposes.

Florrie helped her to her feet and into the bedroom; overcame the problem of the splintered doorjamb by pushing a chair against the door; used scissors to cut off the arm of her jersey and applied the cold compress of a wet towel to the swollen elbow; and as soon as Mildred was equal to the prospect of being left alone for a few minutes, sallied forth to the top of the staircase. The foyer looked safe enough, it was empty except for an unknown man on duty at the reception desk – had Mr Djuro "retired", or was he with others helping to deal with the damage out of doors?

She descended the stairs and strode across the foyer to the Lounge Bar. The barman had a bloodstained bandage round his head, but explained mainly in sign language that the explosion had made him a victim of the poetic justice of a bottle of peach brandy falling on his head. She ordered a tray of tea, milk, sugar, bread and honey without delay, and was carrying it as quickly as

[174]

she could towards the staircase when she encountered Mr Hamilton.

He was standing in front of her, neat and nice, not foreign, not cruel. It was almost like wish fulfilment: she had been praying the telephone was still working and she could summon him. She might have dropped the tray with surprise and relief. As it was, they exclaimed almost in unison that they were glad to see each other, and she added the urgent request that might have led to misunderstandings in an English hotel: 'Come to my bed-room!'

On the stairs she gave him an abbreviated account of what had happened earlier, and he extended sympathy and told her how concerned he had been about the possible effects of the shelling.

Hot sweet tea and aspirins were administered to Mildred, and Florrie urged her cousin to try to eat a little breakfast, while Mr Hamilton reinterpreted events.

The shell had landed on the hotel car park on the opposite side of the building, he said: which was lucky for the ladies if not for some members of the hotel staff and the owners of several cars. Moreover the ladies' luck extended to the timing of the shell's impact: it had undoubtedly spared them further suffering. For General Slutzk must have been determined to obtain the money either to impress his new masters, the Reds, and allay their suspicions of a turncoat, or to feather his own nest. His prompt reaction to his pager was attributable to one of two reasons or to both – he was keen either not to keep his superior officers waiting, or not to reveal to them the remunerative secret of where he was and what he was doing. As for the deal he had proposed, it was a trick: the Orezanian etiquette in such matters was that hostages and ransoms were exchanged simultaneously, not ransom first and more than likely last. Mr Hamilton's consequent deductions were that the general was and would be unable to produce the girls, who must be alive – if they were dead, they would be subject to a forced sale for the purposes of burial.

Unfortunately, Mr Hamilton pursued his hypotheses methodi-cally, if the general was under pressure to please the Reds and consolidate his position in the Red hierarchy, or alternatively if he was feeling insecure and that he had better cut and run, in both cases he would return to the hotel and create the circumstances in which Lady Meavy and indeed her bank would have no alternative but to meet his demands.

'We can't sit here waiting for him to torture us to death,' Florrie cried out.

'Quite so,' Mr Hamilton agreed.

'Well – where do we go? Or do I pay up again?'

'Payment could lead to a new problem, Lady Meavy.'

'Don't tell me I'm broke!'

'Indeed no, far from it – but paying General Slutzk would leave the bank itself short of the cash that might be required to liberate the two young ladies from their kidnappers, supposing they have been kidnapped, and to serve the interests of Miss Meavy.'

Mildred broke in here to say to her cousin: 'Tell him about Fay's call!'

Florrie obliged, and Mr Hamilton betrayed an unwonted trace of excitement.

He had been perching straight-backed on the dressing-table chair, but now rose, clapped a hand to his forehead, took two paces forward and two back, and addressed the ladies, who were sitting together on one of the beds.

'I must offer you my apologies, I have been obtuse. I now realise that my own caller was saying "hospital", just as Miss Meavy was, and I'm reasonably sure that the hospital in question would be the institution in the northern hills which is apparently non-political and cares for the casualties of the war whatever colour they have fought for, and is respected and partly financed by each of the three warlords. Refugees are admitted and work for their keep, I understand – and it occurs to me that Miss Meavy and her friends are possibly or even probably sheltering there, and that yourself, Lady Meavy, and Miss Chaffcombe would be safe if you were prepared to try to reach it.'

'But,' Florrie objected, 'Mildred's arm's been twisted, she's in pain and ought to see a doctor immediately.'

Mildred denied it – she was feeling better – and urged Mr Hamilton to explain a bit more.

He said: 'I couldn't advise you to stay where we are at present, and I wouldn't offer you accommodation in my home or in any private house – secrets do not exist in Orezania, information equals

[176]

money, and I'm afraid your two selves may have become potential hostages of great value. Escape by normal means is out of the question, especially during the hostilities in progress. The course I think you should follow is so unsuitable and difficult that I hesitate to urge it.'

'Come on, Mr Hamilton, one more difficulty won't make much difference!'

'I think you should join the column of refugees heading into the hills and aim for the hospital.'

He answered their questions thus: yes, on foot because there was no road, and sleeping rough, in converted farms along the way or under the stars, but in the mild dry weather that prevailed in late Orezanian autumn, and anonymously, in the usual apparel of the other refugees, and safeguarded to some extent by the fellowship of people in similar situations. Yes, they would have to leave the Ritz surreptitiously, without their luggage and as if they would return; but at the bank he could provide them with money, clothes, sleeping bags, rations, he could get hold of a doctor, and ferry them in his car to the point of their departure between the Blue and Red front lines. Although it would be uncomfortable in every sense, he hoped he was right in thinking it would prove to be the lesser of two evils.

Hesitantly, exchanging looks with Mildred, Florrie asked: 'If we were to follow your advice, when would we have to start?'

He cleared his throat and said: 'Without delay, dressed as you are, and with me.'

'You're not dramatising our predicament, are you?'

'On the contrary.'

'How far to the hospital?'

'Perhaps a hundred miles.'

'No,' she said. 'Mildred isn't fit and couldn't do it.'

'I could and we must,' Mildred piped up; 'I'd walk two hundred miles to be out of reach of General Slutzk.'

Florrie turned back to Mr Hamilton.

'Would it be any use to appeal to King Michael?'

'I hear that he's already taken to his heels.'

'Run away, you mean?'

'He could be with his army, fighting or retreating, or he could be deposed or assassinated.'

[177]

'I suppose I shouldn't try to get in touch with him?'

'No, Lady Meavy – and I very much doubt that he'd wish to help anyone except himself.'

'I see,' she commented in a thicker voice, and after looking out of the window for a moment she added: 'Shall we go?'

A Long March

Mildred was heroic: she held her injured left arm across her body with her right hand, and smiled quaveringly through the pain of walking to the Orez Natwest.

In the hotel Florrie had draped a cardigan and a coat over her cousin's shoulders, and, having asked Mr Hamilton to wait in the passage, put on extra underwear and filled her own capacious bag and Mildred's with other items of clothing.

There must have been a lull in the battle; but the populace was playing safe by not venturing into the streets. Some reassurance for the ladies was provided by the sunshine – Mr Hamilton might be right and their journey would be blessed with an Orezanian version of one of those brief autumnal summers bearing the names of saints.

At the bank they were ushered into an empty interview room and attended first by an English-speaking Orezanian employee, a middle-aged male clerk who was going to buy them the requisite equipment, then by a doctor who gave Mildred a painkilling injection, strapped her arm in a more comfortable position and arranged a sling for it. Mr Hamilton produced money, Orezanian banknotes to the value of three hundred pounds sterling and four gold coins. When Florrie had signed the inescapable forms he said he had assisted other customers to leave Orezania by shanks' pony and the northern route, and had a small amount of vicarious experience which might be useful.

They would not need a map: they would be following in the past and present footsteps of many. They would find Orezanians ready to sell shelter and food at the farms already referred to. Inability to speak the language would be no bar to trade. They must remember that fifty slozars were worth one penny and each gold coin was worth fifty pounds. Refugees who had been political enemies were bound by self-interest to keep the peace for a change, but gangs of young men with and without guns should be avoided if possible. Mr Hamilton emphasised that the average Orezanian was a God-fearing person, kind and charitable, and that if the worst came to the worst the ladies would have to try to contact him by telephone and he would do his utmost to help.

The man who had gone to the shops returned. Florrie and Mildred's doubts that he could buy clothes for them were allayed by the shapelessness of the black cotton dresses he had bought, and the lengths of black material to serve as headgear and shawl. Orezanian bootees, made of canvas and rubber and again drabbest black, replaced their smart leather shoes. Sleeping bags formed backpacks, and satchels would carry the rest of their gear, which included a tin can for cooking and boiling water in, firelighters, matches and soap. A kind of bandage with pouches in which their money could be kept was wound round an upper arm in Florrie's case and an ankle in Mildred's. The comestibles provided were salami, olives, cheese, tea and sugar.

Before departure a meal was laid before them, meat pasties still warm from the bakery and fruit; but it was scarcely eleven o'clock, and for innumerable other reasons they were not hungry. Once more Mildred promised that she was willing and able to walk to the ends of the earth – anything was better than General Slutzk. They repaired by lift to the car park beneath the bank and were driven by Mr Hamilton personally to a spot on the northern edge of the town where the tumbledown houses of smallholders shared the roadside with blocks of jerrybuilt flats scarred by bullet holes.

He switched off the engine. Perhaps because it was midday, lunch-time, the guns were quiet. The high sun shone on the landscape heavy with the harvest of autumn. Pigeons cooed in the trees and sparrows twittered in their dust-baths in the gutter. Mr Hamilton pointed to a family group, a youngish man and wife and three children, the only visible people who, fifty yards ahead, were pushing a primitive cart over-loaded with their belongings. They were typical refugees, he said; and added, when they turned to the right, that they were on the road or rather the rutted track to the hills. He also drew attention to a church that looked like a cowbyre on the high horizon: Lady Meavy and Miss Chaffcombe would have to head for it.

They got out of the car. He renewed his assurances that he would take care of Miss Meavy and her two friends if they should materialise in Orez, provide money, pay ransoms, devise protective measures and organise homecomings. Florrie and Mildred thanked him for everything, thanked him repeatedly and promised to communicate when they could. He offered to shake their hands and they shook his, although they agreed later on that they would have liked to kiss him. They wished one another luck, and the ladies waved and watched as he drove away and until his car was no longer visible.

They started to walk at eleven forty-five and they stopped walking at six. They rested intermittently by the roadside, and once by a clear purling stream in an olive grove, where they made a bonfire of sticks and boiled water for tea. The sunshine was warmer than they expected, and the undulations and uneven surfaces of the track made for hot work; but they hurried on, Florrie allowing Mildred to set the pace. They passed other individuals as well as groups progressing in the same direction, and sometimes beasts of burden, diminutive donkeys with huge loads lashed to their backs, and goats pulling while their owners pushed wheelbarrows – one such wheelbarrow contained a grandmother; but when they were greeted they confined their responses to dumb smiles and polite gestures, and were not detained. They hated themselves for not daring to be good Samaritans: a white-haired old lady, a bundle of black rags under a hedge, begged them for alms in vain, and a youth with a bloody trouser-leg who lay on the verge and shouted at them was only given a wide berth. They were afraid to enter into conversation with anyone and attract attention, and ignored the stalls that sold things to eat and drink and the old-fashioned milkmaids purveying glasses of fresh milk. Yet nobody pestered or threatened them, and towards the end of the afternoon, partly because of the distance they had put between themselves and the perils of Orez, they regained a degree of confidence.

They talked as they went along, but not much. The torturous episode in their bedroom at The Ritz seemed to have less long-term effects on Mildred than on Florrie, whose arm was not twisted. The latter's concern for her cousin was somewhat exaggerated; she was often tearful and grew uncharacteristically glum.

'We're still alive, Flo,' Mildred encouraged her at some stage.

'Are we?' Florrie replied.

'Anyway,' Mildred tried again, 'the weather's lovely, as they say, and people ramble and hike for pleasure.'

'But we shouldn't be forced to, you shouldn't have to hike for a hundred miles with your arm in a sling, you shouldn't have been tortured, we shouldn't be refugees with an uncertain future, and I shouldn't be thinking it's never going to end.'

The condition of the track meant that they had to walk in single file for stretches, and sometimes the way led uphill and they had no breath to spare for conversation.

They paused and sat down after one such climb and surveyed the city stretching out below. Mildred broached a subject that had amused Florrie on previous occasions: the private preoccupations of Mr Hamilton. Was his native wife a fair Circassian, or stubby and black? Did they have issue? Did he sing in a choir? But it fell pretty flat.

They walked on and reached the isolated little church and tiptoed in through the open door. The interior was dark although painted white, lit mostly by the shaft of sunshine through the doorway and the glow of many candles, the flames of which represented the prayers of the people evicted from hearth and home by the civil war. The architecture, as seen by eyes growing accustomed to the darkness, was basic – unglazed slits for windows and tree-trunks deputising for pillars. Florrie and Mildred shed their burdens and sat on a bench in the welcome cool. Other women entered the church, and a few of the silent figures kneeling on the earth floor rose and left it. One man who genuflected and crossed himself was sobbing.

Florrie extracted a banknote from a pocket hidden under her black dress and went and pushed it into a collecting box and lit a candle of her own. Rejoining Mildred, she asked: 'Do you want to light one?' Mildred posed a different question: 'Can I share yours?' And they emerged into the sun.

'Goodbye, Orez,' Mildred said, addressing the distant prospect of the city in a relieved tone of voice.

Florrie's unexpectedly tearful response was to put an arm round Mildred's shoulders and say: 'Forgive me for feeling bad and not helping you to feel better.'

'But I'm fine, honestly, and we're doing so well – I just wish I could cheer you up.'

'Don't pay any attention to me.'

'I can't break the habit of a lifetime.'

'No, I suppose not – sorry!'

They must have walked for another hour without any noticeable improvement of Florrie's mood. At three in the afternoon, stopping by a spring of icy water in thicker evergreen woodland, they rested on the ground strewn with pine needles and a dog appeared from nowhere. He was a medium-sized rough-coated biscuit-coloured mongrel, good-looking and in good condition, and he eyed them from a distance of ten yards or so with a front paw raised in an interrogative canine gesture.

Florrie called him and held out her hand enticingly. She understood the mongrel's caution and softened her voice and waited patiently. He fixed his glowing brown eyes on her, reached a bold decision, trotted forward, wagging his feathery tail carried low, sniffed her cupped hand, gave it a polite and friendly lick, and gazed at her with appealing intensity. He was a charming creature, sensitive yet self-assured, and she had to smile at his winning ways.

'Where did you come from? Who do you belong to?' she asked, stroking his head. 'Say hullo to Mildred!'

He obeyed this rhetorical injunction. Mildred, who also loved dogs and was always teetering on the brink of buying a Yorkshire terrier, patted and petted him. He turned back to Florrie and lay down beside her.

'He seems to have adopted you,' Mildred said.

Florrie laughed and discussed the dog with some of her old animation. 'He can't be a stray, he wouldn't look so well if he was. And he's not hungry, he isn't begging for food. He's rather extraordinary – I think he may be one of those top dogs who pity people in difficulties, but he's young to have developed that sort of intuition, no more than three probably. Have you heard anybody calling him? He's certainly not lost, he's half-asleep and the opposite of homesick. I wish we could take him with us.'

[183]

At length they all stood up and Florrie with tender reluctance bade the dog go home. He stretched and wagged as if she had invited him to join in the walk.

'No,' she told him with more force; 'you go home, go away, find your master, go on!'

His querying gaze had touches of disillusionment and uncertainty.

'We must carry on, perhaps he won't follow,' she said to Mildred. 'I'm not looking back, I can't stand the reproach in his eyes.'

They acted on her suggestion, regained the path, strode hastily for a few minutes, and found the dog at their heels. Florrie volunteered the ambiguous remark that they ought not to steal him, and Mildred half-heartedly agreed. They made more efforts to detach him from themselves, shouting at him and pointing, throwing pebbles into the undergrowth in hopes that he would seek them, and Florrie fancied she could see that his expression was increasingly downcast.

She solved the problem by dropping on to one knee, opening her arms wide, and addressing him thus: 'Come on then, come with us – you win!'

The dog ran forward enthusiastically and submitted to her embrace. Mildred was too pleased by the improvement in her cousin's demeanour to raise any objections. She agreed with Florrie's proposal that they should rename their companion Russ. And Russ engaged their interest for the rest of the afternoon, and, importantly from the point of view of Florrie, who liked him more and more, he did not desert them.

Once or twice they paid lip service to the possible concern of his previous owners. But their consciences were clear enough, they had done their best to disengage from him; and from five o'clockish onwards they had practical anxieties on their minds. Where were they to spend their first homeless night in acceptable conditions and safety? Would they find a satisfactory haven before darkness fell in the Orezanian fashion at six o'clock?

At ten minutes to six they came upon a farm in a fold of the ground, similar to establishments they had passed but more extensive, and were greatly relieved to hear adult voices and children's laughter. They paid to enter what was more a large courtyard than a farmyard. It smelt of animals and food cooking,

[184]

and a stream of cold clear water ran through it in a channel. Groups of men seated on the ground, talking in lowered voices and smoking, and separate groups of women, a few of whom sported coloured scarves over their heads or round their waists, lent the space the appearance of a gipsy encampment. Children played in blissful ignorance, and the last hazy rays of twilight romanticised the sadness of the scene.

They were directed to the barn that served as a dormitory. It was long and low, had hay spread on the floor, was dimly illuminated by candles in sconces, and places had been reserved here and there by bags dumped or clothing spread out. It seemed to be empty, and they settled in a corner and divested themselves of backpacks and satchels and unrolled their sleeping-bags. Russ stayed with them: his character was contrarily anti-social, he was as shy with other dogs and people as he had been determined to make friends with themselves. Mildred went to find a lavatory, and Florrie, having followed suit, returned to describe it as a chamber of horrors.

At half-past six trayfuls of those Orezanian pasties filled with vegetables and a pinch of tough mince, also baskets of apples, were brought into the courtyard. After the rush was over Florrie fetched enough supper for the three of them, and fed the dog, who was hungry but not greedy and seemed grateful.

While they were eating a woman called to them from the far end of the barn, and in response to her crying and beckoning they approached her. She was asking for food, she pointed to a bare foot to explain why she was unable to get it for herself. They could not see much wrong with the foot in the dim light; but then she showed them the stump of her left arm, and Florrie, who was always squeamish, rushed partly to do her bidding and partly in order not to have to look at her mutilations. She had a very pale face and would have been about thirty. She kissed Florrie's hand as she accepted the pasty and the apple.

Soon it was pitch dark out of doors, and people straggled into the barn and lay down on the hay fully clothed. Sleep was apparently the order of the day – and no doubt physical and emotional exhaustion accounted for the immediate outbreak of snores. Florrie and Mildred persuaded Russ to curl up in the vicinity of their feet in the sleeping-bags, and wished each other

[185]

good night. Then Mildred's talent for sleeping was reinforced by the pills she had taken to ease the pain of her arm. But Florrie stayed awake. Her lack of privacy, the refugees stumbling in and out of the stinking barn, the nocturnal sounds of male coughs and spitting, of the occasional shriek of a child having a bad dream, of women sighing and moaning and whispering to their offspring and being ordered to shut up, combined disturbingly with all her own cares and fears.

Perhaps she dozed after two or three hours of spinning thoughts and feeling either too hot or too cold. She came to with a start and was aware that Russ had crept into the gap between her sleeping-bag and Mildred's. His head was level with hers, he was gazing at her, and at intervals his tail wagged against her thigh. To banish him to his previous position by her feet would cause a commotion, always supposing it was possible, and she was loath to do it anyway. She breathed the name she had conferred upon him, and in response he pushed his lowered head against the part of her sleeping-bag tucked under her chin. His gesture was sympathetic and affectionate, she decided, and she responded to it by freeing an arm and stroking his head and neck. After this exchange, which somehow served to dispel the lump in her throat, she – and probably the dog – slept until dawn.

More refugees had arrived during the night that hid them from prying eyes, and everybody bustled about and seemed to be in a hurry to leave the past farther behind them and to proceed into the future.

Florrie and Mildred delayed in the barn to eat cheese and olives for breakfast, and to give Russ a couple of slices of salami. They were again summoned by the woman who had lost her left forearm and hand. She had been trying and failing to wind a bandage round her foot, and needed assistance. But the foot, visible now in the morning light, presented a daunting appearance. It must have been poisoned, was terribly swollen and discoloured, even green in places.

Mildred said to Florrie: 'Don't look, you'll be sick!'

The woman, noticing hesitation, waved her puckered stump at them and voiced words pitched between despair and rage.

Florrie replied, averting her head: 'I can't bear it, I'm sorry – I can't bear any more.'

The End of the Tether

Mildred bound the woman's foot and Florrie gave the woman money, and they set off on the second day of their journeying.

Florrie was silent to start with. She was labouring under the load of two extra regrets, her unhelpful attitude to a fellow-sufferer and her outburst. But Mildred was diplomatic and did not refer to the incident, and it was gradually superseded by time and exertion.

They walked intermittently for the next eleven hours, from seven in the morning till six that evening. They had breaks for refreshment, they bought tea and milk, and sat in the sun and rested their legs, and slept for half an hour under olive trees. They had no trouble in the sense of danger or injury. The path was easy to follow, not particularly steep, and not lonely: there were always other people in sight, in front of them or behind, or gathering the crops or tilling the thin earth of the hillsides. Another conveniently placed farm provided a hot supper and shelter for the night, and on the following day they walked until they could see the hills in the distance, bearing an intimidating resemblance to mountains.

The dog continued to behave perfectly. He did not disappear as he had appeared, did not desert them, or show any viciousness. He was always polite – Mildred called him a polite gentleman of the old school – but he reserved those deep burning looks of his for Florrie. He was her dog now, and responded with alacrity to her words of command which were more like hints or suggestions, he caught her eye and they seemed to smile at each other, and watched her, perhaps watched over her, and lay at her feet when she sat down and slept in close proximity to her sleeping-bag. He was apparently a dog with linguistic skills, he understood her

[187]

English; and insofar as dogs have a sense of humour, they were amused by the same jokes. He could be funny and playful, he could look wise, he had a wonderful temperament, was never irascible, and his love was powerful and direct.

Florrie compared him with Tip, the Welsh collie she had owned and loved when she was young. Tip had always been fault-free in her opinion; yet she had to confess that he was more highly-strung than Russ – he had pined and whined for her throughout her terms at boarding school. Russ was the dog she had long hoped to have as soon as life allowed her to settle down and she would be able to devote herself to it and earn its devotion. She intended to take him back to England if she could, if she ever had the chance, and was already worried that he would hate to spend the six-months' stay in the quarantine of English anti-rabies legislation, and that they would miss each other dreadfully.

He became the main topic of conversation, such as it was and as the terrain permitted. Florrie pointed out his qualities and excused his few defects – his slightly cowardly avoidance of other dogs, for instance: he was brave enough to be a non-belligerent, she claimed. They both laughed at some of his antics, his ability to show his front teeth in a canine smile, and his low moan-cum-bark of pleasure. Mildred remarked that one day Fay was bound to love him too, but Florrie looked into the distance, murmured agreement vaguely and changed the subject.

She often asked after Mildred's arm. Otherwise she made no reference to the events in Orez, and even shied away from speaking of her daughter, or of Jenny and Sue, although the secondary object of the cousins' odyssey – the first having been flight to relative safety – was to seek and with luck find the three girls. Russ not only comforted and delighted her, he also spared her the strain of reminding herself of the chapter of Orezanian accidents and the prospect of more trouble if not tragedy.

At least, by the fourth day, they were fitter, less stiff and tired, could appreciate the scenery in the blessedly fine weather, and knew the ropes if not the language of the staging posts. They had Russ to take their minds off recollections fraught with misery and alarm. They were able to render assistance to women less fortunate than they were. They distributed aspirins and surreptitiously paid the entrance fees for nocturnal accommodation. Mildred's arm was better and she gave her sling to a little girl to skip with.

On the fifth day they began the climb to higher ground. The walking was hard and slow, and the path led through dense forests of ugly evergreen trees that shut out the sunshine. More people fell by the wayside, or at best needed to rest and even sleep there: mothers exhausted by carrying young children, men with unhealed wounds.

Everything was worse on the day that followed. The path became a steep gravelly track, and they were enveloped in low cloud, moist and cold. It soaked them to the skin, they slipped on the wet shale, their muscles ached from the effort of climbing upwards, and an extraordinary coincidence had an upsetting effect.

They stopped for tea and for milk for the dog at ten o'clock in the morning, having walked for a couple of hours. The stall was located on a small plateau, a level area partly grassed, beside a tumbling waterfall and a shepherd's hut. The cloud had dispersed here, some warming rays broke through, and perhaps forty or fifty refugees sat about, eating and drinking, and postponing the start on the next uphill struggle.

A female responded to Florrie's gesturing at the samovar and the jug of milk, and a man, emerging from the hut, exclaimed: 'Bless my soul if it isn't Lady M.!'

He was the Pullet or the bad penny – Vic Pullent of all people – not easy to recognise in his peasant's attire that showed no trace of his military rank or political allegiance – but cockney and indeed cocky as ever, saying he was earning his passage home, and, more typically with a wink, that he was on to a good thing.

Florrie tried to make a good thing better by paying him, but he would not hear of it.

'Special terms for Brits,' he said, 'considering not many come this way.'

How was she, how were they, what brought them to the middle of nowhere, and where were they heading?

They told the tale, or Mildred did.

'Slutzk always was a so-and-so – I warned you, didn't I?' he commented.

Florrie picked on the past tense: 'Is he dead?'

'Not a chance! He'll have a nice bit of protection money in a numbered account even without your half-mill – he'll go while the going's good, and get the job he's good or bad at somewhere else – guys who can do the torture are never short of work. By the way, your pal Michael, he's had it.'

'What? What does that mean?'

'Only a rumour – sorry! They say he's caught one and he's out of action – but he wouldn't have kicked the bucket, not with his nine lives.'

'Where is he?'

'Maybe in the Blue camp up here. There's a regular roundabout not too far ahead, and different paths to the Blue camp and the White and Red ones. But you stick to the path straight in front of you, it goes to Tom Tiddler's Ground where nobody fights anybody and you can put your feet up.'

'Who's King now?'

'Reds don't hold with Kings, they call their King a secretary. But Orezania has a King without a crown, if you catch my meaning, and his kingdom's growing bigger. Most of these refugees are making for it, though they wouldn't say so – they're hitching their wagon to his star, or else joining their menfolk.'

'Tom Tiddler's Ground, what's that?'

'It's the hospital they use, it's neutral space, and loads of people crowd in for a spot of peace.'

'I'm looking for my daughter, you remember, and for two friends of hers.'

'You make for the hospital – the patients are all the colours of the rainbow – they'll tell you if your girls are being kept on ice in one of the camps. Listen, lady, pricey goods aren't thrown on the scrapheap. Sorry if I said the wrong thing about Michael – he was sweet on you, wasn't he? See you again in Blighty, and here's hoping a brand new King'll knock some sense and decency into this ruddy country!'

They said goodbye and wished one another luck. But Florrie showed that she was not feeling lucky, she trudged along behind Mildred with her eyes on the ground, responding negatively to positive statements and forecasts.

A quarter of an hour passed. They were walking through a forest of coniferous trees. Russ yelped and whined somewhere behind them, and fell silent. They turned and hurried back, calling his name. Youths stepped on to the track.

Ragged boys, teenagers, some in threadbare camouflage outfits, hairy, dirty, leering and carrying sticks, ten of them or more, emerged from the darker dark and were on the track and blocking it.

Florrie and Mildred stopped, stopped calling, noticed that no other refugees were for the moment in sight and stood closer together, and Florrie answered the incomprehensible questions shouted at them by a sort of leader of the gang by demanding furiously: 'Where's our dog? What have you done with our dog?'

He had black eyes and broken teeth, and held out a grubby hand and rubbed his index finger and thumb together in the international sign language for money.

'Russ! Russ!' Florrie called.

One of the boys imitated the bark of a dog and they all laughed and rubbed their fingers together.

She said to Mildred in a desperate tone of voice: 'They've got him.'

Mildred replied: 'You'd better give them what they want.'

The leader was now gesticulating, trying to show that Russ would be returned in exchange for money. He got down on all fours and pretended to lick Florrie's hand, and made the money sign.

She yelled for Russ, but the boys covered their ears with their hands, perhaps to show that for some reason he could not hear, and yelled at her, no doubt demanding cash.

'He's dead,' she said, and Mildred urged her: 'You don't know that – pay the money!'

She carried her paper money in a deep pocket in her black skirt, and she reached in and pulled it out and waved it at the leader. He snatched it and gave it to his accomplices, who uttered disappointed noises and renewed their demands with more menace.

'I want him, I love him so, I must find out if he's dead or alive,' she said. 'I've only got the gold in my moneybelt.'

'But you may need it to ransom Fay,' Mildred, in extreme agitation, protested.

'He may be alive,' Florrie said. 'I must find out.'

'Go on – we'll be soon dead otherwise,' Mildred whimpered.

[191]

Florrie fumbled under her garments, undid the belt wound round her arm, extracted one of the two Turkish coins from its pocket, showed it to the gangsters, drawing back a pace or two as she did so, and pointed at the ground at her feet to indicate that when the dog was produced the gold would be available.

She was watched with interest and quietly; but as she finished, jabbing her finger at the spot that Russ would have to occupy, cries of greed and impatience were voiced hoarsely, and the whole gang surged forwards and their leader grabbed the belt out of her hand.

Simultaneously other cries were audible: a group of refugees had rounded a corner, seen that Florrie and Mildred were surrounded, drawn the conclusion that they were being robbed, and were running to the rescue. The gang retreated – rather, they stepped aside and in amongst the trees that hid them and where they could not be followed. It was over. The cousins tried to thank their rescuers. But explanations were too difficult, and they smiled as gratefully as wretchedness allowed and waved the friendly people on.

'Russ!' Florrie called, walking up and down the track.

Mildred restrained her from entering the forest in pursuit of the gang. And they only dared to stay in the vicinity of Russ's disappearance so long as their fellow-refugees were in view. Even Florrie realised that they could not risk another encounter with the gang and probable loss of their remaining funds in Mildred's keeping.

Before long, too soon in Florrie's estimation, they had to leave, to abandon Russ, in order not to lose touch with the guardians of their security who were about to be beyond earshot and out of sight.

Florrie was shattered, hardly able to walk – she stumbled along with Mildred's stronger arm round her waist, uttering a retching sob occasionally and an intermittent monologue.

'He was the best dog in the world – how could they kill him, how could they steal him? ... I hate them, they were cruel – everyone's cruel! ... I've turned a blind eye to it here, I've looked the other way and been a fool – don't pity me! ... People want to grab what isn't theirs, and wicked men tell them they can and must, and show them how to do it ... Michael was a beast, but Russ was what Michael should have been and wasn't, kind and

[192]

good to me and admirable ... My life's been a mistake for too long, empty and loveless ... I didn't deserve Russ, that's the truth ... I don't deserve Fay.'

She apologised to Mildred over and over again. In some open country, where thieves could not conceal themselves, she had to rest and was incapacitated for nearly two hours. Then they walked at a slow pace for half an hour and paused to sit on the verge for an equal amount of time. The pattern was repeated, and the afternoon sun passed its zenith, and earlier ideas of reaching the hospital before night fell were replaced, at least in Mildred's mind, by fears that Florrie might collapse between hostelries and they would have to sleep out of doors, hungry and unprotected.

She tentatively urged her cousin to make a little more haste. But Florrie was deaf to practical considerations, and her legs seemed to have ceased to function normally. For that matter Mildred was not sure she could continue to support her cousin with her right arm, and for some reason her left one had begun to ache again. That the two women were evidently in such poor shape put them more at risk.

They arrived at Vic Pullent's 'roundabout' at four in the afternoon. It was another level shelf-like area where refreshments were for sale, on the far side of which paths led off in various directions. The way to the hospital was easy to see: men on home-made crutches, bandaged mothers carrying wan children, bedraggled casualties of all ages were limping and hobbling along it before night closed in.

Mildred wanted to follow them, but Florrie had to sit down and asked for tea. Then in a flurry of emotion she decided she had done wrong to desert Russ, who could be searching for her now, who could be lost and starving.

'I must go back – forgive me – you go ahead to the hospital – I'll join you when I can.'

Mildred managed to talk her out of it after an exhausting and almost unprecedented argument, which concluded with Florrie yielding in a further flood of tears and self-accusations.

They stumbled on. The path seemed steeper than ever and rougher, and the light that guided them to fade more rapidly than on other evenings. They both needed to stop frequently. And they were apparently alone, the halt and maimed had succeeded in

[193]

outstripping them, and no refugee was so stupid as to lag behind. Once more they found themselves in a forest, clinging together and fearfully trying to hold their breath. Beyond it, at an unknown hour in blackest night, they were faced by a mountain of gravel.

Florrie said: 'I can't,' and Mildred: 'I'm not sure we're still on the path.'

But at the top they were rewarded by the sight of lights, twinkling lights in the windows of human habitations, shacks and shanties on the descending slope of the mountain. The downhill path merged into a street of sorts, and their relief tapped their last reserves of energy. The lights beckoned and welcomed, and they passed the homes of decent people, and were moved to hear voices in peaceful converse. Their eyes were fixed upon a complex of long sheds below, and as they drew nearer with faltering steps Mildred swore she had caught a wonderful whiff of antiseptic.

They reached their destination, discovered a door, dragged themselves in and across to a reception desk, over which a typically dark Orezanian woman presided. She kindly emerged to render assistance, and thus revealed two fair-haired members of staff seated at a table spread with piles of paper. They were Jenny Bowditch and Sue Cartwright.

The joys of reunion were authenticated by weeping.

Florrie, as soon as she was able, asked: 'Where's Fay? Do you know where Fay is?'

'She left here this morning to meet Alexander,' Jenny replied.

PART THREE

Priorities under Pressure

It was nothing like a hospital in England. It was shed-like in a derogatory sense inside as well as out. The walls were corrugated iron cobbled together, the roofs were perished felt and leaky, and the frames of windows had polythene nailed across them. The electric generator was unreliable, an invalid often had no more than a mattress on the floor to lie on, wards could be passages, medicines were in short supply or not on offer, and food was, to put it mildly, basic. Everywhere was dirty: not all floors were concreted, some were earth, and mud was spread around by the shoes of persons entering the buildings or moving from one building to another; while the slightest breeze whistled in and out.

Jenny and Sue had been there for a week, and looked and said they were well. They spun a fairly convincing yarn when asked questions about the night of their disappearance. They had agreed to go on to a disco after the dance at the Orez Ritz, they confessed, some of the White officers invited them and promised to return them in an hour or two and seemed to mean it; but the disco was illegal because of the curfew, and miles out of town, and while they were there the Blues attacked the Whites, their escorts had to escape and then retreat to the White headquarters in the hills, and took the girls along.

By force? Were they held against their will? Were they treated badly? Why had they not sent a message to allay the fears of family and friends?

They were unable to, they would have if they could, but in the White camp they were not exactly detained nor exactly free – it was difficult to describe – and there had been no telephone – and they were sorry.

What was the telephone situation at the hospital?

Non-existent, they said – but a patient called Silvo, who was an engineer and spoke a bit of English, had walked miles for Fay to wherever the telephone wires were and somehow cut into a wire and wound the handle of his weird machine and tried to get through to the bank manager in Orez. He had not been successful, they said, and his last failure was his worst, because Fay had discovered her mother was at the Orez Ritz and spent hours with Silvo and was never able to speak to Lady Meavy, although she did have two frustrating words with Miss Chaffcombe.

Fay was fine, they reassured, apart from worrying about her relations who were so near and yet so far. Fay's story was that she had been ferried across to the island from the Crimea, had taken refuge at the hospital, worked at fetching and carrying, received an invitation from Alexander, who had heard on the grapevine that she was in Orezania, and, because she had given up hope of meeting her mother and Mildred in the meanwhile, joined one of the bands of refugees en route to Alexander's camp located within a day's walk. Jenny added that she was sure some kind ex-invalid would carry a message to Fay, and Sue that Fay would certainly wish to hurry back to the hospital.

The girls, having run through these explanations, collared a passing doctor. He prescribed hot sweet tea, food and sleep for their worn out and undernourished older friends. Florrie and Mildred were duly conducted to a canteen, and, after they had swallowed their medicine, to an elongated hut with two lines of three tiers of bunks, and settled there for the night.

Morning began early: they were up again at five-thirty and back in the canteen, having more tea and a hunk of black bread for breakfast. No, Florrie replied to questions, she had not slept much, she was sick of communal sleeping, and the shameful fact was that she was sick of the sick, too, and pined to be at home. But she was determined to retrace her yesterday's steps to the place where her dear dog Russ disappeared, and then to follow Fay, and at the earliest opportunity together with her daughter, Mildred, Jenny and Sue to make for a port from which boats plied to civilisation. Yes, she declared with unaccustomed warmth, she had turned against Orezania and Orezanians, she detested them for murdering their Kings and one another and beautiful animals and for doing untold harm for the sake of a meaningless colour.

The others assailed her gently with negatives. She was not yet fit to walk for more long distances; and Russ was undoubtedly beyond recall by now; and Fay might not wish to be chaperoned by her mother; and her money in Mildred's security belt would not be enough to pay for five fares to freedom. Moreover, unfortunately, ringing up Fay or Mr Hamilton or friends in England was out of the question. In short there was no alternative to doing as the girls had done, as all the forty or fifty female Orezanian refugees in their dormitory hut and the male refugees elsewhere in the hospital were doing, that is working at odd jobs in return for board and lodging, and either waiting until the civil war petered out or – sooner than that with luck – until Alexander the peace-maker, the man armed with nothing but his blue blood and personal magnetism, was on the throne, having contradicted the communist dogma that might alone was right.

Florrie had no time to argue the point. Duty called – the crowd in the canteen was dispersing, a doctor with stethoscope round his neck summoned Sue to join a detachment of helpers and Sue took Mildred with her, and Jenny led Florrie by the hand through the kitchen and into an elongated lean-to, where trolleys loaded with dirty crockery and dishes were waiting to be washed up in icy spring water and a supply of abrasive sand.

The sinks at which half a dozen other pairs of women were at work were made of spongy wood. Cloths for drying had once been sacks and were obstinately non-absorbent. Some of the plates and mugs were army-issue tin, and some of the dishes were encrusted with the blackened fat of ages of use. Jenny said she would wash, her hands were inured to the icy water and she had no more fingernails to be manicured by the sand, but Florrie claimed her turn at the sink. It was another new experience for her, and not pleasant. But it was much better than Orez had been and probably would have become.

She cooperated gamely. She did not stand on her dignity, she had never felt she had any dignity to stand on, and was impressed in spite of herself by Jenny's idealistic reflection that soldiers and civilians of every colour, former enemies now in the closest

[199]

proximity, in adjoining beds in the wards and sharing the same amenities, would soon be eating off the dishes they had cleaned. She was glad not to have to see horrific sights. She encountered no language problem, since the natives, although amiable, did not talk to her. She chatted to Jenny and tried to hide her sense of interior disintegration.

She described Russ, she could not stop herself describing his courtesy, his chivalrous manners and tireless strength that was always sensitive, and what seemed to be the ardent tenderness and fidelity with which he had gazed into her eyes. Yes, she replied to Jenny, she was still grieving for and mourning Russ, and would miss him for ever. As for King Michael, she told the girl, he was the other side of the medal, an adventurer with a cold heart, a grabber rather than a giver, who misused his charm and had reigned over a court of criminals.

On the subject of royalty she inquired why Jenny was under the impression that Alexander was not another Michael: was it just loyalty to Fay?

'Oh no, absolutely not, I promise you, I'm so fond of Fay that I wouldn't ever mislead her on purpose. Alexander's special – I met him once in London – he's amazing. Most of the people here have faith in him – the refugees who have been to his camp come back saying they're ready and willing to die for him, they're convinced that he really could stop the stupid fighting and save the country.'

'Do you believe that?'

'Yes, I do.'

'Without guns?'

'That's the idea.'

'But the opposition will shoot him if he doesn't shoot them.'

'Maybe the opposition will collapse, the armies won't have any soldiers to fight with, the people will all unite and make a clean sweep, and put the crown on Alexander's head.'

'Dear Jenny, how can you be so optimistic after spending time in Orezania?'

'I don't know politics, Lady Meavy – I'm only spouting second-hand opinion. But my opinion of Alexander is mine.'

'Well, bloodless revolutions are a contradiction in terms. But it may be true that Alexander's unlike too many kings and nearly all

[200]

politicians, and he's the exception who can silence guns by will-power and lead his people into a brighter future. In that case I have other worries. If he and Fay are falling in love, and he perishes quixotically she'll take years and years to get over him at best, and if he becomes the King she'll have to live in this terrible island with torturers and bear children who'll be kidnapped, and she'll probably be assassinated with her husband in the end.'

Jenny ventured to differ respectfully. Some Orezanians – and not only Alexander, who was in a class of his own – were not so bad, she said or rather seemed to reminisce.

'I mean,' she explained with a telltale smile and a blush, 'the soldiers who brought us up here, the White officers, we called them the 'white men', they were really nice to us. They could have sold us to you – we were supposed to be worth money, believe it or not – but instead they thought we'd be safer in the hospital than in a military camp and we'd be rescued sooner or later.'

'Do you miss them?' Florrie asked.

'A bit – we didn't want to say goodbye – but they were right.'

'I'm sorry, Jenny – I never should have invited you to join in my wild goose chase – none of us should have come to Orezania.'

'Oh but we wouldn't have missed it for the world, Lady Meavy!'

The four Englishwomen met to eat together at midday. As they munched their pasties with more or less appetite, Sue suggested a swap, that perhaps Mildred would prefer a quieter afternoon in the lean-to shed, and Florrie would be interested in the drama of the wards. Florrie refused decidedly: she was afraid she was or would have been a rotten nurse, always fainting at the sight of blood.

Before they separated, bells that signalled an emergency rang, and an English-speaking doctor wanted Jenny and Sue to help with an influx of Blue casualties who had arrived via the road from Orez reserved for military usage. The girls prepared to follow him, everyone else in the canteen was doing so, Mildred was obviously eager to tag along, and Florrie waved them away – she would carry on with the washing up and see them later.

She found the kitchen empty and that she was alone in the lean-to: the Orezanians who had bustled about in the morning must also have been summoned to the medical side of the hospital. She set to work again. But the loaded trolleys, the absence of soap, the chilling draughtiness and the view of massed grey clouds through grubby polythene combined together to deepen her depression.

She plunged her cold hands in the colder water. Time passed uncomfortably, and she heard an odd noise, a dragging sound from out of doors, then a high-pitched note that could have been animal or human. Her imagination immediately supplied her with daunting interpretations: Russ had pursued her to the hospital and was hurt and in pain, or else it was a wounded person with broken bones and blood pouring out of ghastly injuries. She ran into the kitchen for assistance, but it was still empty; and she was not sure where to find a doctor or a nurse – the geography of the hospital was baffling.

She returned to the shed, wringing her swollen hands with indecision, despising herself for her fastidiousness or cowardice, wishing whoever or whatever it was out there would go away or expire. But the little cry was repeated, it occurred with the regularity of someone panting, and she peered through the polythene at an indistinct view of gorse-like bushes growing in shale without seeing anyone or anything to account for them.

She arrived at three realisations: that her field of vision was limited, that she could not ignore those sounds of suffering, and that a door in one of the kitchens might lead out and enable her to check up on their source. She thought of Russ and hurried to the door in question, opened it and peered through, and saw not the dog, disappointingly or mercifully not her Russ, but a trail of blood on the shale almost at her feet and the body of a soldier lying in an unnatural position against the wall of the shed in which she had been working.

Against her will, despite her expectation that she would pass out or vomit and prove her uselessness, she approached him. He had blue flashes on his tattered uniform, he belonged to Michael, to whom she owed nothing; and one of his trouser-legs was black with blood and a visible hand was bloody. A raised arm covered his face, which was turned downwards and even partially buried in the shale. Perhaps he had not seen her and she could steal away. Her heart was thumping with the combined force of terror and irresolution.

And while she longed in vain to flee, to be elsewhere, he spoke.

[202]

She could not understand the two or three guttural words, they were in Orezanian, but they were addressed to her and held her back.

'*Aidez-moi,*' he mumbled

Involuntarily in English she blurted out: 'I can't, I don't know what to do, I'll try to find a doctor.'

'Help me,' he pleaded, articulating carefully.

She hesitated. She stood beside him in the cold quiet highland air under the heavy grey sky, and felt her hair blowing in the breeze.

'Please help me.'

She was again about to excuse herself, rush off, do her best even if it was not good, when he moved his arm and revealed the profile of his face. It was so young, so exquisite and pathetic, stained with blood and mud, and scratched too as if by thorns, that she could not bear to desert him, leave him probably to die.

She knelt on the shale and said: 'I'm here.'

He was shivering and she removed the long apron she had been given to work in and covered him with it, and was pleased to think he smiled to thank her.

'*Thé,*' he requested faintly; '*thé* – tea.'

'I'll get it,' she said.

She ran to the kitchen, found a mug and a spoon, poured black tea from the teapot on the hob of the range, spooned in sugar, seized a fairly clean cloth and wetted it with hot water in a huge kettle and wrung it out, and returned to her wounded soldier.

He had not moved. Ever so gently she wiped the side of his face with the cloth. Then she attempted to insert a spoonful of tea between his lips.

'It's sweet,' she said. 'Please drink some,' she begged him.

He lifted his head and opened his eyes, which were blue and heavy-lidded, and focused on her by rolling around in a distressing manner. She put the mug close to his mouth and he did manage to take a sip, although tea spilled and dribbled on to his chin. He had hardly any beard, just a suspicion of blond down for a moustache and slightly curly side-whiskers.

'English?' he asked.

'Yes.'

'I speak.'

[203]

'Yes.'

'It is hospital?'

'Yes.'

'Doctor,' he said.

He had closed his eyes and his head drooped again to the ground.

'I'm going to get a doctor now – wait, wait for me,' she said, meaning: do not die while I am gone.

He acknowledged her speech, and perhaps agreed to do as he was told, by means of a minimal nod. She ran indoors, into the kitchen where the cooks were back at work, and began to shout and point; and Jenny emerged from the lean-to, asking what had happened to her, where had she been, and Florrie explained as together they made haste to find a doctor or stretcher-bearers or both.

They were successful. They had to pass through stinking wards, see dread sights, disregard heartbreaking appeals, but they persuaded the doctor acquainted with Jenny that he was urgently needed.

Although he looked like a murderer steeped in blood, he ran ahead on his errand of mercy, snatching a stretcher on the way – they had a job to keep up with him. At last they joined the kitchen people standing round the poor young soldier.

Lifting him on to the stretcher was painful, even painful for the spectators. He had a broken ankle – his foot dangled – and wounds in his side and a thigh. When the doctor examined him he opened his mouth and emitted the high-pitched sound she had heard before. But the lifting was worse: the doctor enlisted the help of a cook to do it, and a certain clumsiness was inevitable.

Florrie's soldier must have anticipated the effect of the movement of the two parts of his leg, for he reached out his hand during the preparations for the lift. But nobody took it, nobody understood – they shrank back to give the doctor more room, or because they were shy or something. She stepped forward and held his hand, and when he wailed and gripped hers far too tight for comfort she bit her lip and let him.

The Present Takes Precedence

Florrie and Jenny partook of restorative tea after the wounded soldier had been removed on the stretcher. Florrie tried to describe her dilemma when she saw the blood – she was too agitated to keep her squeamishness to herself. She said that at school she had once swooned to see a hypodermic needle, and she was still scared of injections. Other people had phobias about snakes and spiders, she said, and her phobia was about illness, sickness, the squalor of it and the disfigurement, and gruesome surgical practices. She had no doubt been spoilt by the luck of her own good health, and by the privileges of her existence. She never had to look after her parents or anyone, and she employed a nurse to deal with the grubby infancy of Fay, who had later proved she was a chip off the parental block by never needing a doctor.

'But you didn't flinch this afternoon,' Jenny commented.

'I did, I was flinching for all I was worth.'

'Well, you didn't show it, and you saved the soldier's life.'

'That remains to be seen.'

They resumed their dish washing and stuck to it until five o'clockish, when the light failed. In the dormitory hut Mildred was resting on the lower bunk of the pair she shared with her cousin, and said she was haunted by her experiences in the wards. Her sanguine temperament was severely shaken by the sights she had seen and the sounds of men having major surgery without anaesthetics. Jenny and Sue were sympathetic, but also young and resilient: they pointed out that the hospital was like an oasis of peace and hope, and most patients recovered. And Jenny told the tale, which actually surprised Mildred more than it encouraged, of Florrie's conquest of her qualms.

The four of them adjourned to the canteen for supper of cabbage soup and black bread. Afterwards Florrie sprang another surprise: she would like to discover if her soldier boy had survived.

She said: 'I couldn't bear any of you to come with me, I'm not asking for a guided tour, I'll go by myself, I'd rather, and I promise not to be hysterical, and to hurry back to our sleeping quarters if it's all too much for me.'

They were unable to dissuade her; but Sue thought she would get lost on her own and insisted on showing her the way. They walked between the lines of beds in the wards and along endless passages. They encountered medical personnel, stretcher-bearers, patients on the mend and on the move, and scores of cleaners, sweepers, attendants and dogsbodies. There was an unremitting hubbub of voices, footsteps, music on a loudspeaker system, running water somewhere, crockery in use: at least it partly drowned the groaning and crying. The lighting was inadequate, although the soiled state of bandages and bedclothes was nonetheless visible; and the smells were choking.

In one of the sheds the loudspeaker crackled and the distorted sound of a bell tolling replaced the music. It had a dramatic effect: the noise subsided, activity was stilled, patients assumed attitudes of prayer as best they could, people on their feet knelt down, and, when certain words were intoned, everybody made the sign of the cross. Sue indicated that she and Florrie must follow suit. An announcement was made in Orezanian and voices in unison, voices perhaps throughout the hospital, resonant and throbbing with sincerity, projected their pleas for a better life heavenwards. The priest blessed his congregation, and again the voices pleaded with God for forgiveness of the sins which accounted for most of the wounds that pained and threatened. The bell tolled tinnily again, music recommenced, Florrie and Sue stood up, and Florrie saw her soldier.

He was at the far end of the left hand line, the last invalid in the line, lying on a thin mattress or a piece of cloth on the floorboards, and wearing the sleeveless shirt-like hospital garment instead of his battledress. He was not looking at the wall in any sense, his head was actually turned in their direction, but his arm was raised

[206]

to cover his eyes and part of his face. He had soft wavy hair, the black colour of which was not swarthy, and his suspicion of side whiskers and beard were almost golden. His hair, his pallor, the curve of his full lips, the visible tip of his shapely nose, and the arm thrown across his face as if to ward off evil, convinced Florrie that he was the one she was searching for.

'Are you going to talk to him?' Sue asked.

'No,' she answered.

'But he isn't asleep, and I'm sure he'd like to thank you.'

'Oh no – I didn't come here to be thanked, it's the other way round.'

They were interrupted. A patient on Florrie's side of the aisle rose from his mattress, held out a tin mug and shook it at her violently and with vehement exclamations. He had a head wound, a bloody bandage covered one of his eyes or perhaps a hole where the eye had been, but the other eye was hard and livid, and he brandished the blunt instrument of the mug and seemed to curse her.

She drew back.

Jenny said: 'I think he's asking for tea. I'll get it.'

'No, I will,' Florrie replied, taking the mug.

They had passed a lobby where people queued for refreshments. She went there; had the mug filled in due course; returned to find Sue comforting a woman in tears, embracing and patting her; gave the one-eyed man what he wanted and was rewarded with a smile that quivered pathetically.

Sue explained: 'This lady's just lost her husband – he died in another ward – and she doesn't know where to go.'

'We'd better take her back to our hut.'

Sue supported the crumpled figure, and Florrie carried a bundle of her worldly goods. In the dormitory she was shown an empty bunk, and Jenny provided a blanket and Sue another mug of cure-all tea, and Mildred persuaded her to accept some of Florrie's money.

They could do no more for the widow, and were all dropping with exhaustion by this time. They clambered on to their bunks by the light of a few distant candles that flickered in the draughts.

Mildred directed her whispered query through the wire mesh of the bunk above hers: 'Are you awake. Flo?'

[207]

'Yes.'

'Were you all right in the wards?'

'Yes and no.'

'It's frightful, isn't it?'

'Yes.'

'Florrie, will we ever get out of this place?'

'Yes – we'll collect Fay and go home – don't worry!'

'You haven't sent a message to Fay to say we're here?'

'No. How has your arm been today?'

'Not too bad.'

'Dream of St Eo!'

'Oh Florrie!'

The next morning at breakfast in the canteen the four English members of staff were summoned to assist with ailing children who had been evacuated from an institution in Orez. There were twenty or so, aged between six and ten years old, orphans of the war considered to be at risk from the Reds. A whole ward had been allotted to them – where, it seemed to Florrie, a superfluity of nurses and excited women were offering services and stepping on one another's toes. She informed Mildred that she was returning to the wards.

She worked all day for the ill people, women as well as men. She did not see the soldier she had tended, she did not have time even to think of him. She was performing menial tasks, running errands, doing favours, cleaning up and wiping down, being more patient than some of the patients, not objecting, not complaining. Language was no problem: need was easy to understand, and the orders she received from professionals were obeyed to the best of her ability.

She met Mildred and the two girls at midday for a bite of food. But she resisted their urgings to join them in the children's ward, although, as they said, the work would be less of a strain. Her reply was that she actually quite liked to feel useful for a change.

The next day was the same, and the day after that. Mildred, Jenny and Sue stayed with the children, tending and entertaining them, teaching them English and English nursery rhymes, and Florrie devoted herself to care of the invalids. They were all chronically tired, but Florrie was tireder than the others. Sleeping for five or six hours notwithstanding the discomfort of the bunks, exceptionally deep sleep undisturbed by the noise in the dormitory, did not stop her almost nodding off if or when she sat down in the daytime. Jenny and Sue would say for a joke that their elder, Lady M., was at least beginning to look better. Perhaps it is healthy to work so hard, eat so little and sleep so much; and perhaps nature reinforces the strength of those in comparative relationships with the weak. Be that as it may, one beneficial effect of Florrie's activities from her own point of view was that she had no energy to spare for extraneous cogitation or communication.

The silencing of Florrie Meavy would have to be numbered amongst the achievements, for better or for worse, of Orezania. She had previously lived as it were on a cloud of hot air, and she had less and less to say for herself. With Mildred and the girls, while they expatiated upon the sweetness of their little charges and swapped particular instances of it, she confined her contributions to practical matters and immediate concerns; and she was relieved that the same applied to her mental processes.

Jenny and Sue were full of admiration of her selfless and stoical toil, but Mildred was soon worried as well as surprised by the changes taking place in her cousin.

'How can you do it, you of all people, how can you bear to muck out the lavatories and be as good as a nurse?' she asked.

Again: 'You're not overdoing it, are you?' and then: 'You won't suddenly snap, will you, Flo?'

She also opined: 'I'm afraid you'll be haunted for ever by the awful things you're seeing.'

Florrie smiled and issued negatives.

One evening she leant over the side of her bunk and whispered to Mildred below: 'They're so short of money here – the doctors are working wonders on a shoestring – I'm going to give them some – I don't know how to give it but I'll find out – a great deal of money.'

Mildred was at first encouraging, but on reflection she inquired: 'What will Philip and Geoffrey say? What will T.D. say?'

A pause ensued. The implication of the pause was that Florrie had temporarily forgotten the two men who had loved her for ages, the third who was her financial guardian angel, and her former existence in which they had loomed large. At length she commented: 'They'll have to lump it.'

[209]

On another evening Mildred invoked the name of Fay in an attempt to divert Florrie from her involvement with the work of the hospital.

'Hasn't the time come to try to find Fay? Shouldn't we move on?'

Part of the answer was reasonable. Florrie did not feel up to any more backpacking, and she had been persuaded that, although she could not make up her mind about Alexander, she ought to give Fay a chance to come to the same conclusion unaided. But the other part, that they would have to wait for Fay to contact Jenny and Sue, simply wait, was a complete contradiction of her established character and restlessness.

On most mornings the loudspeaker announced the arrival of one or two truckloads of wounded soldiers, and Florrie was amongst those who would hurry from wherever they were to lend a hand. The dead were driven on to burial in the camps, and the quick were lifted or helped out and along to operating theatres, surgeries, and wards and passages where beds and mattresses and their occupants had been reorganised so as to accommodate the new intake. A few days after she had offered to stay put in the hospital she was especially busy with the additional tasks imposed by such emergencies – there had been a big battle in the lowlands. She had carried the corners of stretchers, pushed trolleys, supported a man who weighed twice as much as she did, run after doctors, swilled blood off the floor, and so on. It was late in the day, afternoon, and she was edging between the trolleys on which men with wounds requiring immediate surgical attention lay. The scene was hellish, dark, lit only by an occasional hurricane lamp or candle that showed often half-naked figures in extremes of agony, emitting a scarcely human cacophony expressive of their feelings.

Her arm was caught and gripped as she passed by. She assumed it was another soldier pleading for attention. She vouchsafed an interrogative smile at the indistinct outline of the head of the person on the trolley. Her forearm was gripped harder and she was pulled downwards, and a voice growled into her ear: 'Do not recognise me!'

But she did recognise him at once. She recognised his hand on her arm, his voice, and that he was the person she had been waiting

[210]

for. She recognised his face gleaming with sweat and his silver hair in the gloom.

'Do not say my name,' he explained in an undertone.

'Where are you wounded?' she breathed back.

'My back.'

'Is it bad?'

'Yes. Why you here? I am dreaming.'

'No, you're awake, you're alive.'

'You look after me.'

'What? I'm not a nurse.'

'Take me home with you – I will be well.'

'I couldn't do that.'

'Lady,' he enunciated as if with a reproachful smile.

'I can't even stay with you now.'

'Florrie,' he said, reproaching and cajoling her.

'I can't,' she repeated.

He did not let her go, and he murmured: 'You love me. Take me to English doctors, pay to make me better. You will be my Queen. We will be rich and happy.'

'No!'

'This is not good place.'

'You helped to create it with your fighting.'

'What you say?'

'Nothing. How can I be sorry for you? I've seen what you've done to people.'

'I will die, Florrie.'

'No, no – men like you don't do the dying – you do the killing.'

'Don't leave me, look after me all time, I will be well.'

'I can't – I mustn't.'

She shook her arm free.

'But I find you, Florrie. You do not escape.'

'Goodbye! Adieu! Do you understand – adieu?'

She left him. He did not try to recall her. She managed to get past other casualties on trolleys and on the floor in the dim passage – she had been heading for the children's ward to ask Jenny or Sue or both to help to cope with the rush of work. But she began to cry.

She failed to control herself, it was as if she were paralysed by sorrow, she could neither walk nor remain upright, and sank down on the concrete with her back against a wall of cold corrugated iron, and surrendered to the sort of emotion that was not considered constructive by the hospital staff, and sobbed and sobbed as she had not done for years, more violently, sobbed for Michael, Russ, herself, Orezania, for all the human and animal victims of war and cruelty.

Nobody noticed: she was scarcely visible, and had merely joined in the chorus of grieving. In time she mopped her eyes and blew her nose, stood up and resumed her progress. The passage debouched into a lobby with an electric bulb between sheds. A young male patient limped out of the ward she was about to pass through. Momentarily, because she did not wish to show too much of her tear-stained countenance, they confronted each other. He was using a crutch, and his soft dark hair reminded her of someone, and he startled her by addressing her in English.

'You are my friend.'

He was the boy by the lean-to, clearly feeling better.

'Good afternoon,' he added with care and the smile of an uncertain linguist.

She was surprised into raising her eyes to his as she replied: 'Oh, it's you – good afternoon.'

His smile faded, his expression was concerned, and he said: 'You are sad.'

'I'm okay,' she returned.

He said: 'I have wished to thank you. You are very kind and clever.'

'I wish I were.'

'Believe me! I owe you much. I will never forget you.'

'Well – thank you.'

'Do not be sad. You should be happy. Be happy for me, please!'

'Yes.'

He held out the hand that had once gripped hers so hard and painfully. They shook hands with extra sincerity and said goodbye. She walked on, through doorways and wards, and wondered at the two coincidences in quick succession.

Did coincidences come in threes, like pieces of bad news?

Her question was answered in the children's ward: Fay was there.

But the Future Rules

Florrie was glad not least to have an excuse to shed a few more tears. But she was as good as the word she had just given her convalescent soldier: the tears were happier ones. And Fay mingled her own tears with her mother's.

They dried their eyes, and were preoccupied by the changes that each noticed in the other. Fay had lost more weight and gained womanly qualities; she looked well and strong with pink cheeks and clear complexion, and her vividly blue eyes glistened not only because they had been washed by teardrops. She wore the customary black cotton attire, but it seemed shapely on her stretched lithe figure, and the orange handkerchief tied round her neck added style and dazzle. Florrie admired her, and Fay said she loved her mother's appearance more than ever, notwithstanding swollen eyelids, undone hair, chafed hands and thinness.

They withdrew into the area between sheds, another lobby, and sat on the dusty earth floor – Fay had already spent time with Mildred, Jenny and Sue, and the orphans were making a nuisance of themselves in order to win the attention of their adult playmates.

Florrie said she had heard about Fay's experiences from her two friends, and Fay said she had heard about the trials and tribulations of her mother – the death of Mr Hildwitch, the disaster of Russ, the flight from Blues and Reds and blackmail and violence – from Mildred. Florrie congratulated Fay for having survived, and Fay sympathised with her mother and expressed relief that she had battled through to relative safety. They spoke of Silvo and his telephonic experiments, which were praiseworthy but nearly worse than useless. Silvo had been doing Fay's bidding by asking Mr

Hamilton if she had funds at the bank: she had wished, as her mother now did, to give some money to the hospital. And Fay explained that she had not had to walk from Alexander's camp, she had hitched a lift on a motorbike.

Florrie then filled a momentary silence by saying: 'My darling girl, I suppose I shouldn't ask, but are you by any chance thinking of settling in Orezania?'

'Not at this moment, Ma.'

'Oh? Well – you're too good to waste, and even though you may never forgive me for meddling, I'd never forgive myself if you were miserable because I hadn't dared to meddle.'

'Alexander hasn't proposed to me, Ma.'

'What? He must be mad in that case.'

'And I'm not a bit miserable, and I can promise you I've no intention of wasting my precious self.'

'You're laughing at me – you think I'm behaving like Mrs Bennet.'

'Maybe – but I'm a dutiful daughter and wouldn't dream of marrying any man you disapproved of – I couldn't stand the strain of divided loyalties, and the most miserable thing for me would be to fall out with you.'

Florrie embraced Fay for saying so, and thanked her and referred to their journey home. She had a suspicion that Fay had more to say on the subject of marriage, something less reassuring, and spoke of their departure from Orezania with repressive intentions.

'All the same, Ma, I'd love you to meet Alexander.'

'Well, yes, of course,' Florrie allowed in a flustered manner. 'Is he coming back to England?'

'Oh no, he couldn't – you don't know how important he is – important to his people – he won't ever leave them now.'

Florrie commented: 'All the Kings of Orezania say that.' They both laughed, though not exactly in unison, and she continued: 'If Alexander's stuck here, and I can't wait to get away from Orezania, our meeting looks like being difficult to arrange.'

'Not really,' Fay explained with calm humour: 'whose motorbike do you think I travelled on?'

Florrie protested – she was not in a fit state – had not expected it. But Fay was unmoved and obstinate, and led her mother into a ward that was strangely empty, through another without patients in it, to a third teeming with men in hospital shirts who had clearly risen from their beds of sickness.

Alexander was at the far end, and spotted and smiled at them with an inclination of his head. He could not move to where they were, or indeed wave, because he was surrounded and his hands were being held, shaken, kissed. More invalids were queueing in the aisle between beds to bow to him, to kneel before him, to touch him and no doubt swear allegiance.

He was an unexpectedly fair young man, blond-haired in a land of brunettes; tall and solidly built, wearing jeans and a leather jacket – no military uniform: a handsome normal youth in his modern gear – and yet, Florrie was forced to admit to herself, extraordinarily dignified and benign. He did not hurry although he had pressing reasons to, he was acting as if he had time to spare for everyone, he concentrated on greetings, returned bows, laid hands that were free on fevered brows, raised up those who were kneeling, distributed the largesse of his kindness, gentleness, encouragement, confidence. He was nothing like Michael, and his subjects, if they were his subjects, showed no fear of him and were neither servile nor sycophantic.

When he had nearly reached Fay, she signalled to him and withdrew with Florrie to the lobby outside the children's ward. He joined them there after a few minutes, and Fay while leaning against the relevant door to keep his followers at bay introduced him to her mother.

Surprisingly, Fay asked permission to do so, and as a result Florrie felt compelled to take the formal hint and bob a curtsy.

Alexander accepted these dues without hesitation and graciously, and enfolding Florrie's hand in his he raised her up, bowed and went through the motions of kissing it, and looking at her steadily and straight said with a charming smile in the perfect English only spoken by foreigners: 'I am proud to know the mother of a remarkable person.'

Florrie laughed modestly and as if to suggest that he could moderate his pride, but was checked by his sincerity, his fervent conviction, and made the lame reply, feeling hypocritical: 'How nice to meet you at last!'

'I apologise for the circumstances of our meeting,' he said, indicating the plastic bags of refuse in a dimmer corner of the lobby; 'also for the bad aspects of your visit to my country. My wish would have been to receive you with honour. On the other hand I thank you for the services you have rendered my people in this hospital.'

Florrie was silent, overawed by his authority and his pronouncements which escaped the charge of pomposity by being forthright and touching.

'I am grateful to you for Fay. I care for your daughter,' he declared. 'She deserves to be cared for. That is why I bring her to you, and advise you both to travel home to England. The fate of Orezania is not yet settled, and I do not know if the people will want me to be their King, or whether I shall live or die.'

Fay intervened here, probably not so much because she was embarrassed by the references to herself as because she could not bear the idea of his death: 'Ma, Alexander has such a long rough ride on his motorbike back to camp.'

Florrie then said, as a protracted glance was exchanged by the young couple and noises off suggested that a crowd was trying to reach Alexander: 'Please don't let me keep you.'

He turned back to her.

'My destiny will be decided democratically. Whatever happens, I cannot desert Orezania. If I were a free man, without obligations, I would speak to you differently; and if my prayers are answered I will beg to be allowed to speak to you again. You understand me, I hope. In wartime we all have to speak our minds and be sure we are understood. Fay is young, and I will not compromise her future.'

'Thank you,' Florrie repeated.

'Fay knows my plans,' he said; 'they are simple, everybody knows them, and they will be put into operation in the next day or two. With luck, before long, I could be in a position to think of happiness. In the meanwhile, can I help you, Lady Meavy? Is there anything I can do for you?'

Fay again chipped in: 'He's got nothing to do anything with, Ma – he's only got himself against three armies with guns!'

He smiled at her outburst and again extended his hand to Florrie, who took it and dropped a deeper curtsy.

'Goodbye,' he said.

'Goodbye,' she returned. 'I hope . . .' she started and stopped.

'Ah yes,' he agreed, 'I too hope.'

The door Fay was leaning against burst open and people, his people, hospital staff and patients, even cooks from the remote kitchen shed, milled round him as before while he kept reiterating a phrase in Orezanian that was greeted by enthusiastic cheers.

Florrie and Fay retreated into the doorway of the children's ward and waited for him to extricate himself.

'What's he saying?' Florrie asked at some stage, and Fay answered: 'He's telling them to join his march on Orez.'

At length he was permitted to escape: the throng was somehow held back and the acclamation subsided. He paused to have a friendly word with Jenny and Sue, and to be introduced to Mildred. The children were shy and no doubt made shyer by seeing their Orezanian attendants' extravagant acts of homage. An exception was a diminutive black-eyed girl, perhaps eight or nine but looking younger, who dashed forward and wrapped stick-like arms round one of his legs. He produced an object from his pocket – it was a coin of small denomination – and presented it to her together with a brief little speech that caused his adult compatriots to applaud and, Florrie noticed, Fay to look as if she might be going to cry. But Alexander took her hand, she conferred upon him a gallant brilliant fond smile, they slipped unceremoniously through the back door of the ward, and the sound of a motorbike was heard.

Florrie did not see Fay again until suppertime two hours later. She trusted her daughter, she thought she could trust Alexander, she assumed they were together, and was not altogether sorry to have a chance to attempt to adjust to events. She was unsuccessful: sadness and happiness, regret and relief, continued to exercise a divisive influence, and instead of losing herself in her work she wandered through the wards, searching for Michael and half-hoping not to find him.

Fay's return had a unifying effect: it worried her mother almost exclusively. Of course Florrie much preferred to be with her daughter than without her, she had thanked heaven repeatedly that Fay was safe and well and with her; but Fay had undergone a change between leaving the children's ward and bobbing up in the canteen. She was pale and tense, and eventually wretched.

She explained that she had ridden on the motorbike some of the way to Alexander's camp and walked back; but no, she said, she was not tired. When Florrie confessed that she had been rather bowled over by Alexander, Fay bewildered her by appealing for postponement: 'Please, Ma, not yet.' Mildred rushed in, singing Alexander's praises, and Jenny and Sue were amazed by the Orezanians' show of affection for and faith in him: 'Not yet, not yet,' Fay mumbled obscurely, shaking her head. Alexander's speech to the child was referred to, and Jenny was curious and Sue asked for a translation. Fay supplied one and it ran: 'Always remember you were given a slozar by Alexander Nix, Prince of Orez, who was born to be your King' – and began to cry.

In reply to all the questions, to most of which she answered no – that she had not quarrelled with Alexander, that she was not having doubts about their relationship – she eventually replied: 'It's tomorrow.'

Alexander had told her as they parted that he would begin his campaign in the morning. She had dreaded it, she had not expected it so soon, she knew it had to happen, she believed it was right and splendid, but the strain of encouraging him, of not saying 'Don't', of not begging him to run away and live with her happily ever after, was intolerable.

She cried bravely, proudly, with her head held high, sometimes ridiculing and laughing at herself, and explained further.

Alexander had marked time in England until he had reason to hope that the will of the Orezanian people would prove more powerful than the weapons of war. That hope was now reinforced, and tomorrow it would be put to the test by a campaign that was nothing more nor less than a march on the capital armed only with the promise of peace and, metaphorically, his family tree. He had perhaps a thousand supporters in his camp, and the theory was that he and they would be joined by soldiers deserting from the Blue, White and Red armies, by all the disaffected soldiery who had fought one another for decades, and by civilians from everywhere, the silent majority who had suffered to satisfy the presumptions of politicians, the patriots who had seen their country ground into the dust and dirt by Bolsheviks and other barbarians.

Jenny and Sue crowed: 'Hurrah for Alexander! Well done, Alexander!'

But Fay shut them up with anguished realism.

[218]

'Alexander isn't going to stroll into Orez and be handed the crown on a purple cushion. He's bound to be shot at, he's been in great danger ever since he set foot in Orezania, and he refuses to take precautions, he won't protect himself while his friends are unprotected. And what happens if he can't feed the unknown number of friends who march with him to Orez? He doesn't know how many there may be, his stockpiles may run out and everyone will starve and turn into his enemies. Oh I agree he's a hero – he's the bravest and best person – but so was my father – and history repeats itself!'

She was apologised to by the girls, had her tears wiped away by her mother, was assured by Mildred that miracles were always on the cards, and begged them all to forgive her for complaining when she had been so lucky.

They adjourned to the dormitory and soon said good night. Fay seemed to want to be alone in her bunk at the far end, and prepare for the stress in store. Florrie wished at once to obey her daughter's ultimate injunction, 'Pray for us, Ma,' and to say a secret contrary prayer for Alexander's foe and rival. And Mildred and even Jenny and Sue, after another long day and notwithstanding developments, ached to take the weight off their feet.

The hours passed without Florrie knowing if she ever achieved oblivion. She suddenly heard noise, Orezanian chatter in the dormitory, engines out of doors. Fay was standing by her and speaking with excitement in her voice rather than anxiety: 'Come and see the fun!' Mildred was shaken into wakefulness, and clothing was donned in the dimness – dawn had not broken.

The five of them joined the exodus from the hospital: the Orezanians, staff and patients, were obviously informed of Alexander's plans. They emerged into a chill mist that was illuminated by the lights of military vehicles, the headlights of lorries on the road bringing loads of soldiers and the red rear lights of lorries going to fetch more: the hospital was a point of convergence, Fay said, and the good news was twofold, first that so many warriors were rallying to the cause of peace, and secondly that they were apparently in control of a huge amount of invaluable transport. As eyes grew more accustomed to the dark, Florrie, who had never had much chance to study the lie of the land, saw that the road dipped into a deeper valley and that a huge number of men were massed down there – she caught glimpses of them in the lorries' lights, and saw the glow of cigarettes and smelt tobacco smoke.

She was standing with Fay and the others at the side of the hospital above the road, and they and the crowd of Orezanian staff began to cheer the army with the courage of its pacific convictions forming below.

Patients had joined them, many inadequately dressed in regulation shirts and with bare feet, and doctors were rushing around like sheepdogs, trying to herd them back to at least the comparative warmth of the wards. Florrie was enlisted by a doctor to help, and had to support a one-legged man who had hopped out and fallen over and was alternately howling with pain and bawling encouragement to his erstwhile Blue, White or Red comrades. She was separated from Fay, and indoors, having returned her charge to a nurse in the ward for amputees, she was on the receiving end of instructions, appeals, requests. At last she determined not to be detained, but as she hurried towards an exit and the louder sounds of cheering and clapping she met her soldier-boy on his crutches who greeted her with the words: 'Goodbye war!'

'You're not thinking of marching?' she asked him. 'The path is too long – I've walked it.'

'I shall take truck and march at end to victory,' he laughed.

'Take care,' she said, then amended the platitudinous injunction to: 'Good luck!' – and added: 'Wait a second! Will you help me?'

'Please!'

He meant: if I can.

'Michael – who was King – King Michael was here . . .'

'So,' the boy seemed to agree.

'Do you know him?'

'We all know. We all hate.'

'Weren't you in his Blue army?'

'He made me fight. His agents promise to kill my mother if I do not fight.'

'Oh God! Where is he? Do you know where he is?'

The boy jabbed the thumb of his free hand at the ground, smiling as if with satisfaction.

'Are you telling me he's dead?'

'Yesterday.'

She had a lump in her throat and her vision blurred.

The boy said: 'He was bad man, not king. I march for King Alexander. Thank you. Goodbye!'

She emerged into sunshine shafting through the mist. Lorries were still passing the hospital, and now pedestrians in Orezanian attire, women and children as well as men, were moving downhill from every direction, along roadside verges, on mountain tracks, across fields, over obstacles. The chorus of a defiant song arose, sung by innumerable voices and echoing.

Fay ran across and seized her hand and pulled her to a vantage point with a view of the valley beneath them and insisted: 'Look, Ma, look!'

It took Florrie a moment to focus on what she was meant to look at. The whole valley floor seethed with people, and there must have been hundreds of vehicles of one sort and another, military and civilian, bicycles, horses and carts, donkeys. The march had started – a line of weaponless marchers ten or so abreast was already on the road to Orez; and leading from the front, swinging along with carefree steps, was the single small figure of Alexander.

Fay turned to her mother with tears in her eyes, and was surprised to see that she was also shedding or had shed tears.

She explained their emotion by saying with a rueful smile: 'It's his fault, isn't it?'

'Yes,' Florrie replied.

Then Fay said decisively: 'I'm going with him – he ordered me to stay here – but I don't have to obey him, do I, Ma?' She laughed and repeated for a joke on matrimonial lines the two words: 'Not yet.'

All for Love

'I'm coming with you,' Florrie declared.

'Oh no, Ma,' Fay objected in a voice that was not far removed from a groan, and begged her not to and warned of hardship and danger. But Florrie issued warnings on identical lines; Mildred wondered if she too should walk back to Orez; and Jenny and Sue suggested not very tactfully that everybody should hang about until Alexander became a king or a commoner or a martyr.

Time settled the matter: the marchers were passing and Fay did not want to be left behind. She said she could think of nothing nicer than having her hand held by her mother, and they might as well sink or swim together. Jenny and Sue were being recalled to urgent duties in the children's ward and said goodbye in a hurry: 'Fingers crossed and see you soon!' Mildred accompanied her cousins to the dormitory and handed over her sleeping bag and one of the two remaining gold coins to Fay, who rushed off in search of paper money and iron rations.

Florrie said to Mildred: 'Am I doing the wrong thing? I know I'll be a drag on Fay, but at least she'll have a shoulder to cry on if Alexander comes to grief.'

Mildred offered encouragement as usual, and asked: 'Will you be looking for Russ?'

'No.'

'Or Michael?'

'Definitely not.'

Florrie disclosed that she had seen Michael the previous evening, that he was badly wounded and waiting for surgery, and she had heard a short while ago that he was dead.

'Oh, Flo, I'm sorry.'

'Well, you should be glad – most people will be – and he's simplified my existence for a change – now it's only Fay's love life that worries me.'

Florrie packed determinedly and Mildred changed the subject.

'Do you feel up to another great hike?'

'Oh yes, I think so – and supposing we fall by the wayside or I do, my last will and testament is in order.'

'Don't, please, Flo!'

'Sorry – I'll try to take a leaf out of your book and be optimistic in future.'

Fay returned, having been successful. She flashed banknotes and stowed the food in her satchel, and her cheeks were rosy and her blue eyes glistened and shone with excitement. Fond farewells, modified by hopes of reunion, were exchanged, and Florrie followed her daughter out of doors and downhill as fast as she could and took her place in the column of marchers.

It was a sunny day and hot. The picturesque scenery seemed to have been gilded, and the weather was good for the spirits of the marchers, who sang rousing songs and clapped in unison. And new recruits to the cause, singly and in groups, sometimes families, fell into line behind Florrie and Fay and as it were voted with their feet either for their peaceable King or against usurpers and warlords.

Florrie and Fay chatted in snatches, in between the songs and when they were not hemmed in by Orezanians, and more consecutively during rest periods in the shade of trees and by brooks of running water.

Fay spoke of Alexander, to begin with she could speak of nothing else. He had smuggled himself into Orezania a few weeks ago with nothing, no home, money, organisation, power, she said – and look at him now!

'His camp, Ma, where I met up with him, was amazing – in a sort of forest on the top of a mountain – not easy to attack, you see – and had home-made huts and drainage and a treasury and regular supplies of food for the people flocking in – how he accomplished it all I can't imagine! And he was so busy, planning everything, planning this march before autumn turned into winter – I almost had to queue for an audience – I didn't see him till the

[223]

third day of the week I was there. He was worried that I was okay, never saying he was exhausted and responsible for thousands, never thinking of himself. Then he discovered you were in the hospital and wanted to see you and deposit me where he thought we'd be safest – and to tell the truth I feel ungrateful and guilty because here I am, following the drum against his wishes, and because you're with me.'

Florrie said: 'Don't talk of guilt – since I first heard of Orezania I've done just about everything I ought not to have done!' She enumerated the mistakes that had led to the death of Theodore Hildwitch and the manhandling of Mildred.

'Why did you go to the palace, Ma?' Fay inquired.

'We were commanded – it was a royal command,' Florrie replied after a pause.

'By Michael, you mean?'

'Practically speaking, he was the King of Orezania while we were in Orez – we didn't know for sure that he wasn't – we wanted him to sell us fuel for the aeroplane – it was difficult – I hope we weren't disloyal to Alexander.'

'But you know now, don't you, who's always been the true King?'

'Yes, my darling.'

'Did you see Michael often?'

'No, once or twice – I'd met him in England – he came to dinner at Buckingham Square – you remember.'

'Is he as nasty as he's supposed to be?'

'You must use the past tense, my sweet.'

'Is he dead?'

'So they say.'

'We're meant not to speak ill of the dead, are we?'

'That's right.'

The trucks and lorries that had passed the hospital, carrying advance parties of Alexander's subjects, now returned to pick up stragglers. Florrie and Fay accepted the offer of a lift in one, squeezed in and stood amongst twenty or thirty male Orezanians who laughed and cheered and mercifully did not molest them, and they swayed and bumped for a good few miles along the road to Orez.

They arrived at a farm that had become a bivouac for the

multitude; bought tea and pasties; found space in a crowded grove of olive trees; and in due course Florrie remarked: 'Michael can't be blamed for torturing Mildred. The villain of the piece was General Slutzk. Have you heard of him?'

'Have I not! Don't think me unsympathetic, Ma, but Mildred was lucky. While I worked in the hospital, we were treating the survivors of the attentions of General Slutzk.'

'What do you mean?'

'I don't want to make your flesh creep.'

'I'd rather know the worst.'

'We couldn't do much for men with their eyes gouged out – and in fact that isn't the worst example.'

'Michael was the boss of Slutzk.'

'All the warlords have employed him – he's been indispensable. The rumour is that he's got off scot-free – he'll be up to his tricks in some other country.'

'Orezania,' Florrie began, changing the subject, and having paused for a moment began again; 'Orezania's been an education, I will say that for it.'

Fay spoke reflectively. 'Alexander's admirable, Ma – and I love him for being an idealist – but he wants to impose a rule of law with corporal and capital punishment – and I've come round to agreeing with him, I'd vote for the execution of General Slutzk and Co. Sometimes violence is essential, and you can't avoid politics – we're being political by marching, and although we're probably not in extreme danger, because we're foreign and might be able to buy our way out of trouble, the Orezanians we're with are ready to die for democracy. That's the lesson I've learnt.'

Florrie's contribution to the discussion was as follows: 'You know the priest who broadcast prayers in the hospital? He spoke English, and one day I ran into him and thanked him for his prayers and told him we were no longer religious in England, whereupon he asked me two questions. They were, "How do you live then?" and "How do you die?" People here know things we've forgotten, they're not spoilt or decadent.'

The march recommenced at two in the afternoon, and about an hour later Florrie pointed to the thickly wooded hillside above them and said: 'I think that's where I lost Russ.'

[225]

Fay, who knew the almost mythical saga of the dog, commiserated.

'Oh well,' Florrie replied, 'at least we made the most of our time together. Let's talk of other things before I start to feel sorry for myself.'

Another exchange that was cut short revolved round their journey home, of when and how they would again see St Eo, and walk across its lawns in the blue shade of the cedar trees, and be cosseted by Wilson and Mrs Withgill and Jean and Crisp, and Maria and Barney at Buckingham Square. But Fay was unwilling to enter into details of her departure from Orezania: the subject clearly belonged in that list of hers which was headed 'Not yet'.

They spent the night in their sleeping bags in a field under the stars in the balmy atmosphere, and the next day made rapid progress on foot and mainly in lorries until about midday. Then they were shot at, a machine gun opened fire at uncomfortably close quarters, and Florrie and Fay took cover with the other marchers amongst the trees at the side of the road, and general consternation prevailed. Fear was aggravated by disillusionment, for Alexander's theory and almost his guarantee had been that no Blue, White or even Red soldier would kill unarmed compatriots who were waging a popular war for peace. Fay probably expressed the mood of the majority of marchers when she scolded Alexander for his quixotic notions, and regretted the piles of rifles and cartridge belts they had passed by, the discarded weaponry of soldiers who had joined the march. Bullets ricocheted and whirred, and she shouted at them furiously: 'Go away! Stop it!'

Strangely enough they seemed to obey her. Silence accentuated by the humming of bees and a wistful autumnal birdsong descended on the lush landscape, and soon there was cheering in the distance and people stood up and dusted themselves down, laughed and slapped one another on the back, and marched on towards Orez: Fay hoped the reason behind their behaviour was that the gunmen had been converted into pacifists and monarchists.

Shortly afterwards, as mother and daughter resumed their trudging, she tried to clarify her attitude to Alexander.

'Nothing's decided between us, you know, Ma. He's not the only one who hasn't dared to decide anything. I believe we understand each other, which must be more than half the battle, but I wonder

[226]

if I could stand the strain if he becomes a king and a target for snipers of every sort, or if he doesn't become a king and feels frustrated and a failure. The third possibility I can't bear to think about. Oh dear! Now I wish he and I hadn't been sensible.'

They hitched a lift on a lorry that carried them all the way to the little church on the hill with its view of their destination. The main body of marchers was encamped in the surrounding fields and woods. Dusk was falling, and the lights of Orez flickered below. Vendors with trays of eatables slung from their necks moved through the crowd, calling attention to their wares, and innumerable bonfires flared and smouldered under varied cooking utensils. That so many people had been fed for the duration of the march was one achievement, and another was the digging of lines of latrines sheltered by sacking fences at every staging post. Alexander must have been a mile or so nearer the city, where he would be raised up or cast down and out in the morning.

The mood of the masses was at once sombre and infectious. Fay had gathered from some Orezanian that according to rumour the Whites and Blues had entered into an unholy alliance with the Reds to massacre the opposition. No doubt everyone was feeling defenceless and vulnerable, and asking themselves variations of the rhetorical query that Fay put to Florrie: 'Are we crazy?' They felt like sitting ducks, and that they could easily be murdered in the sleeping bags they spread on pine needles at the edge of the woodland.

The night was again warm and not particularly dark. Florrie regretted the fact that she had omitted to arrange for her donation to the hospital to be paid, and Fay denied her mother's morbid implication by saying such arrangements could be made at the Orez Natwest in a few hours. Shadowy figures moved amongst the trees, and were caught in the illumination of a bonfire or a struck match, and the smells of woodsmoke, tobacco, cooking and humanity overhung the area like a thunder cloud or a pall. Voices were lowered and children cried.

Fay said: 'Ma, I can't imagine carrying on from where I left off in England – it won't ever be the same for me with friends who've stayed at home.'

And Florrie echoed the statement or at any rate the thought.

'My Orezanian resolution is to live differently if I get the chance.'

[227]

They wriggled into their sleeping bags and said good night.

Some time later Fay whispered: 'Ma?'

'Yes?' Florrie whispered back.

'Were you awake?'

'Yes.'

'Ma, pray for Alexander.'

'I will.'

'And for me.'

'I have, my darling.'

'And us, Ma – for all of us.'

'Yes, darling.'

The night dragged by. Neither of them thought she had slept, and both were wide awake at three-thirty in the morning. People were already packing up, cooking, on the move, and men with torches in the distance were marshalling the multitude into order. Florrie and Fay waited for an hour, for two hours. Day dawned slowly, and at last they were able to join the crowd marching down the hill.

The rest was anticlimax. Not a shot was fired, the road into the city was unobstructed. Soldiers fraternised with the marchers; machine gun posts in sidestreets were being dismantled; children clambered over armoured cars; shopkeepers were removing the protective boards from their shop windows; and girls were much in evidence, girls in coloured dresses, distributing flowers and kisses to the victors.

The crush was probably the greatest danger. People behind Florrie and Fay were pushing them forward, and people in front were pushing back. The singing of songs was now interspersed with cries, hoarse cries possibly of vengeance, high-pitched cries possibly of pain, and the celebrations were becoming alcoholic, bottles were brandished and empty tins intermittently flew through the air.

Florrie and Fay seized a chance to escape – a woman had fainted and was carried at head-height into a side-street, and they followed close behind. They then obtained directions to the Orez Ritz and arrived at the hotel. The armed sentries at the door were gone, and a Mr Melbo presided over the reception desk – Mr Djuro aged twenty-odd years had, like Mr Wilko, 'retired'. Unfortunately the telephone was out of order for the moment – Mr Melbo was able

[228]

to say so in English, probably because he had had reason to rehearse the sentence; but he indicated that a message could be taken by a pageboy to the manager of the Orez Natwest Bank. And yes, he had a vacancy in an annexe, 'a room not better', the chief appeal of which for Florrie was that it was not the one she had shared with Mildred.

Mother and daughter deposited their baggage; bathed and washed their hair in the bathroom adjoining; obtained a hot meal downstairs in the restaurant; returned to the room and sank on to their twin beds, beds of the type that had once struck Florrie as uncomfortable; and met Mr Hamilton in the Lounge Bar at six o'clock.

He was as neat as ever in his grey suit, white shirt, sober tie and black lace-up shoes. He had not forgotten to bring Florrie's luggage along, and he presented her with a statement of her account. He was pleased to meet Miss Meavy, and congratulated her on having arrived in Orez at an opportune moment. He accepted and sipped a small sherry. Lady Meavy and Miss Meavy were fortunate to have had tolerable weather for their journey from the north of the island, he said. He was glad that Miss Meavy's young friends were in good health, and Miss Chaffcombe's arm was giving her no more trouble. He was sure that the help of the English ladies had been much appreciated in the hospital, and he hoped that His Majesty King Alexander would bring the boon of stability to his country.

What was the latest news, Florrie asked.

The celebrations were tending to cause unpleasantness.

'Come along now, Mr Hamilton,' she laughed, 'you can call a spade a spade – my daughter's a modern miss. What do you mean by unpleasantness?'

'Summary justice, Lady Meavy,' he replied, opening his eyes regretfully wide; 'I fear that many of the soldiers who threw down their arms and expected to establish friendly relations with the conquering heroes have been disappointed. My understanding is' – he raised his hand to cover his mouth as he cleared his throat – 'that some streets are awash with blood.'

Florrie said: 'Frankly, Mr Hamilton, I'm used to blood by now. The question that springs into my mind isn't how could they, but whose? You don't happen to know the fate of General Slutzk?'

[229]

'I have a suspicion that he will be amongst those who have made large sums of money from the civil war, and in the last few days have been fleeing to lands that are willing to harbour war criminals.'

'What a pity!'

'Indeed.'

'How exactly have they fled?'

'By air – General Zaporag and his Red staff from the airport here – and the Blue and White leaders by helicopter from their camps in the hills, according to rumour.'

'Is the civil war finished, Mr Hamilton?'

'I hesitate to say so, Lady Meavy, but it does appear to be.'

'Could we fly out from Orez Airport?'

'No doubt.'

'My cousin Mildred and the two girls would have to be contacted and fetched, and we couldn't organise anything until the telephone was back in working order.'

Mr Hamilton said that the military road to the north either was or shortly would be open to private traffic, therefore a taxi-ride to and from the hospital posed no problems, and that full telephonic services were promised for the following day.

He addressed Fay: 'May I inquire when you thought of getting home?'

She blushed and could not answer.

Florrie came to the rescue. She undertook to keep him posted, and mentioned the plan to donate money to promote the health of Orezanians. He praised such a charitable intention and assured both Meavys of his best attention at all times. Then he declined a second sherry and departed.

They had supper and retired to bed. The next morning they woke too early, felt flat, nearly at a loose end, and at nine o'clock went across to the cathedral. But as they gave thanks and prayed in the semi-darkness, priests or vergers approached worshippers in the front pews and, after muttered confabulations, escorted or hustled them through various exits. Then the organ began to play or rehearse, an electrified chandelier over the altar was switched on, florists entered with flowers and gilt chairs were carried up the aisle.

They left before they were asked to. Outside a crowd had

gathered in the square and was rapidly growing, and the ribald chants and maudlin cries were further evidence that the celebration of victory was deteriorating into booziness. Civilian police struggled to keep a passageway clear for the dignitaries invited to, and now arriving, on foot and by car for the ceremony in the cathedral; but the crowd surged forward, cheering, and Florrie and Fay tried to hurry round the edge of it in order to reach the hotel. There were too many drunk men ahead of them, reeling about and supporting one another; they decided to take shelter up some steps and under the portico of one of the houses; they joined a group of sober spectators and had a good view of the proceedings; and were pleased to wait and watch not least because Alexander was probably due to attend the function.

Florrie noticed two men who were standing together and staring at her, and thought she recognised them. They had expressionless faces and were burly: where had she come across them? They flinched away, she racked her brain, and she and the crowd seemed to remember simultaneously that they had worked for General Slutzk. They had smelt of garlic in the car to Kraga; they had twisted Mildred's arm and no doubt attended to Orezanian eyes etcetera. Now, suddenly, the crowd closed in on them, an angry chorus swelled, a glass bottle was broken on the shorn head of one of the men and somebody must have kicked the other's legs from under him. They disappeared from view. They were being punched, kicked, jumped on, lynched.

And Alexander was there, pulling and pushing aside the ring-leaders. He was alone and different from everyone else, young and clean-cut, self-confident, authoritative and regal, standing in the midst of those furious irrational men and raising his hands palms outwards in a gesture both pacifying and appealing. He stopped them, he stopped it, he surprised them into stopping; and he was recognised and applauded, and members of his entourage reached the scene, and belatedly the police arrived, and everybody was cheering Alexander for liberating them from war and oppression.

Florrie said to Fay: 'Has he seen you? Do wave at him, darling! Listen, listen, I withdraw all my reservations.'

But Fay, who had turned her back, said to Florrie: 'Let's go home – please, Ma – immediately!'

[231]

The Value of Modesty

They went straight to the bank and were lucky. Mr Hamilton introduced them to 'two gentlemen from Balaclava', who were actually senior Natwest officials, had just flown in to Orezania with supplies of the banknotes of popular currencies, had seats to spare in their chartered aeroplane and would be more than willing to escort five ladies on the first leg of their journey back to the mother country. The telephone was working: a car was ordered to drive to and from the hospital without delay, and Florrie spoke to Mildred and eventually managed to tell her that she and Jenny and Sue had to be packed and prepared to get into it in about two and a half hours. Further calls were put through to Philip Mozergh in his office and Maria at Buckingham Square. Mother and daughter were then given a lift to the Ritz in the bank's security van.

The time was ten-thirty. The ceremony in the cathedral was over, and what was left of the crowd in the square was dispersing calmly. The policemen standing about seemed to be wearing brand new uniforms, and might have been Alexander's marching men now ready to enforce his rule of law. Within the hotel Florrie received telephone calls from Philip who was arranging her itinerary from Balaclava to Odessa and on to Moscow and Heathrow. She and Fay had another proper meal, and tipped and said goodbye and thank you to waiters and chambermaids. And they discussed Fay's decision.

Florrie ventured to say that she thought Alexander would be sad to know Fay had been so tantalisingly close and was putting as much distance as possible between the two of them.

Fay's replied: 'I couldn't stay on, Ma, I'd feel like a vulture, waiting to prey on Alexander. I would have died of shame if he'd found out I'd followed him not only to Orezania but to Orez too, and was hanging round to be picked up. My friends say I'm out of date, but I believe lots of girls feel as I do, or would if they dared to be unfashionable.'

At last Mildred and the girls arrived, and Mr Hamilton and the two gents from Balaclava chugged round to the Ritz in the all too familiar diesel bus. Florrie and Fay had to sign their names repeatedly and were handed wads of money for doing so. When they thanked Mr Hamilton for his efficiency, helpfulness, protectiveness and kindness, he replied that he had been trained to attend to the needs of his customers. But Florrie would have none of it: she enfolded him in her arms and kissed him. He was also kissed by Fay, Mildred, Jenny and Sue, and the travellers climbed into the bus and exchanged waves with the neat receding figure on the steps of the hotel.

They arrived at Orez Airport at five o'clock, and twenty-four hours later at Heathrow.

Philip Mozergh met them, and Crisp was discreetly in the background. But homecoming was not so happy for Florrie as it might have been. Philip's appearance distressed her. He seemed to have shrunk – he was a gnome in comparison with the Orezanian King or Kings she had in mind. And his excited attentions were alien.

'I'm going to drive you to Buckingham Square,' he said, meaning in his company limousine with his chauffeur at the wheel.

She masked her displeasure by asking: 'What day of the week is it?'

The answer, 'Tuesday', signified that according to custom she would be spending the next three nights in London for the sake of the social festivities.

How was she ever to break with tradition? How could she be so ungrateful as to refuse the offer of Philip who had yet again proved his devotion by being present and by having booked tickets and seats on trains and planes?

Matters were not made better by Mildred going with Crisp to St Eo, and Fay choosing to go there too.

But Florrie was bemused by the vicissitudes of all her journeys, her head ached, she had no chance of a private word with Fay and

[233]

was anyway reluctant to put any obstacle in her path, and could not summon the energy to rearrange things.

Philip had agreed under pressure to give Jenny and Sue a lift, and in the car Florrie was relieved that they rattled on.

Philip managed to worry her nonetheless with his terse asides: 'My God, you've been away so long! ... You're thin ... And Fay's a shadow of herself, though I must admit it suits her ... I've tried to square T.D. about the money you've spent in Orezania ... You'll have to tell me the whole story, I'm dying for every detail.'

'Oh dear, traveller's tales are such a yawn – and you probably would be dead by the time I'd finished telling you mine,' she laughed in response.

Rain fell steadily, and the street lighting was needlessly bright and dazzling. Would she have to ask Philip to stay for dinner? His car was too big for Buckingham Square, it had to mount the pavement to get in: its size had annoyed her before – why did he have to have such a monster? Outside number seven, waiting in the illumination shafting through the open door, were Maria and Barney, and she thought more positively: how nice to be cared for by Maria instead of by the wrong man, and to be able to afford the occasional boon of solitude!

At least Philip had the tact to inquire: 'Are you exhausted, darling?'

'I am,' she confessed apologetically.

He let her go for the price of another alien embrace and a promise to talk on the telephone in the morning. She was kissed goodbye by Jenny and Sue and effusively thanked for taking them to Orezania and exposing them to dangers and horrors.

The limousine nosed into the night; she could reciprocate the warm greetings of her servants and friends; the front door was closed and, she hoped, the world with all its complications locked out for the time being.

Barney carried her cases. Maria followed him upstairs to unpack for her. They said they would serve her dinner in half an hour. How luxurious her life was! She was struck afresh by the prettiness of her sitting-room, and the softness of the armchair she sat in.

But the mail piled up on the coffee table depressed her spirit more than ever. Holidays – not that her absence had been a holiday

– were always ruined by the postman in her experience. There were at least a hundred appeals from charities, warning her that children would perish in dreadful circumstances, animals would be treated abominably, wives beaten black and blue, cripples denied toilet facilities, the countryside ruined and beautiful cities defaced, unless she sent money pronto and remembered to leave them legacies in her will. The Inland Revenue also seemed to have an interest in her demise: there were enough brown envelopes to frighten some taxpayers to death. The business correspondence would take her days to wade through, and the private sort was worse: her friends and acquaintances only wrote to her nowadays if they wanted something.

On top of the private pile were two letters that had been delivered by hand. The first was addressed in spidery writing she recognised which caused her heart to sink: it was from Geoffrey Oldcoate. She opened it and read: 'My dearest Florrie, I have heard from Maria that you are homeward bound. Praise be, my prayers have been heard! Maria tells me that Philip Mozergh is in charge of your travel arrangements, so I shall refrain from intruding and will not try to communicate on the evening of your arrival. But, if I may, I shall telephone at the earliest suitable hour on the next day. Looking forward to our reunion with eagerness and joy, Your loving Geoffrey.'

She mentally kicked herself: she had guessed that Geoffrey's feelings would be hurt, she should have overcome her resistance to ringing him from Orez and thus pre-empting his jealousy of Philip. Now she would have to trot out excuses and honour her obligation to play the part of the object of the affections she had appropriated.

The second letter was marked 'Urgent'. But she resolved not to open it, then changed her mind, and immediately wished she had not. The embossed heading of the blue page ran: Sir Robert Ireby KCB plus his address in Lord North Street.

'Darling Florrie,' Bobby Ireby began presumptuously in his thick insensitive handwriting; 'Come to Covent Garden on Thursday, please, seven o'clock Royal Box. The death of King Michael of O is a shocking blow, we're all stricken. Wilberforce from Trade and Industry is joining us on Thursday and he and I are keen to pick your brains about the prospects of doing business with the new

[235]

boy. Love.' No signature was appended, but the first of three postscripts cast doubt on the eligibility of the writer for his directorship of the opera house: 'It's that Japanese show,' the second accounted for the timing of his missive: 'Philip Mozergh told me you'd be back from Orezania today,' and the last stated: 'No forgiveness if you let me down.'

She was summoned to the dining-room. Strangely, she had no appetite for the choice food, although, at the hospital, she could have done with second helpings of the cabbage soup with dumplings, and on her hikes she was always hungry.

With apologies to Maria for not eating up, and having reassured Barney that she was not sick, she bade them good night. She retreated to her bedroom and would have disconnected the telephone if she had not hoped in vain to receive good news from Fay; but she could not rest. She was not happy, and to start with her unhappiness centred on Bobby Ireby. How dare Bobby Ireby call her darling? How dare he bully her? What a horrible letter! And how did he think he knew for certain that Michael was dead?

She had not been happy in Orezania, and had often yearned and pined to be where she now was. Yet she had conquered her squeamishness in the hospital, and felt she was needed there. She had survived the love of a bad man and the loss of a good dog. She had almost believed that by taking life and death seriously, by witnessing tragedy and doing her bit to alleviate pain, she would expiate the sin of her idle, self-centred, purse-proud frivolity, and rectify many mistakes. Was she to start again where she had been pleased to stop? Was she to behave as if nothing had happened to her and she had learnt nothing?

Bobby Ireby was no friend of hers. Yes, they entertained each other, he invited her to the opera and she invited him back, they spent the equivalent of some hundreds of pounds on a few hours of each other's company at intervals; but their intercourse was confined to the smallest of talk, he showed he had no interest in her personality and preoccupations, and she had none in his although she tried not to show it; they met exclusively and as it were as public conveniences, they were like lay figures with socially acceptable qualifications, and a working knowledge of the rules of the game.

But she was no longer inclined to play that game. And Bobby

Ireby was a rotter. She did not care where he sprang from, or blame him for his failures to measure up to modish standards of pronunciation and etiquette. She concentrated on the exaggerations or the lies of his references to Michael's death, and on remembering that he was a dealer in arms, a merchant of death, and successful enough, since everybody seemed to want to kill somebody, to have bought himself a seat at the very best tables.

High society was low, she thought. And the conspiracy of the whole human race, republicans as well as monarchists, revolutionaries as well as conservatives, especially revolutionaries whose turn had come, was to see it through rose-tinted spectacles, bathed in golden light, romanticised, glamorised, imbued with enchantment. Fabrications, distortions! Entry into the highest society, which exists everywhere, always has, always will, was merely a matter of power-broking, horse-trading, swaps, barter, and jam for money: you will be admitted into the circles, groups, cliques and sets of those you have worshipped from afar and envied in return for your ability to pay up, pay up and pay the bill.

Yes, she admitted, real gentlemen existed; but they were created by nature, not by heredity. Her own husband had been one, a flower of chivalry, although his grandfather in portraits resembled a yokel, and there were no paragons in the family history – the baronetcy was bestowed on an insignificant squire possibly in error.

Eldred was an exception, the exception proving the rule that nobility was not to be confused with aristocracy, which in principle was nothing but a man-made recognition of wealth. A duke might be a hero or a saint, but if he were reduced to doing dustman's work he would not be courted by social climbers. Actually, Florrie recalled, Eldred had been in favour of an hierarchy created by finance, for he detested and dreaded the alternative of a class system based upon political or military success. And she herself could see the point of a sort of crossroads where power and influence were exchanged without too much bitterness or bloodshed – capitalists who had run out of capital and aristocrats who had nothing more to sell taking the road downhill, and the new rich with new blood in their veins going up.

But that was not to pardon or to love Bobby Ireby and people like him, who expected to hire her for the evening for a price they could pay, and threatened that she would do the paying if she refused to fall in with their plans. She was damned if she would cave in and attend the 'Japanese show' – probably a Philistine re-titling of *Madam Butterfly*. At the same time she was neither so innocent nor so rebellious as to fail to realise that she would also be damned by refusing the invitation, damned at any rate by social criteria, since Bobby would hound her with his spite.

She needed a protector. She ached for Eldred. Not the least precious of the possessions of which she had been robbed in Orezania was her immunity to love. She paced her bedroom floor and her thoughts veered in the vicarious direction of Fay and Alexander.

Alexander reminded her of Eldred, not by his looks but by his noble bearing. She modified her opinions to the extent of admitting that high intelligence and vision, courage and competence, were a combination that was all the better for being linked to the qualities that a long lineage is supposed to bestow, an aristocratic appear-ance, gentle manners, a charitable disposition, innate sophistication. Of course Eldred was more eccentric than Alexander, she hoped, but they were both rare creatures to be conserved and treasured.

She had loved her husband. But she was at last willing to think that he ought not to have compromised the welfare of his young wife and daughter in order to swing through the rain forest and attempt to prove he was better than Tarzan. He should not have deserted her or disappeared. And because she had not hesitated to say yes when he popped the question at their fourth meeting, and because she had mourned him for so long, she had surely earned her liberation from her monogamous straitjacket.

She shook herself: her regrets about Michael, her own reshar-pened appetite for happiness, were beside the point under con-sideration. If only Alexander had proposed to Fay in England with Eldred's impatience and assurance! Worldly wisdom had an answer to that suggestion: a penniless waiter, an honest and proud waiter, would not have liked to do that to a girl reared in Fay's circumstances who happened to be an heiress. Again, if only he had proposed in Orezania, while they were together in his camp or while she was on the back of his motorbike! Florrie corrected herself again: would he have been right to risk making Fay a wife and a widow almost simultaneously?

No, he might not be to blame. But chances had been missed, and kings with a country to govern could not spare the time to pursue girls who were playing hard to get across a continent. And love was so easily lost, Florrie reflected, and the loss of love and the beloved were so sad and painful for natures like hers and her daughter's.

The grandfather clock downstairs chimed the passage of time, and she was still unable to lie on her soft lonely bed, between the smooth scented sheets, in the fraught silence and peace of her privacy; nor, when she finally did, could she close her mind to unusual speculations, and to ungrateful relief that she was not married to Geoffrey or Philip, until the not so small hours.

In the morning she sat at the desk in her sitting-room and wrote a line of acceptance to Bobby Ireby, and came to the conclusion that Fay's modest scruples were folly.

A Pilgrim in Mayfair

Florrie Meavy rose early the following morning, and opened and read more of her accumulated correspondence.

She was amazed and amused by some friends' missives. Here was Brenda Slawston, the president of the 'Say No' charity, asking her to take hundred-pound tickets for a fancy dress ball in North Norfolk in aid of drug abusers; and there was Mona Brighton inviting her to the wedding of a great-grandchild aged twenty to a West Indian of fifty-five in some Caribbean island. 'Do come – it should be fun,' the ladies had written on the costly white cards. Why on earth should Brenda think she would wish to spend a small fortune to make herself look silly, travel miles, book herself and party into an expensive hotel, and thus contribute to the cause of feather-bedding a gang of repulsive lawbreakers? Poor old Mona, at least more realistically, must have hoped that Florrie would not only be her travelling companion but would also pay for their flight to Florida, for a six-hour voyage by hydrofoil, for an island hop by rowing boat and accommodation in a holiday camp, so that they could attend a marriage no doubt fated to last for weeks or months rather than years.

Letters thanking for the jaunt to Orezania struck Florrie as equally odd. Adam Crabhouse, for instance, wrote at some length that he had revised his ideas about King Michael. He was in receipt of information that convinced him Michael was the Real McCoy who would be ruling his lucky people for many years to come. Adam proved he was a true journalist by getting everything wrong. He enclosed copies of the obituaries of Theodore Hildwitch – one claimed Theodore was the best composer since Beethoven – it had probably been penned by another journalist.

Geoffrey Oldcoate expressed his opinion of Orezania by almost avoiding any mention of it: he thanked Florrie for existing. Eric Hinxton wrote with artistic understatement that the destruction of his Orezanian journal was a whole bale of straw – it had broken his back and spirit, his writer's block was now permanent, and he had nothing left to live for except death. Roger Ryther, who wrote from Hinxton Grange, told a different story: Orezania was something different; well done, Florrie, for breaking new ground; he and Eric had been having such fun, sticking pins into the tiniest effigies of General Slutzk; and he was grateful and glad to have sampled the rough after all the smooth.

Anna Hulcott's letter stated that Orezania was a lovely island and that King Michael and the other Orezanians she had met had been fascinating. Angela Grizebeck's was an unreadable monograph on her pet subject – grammar.

Geoffrey rang Florrie at ten o'clock, after she had been at her desk for two hours, and began by saying: 'Have I woken you?'

He came to lunch at one, and wept a little at the sight of her. He embraced her with diffidence and said he had been afraid he might never set eyes on her again. His affection and fidelity should have plucked at her heartstrings. Instead she smelt his breath, noticed his stained suit, expected him to fall over because he had gallantly chosen not to wear his glasses, and had no patience with his slow pedantic talk. An incredulous question distracted her: how could she ever have had her interest in the opposite sex partially satisfied by the friendship of her dilapidated guest peering at his food and masticating with difficulty?

She restrained her unfairly critical faculties and tried to be nice. She supplied his demand for an account of her vicissitudes after his departure from Orezania.

But his comments hit the wrong note. 'I never should have left you,' he groaned, as if to suggest that he could have wrestled with Mildred's muscular torturers, and held the Red peril at bay. 'I should have been with you,' he said, meaning on the marathon to the northern hills, a couple of hours of which would have been too much for him. 'How horrid for you!' he exclaimed on hearing of her work in the hospital; and he summed up Michael thus, 'Good riddance!'

Soon after lunch she was able to bid Geoffrey goodbye: she had

had the foresight to make an early appointment with her hairdresser.

Her reunion with the other man who had consoled her widow-hood was not much better.

Philip was again tired after his day's work at the office, and he showed it. He had to swallow yawns as, conversationally, she battled with his absent-mindedness. He could only stay for an hour, he informed her, because he had to change before going to an important dinner party. He regretted the brevity of his visit, while she was already regretting its length. She remembered the syndrome of the tired businessman greedily fitting in more social engagements than he could enjoy or render enjoyable – she had attended the funerals of many such men. Had Philip always looked so seedy and behaved so boorishly? Now his grey face evoked no sympathy and his exhaustion offended.

She spoke of Orezania. She went into the details he had said he was dying for. Whereas Geoffrey had made too much of the narrowness of her squeaks, Philip made too little. He described her cathartic experience as an escapade. He was then inquisitive about Fay: was she still keen on the dark horse who seemed to be sitting on the Orezanian throne; was Alexander another conman; would Fay like to queen it over savages; was an ambitious mama pulling the strings in the background?

When Florrie had supplied unwilling and evasive answers, Philip was still more annoying. She had said she wanted to give money to the hospital in the Orezanian hills, or to improve medical services in the island. No, he asserted, not a good idea – her money would line an undeserving pocket – why not get hold of a load of banknotes and set fire to them, if she was in an extravagant mood?

His parting shot, as it were, was worse than Geoffrey's au revoir. He was sufficiently invigorated by her company or her whisky to issue a new proposal. Orezania, he declared, should have proved conclusively that she was in need of help to organise her later life, just as it had proved that he could not mark time much longer, he had to have somebody to come home to and to keep him at home. His passion expressed itself in chilling terms: they were no longer young, they could look after each other, they had the wherewithal to make themselves comfortable, and she would grow accustomed to him even if she never loved him as he had always loved her.

[242]

She parried, she dodged physically, she reminded him of his dinner party, and finally achieved the solitude she wished for.

The telephone rang – the news had spread that she was back at Buckingham Square. She would not answer, she had instructed Maria and Barney to take messages and that she was only prepared to talk to Fay. But Fay did not ring, she can have had no good news to communicate, and Florrie did not like to pester and probe into disappointment.

The next morning she took deep breaths and did make a telephone call. She spoke to T.D. Faulkbourne, told him how and why she had spent getting on for a million pounds in Orezania, justified herself and won his assent if not his approval, referred to his broadside of business letters, and eventually said her piece as intended.

'T.D., I've taken a dramatic decision. I want to donate some of my money either to the hospital in Orezania where I worked or to the medical services on offer there.'

'Your generosity does you credit, Florrie,' he rumbled cautiously.

'The hospital saved my life, not that I was ill, and Orezania changed my mind about things. I've too much money, T.D., and after my experience of the poverty of those people I'm horrified by the superfluity of all my possessions.'

'My dear, you don't have to tell me your heart's in perfect working order.'

'Are you implying my brain isn't, wicked T.D.?'

'You mustn't think I'm wicked because I understand money, and because with the best will in the world I couldn't say the same for you.'

'But it's so simple – I've still more money than I require, and sick Orezanians have less – if I let them have a bit everyone's happier – QED.'

'Have you talked the matter over with Fay?'

'Yes – and she doesn't mind.'

'She isn't married yet, is she?'

'You mean her husband could have other ideas?'

'That's conceivable. Tell me, how long has it taken the Meavy family to accumulate its treasure?'

'What treasure?'

'Its money and properties.'

[243]

'Not a fair question, T.D.'

'Why not? Fay's future husband might well know how difficult it is to make money, how much effort and intelligence have gone into winning it and not losing it, and might have more respect for the Meavys who put together and preserved her inheritance than you seem to have.'

'There's quite enough in the kitty for Fay and half a dozen husbands.'

'How much money do you think of donating?'

'A tithe, perhaps.'

'Ten per cent! How much do you imagine you're worth?'

'What a way to talk, T.D.! How should I know? It's not for me to say what I'm worth. No – seriously – in your crude lingo, I've no idea.'

'Exactly! Well, in my lingo there's a saying that neatly fits the bill: when in doubt, do nowt. Ten per cent of your estate before or after taxes, Florrie?'

'After – I'm not sure – why not after tax?'

'Because that might cost you a much higher percentage of your fortune. You'd have to pay capital gains tax and transfer tax and stockbroker's charges and accountant's fees, and at the end of the day you might not be able to afford St Eo.'

'You're frightening me.'

'Maybe a little. I would like to frighten you into doing nothing in haste, before you've studied the options and fully grasped the facts of the matter. I'll help you on condition you're as sensible as you used to be and do as I say.'

She had to laugh.

He continued 'A wicked thought has struck me, Florrie – this youth who's seized power in Orezania – could he be the one Fay was interested in? And could he by any chance be behind your idea of setting up an Orezanian Health Service?'

'Oh T.D.,' she scolded in an edgy tone of voice; 'Alexander and Fay are friends, but otherwise you're absurdly wide of the mark – Alexander didn't seize power, and although I've only met him once I'm certain that the very last thing he'd ever do is to beg me or anyone else for money. And I'm not setting up a health service – perish the thought! Now I'm going to say goodbye before I get cross with you, but I'll come back to the charge because I'm determined and because I can't help being fond of you for unknown reasons.'

It was Thursday. She would have gone down to St Eo if she had not had Bobby Ireby hanging over her head. But she meant to go early the next morning, therefore she had an excuse to ring through to Mildred and inquire about Fay.

'I've seen very little of her,' Mildred said. 'She hasn't paid me a visit, and Wilson told me she was out the whole of yesterday and isn't having any meals in today. She's warned Wilson and Mrs Withgill that somebody may call her from abroad; but apparently no one's done so. Poor love! I'm afraid she must be in rather a muddle. But she will talk to you, she'll tell you everything – I'm glad you'll soon be together, you'll cheer her up. And Florrie, will you tell me something – whether to wish Alexander would ring Fay or to wish he wouldn't?'

The point remained moot: Florrie avoided settling it one way or the other, and confined the rest of their conversation within the safer region of domestic arrangements.

She spoke on the telephone to a third party before she left Buckingham Square for Covent Garden Opera House. The Filipinos happened to be out, the ringing was prolonged and relentless, she suddenly hoped it was Fay and feared it might be Alexander, and spoke her hullo breathlessly.

The high-pitched clipped voice belonged to Roger Ryther, who apologised for not being the man she had sounded as if she was dying to talk to.

There was more of his bantering stock-in-trade: why had she not broadcast the news that she was back in town? Where had she been, and what had she been playing at, and with whom, on the extra days she had spent in Orezania?

She was at a loss, had no snappy repartee on the tip of her tongue, had lost the knack, was out of practice, and waited for him to reveal his ulterior motive.

Eventually he said: 'Florrie, a new friend of mine – female, so my best old friends needn't worry – Mrs Wright, Cheryl to me, is giving a great big ball, believe it or not. I'm not joking, dear, Cheryl Wright isn't throwing any old party – dress-anyhow-and-bring-a-bottle sort of thing – no, it's a white tie and tails affair and in the right venue for a change, not Clapham or Ealing but Millionaires'

Row. She's a sweet little widow in spite of her Christian name, Cheryl is, and worth her weight in emeralds, my dear, and she worships you from afar, she thinks you're beautiful and brilliant – she's right, for heaven's sake – and she's mad to meet you and has sent me an invitation card an inch thick with your name on it together with mine. Florrie, please, I know what you're going to say, but please do me the favour and the honour and all the rest of it, because Cheryl looks like being my meal ticket for many a long day, and my soft landing and old age pension into the bargain. After all I did come with you to Orezania.'

Florrie had heard of this Cheryl character, who had been the secretary of a tycoon, married him although he was a hundred years older than she was, and, when he predictably died of it, inherited his fortune. She had houses in Kensington Palace Gardens and in all the other expensive places, and must have called in Roger to do them up and to introduce her to the more respectable members of his social circle.

Florrie was displeased. Roger should not have suggested that he had participated in the Orezanian trip because she had compelled him as he was now compelling her: in theory she had offered and he had accepted an expensive treat. He was wrong to try to cash in on her friendship, to link her with an adventuress, to so misunderstand her inclinations, and, in particular, to ask her telephonically and virtually inescapably to promote his interests against her will, since she had no time to invent an excuse. The consequence was that she said yes meaning no, and more fuel was piled on her fiery inner raging at the rites of the establishment.

Madam Butterfly, in a manner of speaking, cut both ways. Where she was again seated, to whom she had been introduced when she was last sitting there, and the relevant sad parts of what she saw on the stage, upset her: yet Bobby Ireby behaved unexpectedly well, and Puccini's music was pleasing and soothing. After the final curtain, in the dining-room behind the box, she was first in the line to say goodbye to her host, hoping thus to avoid his threatened interrogation about Orezania. But he detained and drew her to a gilt chair beside his crony Wilberforce, Sir John Wilberforce, a top Civil Servant, who had also been present on the night she met Michael.

The other guests departed, and the following three-sided conversation ensued.

'I understand that you were a friend of the late King Michael of Orezania, Lady Meavy?' Sir John queried in his deep voice, eyeing her heavily.

Bobby answered for her with characteristic insolence: 'She hired a damn great aeroplane to go and beard him in his lair.'

She flared up and said: 'You're both incorrect. Michael wasn't a king, he had no right to the throne, and I didn't go to Orezania to beard him, I had different reasons for visiting the island.'

'Tell us what your reasons were, Florrie.'

'I shall do nothing of the kind.'

'Come on – I know why – and I've put John in the picture – your daughter's walking out with the new chappie.'

'Thanks, Bobby. My chauffeur's waiting.'

They persuaded her not to take the huff and not to leave, apologies were thrown in for good measure, and Sir John Wilberforce began again, shaking his jowls at her.

'Michael was a good customer of British industry. We also sold items to a General Zaporag and another Orezanian – I think he was called Saltpick.'

'Salbych,' she said.

'Oh, do you know him, did you meet him?'

'He was the warlord of the Whites, and Zaporag was the warlord of the Reds.'

'What's become of them, I wonder.'

'Salbych was tortured almost to death by Michael, and paraded round at a party and taken out and shot. Zaporag's a war criminal and mass murderer.'

'That's tough talk, Florrie,' Bobbie chipped in, and Sir John remarked dismissively: 'War's a terrible thing.'

Again she almost lost her temper.

'It was all the more terrible because you were selling guns to each of the three warring armies.'

They were unmoved by her accusation. Sir John had recourse to the argument that if Britain had not sold the arms other countries would, and British workers would have lost their jobs and the country would have suffered, and Bobby advised her with considerable force not to be childish.

[247]

'Keep your hair on – there are two simple questions we'd like you to answer,' Bobby went on. 'Is Alexander a good egg, and do you think he's ready to receive a deputation led by yours truly?'

'You'd be wasting your time and his.'

'What?'

'He doesn't need you, and he won't. You wouldn't like Alexander – he's in favour of peace. Yes, he seized power or power was seized for him, though not by firing a single bullet from one of your guns. You don't believe me, but you should. I was there, and I was in Orez and a witness to power being handed over to more unarmed fellow-citizens than even your customers thought they could kill. Alexander's the King of Orezania by rights, but he won back his kingdom by the force of his popularity, nothing else, and he's extremely unlikely to start shooting the people who put him on the throne. Anyway, there are more than enough guns available as things are.'

'Good old Florrie!' Bobby's congratulations were scoffing. 'But are you by any chance hoping to become His Majesty's mother-in-law?'

She stood up. She would have liked to crush him with some powerful retort. But she was shaking with indignation, with an exasperation accumulated over days and weeks, and on the verge of tears. All she dared to say in a withering tone of voice was: 'Oh really!'

Sir John lumbered to his feet and looked down upon her.

'Lady Meavy,' he said, 'forgive me for explaining that armaments have a limited life, they wear out and are superseded. The King is bound to wish to defend the people who love him from those at home and abroad who will cast acquisitive eyes on his fertile and strategically unique island. Moreover, the civil war will have aggravated and instigated blood feuds and vendettas, and the laws won't be enforced and order maintained by exhortations alone. It would be very much appreciated if you would inform King Alexander that the old friends of Orezania in this country would be happy to hear from him as soon as he requires our assistance.'

She shrugged her shoulders in reply and to signal her departure. Her hand was shaken by Sir John's huge paw, and Bobby followed her downstairs, as it were snapping at her heels, terrier-like.

[248]

He mixed more routine apologies with unsolicited advice that she should keep her head out of the clouds and her feet on the ground, and with the corrupt hint that her cooperation could well be a rewarding investment in the long run. At least she had the minor satisfaction of climbing into the Jaguar before he had a chance to kiss her goodbye.

Not too many almost sleepless hours later, on the Friday morning, she was again in the car and on her way to St Eo. The image of her daughter's face in her mind's eye resembled a beacon of brightness and hope in the omnipresent gloom of her homecoming. Of course she would not be able to speak of the slander of Alexander and the slurs, although she had fought one against two in defence of his good name. But Fay would understand as she was understood – Fay seemed to be the one person in the world, or at any rate in England, who was capable of understanding anything. Florrie urged Crisp to hurry, she could scarcely wait a moment longer to be with Fay and to encourage her to stick to her principles, to be more moral than fashion decreed, to be the opposite of Bobby and Roger, and to hang on and not to despair of true love on her terms.

She was too late – again too late – Fay had left St Eo.

In time, before long, Florrie even understood that Fay had not been able to bear the prospect of discussing Alexander's silence.

In the Web

According to Mildred, Fay had felt and had said that she ought not to be waiting for Alexander, Alexander ought to be waiting for her.

Florrie, regrets notwithstanding, was amused as well as impressed by the strength of her daughter's ideas on the subject of courtship, and by her readiness to translate them into action.

Apparently Fay had rebelled against hanging around, kicking her heels, twiddling her thumbs and hoping to hear from Orezania, and had taken off in her Mini without saying where she was going or for how long, but leaving these messages for her mother: sorry and all that, nothing to worry about, she would ring up, and if Alexander should telephone please ask how his call could be returned.

Florrie's welcome by dear Wilson and Mrs Wilson, by Mrs Withgill in the kitchen and Jean in the housekeeper's room, by Angus Macrae who had come across from the Estate Office and by Ben Simmonds in the greenhouses, and in due course by her daily ladies and likely lads, and by the people who helped to open the house and grounds of St Eo to the public – their warm words and smiles were some compensation for Fay's absence. But, like the other pleasures of her homecoming, the compensation was double-edged. She was reminded of T.D.'s warning that the price of her tithe for Orezania could spell the sack for her employees. She had not believed him. She would rather die than do it.

She would never sell St Eo and throw Crisp and Wilson and the rest of her loyal devoted friends to the wolves, unless she went completely bust. She would have to lower her sights and reduce

[250]

the scale of her charitable contribution, and discuss it further with Fay before forcing the issue.

She opened her mail. Two letters were almost laughably awful. Sylvester Kexmoor wrote: 'I cannot thank you for luring me into the Orezanian hell-hole. Probably my best work ever was stolen there and sacrificed to the all-powerful god of vandalism, and I am bereft of my talent and my art. You too are sick at heart, Florence. You have poisoned your life with lucre and loneliness. You should be baking a man's bread by day and lying with him at night. Spend your declining years in my houseboat! Get rid of baubles such as St Eo and Buckingham Square, and bring me the bare essential Florence of time gone by! I am still potent, and would initiate you into the mysteries of joy through sex and toil. I haven't sold a picture for six months, and could do with your dowry.'

Eric Hinxton was the writer of the other, actually more absurd than awful, letter. 'I'm ruined,' it ran. 'I have had to repay the money I received in advance for writing my Orezanian diary. And that busy bee Roger Ryther has buzzed off. Dear kind Florrie, I've been thinking, which is just about the last activity I'm capable of and can afford. You're rich, a widow, no spring chicken if I may say so, and rattle around in your great barracks of a house, while I'm poor, unmarried, an old friend, a known quantity, and wouldn't be wanting my marital rights, believe me! What about it? The alternative to the above seems to be a one-way ticket to Beachy Head for your possibly everloving.'

Florrie did no better with telephone calls than she had with letters. On the Friday evening she rushed to answer the first one and was depressed to hear a gravelly voice announce: 'Mona speaking – I've been trying to track you down for God knows how long.'

She had to cudgel her brains to remember that Mona Gristhorpe was the superannuated Bloomsbury groupie married to the ex-diplomat Harold, erstwhile ambassador to Turkey, who had come down to earth with a bump in a bungalow in the village.

'Oh hullo!' she replied.

'When can we cadge a drink? Harold wants to hear about Orezania.'

Florrie was ashamed of her feebleness in rewarding Mona's rudeness with an invitation to lunch on the Saturday.

Then Geoffrey rang, and her spirits were lowered a few more notches by his quavering vocal concern.

'I had a feeling when we met that you were unhappy, my dearest,' he began, 'and I've not been happy ever since.'

Was he consoling her or seeking consolation? She exercised restraint, summoned scarce resources of energy, and assured him that it was nothing, she was fine or soon would be.

'I hope you'd tell me if I could help you in any way.'

'Yes, yes,' she said and was unable to check an ironical laugh.

'What's the matter, Florrie dear? I know you had a nasty time in Orezania. But you seem to me so very changed.'

She excused herself by airing her maternal cares: Fay had disappeared and so on – and he was audibly satisfied to be recast in the role of her confidant and guide.

He wound up the conversation with the double-edged declaration: 'My dear, you've made me feel things are getting back to normal.'

Florrie shared a television supper with Mildred, during which they wondered whether to be glad or sad that they were not disturbed by a longer-distance telephone call; and the night passed and on the Saturday morning she opened the rest of her personal mail.

Her spinster friend from their school days Hester Knayton wrote at length about her life with her mother, who was over ninety, confined to bed, suffering from dementia, incontinent, and needed ruinously expensive nursing. However, Hester had arranged to have a break in London and would love to spend it at Buckingham Square with Florrie, whom she had neither seen nor heard from for an age.

Patricia Foxmore was another sad case. She wanted Florrie to stay with her and the schizophrenic son she looked after in Cheshire, and cheer them up. That social clown Fruity Murcot had sent her a seaside postcard bearing the message that he objected to being dropped like a red-hot brick. Jock Whissey asked her straight out for a loan, similar to the one he had never repaid, and Simon Cogdean pleaded for half an hour of her time in which to interest her in the new company he was now able to start, having been cleared of complicity in the swindles associated with his old one.

The pile of letters that called upon her to do something, visit, entertain, assist, save, finance or simply reply to the writers, mounted higher. Friends and acquaintances added their own appeals to communications from innumerable charities: 'Don't forget us ... Every little helps ... Be an angel ... You were so good last time round.' How had she coped with so many petitions and reproaches in the past, and in those distant days a few weeks ago before she had flown to Orezania for Fay's sake or for her own? She would have to live longer than she was feeling she would in order to respond to everyone and perhaps please a few. She had always counted the blessings of her husband's wealth, and loved to be a lady bountiful; but if she were poorer she would be freer, and undoubtedly less popular. She contemplated rebellious confessions to Fay and T.D. to the effect that she would not shed a tear should St Eo be put on the market and house-clearers called in.

The Gristhorpes did not enhance her life. Mona's old age was as grubby as had been the youth she claimed in print to have spent largely in the bedrooms of Bloomsbury. Her complexion and her clothing were equally stained, and her voice seemed to issue from a stony heart. Harold was one of those leaders of people who have no interest in persons. He proudly recalled the infinitesimal part he had played in political history as if rehearsing a speech in front of a mirror.

Each of them made a memorable suggestion in the course of their protracted visitation – suggestions that grated on the sensibilities of their hostess.

Mona said: 'We call St Eo "The Palace". What a shame it's empty such a lot! You could house most of the homeless here and not notice.'

Harold presented her with copies of snapshots he had taken in Orezania, and delivered himself of his opinions of the situation there without asking for or paying any attention to hers.

'This boy-king's a nine days wonder. He'll be put in his place by the professional politicians, he'll be brushed aside or assassinated, and I fear that the people who believed in him will have to pay for their gullibility. My money's on General Zaporag to rise to the top. They say he's fled the country because he may be charged with war crimes. But he's an old Bolshevik, he'd strangle his mother for power. He'll be back, and liquidate the opposition and unify the country by force.'

After the Gristhorpes had gone, Florrie burned Harold's snapshots: two of them upset her, the one of the Orezu Palace, and the other of Kraga, where she had won and lost the battle of her relationship with Michael.

Later she was able to deal with – by laughing off – Sylvester and Eric's proposals.

To the first she wrote: 'Thank you for the offer to let me bake your bread and lie with you at night. It is characteristically subtle and sensitive. But alas, I don't fancy your houseboat, I detest the east winds of Norfolk, and then there's your potency – I must tell you I'm completely frigid and could neither respond to nor permit the exchanges you have in mind. Seriously, nothing doing, but here's a cheque which I hope will be some consolation for Orezania and for the unsporting attitude of your old friend.'

'Dear Eric,' her second letter ran, 'I'm flattered to think you'd like me to be your missis, thank you very much. Unfortunately you've spoilt our chances of living together happily ever after by your cavalier attitude to marital rights. I would expect my husband to do his duty promptly and regularly. Sorry! No, I won't tease you any more, and I'm truly sorry that Orezania was bad for you and you're so hard up. I enclose a cheque – no acknowledgment required.'

Each cheque was for ten thousand pounds. She drew them with stubborn relish, quite looking forward to T.D.'s next objection to her Orezanian expenses and to being able to say she had blown a further twenty thou.

She had no social engagements on Sunday and Monday. She had made none on purpose because of the potential needs of Fay, and because she could not face a resumption of her former futile activities. But the weekend was the last on which St Eo was open to the public, and, as in all the other years, far from restful. She was at the beck and call of Angus Macrae, and obliged to mingle with the public and bid grateful goodbyes to the part-time staff who guarded her property and knew its history better than she did, and operated the tea and gift shops.

On Sunday evening Philip Mozergh rang her. He had been

staying in T.D.'s villa in Sunningdale and had heard tell of the state of her finances and her charitable plan. He said he would have to give her a good talking-to, and invited her to dine on the Tuesday.

She had to refuse.

'I've agreed to go to a ball with Roger Ryther. I don't know the hostess – her name's Cheryl Wright.'

Philip was not pleased, and lectured her about demeaning herself.

She interrupted with the involuntary sharpness of desperation.

'Please stop it! I tried my hardest to wriggle out, but Roger blackmailed me by saying his career was at stake. Ever since I got home I've been bullied, blackmailed, threatened, warned, and I must have had three hundred letters begging me to do things I don't want to do. Fay's gone missing again, and I long for a holiday to get over my holiday.'

Her outburst was counterproductive. Instead of liberating her from the proprietary grip of Philip, it tightened the same by her having to promise that she would seek his advice in every context in future.

When he finally suggested that something else must have happened to her in Orezania apart from nearly getting killed and made to skivvy in a hospital and so on, and asked what it was, she was embarrassed to have to resort to the age-old juvenile lie: 'Nothing.'

Throughout Monday her feelings of futility gained ground. She seemed to be in limbo, waiting, always waiting for Fay, for Alexander, for their future to be decided and for fate to decide her own. She could no longer see the point of St Eo and the ceaseless struggle to keep it up and running. She was contrarily glad to get away on the Tuesday morning.

Crisp drove her to Buckingham Square, to her hairdresser, her dressmaker, various shops, and in the evening, via Roger's basement flat in Battersea, to Kensington Palace Gardens – they were invited for dinner as well as dancing.

The steps leading up to the high, wide and brightly lit doorway of the Wright residence had been tented, and a pair of almost naked men with oiled bodies and bearing flaming torches stood statuesquely on either side of the entrance – luckily it was a dry warm night. The doors of the Jaguar were opened by representatives of a small army of liveried commissionaires. The floodlighting of the facade of the dignified mansion was luridly coloured, and balloons and silver hearts filled the embrasures of every window.

Florrie, who was wearing her dress with a bodice embroidered with pearls and rhinestones and a long full pink tulle skirt, and Roger, who was not in white tie and tails but in a variation of the dinner jacket theme he had himself designed – it buttoned to the neck military style and had pockets in unexpected places with black satin lapels – mounted the red-carpeted steps between uniformed and hard-eyed security staff armed with mobile phones. The front hall teemed with guests, cloakroom attendants, and butlers, footmen and maids bearing trays of glasses of refreshment, alcoholic and otherwise; and banks of flowers made it look and smell like a florist's shop. Florrie's shot-silk stole in shades of mauve was exchanged for a cloakroom ticket, she accepted a glass of champagne as if in self-defence, then Roger handed his invitation card to one of several large men in red coats who bellowed 'Lady Meavy and Mr Roger Ryther', while a seedy newspaper reporter in a crumpled suit scribbled their names on his clipboard.

They entered an inner hall with staircase and open doors leading into reception rooms and the marquee beyond in the garden. It was already crowded and noisy, and music thumped savagely in the background.

The hostess was over in the distance, progressing slowly in the centre of a posse of older women who were bending to talk to her, introducing some people and pushing others aside, behaving in the manner of agents or public relations consultants. Cheryl Wright was thirtyish, blonde, slight, and had slanting eyebrows like French accents that made her look miserable despite her fixed smile. Her presentation of herself was disastrous: her hair was overdressed, her make-up garish, her jewellery ostentatious, and her gown the work of some fashionable rag-trader's diseased imagination – it had enormously puffed-out upper arm sleeves of yellow satin, a low-cut top of the same material ruched, a bare midriff and a see-through skirt of blue lace.

When she was within range, Roger kissed her and Florrie shook her limp little hand.

Despite Cheryl's reputed eagerness to meet the latter, her contra-

[256]

dictory expression denoting minor pleasure and major pain did not change, until Roger issued a reminder in an undertone, whereupon she smiled more naturally, and attentively and appealingly, and exclaimed: 'Oh Lady Meavy! Forgive me, I'm so sorry – I've met so many people tonight – I'm really not myself.'

Florrie murmured words of sympathy.

Cheryl continued even more apologetically: 'This party isn't what I meant it to be. I feel such a guy – I'm sorry I invited you – would you ever meet me again for lunch or something?'

But Cheryl's impatient attendants moved her on, and she looked back at Florrie almost despairingly.

Roger had explanations to offer. Those women surrounding Cheryl were parasites, he informed Florrie, disregarding the fact that he might be accused of throwing stones from within a glass house. They were the organiser of the ball, the person in charge of the guest list, the flower arranger whose bill would be not far short of six figures, a manager of the company that was doing the catering, and so-called experts in cosmetics and hair-styling. He said Cheryl had been besieged since her husband's death by every 'snake oil' sales person in London, and pointed out the man responsible for her dress – he wore a golden caftan and heavy black hornrims, and had a pigtail reaching to his waist.

The company now seemed to be composed entirely of freaks and deviants. Roger introduced her to some of them, peculiar men in couples whom he knew, a smart female with a deep voice and five o'clock shadow, an oafish pop idol in his twenties who was worth a hundred million, a dirty girl with noticeably unwashed braids. Complexions, generally speaking, fell into one of four categories: gaudily painted, ghostly white, cancerously suntanned and naturally black. Hair was less a crowning glory than an intersexual fashion note: if African it was trained to look Caucasian, and vice versa, or completely shorn by razor, or dyed green or blue or orange or striped, or frizzed or straightened or cut with the aid of a pudding basin.

Conversation was kept to a minimum, partly because of the increasing volume of the music. Roger's friends said to Florrie: 'Hi! Great party,' and left it at that. Her own efforts to talk were fairly feeble, she acknowledged, but she wished they were not received with vacant smiles. Speech itself, let alone volubility, was evidently

[257]

the exception to some rule; anybody who went in for it attracted a curious audience, and was supposed by Roger to be drugged or drunk.

At last, when Florrie felt she could neither stand it nor stand for a moment longer, dinner was announced and everyone surged, strolled, jostled and dawdled into the marquee. It was a huge pink floral bower lit by chandeliers, and tables for ten reached into the middle distance. The band of youths in rags played on a dais at the far end and the noise was stunning; and as people milled about, looking for their allotted seats, Florrie recognised acquaintances who surely would and perhaps should have considered themselves above this vulgar jamboree.

There were the Irelands, and the Adburnhams of stately Adburnham Towers. And what on earth was old Cissie Waterlow doing here – a dowager marchioness noted for her standoffishness mingling with such a motley crew? Even Brandon Kanchester, notwithstanding his ill-bred tendency to lay down the law in respect of upper class etiquette, was present.

They were moths fluttering round the candle of money, she thought. No, she contradicted herself, they did not deserve to be compared to innocent moths, they were more like vampires. They were preying upon Cheryl just as she – Florrie – was preyed upon.

But she too was partaking of Cheryl's hospitality. She had a charitable reason for doing so, to lend Roger a hand; but the Irelands and the rest of them might be doing someone else a favour. Her life, everybody's life, was a web from which extrication was seldom possible. Yes, she thought, they were all caught in a web of duty, obligation, auld lang syne, outdated friendship, faded love, and hopes deferred or disappointed.

Roger guided her to their table and sat next to her. They were too close to the band and the dance floor, on which two men were dancing together in a lubricious manner and a girl was holding her partner by his buttocks. Her other neighbour was a youth with oily flat black hair and a dead white face who lisped at her smuttily: 'Wait for the cabaret!' A large plate of caviare and smoked salmon was placed before her.

The smell of flowers and fish, the excess of everything, the waste, noise, heat and unsympathetic company combined with her pessimistic reflections to sicken her. She had never fainted, but was

[258]

overcome with the certainty that if she stayed where she was she would faint at best, and at worst be ill. She had to go, it was imperative, she exercised enough self-control to shout into Roger's ear: 'I'm not well, don't move!' – and pushed back her chair and hurried out. Nobody stopped her or seemed to notice – diners were still taking their places, and waiters were preoccupied.

Roger disobeyed orders and caught her up, wrung his hands over her, found her a chair to sit on in the front hall, spoke to Crisp on the telephone and would have waited for him to arrive if she had not sworn she was better, and only needed solitude and silence, to be left alone and not made to feel she had ruined his evening.

The front hall was empty. Roger had fetched her mauve stole from the cloakroom, and she sat on a gilt chair in her bejewelled gown with its full pink skirt. And as her nausea began to subside she appreciated the symbolism of her situation, for she was by herself and alternately half-stifled by the perfumes of society women and cut flowers and refreshed by the relatively pure nocturnal air wafting through the open doorway.

By a small stretch of her imagination she was poised between her past and the darkness and mystery of her future.

Thirty for Lunch

Florrie wondered if the iron of her constitution was rusting, and if she might have something seriously wrong with her. She was not afraid, illness would solve some of her problems. But time confirmed her initial belief that her fainting fit was more moral than physical, a sickness of the soul contracted in Orezania and incubated in the atmosphere of her social connections. And although it had been quite dramatic, it actually changed nothing.

She would have to make amends to Roger Ryther and Cheryl Wright: good manners, which are apt to be the death of nice people, insisted that she should do so. She still had Geoffrey and Philip as it were on her hands, and T.D. grumbling at her, and Mildred and her employees depending, and hundreds of more or less fair weather friends queuing up to entertain her and be entertained, and innumerable charities counting on her donations, and above all a beloved daughter, a wonderful exceptional most beloved daughter, who was hiding her head and her bruised heart because the man she loved was otherwise engaged.

Moreover, or unfortunately, she had the wherewithal and the time and usually the energy to supply most social demands – it would be simply mean of her not to do so since she could; while in the case of Fay, the paradox was that her powerlessness nagged at her in the same sort of way as did her power in the social context.

She returned to St Eo. The blessing disguised by her temporary indisposition gave her an excuse. She rang everyone to whom she owed telephone calls, or who would otherwise ring her and complain that she was worrying, neglecting, eluding and not loving them, and explained that she was not unwell, but a little tired maybe, and was going to the country to be quiet for a few days.

Mildred's concern took the form of a renewed plea to be permitted to track Fay down. But Florrie would not countenance it: Fay was not to be blackmailed into hurrying home with stories of her mother's swoon in Millionaires' Row.

From midday Wednesday until midday Friday Florrie was 'quieter' than she could remember being. She even ate a succession of meals alone, because Mildred was either feeding Aubrey Millard-Jones or attending his church services. Yet as she gained a respite from some stresses and strains, so others were sucked into the vacuum. She not only relived her visit to Orezania, she distilled from it two new causes of distress.

Both related to Michael. She had fallen into the trap set for sensitive refined women in particular, she had loved a man she did not like or respect: those were the facts of the matter. Generalisations partially justified: for instance that women are not imbued by nature with much sense of self-preservation and can therefore mate with men who have no redeeming features apart from their virility. But in loving Michael in spite of his cruelty, drunkenness, lack of culture, lack of all the qualities she had always held dear and especially valued in her husband, Florrie had lost faith in her judgment. To put it in a practical way more or less as Philip had done, she was no longer sure she could manage her life on her own.

The other distressing novelty to intrude into her recollections was the question of proof of Michael's demise. She had never seen his corpse – the news or the opinion was conveyed by her Orezanian soldier-boy by means of a thumb pointing earthwards. Bobby Ireby and John Wilberforce thought he was dead: why? Who had told them? She had accepted, she had wished, that he would trouble her no more; but for all she knew for certain he might materialise and do unthinkable damage to herself, Fay, Alexander, Orezania.

The members of her staff, their devotion notwithstanding, did not ameliorate her pangs of dread and panic. Moreover Mildred might marry and abandon her. The ring of the telephone sounded like a knell, and the telephone messages Wilson recorded were never the right ones. In the course of Thursday night she convinced herself that she was in for at least a nervous breakdown, and wondered if she should give Fay the right to sign cheques and legal documents on her behalf. She would have to consult a specialist in nervous diseases, or seek assistance from some crazed psychiatrist.

On Friday she took action that was more in her character, she picked a lot of flowers and arranged them in the chapel and remained there for an hour to pray for guidance. Perhaps she received it: she thought of inviting everybody who weighed on her social conscience down to St Eo on the Sunday. The idea became a project within minutes; Mildred encouraged her; Wilson and Mrs Withgill were not against it; a luncheon menu was agreed; and extra pairs of hands, guests and their transport, and who would want to stay for the Sunday night, were amongst the subjects discussed.

Florrie spent hours on the telephone as if to make up for the time she had refused to speak on it. At length she accumulated twenty-nine acceptances of her invitations, and on Saturday she supervised the opening up of the Great Dining-room with Wilson, the addition of lengthening leaves to the table, the placing of the silver centre-pieces upon it, and chose wines, napery, china, silver and glass. She also worked with Mrs Withgill and her team in the kitchen and with Jean in the house, and cut many more flowers with the assistance of Ben Simmonds.

On Sunday morning, just before any guests had arrived, she regretted the whole exercise and fought against the wish that she was dead.

They streamed in, and she smiled and welcomed them and submitted to kisses and hugs and queries about her health. She was grateful for civility, but had to confirm the truth of the truism that in society rudeness cuts more ice. Mona Gristhorpe greeted her grittily thus: 'Two invites in a week to St Eo, what's the world coming to?'

Fruity Murcot said to her: 'Don't lose any more weight, darling – eat up for your neck's sake!' T.D. scolded her for more extravagance; Brenda Slawston suggested that the money spent on the party would have bought hundreds of hypodermics for drug addicts; Milly Brighton had a similarly charitable notion, that Florrie might like to invest in condoms for rent-boys in Uganda, where she – Milly – would be happy to distribute them. Bobby Ireby, instead of thanking her for inviting him or explaining why he had chucked on behalf of his wife at the last minute, said: 'I've driven a hell of a long way – let's have a spot more cooperation than was forthcoming the other evening.' Eric Hinxton denied that he could possibly keep the ten thousand pounds, and left it at that. Sylvester omitted to acknowledge his receipt of the ten thousand until she asked him if her letter and cheque had arrived.

Adam Crabhouse did not seem to be his usual smug self: was it because he was with his better half? But with characteristic altruism he succeeded in sharing his vexation with his hostess.

He said hullo and then: 'I've heard from our friend Slutzk. He's where the drugs come from, and he's threatening all of us with blue murder if we breathe a word about his labours of love in Orezania.'

As soon as she could she inquired or instructed him: 'You won't, will you?'

He looked cross and cowardly and replied: 'No fear! I can be discreet if I have to – and my contract doesn't undertake to raise me from the dead.'

'Tell Sylvester and Eric, please! Warn them not to do anything foolish!'

He shrugged his shoulders by way of a grudging affirmative and commented acerbically: 'I'd have thought they were unlikely heroes.'

At long last, by Florrie's reckoning, the company was complete and, when pre-prandial alcohol had turned up the volume of voices to an almost deafening degree, Wilson signalled that luncheon was served and she shooed everyone into the Great Dining-room.

The table laid for thirty was a grand sight, and exclamations of admiration accompanied the search for designated seats. Florrie had Geoffrey Oldcoate on her right. Mildred and Aubrey Millard-Jones were next; then came Anna Hulcott, who would offend no one, let alone a parson, Jock Whissey, whose unmannerly short-comings Anna would forgive, and Helen Islebeck and Fruity Murcot, who would be able to practise their seductive wiles on each other. Cheryl Wright was strategically placed between Fruity, who would fancy her youth and her fortune, and T.D. Faulkbourne,

[263]

who was certain to urge her to waste not and want not. Wilma Windsor, a socialist like her husband, could discuss their millions with T.D. and derive further satisfaction from a belted earl on her other side, the Earl of Culkerton, Boy Culkerton, father of the aspiring prima donna. The two battleaxes Brenda Slawston and Milly Brighton would come to no harm in the hands – metaphorically speaking – of Eric Hinxton and Roger Ryther; and the Dragon Pursuivant, Guy Shokerbrooke, could be dim with Melanie Crabhouse, while Adam deserved Jane Shokerbrooke. Bobby Ireby would have to make the best of a bad job between Jane and Mona Gristhorpe, and Solly Windsor could gossip with Agatha Grizebeck in Hungarian or Hebrew. Harold Gristhorpe, whose neighbour was Isobel Culkerton, never minded whom he was talking and not listening to. Philip Mozergh was on Florrie's left, and he and Sylvester would be pleased to have Jenny Bowditch and Sue Cartwright in a sense and partially, although the girls might beg to differ.

They all sat down except for Philip, who remained on his feet, tapped a wine glass with a knife, secured silence and launched into the following speech.

'May I just say how happy we are to be here?' He was seconded and applauded. 'As most of you are aware, Florrie has recently been in Orezania, defeating three armies and putting an end to a civil war. It's no laughing matter – she seems to have had a ghastly time, but according to custom she came out on top. Well, we congratulate her and are curious to know how and why she did it. Please, dear Florrie, let us into the secret of your Orezanian travels, tell us the true traveller's tale! Meanwhile, thank you for what we are about to receive and for showing us you're still and always will be the queen of our revels.'

She was not pleased. She registered Philip's coded message that he was angry with her for not taking his telephone calls, for never marrying him, for having undergone some sort of change in Orezania, for possibly preferring another man.

But Philip had not only hit out at her for his personal reasons, he also set a bad example. Bobby Ireby now shouted above the clapping: 'What's up, Florrie?' and Jock Whissey, who was called Jock Witty by his clubbable cronies, pointed at Adam Crabhouse and called out: 'Speak from the heart, old girl, your secret's certain

[264]

to be safe with a journalist!' Other voices chimed in: 'Come on, Florrie ... Take no notice, Florrie ... You'll spoil our lunch ... Spill the beans, do!'

It could not continue. People were beginning to argue, and she was too desperate to care.

'All right,' she cried, silencing the hubbub; 'since you ask, which you shouldn't, the truth is I fell in love in Orezania.'

Geoffrey Oldcoate, at her side, caught his breath oddly, and Mildred whispered an involuntary protest: 'Oh Florrie!'

She was not to be stopped, it was too late now to stop.

'He had the most wonderful eyes, and the nicest nature I've ever come across, and I loved him to distraction, yes! But don't worry, he was a victim of the war, we only had a few days and nights together.'

Sounds of sympathy and embarrassment greeted her confession.

'Yes,' she insisted, 'he was called Russ, and he had a lovely silky coat and four legs.'

Seconds elapsed before laughter, at once ribald and uneasy, came to the rescue.

Florrie managed to join in, and to say in a more natural voice:

'There – now – let's have lunch!'

Geoffrey poured words of comfort into one of her ears, and Philip hissed into the other, 'Game, set and match to you, my dear,' and grumpily turned his back on her to flirt with Jenny.

She could not concentrate on Geoffrey's small talk, and toyed with her first course, sipped more wine than she liked to drink, tried repeatedly to swallow the lump in her throat and resist her urge to run away. Her party was a success, although she had never before been so conscious of failure: her guests stuffed themselves with food and were chattering like a flock of starlings.

How long will I have to put up with it, she asked herself rhetorically.

The second course was handed round, and, as if in answer to her question, Wilson approached and informed her in an undertone that she was wanted on the telephone.

She escaped through the door behind her: Geoffrey said he would deal with queries about her absence.

Her relief was short-lived: she jumped to the conclusion that Fay was in trouble. But Wilson had followed her, and out in the passage was quick to give her the name of the caller: 'I was instructed to tell you it was Alexander, milady.'

She ran along to her small sitting-room and waited for Wilson to put her through.

'Hullo!' she said with a catch in her voice.

'Good afternoon, Lady Meavy. I hope this is not an inconvenient moment to speak to you?'

'No, not at all – on the contrary.'

'I arrived at my hotel in London ten minutes ago.'

'Oh? Are you . . . How are you? How are things in your country?'

'Thank you, I am well, and conditions in Orezania are beginning to improve. You are also well, I hope – and I would very much like to know how Fay is.'

'She's not here. I haven't seen or talked to her for some days. To the best of my knowledge she's fine. There was no word from Orezania, you see.'

'I was not free to communicate, alas. My work was nearly unceasing. Only today did I feel free to travel abroad, and to telephone you.'

'I'm afraid I can't give you Fay's telephone number – I have no number to give you.'

'But I wish to speak to you yourself.'

'To me? Really?'

'I must talk to you before speaking to Fay. I have the highest regard for your daughter, and I love her too much ever to hurt her, Lady Meavy.'

'That's wonderful, isn't it? I mean I can't speak for Fay, but I admire your sentiments. I'm sorry, I don't know how to address you.'

'Alexander, please.'

'I wish you well, Alexander, I can say that.'

'Thank you. My time is limited, and I'm not sure you understand me. May I speak frankly and from my heart?'

'Yes – yes, of course.'

'I would like to ask Fay to marry me. I am twenty-three, three years older than Fay, I believe I am healthy and strong, and I know the world – I have been involved in political matters since I was ten. I am the only surviving member of my family, all my close relations were killed by the Bolsheviks. I was smuggled out of

[266]

Orezania as a baby, and brought up by distant and old cousins in England, who are now also dead. I met your Fay five months ago and loved her at first sight, and I have not changed my mind or my heart – I do not change my mind. Whatever happens, she will remain a vital part of my destiny. But my circumstances have never been favourable for love. To begin with I was too poor to propose marriage to a rich girl, and now I am a king – and to be the Queen of Orezania is not safe, my mother was murdered for wearing the crown. Forgive me for such a long speech.'

'I do forgive you.'

'I'm afraid I have more to say.'

'Please go on. I'm listening.'

'At present a majority of my people like me, but one day it might be different, I would refuse to rule them by force, and the best result in that eventuality would be exile, sad for me and bad for my family. And supposing my Queen and I were always liked, from the day we married until the day we died we would be the prisoners of our people, we would have very big public lives and very small private ones – and Fay is not used to it, not trained for it, and would be far from her friends in a foreign land and having to speak a strange language. You understand me, Lady Meavy?'

'I think so.'

'I could not ask Fay to marry me without the permission of her parent, and I cannot ask her parent for permission without stating all the facts.'

'Oh dear!'

'Please, I haven't finished. I did not wish to be King. For a lot of reasons I wish I wasn't a king. I could, and perhaps from some points of view I should, have stayed in England and learned to be a better waiter. My life would have been my own, and in certain circumstances I would have dared to ask Fay to share it. But the choice is made – and was made for me rather than by me. Although the accident of my birth might have been repaired or overcome, not so my feeling for my responsibilities. I could not shirk them, I was unable to forget the needs of the poor people I was in a position to help, and I must do what I can for them – my nature won't allow me to consider any alternative. You see my difficulty, Lady Meavy. If only I had more time I would have written or

[267]

visited you at your convenience, and not poured my heart into the telephone. As it is, I swear to you that if I could I would care for and take care of Fay while there is breath in my body, and that her welfare and wellbeing, if she were to consent to be my wife, would mean everything to me. Tell me what to do!'

'Go ahead and ask her, find her and ask her, Alexander. She's wise beyond her years and she has imagination, she'll have considered her future as seriously as you have – her answer will mean much more than mine. But my blessing is yours.'

'Thank you so much – thank you, thank you.'

'I'm sorry not to know where she is.'

'I think and hope I do.'

'Well, I'll leave that to you. Goodbye, Alexander.'

He said something she did not catch, and replied to her inquiry: 'In Orezanian it means happiness is possible – we say it instead of goodbye.'

They rang off, and she returned to the Great Dining-Room.

Her guests cheered at the sight of her, and she felt herself smiling back at them unrestrainedly.

'Was it good or bad news?' Geoffrey wanted to know.

'We'll have to wait and see,' she said, and patted him and added, 'darling Geoffrey.'

She was not in the mood to eat and began to walk round the table, talking to people.

Philip Mozergh caught her by the wrist and appealed: 'Pardon my impertinence,' and she replied: 'It was nothing,' and planted a sisterly kiss on his blotched forehead.

Everyone seemed to be nicer and dearer to her than they had a short while ago.

She reached T.D., who indicated the pretty young woman on his right and rumbled: 'You have a new admirer, Florrie.'

The stranger stood up, and Florrie recognised Cheryl Wright. She wore a well-cut tweed coat and skirt and no jewellery, and her eyebrows were apologetic and her smile tentative.

'Please don't disturb yourself,' Florrie said. 'Please sit down.'

But Cheryl remained standing with a napkin in her hand and said: 'Thank you for inviting me. I've been so ashamed that you came to my party. A hundred and one things went wrong on that night. And this lunch of yours is so elegant, and you have proper friends, and your house is perfect – what can you have thought of mine?'

Florrie laughed at these compliments, hesitated, then exchanged a smile with Cheryl and was inspired by the improvement in her outlook to say: 'Come and see me one day.'

Sunshine and Showers

At six-thirty that evening, a couple of hours after the last luncheon
guest had left, the telephone rang in Florrie's sitting-room.

She was alone there, waiting, and she picked up the instrument.

'Ma,' Fay began and burst into tears.

Florrie also cried, and neither of them was able to speak for a
moment.

Then Florrie said: 'I was waiting for you to ring, and praying no
one else would.'

Fay's inconsequential response was: 'I've been with him all
afternoon.'

'What happened? You're not sad, are you?'

'No,' Fay replied and shed more tears.

Florrie laughed at her, they laughed together, and eyes were
dried and the conversation proceeded without too many
interruptions.

'My darling, tell me now.'

'I can hardly bring myself to say it, Ma, I can't believe I could be
saying it.'

'Oh my precious darling!'

'Stop, Ma – don't congratulate me – if you're too sweet to me I'll
collapse completely!'

'He spoke to me first, you know.'

'Yes – he's as old-fashioned as I am, thank goodness.'

'Did he give you all the reasons for not marrying him that he
gave me?'

'Yes – and I gave him my reasons, too.'

'What? What reasons? I'm getting nervous.'

'Ma, please – please listen! I cried just now partly because I haven't been nice to you. No, I haven't ever since I met Alexander. I've hidden from you as if I didn't love you any more, but actually I hid because I do, and because everything was such a strain, an awful happy strain, that I had to be alone to bear it, concentrate on it, and not share it with you and let go and shriek with joy and scream with horror and be a pest. He couldn't help making me love him, but then he nearly drove me mad by holding back.'

They laughed, and she continued: 'I knew he loved me from the beginning – you always do, don't you? But there were obstacles on his side and on mine – he thought it wouldn't be fair to marry me, and I thought I'd never get over him alive or dead. But none of that matters any more – he's won back his kingdom, and I'd rather live for the day. The only trouble is he's returning to Orez tomorrow and expects me to go with him.'

'For how long?'

'For as long as it takes to be introduced to his people, and start to learn the language, and help to organise the wedding, and see more of the island. And after we were married I'd be stuck there for the rest of my life, or until we were shot or kicked out, and I'd be hundreds of miles away from you, and my children wouldn't know you properly.'

'We'd be together sometimes though. I have no ties and could be in Orezania when needed, and surely you could bring the children to stay with me.'

'Maybe – but I feel I've wasted these last months by not spending time with you, and I'm hating the prospect of separation for ever or almost.'

'My darling girl, I'm touched by your sentiments, but you couldn't and can't build your life round mine, and you've done nothing to me to be sorry for, and all my hopes are that you should be happy – I mean, although the feminists would tear me limb from limb for saying so, be happy by throwing in your lot with the man you love.'

'Are you telling me to say yes to Alexander?'

'What? Haven't you said yes already?'

'I wanted to talk to you first.'

'Oh Fay! Putting me first won't do for either of us in the long run or even the short run. I'm not being unselfish. To know you'd

[271]

followed your star is my ultimate ambition. What's the matter, darling?'

'Thank you for making it easy for me.'

'Shouldn't you hurry to put Alexander out of his agony?'

'He's all right – he wanted me to tell you that happiness was possible – don't go away, Ma!'

'Well, it might interest you to know that I've had to bite my tongue to stop myself saying, "For goodness sake, marry the man!" Believe it or not, I really am a trifle steadier than Mrs Bennet deep down. Whatever the modern anti-romantic promiscuous brigade may shout from the rooftops, you have to marry the person you love, if possible; not to is a denial of love. And we're not the only monogamists – monogamy hasn't been an ideal of civilisation for nothing. We all have to be careful who we fall in love with, because we can leave or be left by him or her, or he or she can die, but that love's part of us and inescapable. Anyway, that's my philosophy and experience, and that's why you have to marry your Alexander and exchange vows to be faithful unto death. Fashionable notions may simplify sex, but they complicate love by pretending it doesn't exist. By the way, Alexander's perfect, good King Alexander, noble and worthy of you.'

Fay was practical: 'Can I bring him to St Eo tomorrow? We could spend the middle of the day with you, and I could pack before our flight in the evening.'

It was agreed, and Florrie also turned her attention to practicalities.

'Where will you be staying in Orezania?' she asked.

'In Orez, with Alexander's friends, a family living in a house near the palace – they'll help me with the language and chaperone me.'

'I'm so glad to hear chaperones aren't extinct after all.' Fay giggled and Florrie continued: 'Oh well – were you staying with Jenny and Sue in London?'

'Of course,' Fay giggled again.

'They didn't tell me and I didn't ask when they were here today – perhaps my discretion proves I've changed for the better.'

'You never change, you don't need to, Ma.'

'Oh dear!' Florrie said, and left it at that. 'Do you dread your new life, darling?'

[272]

'Only a little – I'm too excited – besides, I'm Father's daughter – and the Orezanians I came across were wonderful people.'

'What about your wedding dress?' Florrie inquired, and the rest of their conversation was devoted to equally pressing questions such as where the dress would be made and who would make it, the announcement of the engagement in newspapers, the list of wedding guests, and possible honeymoon destinations.

Florrie got through that Sunday evening with the help of Mildred and no further telephone calls; and the night and the next morning passed. Fay arrived with Alexander in her Mini on the dot of midday, as arranged. Alexander kissed Florrie firmly and warmly and was introduced to the assembled staff. The scene in the front hall might have belonged to a bygone age. Miss Fay's young man, notwithstanding the fact that he was said to be the monarch of some foreign island, removed the suspicions of Jean Watson, the Wilsons, Crisps, Withgills and Ben Simmondses, by means of his fair complexion, perfect English, sincere interest in each and every one of them and winning smiles, and because he was responsible for the brighter eyes and glowing cheeks of the girl they had loved since she was a baby.

Mildred and the Macraes looked in before lunch and were duly charmed. Alexander thanked Mildred for the merciful services she had rendered his people in the hospital in the Orezanian hills, and for having been a dear cousin and friend to Fay. With Angus Macrae he discussed the possibility of introducing the hardy Scottish breeds of cattle into the highlands of his country, and he listened patiently to Winifred Macrae's account of her package tour of Turkey, which she referred to as his 'neck of the woods'.

Mother, daughter and prospective son-in-law were by themselves from then on. They had so much to say to one another, and so many decisions to take, that they tried to be businesslike and not distracted by emotion; but everything they said seemed to have an emotional content. For instance, the wording of the announcement that Florrie was to put in the papers brought home to her the virtual and imminent loss of her irreplaceable daughter. Again, Alexander's reasonable ruling that the wedding and coronation would have to be united in a single ceremony, and that his wife's dress must be made in the country of which she was becoming the Queen, meant that Fay would be short of excuses to fly over for visits to St Eo and Buckingham Square.

Florrie spoke of the money that she and Fay were determined to give to hospitals or medical causes in Orezania.

Alexander's response was at once grateful and rueful.

'Thank you – and forgive me for wishing I was King of a country that wasn't so impoverished. But yesterday and today have persuaded me that I have luck to spare and to share with Orezania.'

Florrie inquired: 'What do you think we should do about St Eo? Hasn't the time come to be sensible? I can't live quite alone in such a big house and I'm fed up with entertaining, the costs of maintenance don't bear thinking about, I'd love to call it a day and retire to a desert island, and surely you two aren't going to want to run an English establishment by remote control.'

Fay interrupted here to scold Florrie tearfully for her premature notions: 'You're not to talk of retirement, Ma – I won't listen to it!' She issued strict instructions: 'Furthermore, if any island figures in your plans it's going to be Orezania.' She then addressed the problem: 'I'd hate to sell the house unless we were forced to – it holds our family history, and our memories would belong to strangers. And what would become of our darling old retainers, and what would Father say? Alexander and I have a different solution to put forward, if you wouldn't mind.'

In due course Alexander spoke tentatively. 'My country will need a base in Europe for the organisation of trade, and we wondered if you would like to discuss with your advisers the possibility of permitting us to use part of St Eo for that purpose. In addition,' he continued, since Florrie raised no objections, 'I feel I have to say for the sake of my future wife and perhaps our descendants that one day they may require a roof over their heads.'

Fay weighed in: 'Alexander means exile, Ma. He wouldn't ever submit to it, I'm well aware that he'd rather be dead, and I wouldn't leave Orezania without him, but I know I'd stop at nothing to get my children out – and meanwhile I'd be so happy to know that you were keeping another home warm for them, for your grandchildren, just in case.'

Florrie said yes to everything, and they finished lunch. Fay rushed off to pack, and Alexander accepted the offer of a tour of the reception rooms. At one point Florrie asked him to use the popular version of her Christian name, which prompted him to tell her that he planned to change the name of his capital city, because Orez in reverse spelt zero. He would also change his family names that had the same negative meanings, Nix in particular, and rechristen his kingdom if he could.

In the chapel he crossed himself and genuflected deeply, and as they emerged he thanked Florrie for Fay and explained: 'My life was always sad and solemn before I met her. The truth was I had nothing much to laugh at. But your daughter is giving me back my youth as well as herself.'

When Fay reappeared she insisted on a short walk out of doors, and linked arms with her mother and her betrothed. They strolled on the springy lawns under the great cedar trees, and in the kitchen garden she showed Alexander where she had kept her rabbit Nibbles and in an outhouse the sledge that her father had pushed across Antarctica.

At four-thirty Crisp brought the Jaguar to the front door – he had already removed the Mini. It had been decided that Florrie would drive up to town with the others. Alexander took the front passenger seat, allowing mother and daughter to sit together in the back. Every so often during the journey, as they remembered things they had forgotten to say, Fay rested her head on the shoulder of Florrie, who stroked her hair and cheek.

The stop at Buckingham Square was brief. Alexander, introduced to Maria and Barney, was curtsied and bowed to in return for his graceful condescension. Then Fay hugged her mother terribly tight, saying in a thick voice, 'See you soon – don't worry – thank you again!' Florrie kissed Alexander, and the young people climbed quickly into the back seat. Hands waved through the windows of the car as it turned the corner and its red rear lights receded into the darkness.

An hour and a bit later, at seven-thirty-ish, Philip Mozergh telephoned.

He had spoken to Wilson at St Eo, understood that Fay was engaged to marry King Alexander, deduced that Florrie would have said goodbye to the young pair, and doled out congratulations, good wishes, sympathy and comfort. She described the variety of her feelings at some length – she was accustomed to shifting her burdens on to his shoulders. Eventually she asked him how he had been getting on.

He replied that he had something to tell her, but that he would do so some other time.

'Oh?' She hoped he was not going to add to her worries by asking her to attend to one of his. 'What is it, Philip?'

'I'm sorry I made my speech before your luncheon party yesterday – and you were right to put me in my place,' he said.

'Is that all? That's forgiven and forgotten.'

'I know – you gave me a forgiving kiss after Alexander rang up – and it seemed to be a forgetful one.'

'What on earth do you mean?'

'I thought you were confirming my suspicions, whatever did or didn't happen to you in Orezania, and kissing me goodbye.'

'Nonsense!'

'My dear, this may not be the moment to say so – but there's never a better moment – I'm afraid we're both old enough to know that in affairs of the heart everybody behaves badly – I must tell you that I too am engaged to be married.'

'Philip!'

'Nobody could say I'm rushing headlong into matrimony. I've loved you, dear Florrie, not exclusively, I admit, I always have admitted, but more than I loved anyone else and for very much longer. I'm sorry that in my case hope didn't spring eternal – I was discouraged for the last time when you returned from Orezania. At your lunch at St Eo, rightly or wrongly I assumed that your kiss meant adieu. And I've explained my requirements to you, haven't I? There's been a girl around for a year or two who's been willing and able to supply them . . . Are you there?'

'Yes. It's my turn to congratulate you.'

'We'll be friends for ever – we'll see each other at social gatherings and the fact is you never regarded me as more than a friend – nothing has changed.'

'No.'

'You can reach me just as before, you can ring me or write to me at the office – I'll provide all assistance within my power.'

'No, Philip, I'll ring you at home in future.'

'As you wish.'

'How old is she?'

'Thirty-six.'

'Oh yes. And pretty?'

'People think so.'

'What's her name?'

'Ruth.'

'Surname?'

'Does that matter?'

'I'd like to write and congratulate her.'

'Her name's Ruth Caulfield. She's been my PA.'

'She sounds ideal. I'm so glad, Philip. I owe you every possible good wish. I wish you everything good from the bottom of my heart – I really do! But can we talk more some other time? I'm exhausted by emotions – and I don't mean bad emotions! Thanks for being my chief prop, thanks for the years you've lent me, thanks for the memory – good night, not goodbye.'

'Thank you, my darling!'

She had scarcely concluded this conversation, let alone adjusted to the news it conveyed, when the telephone rang again. She would have left it to Maria to answer, she dreaded a voluble acquaintance on the line, let alone a stranger; but once more, as she had when Philip's call came through, she thought Fay might be ringing from the airport and that something might be amiss.

It was Anna Hulcott. Florrie was relieved: Anna was so dependably gentle and supportive, so unobjectionable. In response to a typical stream of superlatives in respect of the lunch party and, when informed of it, Fay's engagement to a reigning monarch, she poured out an account of her most recent upsets, the anguish of parting with her only child and the defection of Philip.

How hard to bear, Anna commented, and what a surprise and shock – she completely understood why Florrie felt drained.

'But I shouldn't complain, you never do,' Florrie returned. 'I mustn't grumble, as they say, I couldn't even count my blessings – and now Fay's making a brilliant match and is brilliantly happy, and Philip's marriage is actually all for the best.'

'That may be true. Nevertheless, dearest, you're bound to feel bereft. There was a favour I was hoping to ask you, but I think I'd better leave you in peace. Please ring me if I can ever be of any assistance.'

'No, Anna, wait!' Florrie pulled herself together and asked: 'What is the favour?'

'Oh but I'm sure you'd prefer not to be bothered!'

'No – honestly – please!'

'Well, I'll try to be brief. Would you, could you, take my place as president of my pet charity for battered wives and women? It's called "Second Chance".'

'Oh Anna!'

'I know you're the patron of hundreds of charities, I know how charitable you are, and I wouldn't dream of blaming you for saying "no can do". I just thought it was worth asking from the point of view of my poor women, and because I would have been proud to hand over to you. Forgive me, Florrie!'

'I'll willingly give you money. But I've been intending to wriggle out of commitments.'

'A little money would be very helpful – and please forget the other business – I wouldn't have asked if I hadn't been in a hurry – and Geoffrey promised me you wouldn't be too bored.'

'I'm flattered and touched – you never bore anybody. But what's the hurry, Anna?'

'That's not important. Thank you for being so generous, Florrie.'

'You're not ill, are you?'

'I have to have an operation and treatment, but I'm in good hands and ought to be back in circulation before long. The thing is "Second Chance" needs a president it can rely on.'

'I've changed my mind. Of course I'll take over.'

'No, no, Florrie – don't do it out of pity, please!'

'And don't you argue with me. I've said my say – you have my answer. Now tell me what's wrong!'

'It seems to be curable. I imagined I was perfectly well in Orezania. But I'm making adjustments and acts of faith and so on. It's not worth worrying about. My life's been a waste of time – and I don't expect you to disagree, dearest. I probably shouldn't have married a Pole, I certainly shouldn't have married a Pole called Wenceslaus Wisniowieski. The aim of my charity – our charity – is to enable other women to escape from the sort of situation I manoeuvred myself into. There's my doorbell, Florrie – my son Stanley's arriving, which is the best medicine for me. Stanley's the living proof that good can come out of evil. I'll write to you.'

[278]

'And I'll ring up.'

Florrie replaced the receiver; went down to the dining-room when she was summoned by Barney; drank some of Maria's soup, and begged to be excused from eating the food Maria had cooked; said good night and remounted the stairs to her sitting-room and then to her bedroom; and sat down on the edge of her bed and wept.

She shed her scalding tears not only for Anna, nor for the end of her loving friendship with Philip, nor for the beginning of an impaired existence without Fay, nor for Orezanian perils and the sadness, cruelty, depravity and incorrigibility of the world and its inhabitants – not only for those reasons, but also because she had been frustrated: she would have to bend before the will of T.D. Faulkbourne, and, for the sake of Fay and Alexander and their progeny, reduce the sum of money she had meant to give to the hospital in the hills of Orezania; she was stuck with St Eo, she would have to be the caretaker of the house for its next owner, and fill it with guests to keep it warm, and carry on as if nothing had happened; she was back on the treadmill of obligation and duty, and her plan somehow to alter and improve was a dead duck.

She reached out a hand and switched on her bedside radio. Music caught her attention, measured chords subtly interwoven, an unstoppable succession of chords expressing a gamut of emotions, strangely inclusive of tragedy, comedy, light and shade – beautiful reassuring sounds, mournful and yet celebratory, if not exactly a tune. It drifted into nothingness, and a voice announced that the composer was Theodore Hildwitch.

Another Story

The next morning she recognised the strong but shaky handwriting on an envelope in her pile of mail. The letter within was from Sylvester Kexmoor, but, mysteriously, it was headed Hinxton Grange. She read as follows: 'Florrie! Eric Hinxton and I have decided to publish a book of his text and my pictures descriptive of Orezania as we experienced it. We reached our decision in your stately home, where Adam Crabhouse informed us of the threats issued by the criminal Slutzk and warned us to keep our heads down. We are free artists and will not yield to intimidation, and our vocation is to bear witness at all costs. We do not expect outsiders to share the risks we run by exposing the oppressors of the Orezanian people, therefore we shall pay for the production and distribution of our book with the money you gave us. Thank you for your patronage.' Below the signature were four postscripts. The first stated that his houseboat on the Norfolk Broads had sunk and he was staying with Eric while he repainted the canvases that had been pinched by Slutzk. In the second he declared that neither death nor bankruptcy scared him, and that he had persuaded Eric to be prepared to sell Hinxton Grange in the event of their being stuck with damages for libel and legal fees. The third said they were doing it partly as a tribute to Theodore Hildwitch, and the fourth showed noughts and crosses, signifying hugs and kisses.

Florrie pitied Eric on account of his probably permanent house guest; she resigned herself to receiving a big bouquet of complaints about Sylvester's drinking and dominance from Eric; she guessed the two of them would soon run out of funds and apply to her for a further subsidy; and she remembered the conceit and silliness of

Theodore. From the point of view of polite society, which she shared or had shared, nearly all artists were impossible.

Yet Theobald's music had eased her heartache yesterday evening. It – or he – had seemed to apply healing unguents to all the soreness. She was ashamed of having broadcast her scorn and mockery of his work, of which she had heard no more than a fraction – her criticism was based on ignorance. She blushed to recall her reaction to his satirical rendering of the Orezanian National Anthem at Kraga, her divided loyalties and resentment: for the words of that anthem were a paean of praise of war and bloodshed – Agatha Grizebeck had translated them – and he had risked his life and lost his life in order to stage his protest.

And Sylvester and Eric were paying their tribute to Theodore by doing the same sort of thing. Sylvester, who was becoming the caricature of an artist in decline, and Eric, who grizzled nonstop, had redeemed themselves. Admittedly neither had much to lose in a material sense; but Slutzk would certainly have the will, and possibly also the power, to wreak legal and even physical vengeance if they were to present him to the world in his villainous colours. At least Adam Crabhouse thought so – discretion, in fact silence, was the better part of Adam's valour.

For a change Florrie's bad old boys were acting constructively, not least by agreeing to cooperate and to tackle the hard task of recreating their Orezanian works of art. They were setting a courageous example, and she had to follow it to the extent of revising yet another opinion. A neat way of expressing her contrite feelings occurred to her: artists could not and should not be judged by the shibboleths of the drawing-room.

The telephone rang and she lifted the receiver.

'Am I too early?' Geoffrey Oldcoate inquired.

'No,' she said, swallowing her disappointment that she was not speaking to Fay. 'Not at all,' she repeated a trifle sharply – why was Geoffrey inclined to assume that she slept idly late on every morning?

'How are you? I didn't ring yesterday evening because I was afraid you might not be up to a chat.'

'Geoffrey, I'm perfectly well – thanks all the same. But if you had rung you might have come in for a few moans and groans.'

'Why, my dear – were you in trouble?'

[281]

'No,' she laughed ironically. 'Fay's engaged to marry Alexander and she flew off with him to Orezania probably for ever, and Philip broke the news that he's going to be married, and Anna Hulcott told me she had cancer. But I'm quite well.'

'Oh my dearest Florrie, shall I come round to be with you? Are you by any chance free at lunchtime?'

'You don't understand, Geoffrey – Fay's dreams have come true, I'm happy that she's so happy, I'm pleased that Philip's settling down with a nice young woman who'll look after him in his dotage, and Anna's attitude to her illness was inspirational. My moans and groans were shallow and temporary, and you're not to be too sympathetic. About lunch – I'm not sure – I think T.D. may be wanting to meet and talk business – can I let you know within an hour? It was kind of you to offer to hold my hand, but I'd rather not think of yesterday.'

'It wasn't kindness, Florrie.'

'Philip's marrying his personal assistant who's years younger than he is.'

'As you know, I've never had much time for Philip, and I would suggest you're well out of him.'

'I agree. You're right. But I seem to be running out of everybody.'

'Aren't you forgetting me, my dear?'

'Oh Geoffrey, I beg your pardon. I could never forget you, or cease to be grateful to you.'

'I would propose marriage yet again, Florrie, if I were confident that I could be a proper husband.'

'Oh Geoffrey!' she repeated in a voice with an undertone of exasperation. 'Thank you, I know you would, but I'm not thinking of husbands, proper or improper – I'm thinking of how to reorganise the rest of my life without Fay, and how not to feel I'm completely at the mercy of people nagging me to be at their parties and support their charities.'

'Are you referring to Anna? I fear I'm to blame, I supposed you'd wish to be informed of the state of Anna's health, I failed to imagine that she might nag you.'

'She didn't – she's a heroine – and I'm the only one to blame, because I hadn't the heart to disappoint her. No, I don't mean that, of course I don't – poor darling Anna! What does one more presidency of one more charity matter, even if I have precious little

[282]

faith in second chances for anyone? But the truth is I can't take the line of least resistance and knuckle under and toe the line for ever. Pay no attention to me, I'm in a stupid mood.'

'Florrie, I hate to borrow the question that Philip asked you at St Eo, but I also wonder what really happened to you in Orezania?'

'Sorry I can't go into that, it's too long a story, and my present concern isn't the past. All I can tell you is the commonest, stupidest and shortest tale – to wit, don't worry. I'm better than I was, and perhaps I'm a survivor. I think I'm fit, and I have a faithful friend, and a daughter betrothed to a real live king, and no money worries and an enviable position in society, what more can I possibly ask for?'

'One day you'll be happy as well.'

'Don't say such things and make me sad. Goodbye, Geoffrey dear. I'll ring you back.'

She sighed. She should not have fibbed to Geoffrey, she hoped he would not find out that T.D. had never asked or been asked to lunch with her. It was all so futile – she would probably have to yield yet again and spend still more of her life with a man who, through no fault of his own, had receded into the past that was no longer her concern. She applied herself with determination to paying bills and signing her name on documents, T.D. having marked the relevant spaces with a pencilled cross. Was she capable of nothing more demanding? Was such work or child's play enough to keep her going for however long she might live?

The telephone was a welcome interruption; but it was Cheryl Wright speaking, not Fay.

Cheryl, after once more thanking her for the St Eo entertainment, queried in her small humble voice: 'I don't know if you really meant me to ring you up – and please don't think me pushing – but I would love to talk to you if you could ever spare the time.'

'Oh yes,' Florrie replied noncommittally, then added with more warmth: 'Oh yes, Cheryl – wait a minute! Would you like to have lunch alone with me today?'

'That's too kind – I didn't mean to be a nuisance.'

'You won't be a nuisance, you'll be my insurance policy. Do come if you can! One o'clock – I look forward to seeing you.'

They said goodbye, and a moment later Florrie was saying hullo to a man who greeted her thus: 'Hi there, Lady!'

'Who is that?'

'Vic – Vic Pullent – remember?'

'Oh Vic!'

'How's tricks, Lady M.?'

'They could be worse. How are you?'

'Never better – glad to be home, and shouldn't wonder if you are too.'

'Yes and no – there's a big adjustment to make after all the ghastliness of Orezania.'

'Granted! But I did nicely in the end, though you could say it was blood money I was paid for tea and buns. Orezania, that's what I'm on about, Lady Florrie.'

'Please don't let's go into that particular subject!'

'I wouldn't be going into it, I'd be coming out of it, if you catch my meaning. Look, could I drop in today? You'd understand as soon as we was face to face – phones are funny and can give the wrong impression.'

'I'm busy today.'

'Course you are. So's yours truly. But five minutes wouldn't create a mint of difference, would it? I'm telling you, this is important, and you won't regret the time.'

She paused and said: 'You must excuse me.'

'I'm not taking no for an answer, that's a fact – and sorry for the shortage of soft soap. Believe me, it's more important to you than me, and you'll rue the day if you barricade your front door.'

Florrie now demanded on a tearful note: 'What is it? Is it to do with anyone I know?'

'Don't you fret – wait and see – I won't say more – but I wouldn't harm you or diddle you – take my word! My best advice is do it, girl! When can I visit at Buckingham Square?'

'Five o'clock for a few minutes – I have an engagement and I'll have to change and get ready,' she fibbed again, for she was engaged to do nothing.

'Five suits fine. See you!'

Florrie rang Geoffrey and explained that T.D. was not lunching with her after all, but that Cheryl Wright was. She said she was honouring a promise to Cheryl, and begged Geoffrey's forgiveness, and hated herself for not being particularly pleased when he immediately granted it.

[284]

She turned back to her papers and tried in vain to concentrate. Surely the Pullet was not going to spring the most shattering of all imaginable surprises? He had virtually promised that whatever he was up to would not harm her. No, she thought, she resolved to think, her fear was far-fetched and superstitious, a fear of phantoms and ghosts. All the same she wished Vic had not introduced a dark shadow into her yellow sitting-room. An idea as impolite as it was attractive crossed her mind: should she be absent or unavailable at five o'clock?

She cast her eye over more incomprehensible documents and obediently signed her name where instructed to.

Fay's call almost coincided with the ring of Florrie's doorbell. It was infuriatingly brief and often inaudible in accordance with Orezanian custom: Fay only managed to convey the news that she was well and would telephone tomorrow, and Florrie that she was better, before the line went dead. But it had a tonic effect, it relieved tension and seemed to put the past in its place. When Barney ushered Cheryl through the sitting-room door, Florrie's greeting was warm and attentive.

They shook hands. Cheryl declined liquid refreshment. She was blonde and waiflike and sat on the edge of the sofa, gripping her bag. But she wore a beautifully cut grey flannel suit, an exceptionally pretty shirt, two strings of pearls that looked real and bespoke shoes. And despite shyness, if she was shy, she began to confide in Florrie before lunch was announced.

Her husband, Desmond Wright, had died eighteen months ago. His death was sudden and unexpected, although he was in his seventies: Cheryl called it tragic. He had made millions, and she was his second wife. He had been a widower when she became his personal assistant, and she had fallen in love with him notwithstanding the difference of their ages, and he had proposed to her and they had been happily married for six and a half years.

Florrie escorted her guest down to the dining-room, where Cheryl informed the millionairess she was talking to with a disarming lack of diplomacy: 'People say millionaires always begin by being crooks.' She rebutted the idea: 'It isn't true, Desmond wasn't crooked, he never could have been, he was simply energetic and sensible. He used to say he was lucky, but I know how he turned luck to his advantage. He was kindness itself to me and

[285]

everyone, and not even keen on money, although he was pleased to be successful. He was more like a child in a sweetshop than a miser, he kept on buying' houses and pictures, not that he took much interest in them after they were his – and in the end he gave and gave to good causes.'

But, Cheryl continued as if coming to the point that preoccupied her, while she mourned and grieved over her husband she had been distracted by sólicitors, accountants, surveyors and valuers and bank officials.

'I didn't marry for money. Obviously Desmond was wealthy; but I wasn't aware of the extent of his personal fortune, everything seemed to be paid for by companies, our life was a fairy tale, and I only spent on clothes so as to do him credit. The figures were awful – and I was having them dinned into me – they made me ill when I should have been sad and grateful – and the people who said they could cure me made matters worse.'

Florrie asked: 'Were they the guests at your ball?'

'They were,' Cheryl admitted. 'I'm not a magnetic person, but the money that was mine made me much more attractive than I ever wanted to be. I became an object of interest and was invited here and there and to parties and receptions and on to committees – it was ridiculous! One of my so-called friends badgered me to give that ball, and a friend of hers organised it, and another friend provided a pill to see me through, which stupefied me, and another did the flowers for a price, and a young designer pleaded with me to wear his embarrassing dress, and somebody else lent me the jewellery she sells, and so it went on. I'm sorry you were there.'

'Why did you send me an invitation?'

'Desmond was acquainted with Mr Mozergh, who came to our house and spoke about you, and your friend Roger Ryther thinks you're marvellous.'

'Oh well, that's nice, but you mustn't take Roger too seriously.'

'I agree with him. Sometimes I saw you at parties and once at the opera – you were wearing the loveliest dress – and Mr Mozergh said you set an example by the way you managed your widow-hood, and houses and possessions and social and private lives. I remembered you when I was getting in a muddle and mess, and hoped to meet you and that you'd tell me how to manage mine.'

[286]

Luncheon was over, and the two ladies returned to the sitting-room on the first floor for coffee.

Florrie said: 'I'm afraid I have to disillusion you. My management has mainly succeeded in muddling me. But if you want to extricate yourself from the position you seem to be in, which bears similarities to my position, I have at least learnt how it can be done. Give your money away – you'll solve all your problems!'

Cheryl giggled uneasily and uncertainly, then said in a defensive voice: 'But I'm the mother of Desmond's only son.'

'And I'm the mother of Eldred's only child,' Florrie chimed in. 'Sorry, my dear, I didn't know you had a son and heir. We're in an even more similar boat than I thought we were. We can't sink our treasure in the sea, we can't disinherit our offspring, and no doubt you wouldn't like to dispose of the money your husband was clever enough to amass any more than I'd like to dispose of the money my husband and his forebears made and multiplied and kept intact. We're the trustees of family fortunes, and the loved and envied victims thereof.' She laughed momentarily at her satirical language. 'So what's the answer?' she resumed. 'We could be called, we have been called the children of paradox. We're the brides of wealth and power, who yearn for poverty or at any rate obscurity. There may not be too many of us around, because our bank balances far exceed those that figure in the dreams of avarice, but we join the host of women who have lived and do live like us in every age and every country, especially in countries that pretend or have pretended they're classless, for instance the Soviet Union and America. We're the poor little rich girls, who are inclined to convert their good luck into bad luck. And nobody pities us – why should they? Scarcely anybody understands that we might not be having as much fun as they think they would have in our shoes. My researches have established that we can't be housewives or have careers, we can't save for a rainy day or join the majority, we're too busy spending our money to cultivate friendships and we're recklessly friendly at our peril, and although a man might make the whole difference to us, we'd rather not be the meal ticket and soft touch for Tom, Dick or Harry. In other words there's no escape, except in the unlikely event of our being ruined. However,' Florrie said with a smile and explained it thus: 'yes, we're still

[287]

human, we too have a "however" to fall back on, our clouds have a golden lining if we look for it, and we can always comfort ourselves by thinking of the realities of life at the bottom of the financial pile. However,' she repeated, 'our best hope and our lifeline is to honour our obligations, that's my discovery and my advice. Doing our bit is our last precious link with everyone else, with kings and commoners, and with normality. And after all, we are the lilies of the field, who toil not, neither do we spin, but look at us in our glory, you in your elegant suit that must have cost a fortune and with pearls worth goodness knows what, and me in my warm house with my willing servants. We're here to decorate and amuse the world, and always pick up the bill. Now I've talked far too much – forgive me!'

Cheryl stayed for ten more minutes. She seemed to be bewildered by Florrie's disquisition, but said it was interesting. She was pleased to be told that T.D. Faulkbourne would sort out some of her problems. When she got up to go she kissed her hostess impulsively and was full of gratitude and compliments.

At three o'clock that afternoon Florrie walked to Hyde Park and sat for a spell by the Serpentine in the October sunshine. The English climate had relented: the day had the particularly welcome qualities of a tyrant's smile. And as autumn leaves swayed down on her and sunny beams dazzled, she was aware of a creeping sense of serenity. She was sceptical: her months of dissatisfaction and world-weariness, her revulsion and revolt from the frivolity, greed and cruelty of her species would no doubt unsettle her again. But they did not. Her confessional converse with Cheryl seemed to have cleared the air both metaphysically and meteorologically.

She lingered and watched the passing scene with a novel tolerance. Lovers held hands and kissed, and she thought not only of Fay. Cheryl would soon link up with another man, who would be the arbiter of her fate for better or for worse. And it could be that the same applied to herself, Florrie realised or recognised. How strange, she thought with unwonted frankness, as it were looking facts in the face without flinching – strange that after a whole decade of a sort of death of the heart, she or it should have come back to life! A mere matter of weeks ago she had lost Eldred in the sense that he had ceased to provide her with immunity to love, then she lost Michael, unquestionably lost him, and now

[288]

Philip and Geoffrey in their different ways – the coast was clear, vulgarly speaking. Moreover Fay was in Orezania, and under Alexander's wing. Yet Florrie was persuaded that she could cope on her own as well as in the other eventuality; her optimism took the form of a readiness to wait on events.

She wandered home through the golden glow of the sun setting as her spirits unaccountably rose.

At five her doorbell rang, and a moment later the Pullet presented himself in her sitting-room. Any pleasure she might have had in seeing his sharp smile and crinkly hair again was counteracted by the figure of a man standing behind him. Vic was wrong not to tell her he was bringing a stranger into her house: her smile froze, her hand withdrew from his.

The stranger entered – tall, bespectacled, with thick silver-grey hair and features somehow familiar.

'Lady Florrie, this is Rudolf Chirke – he's Michael's brother.'

She shook his outstretched hand, which was large and warm. He smiled at her, showing the same strong white teeth, and she asked Barney rather unsteadily to bring up three cups for tea instead of two. She sat down with a bump and asked the others to be seated.

Vic said: 'Rudolf's got something for you.'

The man produced it from the side pocket of the jacket of his loosely-cut suit – it was wrapped in tissue paper, and he had smooth-skinned brown hands with long fingers and nice big fingernails.

He spoke with a peculiar accent, American overlaying foreign: 'I didn't count on your receiving me, and I believe Vic omitted to mention me to you. Please pardon me for gaining admission to your house by default. The object in this paper reached me by a circuitous route, it belonged to my late brother, and I was given to understand that one of his last wishes was for you to have it. I arrived in England from the States two days ago and contacted Michael's colleague Vic, who engineered our meeting. And now I can make the presentation.'

She took it and began to unwrap it and asked: 'May I?'

'Please,' he said.

It was the jewelled cross that Michael had worn round his neck on the night he materialised in his sky-blue uniform in the royal box at Covent Garden Opera House.

[289]

She remarked inconsequently, perhaps to choke back emotion: 'I never knew Michael had a brother.'

Vic said in his cheeky way: 'He kept his family mighty quiet,' and Rudolf volunteered further explanation: 'My parents with their three children, myself, my sister and Michael, fled from Orezania in the fifties – it was then under Soviet control – and were granted political asylum in the USA. We changed our surname from Cherskov to Chirke, and in time assumed American nationality. My parents died a good few years ago, and my sister married an American, as I did – we became Americans. The career I made was in the Groves of Academe, as they say, but I'm retired now.'

She could not take it all in, she was distracted by noting his likenesses to Michael and his differences, and by watching his full lips and stealing glances at his steady eyes. She registered the last sentence and deduced that he must have taken early retirement – he looked about fifty-five.

Tea arrived, and she had to ask Barney to pour it out – she could not trust her hand not to shake and spill.

She picked on another sentence in his speech and asked: 'Is Mrs Chirke with you in England?'

'My wife died six months ago.'

'I'm sorry, I didn't know.' She turned to Vic and said: 'I'm glad to see you've recovered from Orezania.'

'I was lucky to save my bacon,' he replied, grinning artfully.

She summoned her resources and addressed her other guest.

'It's so kind of you to give me this cross, and to have come so far and taken so much trouble. But I feel I can't accept your brother's bequest – for one thing it should belong to you and your children, and for another it was probably once a part of the royal Orezanian collection of jewellery.'

He smiled at her, he was almost laughing at her, and she decided that he was better than Michael, he had none of Michael's savagery.

'I have to correct some errors,' he said 'The cross isn't valuable or royal, the stones are semi-precious, and my father bought it for my mother. Michael wasn't the king of anywhere, he was an actor. To be honest, he was the black sheep of my family, the usual destructive charmer, and a thief who pinched that cross from his mother's jewel-box and tried to do likewise with the Orezanian crown. Also, I have no children, and I have come to England not specifically to carry out my brother's wish but with a view to settling in your country – there are papers here that I need for purposes of research.'

'Is Alexander the real King?'

'Yes,' he said, and Vic corroborated: 'Definitely!'

'My daughter's engaged to marry Alexander. Will she be safe, do you think?'

Vic answered this general question. 'Should be – why not? Alexander's getting rid of all the old Bolshies – and he's dead right, they only understand kill or be killed. I wish your girl well, and Alexander too – Orezania could do with a spot of the genuine article. Lady Florrie, five minutes have come and gone and here I am, breaking my promises – I must skedaddle, and so must you to your engagement. Thanks for the tea – and happy days!'

He was on his feet, they were all standing, and she shook hands with Vic and at greater length with Rudolph.

'My engagement's cancelled,' she informed the latter. 'I wonder if you'd like to stay for a little while? Do stay with me!'

'Thank you,' he said.

'No,' she corrected him, 'thank you.'